PRAISE

MUA1A7A1 96

THE SHARK

"This romantic thriller is tense, sexy, and pleasingly complex."

—*Publishers Weekly*

"Precise storytelling complete with strong conflict and heightened tension are the highlights of Burton's latest. With a tough, vulnerable heroine in Riley at the story's center, Burton's novel is a well-crafted, suspenseful mystery with a ruthless villain who would put any reader on edge. A thrilling read."

—*RT Book Reviews*, four stars

BEFORE SHE DIES

"Will keep readers sleeping with the lights on."

—*Publishers Weekly* (starred review)

MERCILESS

"Burton keeps getting better!"

—*RT Book Reviews*

YOU'RE NOT SAFE

"Burton once again demonstrates her romantic suspense chops with this taut novel. Burton plays cat and mouse with the reader through a tight plot, credible suspects, and romantic spice keeping it real."

—*Publishers Weekly*

BE AFRAID

"Mary Burton [is] the modern-day queen of romantic suspense."

—Bookreporter.com

I
SEE
YOU

I
SEE
YOU

MARY
BURTON

Montlake
Romance

Published by Montlake Romance, Seattle

www.apub.com

Amazon, the Amazon logo, and Montlake Romance are trademarks of Amazon.com, Inc., or its affiliates.

ISBN-13: 9781542007603
ISBN-10: 1542007607

Cover design by Caroline T. Johnson

Printed in the United States of America

The face is the mirror of the mind, and the eyes, without speaking, confess the secrets of the heart.

—*Saint Jerome*

PROLOGUE

Tuesday, June 11, 2:00 p.m.
Alexandria, Virginia
Two Months Before

"One hundred bucks," Nikki McDonald said. "That's all I'm paying."

The building manager's gaze dropped to the creased bills carefully smoothed out so they did not look like they had been jammed in a pantry mason jar. "I could lose my job."

Nikki's cash reserves were on vapors, and her credit cards bumped against their respective limits. What resources she still had needed to last until the end of the month, when her corporate freelance gig coughed up the two grand needed for rent. "No worries. Open the door, and no one will be the wiser."

A string of sixty-watt bulbs skimmed along the top of the low, dark ceiling, dribbling light on the storage units housed in the basement of the Alexandria apartment complex they served. Moisture clung to the walls, and a musty scent filled the air. God only knew what the mold count was down here, and because Nikki's medical insurance expired at the end of the month, she did not need some kind of bullshit allergic reaction.

The manager quickly pocketed the money and thumbed through a collection of keys until he found the right one. He jammed it in the lock and twisted. It did not budge. He removed the key, inspected the worn ridges and teeth, and then tossed her a baffled expression.

Nikki grinned but sensed her attempt to appear patient fell flat as the man's brows knotted, and he refocused on a second attempt. He wiggled the key back and forth. This time he teased the tumblers into alignment. The lock clicked open.

His expression triumphant, he pushed open the door. "What are you looking for?"

"A trunk," she said.

She had received a tip through her website, Crime Connection, which she had set up two months ago after she'd left the news station. The purpose of the site was to turn cold or hot case tips into stories that would earn her another job in television. So far, the tips had been either bogus or so vague they had been unusable, but this one was so specific it gave her hope it would be different.

The sender had detailed the building's address and this specific storage unit, along with a note to open a gray trunk. A little digging into the building's history, and the unit's owner revealed a Helen Saunders rented this space. By all accounts the eighty-eight-year-old lived quietly and had been retired for over two decades. She still volunteered at a food bank, had no criminal record, and always paid her rent on time. When Nikki had visited her yesterday, the woman had had trouble concentrating and had admitted she did not own a computer. Clearly, Helen had not sent the message via Nikki's website.

Look in the gray trunk.

Nikki studied the dusty brown boxes covered in what looked like a decade's worth of dust. She fished her GoPro from a large black purse and clipped it onto the V of her blouse, between her breasts. Back in the day, she would have had her cameraman, Leo, do the filming. But

Leo, along with the steady paycheck and insurance, was gone. "Can you find Helen Saunders's original rental application?"

"Those records would be in the warehouse, if we still have them."

"There's five hundred bucks for the guy who can find it for me."

"Why?"

"Never know."

"I don't know. I could lose my job."

She leveled her gaze on the guy, sensing that despite his worry, he would be looking for that application. "Thanks for your help. I can take it from here."

"I should stay. I got an obligation to my tenant."

"I'm not here to steal," she said. "Just following up on a tip."

The manager eyed the camera and its strategic placement several beats before he raised his gaze to her face. "Do I know you?"

"I don't think so."

He shook his head, wagging his finger. "You do the news."

Nikki switched the camera on. "Did."

"You got canned, right?"

"It's complicated."

She had been chasing a story on political corruption and government contracting. The deeper she had dug into the systemic graft, the more committed she had become to the story. In the end, she had been damn proud of the final draft, which was some of her best work. However, the politically savvy station manager had not been as thrilled, and his heavy-handed edits had gutted the story. The stubborn streak that had propelled her up the career ladder now demanded she dig in her heels. Despite her manager's ultimatum, she had read the story on the air during prime time. The next morning, when she had arrived at the station, her manager had canned her on the spot and had had her escorted out of the building. She had been taken aback, though not surprised, but as she had marched out of the office with her box of belongings, she had been optimistic because she'd believed her credentials would land her a job in another market. What she'd discovered was that her story had offended some powerful people who had seen to it that every major and minor news market was closed to her.

Refusing to let her temper rise, she angled her camera toward the building manager's face. "Make sure I don't accidently film you when I go live."

He turned his face away. "I can't be on camera. We're not supposed to be here. I could get fired."

"Take it from me—you don't want that."

The manager eased away from the door. "I'll be back here."

"Whatever works."

Of course, she wasn't actually going live. Given her luck, this entire adventure could be a stunt designed to humiliate her.

She plucked her phone from her back pocket and held it up, knowing a second camera angle might come in handy during editing. In selfie mode, she began to record. "I just received an anonymous tip through my website, Crime Connection," she said, loud enough for the camera to pick up her voice. "My source tells me to look for a gray trunk in this particular location."

She panned around the space and then propped her phone on an old dresser mirror and continued to move boxes filled with crap that should have been tossed a decade ago. Dust soon coated her jeans and very expensive turquoise top. The grime would enhance the television drama but would be hell on the dry cleaning bill.

The camera jostled when she bumped it with a dusty box. "It's an average storage unit that most of us who've lived in an urban apartment would have used at one time or another." She moved a lamp from an ugly 1970s-style end table and angled her body around the table.

Nikki looked directly into the frame, wanting the lens to catch her pensive look. As she turned, she spotted the gray trunk.

After grabbing the leather side handle, she hefted the trunk and found it much lighter than expected. She set the trunk in the hallway, where the light was marginally better. Though she felt a rush of excitement, she did not hurry the opening. The buildup could be as important as the payoff. "A gray trunk."

She picked up the phone and pointed it toward the tarnished brass lock. Multiple angles always worked well in editing. Her fingers hovered over the lock.

As she adjusted the lens in for a close-up, the manager peered over her shoulder, partly blocking her shot. She swatted him back as she pressed the release button on the lock. To her delight, it popped open. She lifted the lid. The box was filled with stained, brittle tissue paper, which crumbled on contact. Her insides tingled. She still lived for this and remembered how much she missed investigative journalism.

As she scooped up paper, she froze as she stared at the box's contents. "Is this a joke? Did Rick put you up to this?"

"Who's Rick?"

"My former boss at the news station."

"I don't know Rick," the manager said. "It looks like a Halloween decoration."

It was a complete skeleton that was discolored and darkened. She reached into the box and wrapped her hands around the skull, expecting it to feel slick like plastic. However, the moment she touched the skull, she knew it was not made of a smooth synthetic. It was porous like a pumice stone.

She raised the skull, and the jaw immediately dropped. Darkness radiated from empty sockets as the lower jaw dangled in silent laughter before the delicate hinge joints failed and sent the mandible to the cement floor. It broke into several pieces.

The manager stepped closer. "Is that real?"

Her heart raced in her chest as she thought back to the person who had sent her the message. The tip had been anonymous, and she had not bothered to trace the sender. Why her? She was a pariah in television news now. All the visitors to her website were really drawn by morbid curiosity over the epic implosion of her career. She had yet to receive a legitimate tip.

Until now.

Maybe Nikki still had a few fans out there.

She dropped to her knees and carefully collected the broken bits of bone. Normal people did not get juiced over what looked like a torched skull. But she did. Especially if it got her out of purgatory.

For the first time in months, she felt like things were looking up.

Her brain shifted into tactical mode. She had been around long enough to know this skull could belong to your garden-variety murdered guy. He would get his five minutes of fame, and that would be it.

But she had always been a glass-half-full kind of gal. The story could be bigger. And if it was, her former backstabbing boss would be forgotten, and she would be back in the game.

Nikki reached for her phone as she unhooked the camera and aimed it at her face. "It's real."

"Who are you calling?" the manager asked.

She looked into the camera. "The cops."

CHAPTER ONE

Sunday, August 11, 11:00 p.m.
Alexandria, Virginia
Two Days Before

Fresh from the shower, he dried his dark hair and walked across the drab, worn carpet of the motel room toward the television tuned to the local news station. Beside it sat a pizza box. He flipped open the top and grabbed the last slice, plucked off the onions and pepperoni, and discarded them into a pile with the others.

"It was a waste to order the extra toppings." He liked his pizza plain and simple. "But I was trying to be a nice guy."

The woman behind him said nothing.

After tossing a sliver of onion into the box, he grabbed the remote and turned up the volume. The mattress sagged as he sat on the edge of the bed. The news anchor was blathering on about local traffic congestion caused by a car accident during evening rush hour. "Same old, same old."

He took a large bite. The pizza was cold and the cheese hard, but he had worked up an appetite and was willing to settle.

The television newscaster continued on about politics, weather, and a soft piece on the elderly, but again did not mention the story he had been expecting for weeks. "Such bullshit. You and I both know she has the story, but there's been nothing on her site or in the news. She's got to have figured it out by now."

Silence.

"It's a good story, one people will want to know about. The public might not care about the bones of a dead whore, but they'll care about a missing rich girl."

He ate the rest of the slice, watching until the thirty-minute news show ended. Pizza grease, smelling faintly of onions, glistened on his fingertips. "Paid two extra bucks for nothing."

He wiped his fingers on the comforter before he walked to the window. An overhead vent blasted cold air as he pushed back a small portion of the thick oily curtain. Through a window streaked with condensation, he looked up toward the stars, drowned in a sea of lights flooding from streetlights and neon signs.

"I miss Nevada. The stars. Big sky. A man can hardly breathe in the city."

He let the curtain slide from his fingers as he moved toward the dresser. He opened the top drawer, where he had placed his neatly folded clothes. He pulled on his underwear and then his faded jeans before turning toward the woman.

She was on her back, mouth gagged and sightless blue eyes still brittle with fear as she stared at the popcorn ceiling. Her hands were tied to the bedpost; laid bare were her breasts and the five oozing stab wounds. Blood painted her pale skin red, soaked the bedding, and arched over the headboard and across the framed print of the US Capitol hanging on the wall.

She was petite and so lean her stomach was nearly concave. Unnaturally blond hair framed a pale, hollow face that was unremarkable. Large silver hoops dropped from her earlobes.

The sight of her naked frame awash in her own blood was a shot to his loins, and he was tempted to have another go at her. There was nothing better than fucking a woman in her own blood.

He drew his fingertips over her pale leg, still warm to the touch. The darkness inside him, starved for too long, had finally turned ravenous. Insatiable. "I went for a long time without doing this, and then two of you in as many months."

The first one had been easy enough to charm. He was a good-looking guy, and when he tried, he could charm the pants off almost any woman. She had cost him the price of five cocktails in a trendy bar.

This one was a pro and had willingly climbed into his car as she'd smiled and asked him how he liked to party.

He traced a finger through the blood, creating a pale path that unveiled a rose tattoo. "After a man gets a taste for death, even the best fuck just doesn't cut it."

Reluctantly, he moved from the bed and washed his hands in the bathroom sink. The hot water stung his palm, and when he looked down, he noted the small nick above his lifeline. He remembered how the handle had grown slick as he had plunged it into his date and, on the last strike, how it had slipped. But he had been so possessed that a small cut had barely registered on his radar.

Now, he could see he had been lucky. The wound was superficial and would not need stitches.

He dried his hands on a fresh towel and wiped off the sink, the toilet handle, and the hot and cold shower knobs. Next, he cleaned the remote control and the doorknob before dropping the towel into his backpack.

The cops were going to collect DNA and prints, but this room was loaded with both from all previous guests. Assuming this case even made the priority list, it would be at least a year before the samples got sorted and tested. By then he would be on a beach in Mexico.

"You aren't that important, girl," he whispered. "Hookers are a dime a dozen, and cops got better things to do than find me."

He pulled his still-clean shirt over his head, tucked it in the waistband of his jeans, and shoved his feet into a pair of sneakers. He double knotted the laces for good measure.

A last glance in the mirror confirmed there was no blood on his face. He combed his fingers through his hair and then rubbed the stubble darkening his chin. He could use a shave.

The mirror's reflection caught the woman's body lying in the pool of blood now fully bloomed on the white sheets. Soon it would be brown and lose its luster.

He hoisted the backpack on his shoulder. "No one is going to bother you, darling. Room's paid for until tomorrow. You'll finally get that rest you were complaining about needing so bad."

CHAPTER TWO

Monday, August 12, 9:30 a.m.
Quantico, Virginia
One Day Before

The eyes were critical. They reflected secrets. Even when an individual tried to fake it, the eyes still echoed loss, love, fear, or hate. They were the visual portals to the soul. And they were the hardest to capture in a facial reconstruction sculpture.

Special Agent Zoe Spencer stepped back from the clay bust she had been working on for weeks. The woman's likeness featured an angled jaw, a long narrow nose, and sculpted cheekbones. She had chosen brown for the eyes, a guess based on statistics. And it was not lost on her that the most telling part of who this woman had been was conjecture.

Zoe's attention to detail was both her superpower and her Achilles' heel. Many questioned her ceaseless fretting over the minutiae such as a chin's dimple, the flare of nostrils, or the curve of lips into a grin. Some in the bureau still believed her work was purely art and not real science.

Her sculptures were not an exercise in art and creativity. The point of her work, like this bust, was to restore a murder victim's identity and see that they received justice. But instead of arguing with the nonbelievers, she simply allowed her 61 percent closure rate to do her talking.

Sculptor, artist, and FBI special agent were her current incarnations, but she'd had others. Dancer. Wife. Young widow. Survivor. Each had left indelible marks, some welcome and some not.

On a good day, Zoe would not change her history. Her past had led her to this place, and she was here for a reason. But on a bad day, well, she would have killed to get her old life back.

She had been with the FBI criminal profiler squad for two years and almost immediately had put her expertise to work. She caught the cases requiring forensic sketches or sculptures not only because of her artistic abilities and expertise in fraud but also because of her keen interview skills. Armed only with questions, a sketch pad, and a pencil, she burrowed into the repressed memories of witnesses and victims, penciling and shadowing those recollections into useful images.

She certainly did not have a master artisan's skill, but she was good enough. And from time to time, local law enforcement brought her a skull and requested a forensic reconstruction. Such was the case of her latest subject.

The lab door opened. "How's it going?"

The question came from her boss, Special Agent Jerrod Ramsey, who oversaw a five-person profiling team based at the FBI's Quantico office. Their team specialized in the more unusual and difficult cases.

In his late thirties, Ramsey was tall and lean with broad shoulders. He had thick brown hair cut short on the sides and longer on the top, a style reminiscent of the 1930s. His patrician looks betrayed the upperclass upbringing that had financed his Harvard University undergrad and Yale law degrees. Naturally skeptical, he was considered one of the best profilers, and though many wanted him in the FBI's Washington, DC, headquarters overseeing more agents, he had skillfully maneuvered away from the promotions.

Zoe raised the sculpting tool to the bust's ear and shaved down the lobe a fraction. The artist always wanted more time to tinker. The agent understood when good had to be enough. "I'm ninety percent of the way there."

Ramsey approached the bust and studied it closely. His expression was unreadable, stern even, but interest sparked in his eyes. He was impressed. "This is better than ninety percent."

"Thank you."

Ramsey leaned in, closely regarding Jane Doe's glassy stare. "It's really remarkable that you could create this likeness given the damage."

Nikki McDonald had done Zoe no favors when she had handled and then dropped the scorched skull. "I've worked with worse."

"I understand standard skin depths and predetermined measurements for determining facial structure, but how did you decide that she had brown eyes?"

Ah, always back to the eyes. "Over fifty percent of the world's population has brown eyes."

He grinned slightly. "So, a guess?"

"A calculated guess, Agent Ramsey."

"I stand corrected. How long did this take?"

"On and off, about six weeks. I had to work it around other cases."

"We all juggle. Nature of the beast."

"Not complaining. I like the work." *I'm married to it* was more like it.

"What else can you tell me about Jane Doe?" he asked.

Zoe shrugged off the smock she wore over her white tailored shirt and black slacks and exchanged it for her suit jacket, hanging on a peg. "Bone structure tells me she was a Caucasian female in her late teens. The few teeth that remain indicate she enjoyed good nutrition and dental care, which suggests she had resources when she was alive."

He walked around the bust, getting a 360-degree view. He pointed to the hair tucked behind the ear, as a girl in her teens might do. "Was the hair also a calculated guess?"

"In part. Given her bone structure, I assumed it was a lighter color."

"Do you know how she died?"

"Knife marks on her ribs indicate she was stabbed at least once in or near the heart."

"The bones were badly burned. Could a fire have killed her?"

"We'd need soft tissue to determine. There are marks along the sides of the skull suggesting someone took a blowtorch to it."

"Why torch the skull?"

"Your guess is as good as mine. Perhaps the killer wanted to minimize the smell of rotting flesh. Or he wanted to destroy DNA, which he did accomplish when he also pulled most of her teeth. Or he could have been exorcising extreme rage."

"He wanted to obliterate the woman's identity," he said, more to himself.

"That's what I think."

"The killer or someone messaged the tip to Ms. McDonald's website," Ramsey said. "Why now?"

"Another guess? The killer is tired of hiding," she theorized. "He wants recognition for a job he considers well done. Maybe he's sending a message to someone else?"

"Who?"

"An accomplice." She sighed. "Or a witness who now feels secure enough to act."

"How long has Jane Doe been dead?" Ramsey eyed the bust as if the face troubled him.

"No way of knowing. Though Jane's dental work is modern."

"Any personal items found with the skull?"

"No." She was Jane's last and best hope for identification.

Ramsey straightened. "Impressive work, Agent Spencer. The bust will be a significant help to Alexandria police. You're working with Detective William Vaughan?"

"Correct."

"He attended several of the profiling team's workshops in the spring."

The spring training sessions had been designed to help local cops solve crimes. Detective Vaughan had been one of her best students. She had discovered he had a master's in theoretical math, a reputation for thinking outside the box, and, over his ten years on homicide, a closure rate edging toward 90 percent. Her respect for his work had grown into desire, and when he had asked her out for coffee, saying yes had been easy. It was not long after that that they had started sleeping together.

"I'll send Vaughan a picture of the bust so he can cross-check it against any pictures he has on file," she said. "His department's public information officer is arranging a news release. If we can publicize her face, we might get an identification."

"Good."

"Ms. McDonald has called my office several times," she said. "I haven't taken her call, but her voicemail messages make it very clear she wants access to the case. Kind of a finder's fee."

"She'll get the news along with everyone else." His mouth bunched in curiosity as he regarded the still face. "I understand the apartment building where the skull was found is a half mile from I-95." The north-south interstate's twelve hundred miles of roadway ran through a dozen states and was a main artery for running drugs and weapons and human trafficking.

"Correct. Jane Doe could be from anywhere."

Ramsey stood back from the bust, folding his arms over his chest. "Her face is familiar."

Zoe looked again at the bust. "You've seen her before?"

He leaned forward, his eyes narrowing. "Ever had a name on the tip of your tongue, but you couldn't quite grasp it?"

Instead of pressing him for the name, she took a different tactic. "You've worked hundreds of cases."

His gaze cut back to Zoe. "Yes. And I've seen the faces of a thousand victims."

"Given she was in the basement for up to twenty years, you could have been a new agent when you saw her."

"Early 2000s."

"Remember, she'd have been a girl of means and likely missed when she vanished."

He flexed his fingers and then suddenly straightened, snapping his fingers. "I can't believe I didn't see it right away. This is Marsha Prince."

"Prince?" Zoe said. "Why is that name familiar?"

"She was a rising sophomore at Georgetown University and was in Alexandria working in her father's business. She was days away from returning to school in August 2001 when she vanished."

Tumblers clicked into place, and the memory unlocked. The case had been profiled at the academy. "She was living at home with her parents, who lived in Alexandria. She literally vanished, and the cops never figured out what happened to her."

"That's the one," Ramsey said.

There had been search crews scouring the region. Cadaver dogs had canvassed the parks, fields, and riverbeds, dry from drought that summer. As Zoe studied the face, more fragments of the forgotten case slid together into a cohesive picture.

Young, blond, smart. With the world before Marsha Prince, her disappearance had set off a firestorm that had rippled through all levels of law enforcement, local politics, and television news shows. Her name had been kept alive for a few years until finally time had cast Marsha into the sea of lost souls.

"Should we notify her family that we may have found her?" Zoe asked.

"Mom and Dad are both deceased," he said. "She does have a sister, Hadley Prince, but last I heard, she'd moved away."

"Without DNA, we'll need a visual identification from family."

"Turn it over to Detective Vaughan. The ball's in his court now."

***

I rocked the finals! This is going to be an epic summer.

Marsha Prince, May 2001

CHAPTER THREE

Monday, August 12, 1:30 p.m.
Shenandoah Valley, Virginia
One Day Before

A homicide detective's case rarely fell into place easily and quickly. Solving it required legwork, poking and prodding of countless witnesses, sifting through hours of surveillance tapes, and the ability to study a murder scene until the critical details presented themselves.

A cop needed patience. Lots of it.

And so did the father of a teenage son.

The past year had been a study in tolerance and persistence as Alexandria homicide detective William Vaughan had shepherded his son through his final year of high school. Teenage hormones, brooding silences, and a couple of broken curfews had dominated their spring. The kid chomped at the bit and thought he knew better than anyone, especially his old man. Many a night, Vaughan had stood on the back porch of their home, drunk a beer, and counted the seconds to this moment.

"Do you have everything?" Vaughan asked his son.

Nate opened a careworn dresser in his dorm room and shoved in a handful of T-shirts. "I'm good."

Vaughan looked at the small cinder block room sporting two twin beds, identical desks, and a long dresser with enough drawer space for two boys. Nate's roommate, Sam from Roanoke, who had red hair, glasses, and a lean frame, stacked a handful of books on his desk.

Nate had been Vaughan's to raise since his divorce. Connie had remarried and had decided a seven-year-old boy did not fit into her new life. She had loved the boy. Wanted to be a part of his life. But she just had not wanted to be hampered with the day-to-day grind.

Single fatherhood had scared the shit out of Vaughan, but he had figured out a way to make it work. To say this was a case of "father knows best" would be a gross overstatement, but he and Nate had done pretty well together. He was damn proud of the young man Nate was becoming.

Faced with the freedom that had tantalized Vaughan for the last couple of years, he suddenly did not want it. "How about I buy you boys a pizza in the dining hall? I hear it's good."

Nate shrugged. "I could eat."

The kid could always eat. "Sam, join us? Might as well send you two off with full bellies."

"Yeah, sure. Thanks," Sam said.

The three made their way across the campus to the dining hall fashioned out of glass and metal. A modern marvel that looked more like a fancy resort than a dining hall. The kid was going to have the best time of his life, and Vaughan was envious. His college and graduate school days had been parceled around part-time jobs that supported him and his then new wife.

Vaughan told the boys to get a table in the crowded room filled with students and parents while he scored a couple of pizzas. Fifteen minutes later, he spotted the boys sitting at a corner table.

As he approached, he caught the tail end of a conversation centered around a hot girl living on the fifth floor of their dorm. Rebecca.

Vaughan set the pizzas and sodas on their table.

He sat and flipped open the lids. The boys dug in immediately. This was his last moment with Nate for a while, and he wanted to savor every bit of it.

Vaughan reached for a slice and had it inches from his lips when his phone chimed with a text. It was from his commander, Captain Kevin Preston.

Homicide. Motel off S. Bragg Street. How soon can you be back?

He turned the phone facedown, determined to enjoy these last moments. But try as he might, the text chewed on him.

Nate bit into a slice. The kid knew the phone rarely brought good news. "You got to go?"

Vaughan took a bite and then accepted the inevitable. "Sorry, pal."

"Murder calls." Nate looked at Sam. "Dad's a homicide detective."

Vaughan wiped the grease from his fingers on a napkin and tucked his phone in his pocket. "Never a dull moment."

Nate rose with him and almost leaned in for a quick hug before he seemed to remember they were not at home but in front of his new roommate and the entire freshman class.

Shit. When had his little guy grown up? Vaughan thrust out his hand. "Good luck, son."

The boy took it.

Vaughan wondered when the kid had gotten so tall and his grip so strong. He pulled him forward and embraced him. "Call me if you need anything."

Nate relaxed a fraction. "I will."

He reluctantly released the kid.

With a wave to Sam, Vaughan navigated through the sea of people in the dining hall and strode to his car. He looked back, half hoping to see Nate one last time, but his boy had been swallowed up by his new life.

The car felt empty when Vaughan cranked the engine. Two hours ago, it had been crammed full of Nate's things, the radio had been blaring the kid's playlist entitled *Freedom*, and they had both been chowing on fast-food burgers.

Vaughan turned up the radio as he pulled onto the interstate, but the song's electric guitar riff did not banish the silence. Even the scent of McDonald's burgers and fries was fading.

The kid was doing what he needed to do. And like it or not, it was time for both of them to begin a new phase of their lives.

He punched the accelerator.

Two hours later, Vaughan arrived at the motel on South Bragg Street. It was a two-story structure with the room doors facing out toward the parking lot. The room rate was less than forty bucks a night, a near steal in the Northern Virginia market, and attracted a steady stream of pimps, prostitutes, and drug addicts. He had responded to a homicide here last year.

The room was roped off, and a uniformed officer waited outside the crime scene. The forensic team had arrived, and judging by the camera flashes, they were working the scene.

He reached in his glove box and removed his weapon and badge, hooking both on his belt in one fluid motion. He stepped out of the car and braced against the coiling afternoon heat, dense with humidity. He pulled on a navy-blue sport jacket, slightly frayed on the inside from the constant friction of the holster and weapon. He fished gloves from the coat pocket and worked his fingers inside the latex.

Several sets of curtains fluttered along the string of outward-facing rooms as guests stole peeks at the scene. No one appeared ready to talk, but he would be knocking on doors soon.

He shifted his attention from the windows to the scene and the officer standing watch. Officer Shepard Monroe was in his early fifties and wore a buzz cut and a thick droopy mustache. "Get the kid dropped off?"

Vaughan's son had been a fixture at the station and knew everyone who worked there. "He was discussing a cute coed with his roommate when I left."

"That's our boy."

"Text him occasionally, Shep, and remind him to study hard."

Monroe rested his hands on his gun belt. "Let the kid have some fun."

"He'll have plenty. But school is first." Vaughan tried not to think about the student loan papers he had signed to cover Nate's tuition. It was a good chunk of change, given his pay scale. "What do we have?"

"Looks like a sex worker tangled with the wrong john. Cut her up pretty good."

"Do you know who she was?"

"No identification yet," Monroe said. "There's a purse under the bed, but it's covered in blood. I left it for the techs."

"Anyone see the guy? Hear sounds from the room?"

"I knocked on the surrounding doors. If anyone saw or heard anything, they aren't sharing."

The dark-gray door sported the tarnished brass number 107. "Who rented the room?"

"Girl did. She paid enough cash to cover twenty-four hours."

"That's a long time for a place like this. Was she working multiple clients out of the room?"

"Manager says no. Said only one guy showed."

"Description?"

"Medium height and build. Sandy blond or brown hair. Dark clothes. Thinks Caucasian, but isn't sure."

"That's it?" Vaughan asked.

"No one asks questions here, including the management."

"Did the girl give a name?"

"Elizabeth Taylor."

She wouldn't be the first to use an actress's name. "Let me guess, not her real name."

"Not likely." Officer Monroe's gun belt creaked as he shifted.

Finding an ID in the purse was not a given. Many of the working girls did not carry one, just in case they were busted.

"I might ask the guests what they know." Sometimes the homicide badge loosened tongues.

"Good luck."

Vaughan stepped into the room, now illuminated with a portable light that cast a harsh brightness on a place accustomed to shadows. A constellation of blood was splashed on the bed, walls, and carpeting, and a thick coppery scent combined with decomposing flesh enveloped him. Ten years on homicide had hardened him, but he still was not immune to the gruesome scenes like this or the accompanying stench.

Knowing emotions would not serve this victim, he detached from the carnage and shifted into assessment mode. The room had brown carpeting, beige walls, two double beds, a long dresser with a television, and a vanity. A small bathroom adjoined. Low-wattage bulbs spit out light, now supplemented by a lamp brought in by the forensic team.

The two techs, both in Tyvek suits, blocked his view of the body. One sketched the scene, and the other took pictures.

"What do you have?" Vaughan asked.

The shorter of the two turned, and Vaughan recognized Bud Clary. He had a thick waist and a stocky build. In his late forties, he had twenty years in the department, and they had worked dozens of homicides together.

"I thought you had the day off?" Bud asked.

Nate's college campus was now light-years away. "No rest for the wicked."

"Tell me about it." Bud glanced at his notebook, which featured a rough drawing of the room. Cases often did not go to trial for months or years, and sketches helped jog memories. "Jane Doe was in her late teens and was stabbed five times in the chest and neck."

Vaughan looked past Bud, toward the victim's long, pale, thin leg painted in blood. Her toenails were purple, and a long scroll tattoo coiled around her left ankle.

Bud held up his hand. "I wouldn't get too close. The carpet around the bed is soaked. Whoever killed her knew how to bleed her out quickly."

"Officer Monroe said there's a purse by the bed?" Vaughan asked.

"I'll check."

The other tech, Fiona Tate, was in her late twenties, with short brown hair and sculpted cheekbones. She snapped photos while moving from the bed toward the bureau and a pizza box.

Vaughan's first unobstructed view of the female victim challenged his resolve to remain emotionally distant. The girl was about Nate's age, and she reminded him of the young kids he had just seen in the college dining hall earlier today.

Those fresh-faced, smiling kids stood in stark contrast to this girl, whose sallow complexion and drawn skin stretched over her face. Her eyes remained open, staring with a cloudy, unseeing gaze that echoed panic and fear.

The life span of a sex worker was only a few years. If she had not died tonight, chances were good she would have been dead by her twenty-first birthday. He had seen too many girls like Jane Doe get used up and spit out by the streets. Already he wondered if this case would ever see trial.

Bud fished under the bed and removed a purple bag covered in sparkling stones and fringe. He unzipped the top as Fiona continued to snap photos. The tech dug in the purse, coming up with a handful of condoms, lube, handcuffs, and a flip phone. No ID.

"Is the phone password protected?" he asked.

"Yes," the tech said.

"Damn." That phone likely contained the girl's client lists and communications with her killer.

Vaughan walked a wide circle around the bed, removing a pen from his breast pocket, and then flipped open the pizza box. A stale pile of onions stood inches from a collection of shriveled pepperoni slices. "Someone bought a pizza with toppings they didn't like."

Bud studied the victim's slight frame. "She looks half-starved. But the autopsy will confirm what's in her stomach."

"She probably was." Vaughan flipped the lid closed long enough to take a photo of the generic logo before searching around for any kind of receipt. He found none.

Vaughan glanced back at the bed and the faint impression on the end. It appeared as if someone had sat there watching television. "Was the television on when you arrived?"

"It was," Bud said. "It was a local news channel."

"He watched television as she bled out."

"Jesus," Fiona said.

Vaughan crossed to the bathroom, where he saw the towel crumpled on the counter. The sink and tub handles looked as if they had been wiped down, but there were no traces of blood on the remaining towel. He looked closely at the shower's drain and saw faint hints of blood around it. The killer had been naked when he had murdered the girl; then he had showered and dressed. The sequence would have ensured his clothes were not stained with blood.

"When you run the victim's prints, let me know if you get a hit?" Vaughan asked.

"Will do, Detective," Bud said.

The probability of solving this case was incredibly low. Statistically, girls like this were considered expendable by their families, their pimps, and the justice system. They had no advocate except him and his overworked staff. But understanding the reality did not dampen his determination to give this girl some dignity and reckoning from the grave.

"Bud and Fiona, keep me posted." And when both techs nodded, he stepped outside. He squinted toward the hot sun, absorbing its heat, knowing there was a monster out there who believed he would not get nailed for this crime.

He straightened his jacket and strode toward the adjoining room. Inside he heard whispers.

"Open up," he said. "Alexandria Homicide."

The knob turned and the door opened, catching on the security chain. A woman with gray hair and pale skin stared back at him. "I already talked to the cops."

"You haven't talked to me." Vaughan held up his badge. "A murder occurred next door."

She rubbed her index finger under her red-tipped nose. "That's what the cop said."

"Did you hear anything?"

"Not a sound."

"When did you arrive?"

"I checked in about midnight."

That would have been fourteen hours ago and well within the window of the murder. "And you heard nothing?"

"Well, a television show, or maybe it was the news. I could hear it through the walls, but it was muffled."

He studied her bloodshot eyes before his gaze cut to the bruises near the crease of her arm. "Did you hear any conversation, shouts, cries, screams?"

She tugged down her sleeve. "No. Like I said, just the television."

If she had been high, as he suspected, she would not have heard a train if it had rattled past the foot of her bed. "When did you shoot up?"

"I don't do drugs."

"I don't care what you put in your arm. I just want a time."

Her eyes roved down her arm, and then, "Maybe about fifteen minutes after I checked in."

"And you heard nothing?"

"No. Just the television, I swear. And I didn't get that messed up."

If that was true, that meant Jane Doe had been killed before midnight. He took the woman's name and number and gave her his card.

Vaughan moved down the string of rooms, but each new occupant was less helpful than the last. He spoke to several working girls, gave them his card, and told them he wanted to figure out what had happened to the girl.

Homicide work was tedious, amounting to boots on the ground that led to small crumbs that might lead him to a killer. The forensic stuff would come in handy later in court, if the case made it that far. But his best chances of solving this murder fell within the first forty-eight hours. After that, the chances dropped by 90 percent.

His phone rang, and he tugged it from the cradle nestled beside his badge. Zoe Spencer's name flashed on the screen.

They had met months ago at a Quantico training session sponsored by the FBI for local law enforcement. She had been lecturing on forensic art, and she'd worn a pencil skirt and black heels that had given him such a hard-on; he had not learned much.

He had approached her after the second week of classes, bribing her with coffee if she would assist him with a case, and she had agreed. Her assistance had helped solve the case, and basically one thing had led to another.

Their paths had not crossed for weeks until early summer, when Nikki McDonald had called in the Jane Doe find. He had called Spencer immediately.

"Agent Spencer. Any luck with my Jane Doe?" he asked.

"I can be in your office in an hour and give you the full story."

"Can I have the CliffsNotes version?"

"Better to show you," she said.

"Make it two hours. I'm at a homicide scene."

"Understood. See you in two hours."

After he ended the call, he knocked on motel room doors for another hour but discovered if there had been a witness, they weren't talking.

When he had less than a half hour before his meeting with Spencer, he notified Officer Monroe he was headed back to the station, and then he texted his partner, Detective Cassidy Hughes, about this current case as well as the pending update on Jane Doe. Hughes replied quickly, informing him she would be tied up in court for at least another hour.

He slid behind the wheel of his car and turned on the engine and air-conditioning. As he pulled out of the lot, the motel room sign glinted in his rearview mirror. Already he felt as if he had let the dead girl down. If he got an ID, then he could search arrest records and last known associates. Jesus, there had to be someone out there who had known her.

He forced his mind to shift gears and focus on the Jane Doe Nikki McDonald had found in the storage unit early in the summer. When he and his partner had arrived on the scene, Nikki had already uploaded footage to her social media pages.

He'd asked her to hold off on any more posts, but when she'd realized her post had gone viral, she'd doubled down. He had posted a uniformed officer at the scene to keep curiosity seekers and crime junkies away.

Nikki's posts had generated a couple of spots on local news, leading to more speculation about the victim's identity. The pressure to solve the case had steadily built.

He and his partner had interviewed the owner of the unit, but she'd had no idea how the trunk had ended up in her space. There had been no prints on the trunk and no usable DNA in or on it. They had hit one dead end after another.

Now, as he drove toward the station, he hoped Spencer had identified the victim. The snag of traffic irritated him more than usual because he was anxious to hear what Spencer had to say. Fifteen minutes later, he walked through the front door of the police station.

The sergeant behind the desk, a bulldog of a man with a thick mop of gray hair, looked up. "That special agent just arrived. She's in the conference room."

Vaughan straightened his tie. "Thanks."

"This about the head case?" the sergeant asked.

Dark humor might have offended some on the other side of the blue line, but it was how cops coped with very grim realities. "That's what she tells me."

Vaughan climbed the stairs two at a time and pushed through the second floor door to find Spencer sitting in the conference room. Her head was bent, and her gaze was on her phone as she quickly typed a message.

Spencer had a long lean body suited for her trademark black suits and tall heels. Auburn hair was always plaited into a french braid, emphasizing her sculpted cheekbones and vivid blue eyes. She wore minimal makeup, but as far as he was concerned, she did not need it.

Vaughan cleared his throat. "Special Agent Spencer."

Her pensive expression slipped away as she raised her gaze from the phone. "Detective Vaughan."

As she began to rise, he motioned for her to stay seated. He took the chair across from her. "I've texted Hughes. She's stuck in court."

"I know she hates that."

"No doubt." He didn't want to talk about his partner. Spencer had been working a case in Nashville the last couple of weeks, and he wanted to tell her how much he had missed seeing her. Instead, he asked, "You have an identification for me?"

"I do." She opened a file. Her fingers were long. Graceful. Like her legs. She had mentioned something once about being a ballerina but had never explained how a dancer transitioned from the stage to the bureau.

"As you know, I've spent most of the summer working on a facial reconstruction project," she said. "We believe we were able to identify the subject. Her name was Marsha Prince."

Vaughan sat back in his chair, his thoughts pivoting from her legs to business. "I had just joined the force, and the case made a real impression on all of us. Marsha Prince vanished after visiting a local nightclub." She had been underage and had used a fake identification. Unlike the Jane Doe back at the motel, Marsha's case had dominated headlines. "Where in the World Is Marsha Prince?" had been one article. It hyped theories ranging from her being buried in a shallow grave in the Shenandoah Valley to working as a sex slave in Mexico.

"It appears Ms. Prince didn't make it more than five miles from her family home." She laid out a picture taken of Marsha Prince her freshman year of college and then beside it a photograph of the bust she had sculpted.

He was struck by how sweet the girl looked. Thick blond hair swept over an oval face sporting a bright, wide smile. She had earned straight As her freshman year while balancing a part-time waitress job and volunteering at a food bank.

"Shit," he muttered. He picked up both pictures. "The faces look identical."

"Even I was surprised by the accuracy."

"It's one hell of a job, Agent Spencer."

"Thanks."

"As I remember, Marsha Prince's family appeared squeaky clean. Younger sister, Hadley, was a cheerleader and a senior in high school. She was also slated to follow in her sister's footsteps to Georgetown.

However, during the investigation, the cops learned of the father's financial troubles."

"Her father, Larry Prince, owned Prince Asphalt Paving Company, and her mother's illness put the family on the ropes."

"The mother had multiple sclerosis," he said.

"That's right," she said. "Father was not particularly beloved by his neighbors because he was so particular about his yard. He hated it when anyone walked on the grass. But the family overall had no issues that anyone really noticed. And then his daughter vanished."

"Marsha stayed on the FBI's missing persons list for a long time."

"She was removed just today."

Vaughan tapped his finger on the faux-wood-grain tabletop. "Nikki McDonald said she received the original tip via her website. We tried to trace the sender but had no luck."

"Not surprising. The killer isn't ready to be caught."

"But he could be?"

"I'm betting when the identity is made public, he'll want more attention."

"Why now?" Vaughan asked, more to himself.

"He needs recognition and validation to fill some kind of void in his life."

Vaughan nodded. "He's suffered some loss or upset in his real life. Lost a job, underwent a divorce or breakup, or maybe even his health."

"Those are the primary triggers," Spencer said.

"I discovered that Marsha Prince's surviving sister now lives in Alexandria," Vaughan said.

"After Marsha disappeared, Hadley married her high school boyfriend, Mark Foster, and they moved to Oregon. The couple has one child. In January of this year, Mark Foster accepted a new accounting job in Alexandria, and the family moved back east. Hadley is a fitness instructor. The daughter, Skylar, is a senior in high school."

"You'd think after the pain of losing her sister, Hadley would never have returned to Alexandria."

"Promotions are hard to turn down, I suppose."

"I owe her a death notification, unless you've done that already," Vaughan said.

"I have not. This is your jurisdiction. I'm here strictly to inform you of my findings."

He glanced at his watch. "No time like the present. Care to join me? I know you're as curious as I am about this case."

She placed the photos back in her folder. "Actually, I would. I've spent six weeks molding Marsha Prince's face, and I'd like to see this girl find justice."

"We can take my car."

***

Wild Blue: My mother and father always fight.

Mr. Fix it: Parents can be so selfish.

Wild Blue: I know, right? They always put themselves first. I hate the shouting.

Mr. Fix it: You shouldn't have to live like this.

Wild Blue: I don't want to live like this anymore.

Mr. Fix it: How about we grab dinner?

Wild Blue: I'd like that.

Mr. Fix it: When?

Wild Blue: Always easiest to sneak out on Mondays.
Both my parents are always out until late.

Mr. Fix it: Tonight then.

Wild Blue: You keep me sane.

Mr. Fix it: Remember, you are very special.

CHAPTER FOUR

Monday, August 12, 4:30 p.m.
Alexandria, Virginia
One Day Before

The faint scent of french fries still lingered in Vaughan's car as he watched Spencer click her seat belt into place. The dark interior radiated the day's heat, but she managed to always look so cool and collected.

"Excuse the fast-food smells. I just dropped my son off at college. The kid was eating like there was no tomorrow." He had mentioned his son in passing, but she had not asked him any questions about the boy, and when he'd inquired about her personal life, she had confirmed little beyond the fact that she was single.

"I'm sure he was a little nervous. Freshman year of college is a big deal. It certainly was for me." She typed the address of the Fosters' home into her phone.

"I always bought him fries after soccer practice or if I had to work a double shift. I think the fries were more for my benefit than his."

"Feeding is a form of love. He might not have said it, but the ritual must have comforted him."

"All I got from the kid today were grunts and silence."

"His prefrontal cortex isn't fully developed; add in hormones and the stress of a new life situation, and you're bound to get a moody kid. Your son is acting as he should."

"You should know. You're the profiler." He had never asked what she'd noticed about him, but he was slightly curious. "And what advice do you have for his old man?"

"Keep doing what you are doing."

Up until now, he had tabled whatever additional questions he'd had about her personal life. "You have any kids?"

"No."

"Did I hear something about you moving?"

"To Old Town. An uncle left me his place on Prince Street."

He whistled. "That's expensive real estate."

"Don't get me started on the electric bills."

"You going to keep the place?"

"I don't know. It's crammed full of furniture and memories. Until I sort through it all, I'll hang on to the place."

The GPS directed him down familiar streets and then on Janney Road and finally into an upscale neighborhood. It was five fifteen when he parked in front of the Fosters' two-story brick colonial. It had a neat front yard that managed to remain green in the brutal August heat, and parked in the gravel driveway was a late-model Ford Explorer. It was upward of three thousand square feet and, in this high-dollar neck of the woods, would have cost over a million dollars.

Out of the car, she waited as he crossed around the front and joined her. "Business must be good," he said.

"It appears so."

No missing her skepticism. She knew as well as he that appearances could be damn deceiving. He had seen plenty of drugs and domestic abuse in expensive homes as well as compassion and tenderness in the slums. You never knew what happened behind closed doors.

The generously trimmed bushes lining the brick exterior offered no hiding place for anyone looking to cause trouble, and there was a tall privacy fence rimming the backyard. He guessed no dog, because if there was one on the premises, it would generally be barking by now.

Still, he flexed his fingers and kept his jacket unbuttoned and his holstered gun quickly accessible, a habit he had picked up early in his detective days. Spencer's actions mirrored his as she tactically positioned herself a few steps behind him. This should be a straightforward death notification, but a smart cop who wanted to go home alive always expected trouble.

He rang the bell, and footsteps thudded on a hard floor inside the house. Two latches scraped across a lock, and a bolt clicked open. Not typical of suburbia. Normally, folks in the nice areas figured bad things did not happen there. Hadley Prince Foster knew otherwise.

The heavy oak door opened to a petite woman with long blond hair pulled into a ponytail. She wore expensive exercise gear that was designed more for fashion than function and athletic shoes that matched the striping on her capri pants. Diamonds winked from her left ring finger and her ears.

"May I help you?" Her smile was pleasant but not warm and welcoming.

Both Vaughan and Spencer held up their badges. "Hadley Foster?"

She tightened her hand on the doorknob. "I am."

"Your maiden name was Prince?" Spencer asked.

The smile was gone. "That's right."

"May we come inside?" Spencer asked. "There's something we need to talk to you about."

"Concerning?" Hadley asked.

"Your sister, Marsha," Vaughan replied.

Under the expertly applied makeup, Hadley's face paled, and her lips thinned into a grim line. A car door across the street slammed closed, and she flinched. She looked past them to the house across the street, and when the man dressed in a dark suit waved, she smiled weakly and waved back.

"Come inside," she said.

As she moved to the side, they angled around her and stepped into a foyer. Directly in front of them was a set of carpeted stairs that rose up to a second floor.

To his right, there was a formal room, and down the center hallway, a kitchen filled with white marble and bright stainless steel appliances. A back door fed off the kitchen into the yard surrounded by the privacy fence they had seen when they'd approached the house.

"This way, please." Hadley escorted them into the formal room, furnished with overstuffed chairs and a couch. A coffee table sported a large picture book featuring modern art. Pale-gray walls displayed a collection of framed paintings that created a look that was too cold for his taste.

This place was nothing like the man cave he shared with Nate. Best they could do in the way of decorating was a couple of framed Washington Redskins jerseys and a poster of the Rocky Mountains. Furniture in their small den included a couple of big recliners, a threadbare couch, and a wide-screen television.

Vaughan and Spencer each took a side chair. Hadley sat on the couch across from them, careful to sit in the center, the coffee table between them.

Spencer opened her folder and handed the picture of the bust to Hadley and said nothing.

Hadley took the paper, and when her gaze dropped to the image, her hand trembled slightly. A breath shuddered through her body. "That's my sister."

"Are you sure?" Spencer asked.

"Yes." Suspicion sharpened Hadley's gaze. "It looks like a sculpture. What's this about?"

"A set of remains was found in a nearby storage unit in the middle of June. I did a re-creation of the deceased's face, using the skull as a point of reference."

"Were you working off pictures of my sister?" Hadley asked.

"No. While I was working on the bust, I didn't know about your sister."

"Is that the skull they were talking about on the news?" Hadley asked.

"Yes," he said.

"I had no idea." Hadley placed the image on the coffee table but stared at it as if she were seeing a ghost. "Are you sure it's Marsha? The news kept saying there was no DNA."

"There was no DNA. That's why we enlisted the help of Agent Spencer," Vaughan said.

"Enough of the skull remained for me to sculpt the image you see before you. I ran the image of the reconstructed bust through a facial recognition scanning program, which said there was a ninety-eight percent probability it was Marsha Prince."

"So there's a two percent chance it's not her. My sister could still be alive," Hadley said.

"Actually, the probability it's not her is 1.8 percent," Spencer countered.

Hadley closed her eyes and pressed her fingers against her closed lids. Stillness washed over her, and when she finally spoke, her voice broke, forcing her to steady it. "I've spent the last eighteen years wondering what happened to her. I can't tell you how many nights I've dreamed of her walking through the front door with a big grin on her face. I'd wake up so happy." She folded her arms around her waist as if reliving the sensation. "And then I'd realize she was still gone."

"Can you tell us about the last day with your sister?" Vaughan asked.

She flattened her hands against her pants and rubbed them back and forth. Like the folded arms, it was a soothing move. "It was a really beautiful day. The sun was shining, and it was hot like today. My dad was also in a good mood."

"He wasn't always in a good mood?" Spencer asked.

"No. He worked really hard to keep the paving business going. He was up with the sun and rarely came home until after nine in the evening. Mom always did everything to keep him happy and the family together, but she was pretty sick by then. If Dad made it to dinner, the best we could get was a half smile or a grunt. Dad wasn't a likable guy."

"But he was in a good mood that day," Vaughan said.

"He was in a terrific mood. He decided not to go into work that day, and he said he wanted to take us all to the mall. He said it was high time his family had a fun day together, and no time like now, seeing that Marsha was leaving for school again."

"Weren't you also leaving for college?" Spencer asked.

"No. Dad had told me in July that he did not have the money to send us both. I had to stay behind and work in the shop for a year."

"That must have been difficult," Spencer said.

"It wasn't easy. But I understood that the money just wasn't there."

"Were you worried by your father's unexpected behavior?" Spencer asked.

"More surprised. I was a little leery, but it didn't take much convincing to win me over. Marsha was thrilled by the idea of an outing. But she was always in a good mood. Always positive no matter what. She loved the idea of doing anything fun."

"You all got into the family van?" Spencer asked as she reached in a folder and removed a picture.

"And we drove to the Springfield Mall. Dad took us into Macy's and told us to pick out whatever new outfit we wanted. That was a lot of fun. I had wanted a skirt I'd seen on television and thought maybe I could find it."

"Did you?"

"No, but I found one just like it. It wasn't on sale, but Dad said to get it anyway. We all came out of the store looking so great. Even Mom was enjoying herself. Then we went to the portrait studio, and Dad had a family picture taken. He also had one done of Marsha and me."

Spencer removed the picture from her purse and handed the picture to Hadley. "Is this the family portrait?"

"Yes." Hadley dropped her gaze to the image, and the fleeting glimmer of happiness in her gaze dimmed. She traced the faces of her mother and older sister. They were all smiling and looked like the picture-perfect family.

"When did you notice Marsha was missing?" Vaughan asked.

Hadley did not respond right away, but Vaughan and Spencer let the silence stretch. Cops understood that silence made most people uncomfortable, and they naturally wanted to fill it with words. His patience paid off when Hadley shifted her gaze to the picture.

"She was home for another week and then back to school. To earn extra money, she did some house-sitting. She had an overnight gig lined up, but at the last minute, she called and asked if I could take the job. I didn't want to go, but I wanted the money, so I said yes."

"Why did she cancel?" Spencer asked.

"She was going out to a club with friends," Hadley said.

"Which friends?" Vaughan asked.

"I never asked. The cops asked me over and over where she went, but I couldn't say. I wished I'd asked, but she was in a rush." She tucked a stray strand of hair behind her ear.

Eighteen years ago, the police could never confirm where Marsha had gone that night. Her regular friends had not seen her, and she had never made it to any of the area's clubs.

"Did your parents know she'd gone to a club?" Vaughan asked.

"No. Dad had already gone back to work, and Mom was exhausted and lying down. We both left and went our separate ways. When I got home the next morning, as soon as I pushed open the front door, Mom was freaking out. She said Marsha had not come home. She always came home. I used to kid her because she was such a Goody Two-Shoes."

"Did Marsha have a boyfriend, maybe one she didn't want your parents to know about?" Spencer asked.

"She dated a lot. Nothing that was ever serious. She was focused on school, and boys were kind of an afterthought."

"Did Marsha ever mention any of the boys she dated?" Spencer asked.

"No. Mom called around, but no one had seen her. Finally, she called Dad at work, and he called the police. From there it just spiraled out of control. The cops came, then the FBI, and finally the reporters. It was next to impossible to go to work after that. I started spending more time with Mark and hiding out from the world. I found out I was pregnant a few weeks later. I'd just turned eighteen. Mark asked me to marry him, and it made sense for us to leave Virginia."

"Your parents died within a year," Vaughan said.

"Yeah. It was too much for Mom. Her health was bad then anyways, and Dad had a heart attack. After I left Virginia, we spoke on the phone a few times, but I never saw them again."

Spencer's brow knotted in thought. "Was there anyone who made threats against you or your family?"

"The cops must have asked me that question a million times," Hadley said. "I didn't know of any, and I don't remember any unusual characters coming by the house. There were no red flags." She touched the edge of the picture and pushed it away so that her sister's brown eyes were not staring at her. "I still can't believe she's really dead." She shook her head. "I always held out hope."

"Would she have had a reason to run away?" Spencer asked.

"No. At least not that I knew of. She was going back to school. Mom and Dad were so proud of her, and they gave her the best education they could afford." She sat back, plucking an invisible hair from her pant leg. "Do you really think, after all this time, you can figure out what happened to Marsha? It's been eighteen years."

"I don't know," Vaughan said. "Time can sometimes work to our advantage. People who didn't talk before are willing now. Forensic technology has improved."

"Why would someone talk to the cops now, if they didn't back then?" Hadley asked.

"A killer confesses to a loved one or friend. The killer has a falling-out with this person, and they tell the police what they know. Or the killer dies, and whoever was holding their secret is now willing to talk," he said.

"Don't they forget details?" Hadley asked.

"Sure," Spencer said. "But sometimes fewer details are better than none."

Vaughan shifted tactics. "Your father's business was in financial trouble. He was highly leveraged."

"That's why I couldn't go to college. If you want the exact numbers, you should talk to Mr. Slater. Henry Slater. He worked for Dad, and he bought the business after Dad died. The paving business goes by a different name now, but it's still at the same location."

The front door opened, and footsteps sounded in the foyer. "Mom! Dad and I are home!"

"My daughter and husband," she said. "Mark knows, of course, but we've never told Skylar about any of this. She doesn't know what happened to my family."

"We understand," Vaughan said. "We'll take our lead from you."

Hadley stood. "In here."

Mark and Skylar Foster appeared in the door, both pausing when they saw Vaughan and Spencer. Skylar was petite and blond like her mother. She wore capri pants, a loose top, and sandals. She clutched a jeweled pink phone case and had a red backpack slung over her shoulder.

Mark Foster was tall and lean and wore crisp black suit pants but had loosened his red tie and rolled up his shirtsleeves.

"What's the deal?" Skylar asked. "Everything all right?"

"Of course," Hadley said. She rose and crossed to Mark, kissing him softly on the cheek. He stood straight and did not lean into the kiss.

"This is FBI special agent Zoe Spencer and Detective William Vaughan," Hadley said. "They had questions about an old cold case that, turns out, has nothing to do with me. They were just leaving."

Vaughan and Spencer both rose. The appearance of her family clearly made Hadley very uncomfortable. Like it or not, she was not going to say another word.

Mark extended his hand to Vaughan and Spencer. "What cold case?" he asked.

"A girl went missing eighteen years ago," Spencer said. "We thought she might have known your wife."

Mark glanced toward Hadley, as if trying to gauge her state of mind. He laid his hand on his daughter's shoulder but said nothing.

Skylar's frown was a mirror image of her mother's. "What girl?"

"It would have been before you were born," Mark said.

"Who was she?" the girl pressed.

"We'll talk about it later," Hadley said. "I don't want to hold up the detective and the agent."

The girl did not appear satisfied but seemed to sense she would get nowhere with her mother with them present.

"I'm sorry I couldn't be more of a help," Hadley said.

"Thank you again for your time," Vaughan said.

Spencer followed. "I can call you if I have more questions?"

"Certainly," Hadley said.

They each handed Mark and Hadley a business card, and the couple escorted them to the front door. "Thank you for coming," she said.

Mark's gaze grew more pensive. "Thank you."

Vaughan nodded as a smiling Hadley Foster closed the front door with a soft click. The locks slid back into place.

The two walked down the steps and along the sidewalk. They moved past a black Lexus and an Explorer parked in the driveway. "Wasn't that interesting," she said.

"I would have expected more shock from Hadley about the recovery of her sister's body. But she seemed more worried about why witnesses talk years later."

"The more perfect families and homes appear, the less I tend to trust them."

On that, they agreed. "Hadley's created a picture-perfect life here."

"She's holding on so tight I'm surprised her knuckles aren't white."

"Sounds like experience talking."

She arched a brow but pivoted away from the very overt attempt to know more about her. "I'd like to talk to Mr. Slater. He knew the family back in the day and might have a few insights."

A breeze carried the soft scent of new perfume that he liked very much. "Would you like to go now?"

"I would." In the car, she typed in the address of the business. "The website says they're open until seven."

Vaughan glanced at the time on the digital dash clock. He had pictured his first night without Nate to be a quiet affair featuring a cold beer, pizza, and the preseason football game he had taped.

In all honesty, the idea of quiet had been unsettling. He'd heard empty nesters got used to the silence, but he was not there yet. The more commotion in his life, the better, as far as he was concerned.

"Let's go." She scrolled through her phone messages. "Two missed calls from Nikki McDonald."

"Persistent. I'll give her that much."

"She can wait."

***

Wild Blue: I can't make dinner.

Mr. Fix it: Why?

Wild Blue: Mom and Dad got bad news.
Something about her sister.

Mr. Fix it: What about her?

Wild Blue: I'll tell you later.

Mr. Fix it: Okay.

Wild Blue: U r the only one who understands me.

Mr. Fix it: We are one and the same. How is your
mom?

Wild Blue: Lame. Like always. Next Monday?

Mr. Fix it: Yes.

Wild Blue: Luv you.

Mr. Fix it: Me, too.

CHAPTER FIVE

Monday, August 12, 6:00 p.m.
Alexandria, Virginia
One Day Before

Zoe had never seen Vaughan ruffled. He kept his tone easy and direct and could rope in a suspect, coworker, or even her with an easy smile. But she sensed those still waters ran deep, and he was not satisfied with the visit with Hadley Foster.

She flipped through the pictures in her case file until she reached the images of the blackened skull. "One thing to kill a young woman, but it's another to pull her teeth and burn her remains."

"That kind of death reminds me of a mob or cartel hit," he said. "Makes me wonder if Larry Prince was into something he shouldn't have been."

"Kill the girl to punish the father? That's possible, but it's a stretch. Larry Prince was investigated thoroughly, and there was nothing that smelled of organized crime."

"And cartels don't usually call the media and tell them where to find the body," he reasoned.

"Maybe Larry Prince pissed off the wrong person. Maybe someone pointed the finger at him, and he and his family paid the price."

"It's possible."

Vaughan wove up King Street, angled down Telegraph Road, and turned on Richmond Highway, where the landscape quickly turned from new and modern to strip malls, fast-food joints, and light industry. Five miles down Route One, he drove onto the Slater Slurry Inc. lot.

He parked beside a line of trucks, and the two made their way to the front office. A bell rang over their heads. The office was small and covered in faux paneling that looked like it dated back to the seventies. The few guest chairs were chrome and red vinyl, and the front desk, piled high with files, was metal.

A door behind the desk opened to a stocky man with a thick crop of gray hair held back with reading glasses. His face was round and wrinkled and reminded her of a bulldog.

"Can I help you?" the man asked.

"We're looking for Mr. Henry Slater." Vaughan held up his badge and made introductions.

"You found me." The man arched a brow. "What's this about?"

"We wanted to ask you about Larry Prince."

Slater pulled off his glasses and moved behind the desk. "He's been dead seventeen years. Died of a heart attack."

"I understand you two had a good working relationship," Vaughan said.

"He was my boss," Slater replied. "He treated me fairly, taught me the business. In return, I gave him a solid day's work. Our relationship was strictly professional. When the whistle blew, we went our separate ways."

"What do you remember about Marsha Prince?" Zoe asked.

"I've done my best to forget about it all." He sighed and rubbed the back of his neck with his hand. "She was a great kid. Hardworking, and all the customers loved her. Broke her father's heart when she vanished."

"Hadley also worked in the shop?" Vaughan asked.

"Not as much, but she was gearing up to run the register full time. But when her sister went missing, she got married and left town. I tried to keep up with Hadley and even sent her a Christmas card that first year she was out west, but she never wrote back. I figured it was just as well. Larry and Edith weren't exactly the best of parents."

"Why do you say that?" Vaughan asked.

"Larry was super controlling with his girls. Didn't like boys looking at them at all. If Mark hadn't been working here, I'm not sure Larry would ever have let him date Hadley. But Mark was a hardworking guy, and Larry liked him. Why are you asking about Marsha now?"

"Marsha Prince's remains were found eight weeks ago. It's taken this long to identify them."

"Shit. Where?" Slater asked.

"About five miles from here in a storage unit," Zoe said.

"I remember a reporter doing a story a couple months ago," Slater said. "She found bones in a box."

Unfortunately for them, the public videotape of the discovery had revealed many key details. Law enforcement normally held back facts they believed were known only to the killer, but in this case, there were few secrets they could now keep.

"The remains belonged to Marsha Prince," Zoe said.

Slater rubbed his hand over his jaw. "How did she die?"

Nikki McDonald still didn't know the answer to this question, and Zoe wanted to keep it under wraps for now. "We haven't determined that yet."

"Jesus." Slater rubbed the back of his neck as he shook his head. "The bones on the video were all black."

"They had been burned."

"Why?"

"Either someone didn't want her found, or they were sending a message."

"What kind of message?" he asked.

"You tell us," Vaughan countered.

"If you're suggesting that Larry Prince was into anything shady, you are wrong."

"I'm not suggesting anything. You bought the business a year after Marsha vanished," Vaughan said. "If anyone knew what was in the books or if Larry had owed anyone a lot of money, you would. Did he make anyone angry?"

"He got on well enough with the clients. He wasn't the warm and fuzzy type, but he was professional. And no, there wasn't anything funny about the books. I was able to keep the crews working and the business open because he had given me signature power on the accounts soon after Marsha vanished. He was a total wreck, and so was Edith. You can go back and check all the statements. I never did anything funny or off color with them."

"How did you afford the company?" Vaughan asked.

"It was a matter of meeting the banks and accepting the existing loans on the business. I had a track record, and I put my home up as collateral. The bank didn't want a default on their hands. I called Hadley and offered to send her money each month, but she said her husband made enough and for me to keep it."

Zoe pulled out the last picture taken of the Prince family and handed it to Slater. "Hadley said her father took the family out for a big splurge. Why was he in such a good mood?" Zoe asked.

Slater stared at the picture a long moment before handing it back to Zoe. "The cops asked me that question a dozen times back in the day. He had won a lucrative state contract. We knew we would have to buy more trucks and hire more men, but it also meant the bank was willing to give us the loan. The loan had come through that day, and he figured, why not do something nice for himself and his family. Only a month before, he had had to tell Hadley he couldn't send her to college. He was planning to tell her she could now go."

"How did Hadley react about not going to college?" Zoe asked.

"She was really upset, as you can imagine. She had worked harder than her sister and made better grades but was still facing a few years of working behind the counter here."

"Did Larry Prince have a girlfriend?" Vaughan asked.

Slater hesitated. "That's out of the blue. Why do you ask?"

"Trying to get a full picture," Vaughan said. "There's always more than meets the eye."

"There was a woman who worked the front desk." Slater's tone was reluctant. "They messed around a couple of times, but it wasn't serious."

"Did you tell the cops this?" Zoe asked.

"No. It didn't seem to have anything to do with Marsha."

"What was the woman's name?" Vaughan asked.

"Becky Mahoney. After the murders and all the media attention, she moved to Fredericksburg, Virginia. I haven't seen her in years."

"Who was Marsha dating?" Vaughan asked.

"There were a few upwardly mobile guys, but she never went out with any of them more than once."

"What about the ones that weren't upwardly mobile?" Zoe asked.

"There were a few who worked in this shop. One guy in particular caught her eye. Good-looking kid. Jason Dalton. He could charm anyone, and Marsha was no exception. But Jason was smart enough to know to stay away from the boss's daughters. And he was more interested in getting enough money together so he could move south."

"Was Marsha interested in any guys?" Zoe said.

"There were several, but it's been so long I don't remember the names. They all liked Marsha, too. Most of them had drug problems or had done time."

"Do you know where Jason Dalton is now?" Vaughan asked.

"Jason moved south a few months before Marsha vanished. I never saw him again. I haven't kept up with the other guys."

"You suspect Jason?"

"No. He was guilty of being poor and maybe stupid like most teenage boys are, but I never saw him as a killer."

"Was Hadley seeing anyone other than Mark?" Zoe asked.

"How would I know something like that?" Slater countered.

"You're one of the few people who knew the family well at the time," Vaughan pointed out.

"Hadley was crazy about Mark," Slater said.

"That's not exactly an answer," Zoe said.

"No, she wasn't dating anyone else," Slater said.

***

Forty-five minutes later, Zoe and Vaughan arrived at Nikki McDonald's apartment building. Vaughan parked, and they made their way into the lobby. They showed identification to the doorman, who called up to Nikki.

"I hope she saved her pennies," Vaughan said. "The rent here is not cheap."

"She's been out of work four months," Zoe said. "Her website has had a reasonable amount of hits but not enough to generate advertising to cover this."

The elevator doors opened, and Nikki stepped off. She wore dark cotton pants, a gray top, and sandals. Her hair was freshly brushed, and her lipstick looked as if it had just been applied.

"Detective Vaughan and Agent Spencer," Nikki said. "I was beginning to think you both were avoiding me."

Vaughan grinned. "I said I'd talk to you when I had some information."

Her eyes sparked. "And you do. Your expression gives it away."

His smile widened. "Is there somewhere we can talk?"

Nikki rubbed her hands together. "I feel like this is going to be good."

"It is," he teased.

"Now I'm intrigued."

On an intellectual level, Zoe understood Vaughan's easy style worked well with those he interviewed. It was that charm that had drawn her to him initially. His life was not perfect, but he chose not to haul the baggage around with him. And seeing as she carried enough for two people, it was a welcome relief.

However, she wasn't so crazy about the way Nikki McDonald leaned toward him when she spoke or the way she touched her hair in a flirty way.

Nikki led them down the hallway to a small waiting room furnished with four large chairs and a coffee table. Five sales brochures fanned across the sparkling glass tabletop. "The building manager uses this for sales meetings, but we can use it."

The reporter extended her hand to the two chairs and took the one on the other side of the coffee table. She leaned back, a woman comfortable in her space. "Let's have it."

Zoe and Vaughan sat, and he nodded to her, giving her the go-ahead to deliver the news. "The bones you found belonged to Marsha Prince."

Nikki's gaze lost all hints of amusement as her gaze leveled on Zoe. "Marsha Prince. *My* Marsha Prince?"

"If you mean the woman who was the subject of your news reports years ago, then yes," Zoe said.

Nikki had covered the girl's disappearance extensively, as had many journalists in the beginning. She had floated several theories, including one that had suggested the girl had been killed by a serial killer in the Shenandoah Valley. Cops had later disproved that conclusively.

She sat back and tapped a manicured finger on the table. "This is huge."

"Which makes it all the more important that we understand who sent you the message about the skull," Vaughan said.

"I gave you everything I had," she said.

"Have you been contacted in the interim?" Vaughan asked.

"No. Not another peep out of whomever this person is."

"You reach out to the sender?"

"I have."

"You covered the original story multiple times, and you did an anniversary report on the girl's disappearance," Zoe said.

"The story helped boost me up the ladder."

"Why didn't you include Hadley Foster in the anniversary piece?"

"I tried to talk to her, but she wouldn't have anything to do with me. She was clear she didn't want to be involved."

"She never submitted to any interview, correct?" Zoe asked.

"No, she never would. I know the police spoke to her extensively. I tried once to get ahold of some of the interview tapes but couldn't."

A frown deepened the lines on Vaughan's face. The idea that someone in his department would leak information to the media was clearly distasteful.

"The owner of the storage unit had no ties to the Prince family?" Zoe asked.

"She did not," Nikki agreed. "Helen Saunders also had no children. She did have a great-nephew, but he moved away years ago, and I haven't been able to find him."

"If you do come across new information or this mysterious informant contacts you, you will tell us." Vaughan had not tacked a question mark on at the end of the sentence.

"Of course. I always help law enforcement. If you figure this out, how about giving me an exclusive?"

"I can't make any promises," Vaughan said.

"You scratch my back—well, you know the rest."

He stood, extending his hand. As they shook, he said, "Don't hold out on me, Ms. McDonald."

"Never." She released his grip. "Agent Spencer, I would love to see a picture of the bust you created," she said. "I understand you have a real talent for re-creating the faces of the dead."

"We'll be sending out a press release in the next twenty-four hours," Zoe said.

"I don't get a sneak peek?" Nikki asked.

"No, I'm afraid that's not possible."

Nikki offered an exaggerated pout. "No fair."

Zoe lifted her gaze, knowing it was not friendly. "Marsha Prince would agree."

***

Zoe and Vaughan arrived at the Alexandria Heights apartment complex where Marsha Prince's body had been found. The brick entryway pillars were under construction, and the siding on the west side was covered in scaffolding. Several sets of windows on the top floor still bore the manufacturer's sticker.

"The building's undergoing a major renovation," he said.

"I do not envy the residents. I'm considering a renovation of my place, and I'm not looking forward to it."

"Why not just sell? The location alone is worth a fortune," he replied.

"I'm not ready."

"We're at the top of the real estate market, so you must be sentimental," he said.

She shrugged. "It happens to the best of us. I'm sure it will pass."

"Were you close to your uncle?"

"Jimmy wasn't actually my uncle. He was my late husband's uncle," she said.

Vaughan rattled the keys in his hands. "I didn't realize you'd been married."

"Jeff died several years ago."

"I'm sorry," he said.

Every time she heard the words, they fell short of doing anything other than filling the silence. At least these days they did not make her angry. "Thanks. He was young, and it was so unexpected; it's still not easy to talk about."

He cleared his throat. "Let me show you the storage unit."

"I understand Alexandria PD still has it closed off."

"We were waiting for identification. I'll lead the way," he said.

As they entered the lobby, the sounds of children laughing echoed over the tiled floors. There were three elevators, and all appeared to be in use. A man on a cell phone stepped off the center one, glanced at them, and then kept going.

Vaughan circumvented the elevators, choosing a set of stairs to the right. She followed him down two flights until they were on the garage level. In the distance, a car door opened and closed, and two people were having a heated discussion about where to have dinner.

He crossed the garage and led her toward a dimly lit corner. He unlocked the door and flipped on a light. Immediately, she spotted the strip of yellow tape wrapped around the third caged unit.

"Whoever stashed Marsha Prince here must have known Ms. Saunders," she said. "He or she would have known she barely used the unit. I wonder if we can identify that great-nephew Ms. McDonald mentioned."

"We tried. We went through her phone records and financials and found no consistent caller. No distant relative or con man. Nothing."

Her heels clicked as she walked up to the cage door, turned the latch, and swung it open.

"There were twenty-eight boxes in here of all shapes and sizes," Vaughan said. "We searched them all. But we didn't find any more human remains, and there was no connection to the Prince family."

She ran her finger over the dusty edge of the back window. "Did you ever hear of any theories from the cops that worked the case about who killed Marsha Prince?"

"There was never one person in their sights, but they all made several big bets that she knew her killer."

"Most women do," she said.

"I'll put in a request for the old case files."

She imagined the attention and paperwork a case like this generated. It would take Vaughan weeks to dig through the old files. "I don't spend six weeks re-creating a woman's face without becoming invested. I'd like to help."

He leaned against the side of the cage. "I never say no to help."

"Good."

"Seeing as we're going to be partners, want to grab dinner?" he asked.

"I'm starving, and we could talk about the case." It was a ritual she had shared with her late husband. Dinner had always involved a cold beer, maybe a steak, and discussion of a case. They had both loved the intellectual challenge, the sparring, and the lovemaking afterward.

"I know a place."

"Lead the way."

He drove them to a small diner surrounded by a cluster of fast-food restaurants near the interstate. When she shot him a questioning look, he held up a hand. "Trust me."

"I'm holding you to a good meal, Detective Vaughan."

He opened the door, held it, and waited for her to pass. The hostess called out his name; he waved and headed toward what had to be a favorite booth. Men, she noted, were creatures of habit and liked routine.

She slid across the red vinyl seat of the corner booth. From this vantage, they both had a clear view of the front and back exits. Like all cops, he probably wanted to know who was coming and going while he ate.

She reached for a laminated menu and opened it. "So, how many nights a week did you and Nate come here?"

"At least three. He never gets tired of the cheeseburgers and fries."

The idea of a burger and fries did tempt, but too many years of eating lean had left her unable to deviate from her strict diet. When the waitress appeared with two ice waters, she ordered a salad with grilled chicken. Vaughan got the cheeseburger and a soda.

She took a long drink of her water.

"The last time I saw you, you were on the hunt for a killer in Nashville," he said.

"South Broadway Shooter, according to the media." This serial killer had shot couples as they strolled along the Cumberland River near Lower Broadway and the very popular tourist and entertainment strip. When she'd arrived, the shooter had killed six people in the span of one month. Local law enforcement had called her in to create a profile of the killer as well as a sketch based on scattered eyewitness testimonies. Two days after the media had telecast her sketch, he had been captured.

"The capture made national news."

"The citizens of Nashville were scared. He all but shut down the tourist trade in the downtown area."

"The media never explained what his motivations were."

"Other than he was insane? He felt slighted by the music industry."

The waitress delivered his soda, and he thanked her by name. Vaughan was good that way. He smiled, used first names, and made eye contact, as if you were the only person in the world. It was what had made him one of her best students at the training session. And a good lover.

"How many crimes boil down to hurt feelings?" he asked.

"Too many." She took a sip of water and, when the waitress delivered their meal, carefully unwrapped her paper napkin from around the stainless fork and knife. She sliced into the chicken and was pleasantly surprised to find it was moist.

He bit into his burger, and for several minutes, the two sat and ate in silence. Cops on a case were damn lucky to sit at a table and eat a hot meal.

"What about the security cameras aimed at the apartment complex or on Helen Saunders's floor?"

"We pulled the camera footage, but the building only stores the video for two weeks. And there were thousands of people who came and went during those weeks."

"What about known associates of Helen Saunders? I suspect that her unit was not picked at random."

"We couldn't find anyone connected to Ms. Saunders who knew Marsha."

"With all the media attention during the initial investigation, no one came forward?"

"There were hundreds of leads called in, but none of them panned out." A bitterness sharpened the words.

"You sound troubled. Why?"

"I worked the stabbing homicide of a young sex worker today. Her case deserves that much attention."

Zoe understood the grim realities of a cop with limited time, too many cases, and a strong desire to find justice for all. "And she won't get it."

"She will if I have a say."

They sat in silence for a few more minutes, finishing up their meals, searching for conversation that strayed beyond their jobs.

"Any big plans now that you're an empty nester?" she asked.

"No idea." He set down the last bit of burger and again carefully wiped his hands with his paper napkin.

Her gaze dropped to his hands, remembering what they had felt like on her body.

"Want to come back to the house with me?" he asked, as if his own memory mirrored hers.

"Your actual house, and not a hotel room?" she asked.

"Nate's gone. The place is in a little disarray after this morning's packing, but it's clean and so very close," he said with a slight grin.

The colloquial term for their arrangement was friends with benefits or, more aptly, occasional work colleagues with benefits. Whatever the primary distinction, it was the benefits that were key.

This was the first time she would go to his house. The half dozen hookups over the last few months had been at either her old apartment in Arlington or a hotel room. Never at his home and never at the Old Town place that had belonged to Jeff's uncle. Made sense. Neutral locations kept their relationship from getting too personal.

"Early day at the office," she countered.

"My morning call is early as well, but you also get breakfast and personal delivery to your destination of choice in the morning. That gives us the bulk of the night, and then I'll drop you off."

She pictured those hands again on her naked body. "I'm ready when you are."

He tossed his napkin aside, his half-eaten meal seemingly forgotten. "I'll get the check."

***

When Nikki arrived at the Foster house, she was still reeling from the news. The skull had belonged to Marsha Prince!

She had not heard the name in thirteen years. The Marsha Prince disappearance had been the first big story she had covered, and she had been handed the assignment because of pure dumb luck. The station's crime reporter had been sick with the flu. Her boss, in a moment of desperation, had sent Nikki out to cover what the police dispatch had been calling a "possible abduction."

The instant she and her cameraman had shown up at the Prince residence and seen the three cop cars, she had known in her bones she had hit pay dirt.

Maybe she should have given Hadley more time to process, but she wanted to strike while the iron was hot. As she raised her hand to press the bell, angry voices, full of frustration, echoed from the home.

She rang the bell, and when no one answered, she knocked harder. Finally, the voices silenced, and footsteps hurried toward the door. When it snapped open, she found herself staring at Mark Foster. He was a tall man, but not as fit and lean as she remembered from the days she had covered the Marsha Prince disappearance. He wore suit pants, a white shirt rolled up to his elbows, and a red tie that he had loosened.

"I'm Nikki McDonald. I'm here to see Hadley and talk to her about her sister, Marsha."

"No. My wife is not up to giving a quote."

"Mark, who's at the door?" The woman's voice grew louder, along with clipped footsteps.

Nikki recognized the petite blonde, who looked very much like the girl she had tried to interview eighteen years ago. Her body remained trim and fit, though her angled face had lost the softness of youth. "Mrs. Foster."

"I've seen you on television before."

"Nikki McDonald. I also talked to you years ago."

"You flew out to Oregon."

"Yes, I did." She'd arranged to do a fifth-year anniversary piece, and Hadley had agreed to the interview. But when she had flown out to Portland, Hadley had refused to see her. She had changed her mind.

Instead of wallowing in the failed story, she pressed forward. "I'd still like to sit down with you and talk to you about your sister."

Hadley's cheeks flushed. "I have nothing to say."

"Years ago, I remember you mentioned that you and your sister did not get along."

"That's not how I remember it," Hadley said. "I loved my sister."

"Some of her friends said that you two were fighting a lot that summer. Your parents had money for her education but not yours."

"I was immature in those days. I should have been kinder to my sister," Hadley said. "Ms. McDonald, our family has been through a terrible ordeal. We don't need you digging into old wounds."

"If not me, then it'll be the cops. They won't let this go."

"Good night." Mark moved to shut the door.

Nikki stepped forward and put her foot on the threshold so he could not shut it. "No other reporter knows as much about this case as I do. I'm the best person to tell your sister's story."

"She would not want her story told," Hadley said, stepping forward. "She'd have hated the attention."

Mark stepped between Nikki and Hadley. As he had been back in the day, he was her protector. "This is enough. Leave, or I'm calling the cops."

"There are going to be other reporters," she warned. "Talk to me. Tell me your story."

"We're going to ignore all the reporters, including you," he said. "This is a private family matter."

"There is nothing private about it," Nikki countered.

"Just like before, the story will die, and it'll be forgotten," Hadley said.

"Do you really want Marsha forgotten?" Nikki said.

A girl appeared at the top of the stairs, and she regarded them for a beat before she began to descend. "Mom!"

"There's not a day that goes by that I don't think about my sister and what I could or should have done to save her," she hissed. "But I can't change the past."

Nikki lowered her voice, leaning forward. "What is it about your past with Marsha that you want to change?"

Hadley pressed her fingers to her temples and turned from the door. "Leave me alone."

Hadley's last words had barely been spoken when Mark pushed Nikki back and closed the front door in her face.

Nikki stood on the porch, more irritated with herself than put out. As she walked down the steps, she heard shades snap shut behind her in window after window.

Her desperation for a story had gotten the better of her, and she had pushed Hadley too far and too fast. But she would regroup and return. This story was her ticket back, and she was not going to let it go.

***

Minutes before seven, he watched Skylar's sappy boyfriend, Neil, pick her up, and then almost immediately, Hadley pulled out of the driveway.

He waited for Hadley's car to go around the corner before he started his engine and followed. Normally, Hadley waited longer to leave and was careful about her speed in the neighborhood, but tonight she appeared in a rush.

He wasn't worried, because she always went to the upscale hotel in Crystal City where her lover waited in the dimly lit bar. They would meet, flirt, and then find their way separately to his room. She always left by eleven and by midnight was home, showered, and in bed, curled on her side, likely pretending to sleep.

However, this Monday was different. The cops had come to her house. He didn't need to see badges to know they were the law. The plain suits and the way they had moved had given them away. The camera he had mounted on a neighbor's tree had alerted him. They were there to inform Hadley about the gift he had given Nikki McDonald.

God, if I could have been a fly on the wall. It would have been priceless to see Hadley's expression when the cops told her about Marsha's bones rolling around in that chest.

He tried to imagine Hadley's reaction. She was always cool and could hide her true feelings. He, better than anyone, knew that. Hadley had spent eighteen years pretending she did not know what had happened to Marsha. Now she had to be wondering if the secrets were finally going to bubble to the surface.

As he followed her through Arlington, he already knew she would not waver from her Monday night dalliance. Her regimented schedule was the only thing keeping her glued together after today's knock on the door.

CHAPTER SIX

Monday, August 12, 8:30 p.m.
Northern Virginia
One Day Before

Zoe was not surprised that Vaughan's home was modest. Cops in the Northern Virginia real estate market did not have many options, and she imagined he counted himself lucky that he was inside the beltway.

As he pulled into the driveway, security lights mounted on the side and front of the house clicked on. The one-story brick house was located on a cul-de-sac that was ringed by a half dozen larger homes more recently built.

There was no garage, and the closely cut grass had browned and bristled in the August heat. No flowers in the edged beds or extrafussy accoutrements such as flags or garden statues women tended to like. But there was a wooden fort built in one large tree, and judging by the graying wood and weathered rope ladder, it had been there at least a decade.

As she stepped out of the car, her general assessment of the Vaughan home was that it was normal.

He pressed several buttons on the keypad mounted by the front door, and it opened. A sensor inside the house triggered interior lights, and a security alarm pinged as he punched in the code.

Okay, maybe Vaughan's emphasis on security was not exactly run of the mill. But once anyone saw what a homicide detective witnessed, they understood monsters did not just inhabit fairy tales.

The interior setup was very masculine. Large overstuffed couch, twin recliners, and a massive television mounted over a fireplace that looked unused. The pictures on the walls were themed around his son or sports. The place was clean and neat, and the only hints of Nate's major transition were several unfilled boxes.

"Can I get you something to drink?" he asked. "I have bourbon."

"Thanks. No ice."

He opened a kitchen cabinet and removed a half-full bottle of bourbon and poured two fingers in everyday glasses. As he handed her a glass, her fingers barely brushed his. It was a light touch, scarcely noticeable, but it sent a thrill through her. It had been a while since they had been together, and she hungered for what was coming.

She took a sip, impressed. "Nice."

"Glad you like it." His gaze studied her over the rim of his glass before he downed it in an uncharacteristic show of impatience.

She finished the last of her drink and set the glass down beside his. "You going to give me the grand tour or take me straight to the bedroom?"

He loosened his tie. "Do you want the grand tour?"

"How about a rain check on that?" It surprised her how much her impatience had seeped into her tone.

"Good."

Vaughan took her by the hand and led her down the central hallway peppered with more pictures of Vaughan and his son.

The bed in the master room was a king with two pillows and a neatly made blue comforter. Twin nightstands had lamps, but the table closest to the door was piled high with books on history, mathematics, and politics. Topping the stack of books was a pair of dark-rimmed glasses.

"There's a bathroom in there if you need it," he said.

"Thanks."

She removed her weapon and holster from her waistband and set them both on a dresser outfitted with a large mirror that caught the bed's reflection.

She shrugged off her jacket and laid it beside her weapon and kicked off her shoes. As she unbuttoned her blouse, she caught Vaughan's reflection in the mirror. He had removed his badge and gun but was watching her closely as he unfastened his shirt buttons.

She slid off her shirt and then her pants. When she faced him in just her bra and panties, he was reaching for his belt buckle as his eyes roved over her.

She crossed the room and pushed his hands aside, taking the smooth metal buckle in her fingers. She was careful not to touch him as she studied his face.

"I feel a little like a lab rat," he said.

"Really?"

"You are always studying my every expression. And I know you've analyzed my home."

"It's what I do. I study people." She unhooked the top button of his trousers.

His jaw pulsed. "Do you ever see people as people?"

"It's easier if I don't."

He traced his finger over her bare shoulder. "There's no emotion, then, when we do this?"

"I like it very much." She opened his pants but did not slide her hand under the waistband of his shorts.

"You're using me for sex?" A note of seriousness hummed under the playful tone.

Maybe she was. But after Jeff had died, she had used other men for sex and had never returned for extra helpings as she had with him.

Zoe met his gaze, seeing an intensity she had not noticed before. "Do you want me to stop?"

His silence swarmed around her. "No."

"Good. Because I don't want to stop." She reached for the clasp between her breasts and unhooked her bra. She slid it off and let it fall to the floor.

He cupped her breast and leaned in to kiss her lips. Since the first time he had touched her, she had liked the way he teased her nipples and the sensual way he kissed her. He certainly did not feel like Jeff or even look like him. But he had a way of fanning flames that had died with her husband.

She pressed against him, liking the feel of his erection brushing against her groin, the way his taut abdomen hitched when she teased him, and how breath shuddered over his lips when her teeth gently bit his bottom lip.

They stood, teasing each other, almost testing to see who would be the first to lower to the bed. It had always been her in the past. And each time she had eased down to the mattress and beckoned him forward, that patience of his had shattered.

This time, she found he was taking extra time playing, and when she tried to tug him toward the bed, he resisted. It had been a month since he had been inside her, and she missed the sensations he churned in her body.

She pushed off his pants and underwear, growing impatient with the foreplay. He stepped out, but instead of pulling her toward the bed, he cupped her lace-clad buttocks.

The flirtatious back-and-forth was starting to feel more intimate than she had intended. Prolonged foreplay and kissing had been something she had only shared with Jeff. And since his death, she had avoided emotional attachments, including one with Vaughan.

She stepped back from Vaughan and slid off her panties. His breathing was quick, and she was pleased to know that she was not the only one who was anxious to be in bed. Later, she might analyze why he had this sudden need for them to savor each other. For now, she did not care.

She took him by the hand, and as she climbed onto the mattress, she pulled him with her. She knew what he liked—knew how to make him forget whatever promise he had made to go slow. She cupped her breasts and moistened her lips as her fingers slid down her belly to her sex. Seconds later, he was on top of her, and she maneuvered his erection to her opening.

She felt his urgency as he pressed inside her and sensed his resolve wavering. She smoothed her hand over his buttocks, coaxing him deeper inside of her. He moved in and out of her slowly as her body adjusted to him, and soon he was thrusting harder.

Sexual tension built in her body, and she gave him high marks for the way he had learned the pressure points on her body so quickly.

She closed her eyes, trying to remember what it had felt like when she had been with Jeff. Six years was a lifetime, and the intervening time had stripped away almost every last memory she had cherished.

Now more than ever, she desperately wanted to remember Jeff, but she could not recall a single detail. Later, she would play back his last voicemail message on her phone and recharge the fading recollections.

As if he sensed her mind drifting, Vaughan pushed deeper into her, shooting electricity through her entire system. He brought her focus back to the sensations stirring in her body. She wanted to turn off her brain and shut out the sadness, if only for a little while.

Desire and release roared around her, chasing her closer to the cliff. She wanted to free-fall over the edge. She wanted to feel.

"Open your eyes," he said.

His deep voice was a distant distraction, and she wanted nothing more than to swat it away like a bug. Her focus needed to remain on the orgasm that promised release. She did not want to acknowledge work, life, grief, or him.

As he slowed his pace, her race to the edge decelerated. She raised her pelvis.

"Open your eyes."

The way the words were spoken was so clear and concise; she knew if she did not obey, he would stop and rob her of the payoff.

With a sense of resolve, Zoe opened her eyes and discovered he was studying her with an odd mix of desire and annoyance.

"You're not the only one who reads body language," he said.

"What does that mean?" Her distant voice echoed with insincerity.

"Who are you with?" he asked.

"You," she said.

He brushed the stray wisps of hair from her face. "Are you?"

"I don't see anyone else."

"Not even your late husband?"

Jesus, did it really matter? They were both getting what they wanted. She expected nothing from him. No strings or baggage.

The buildup to her release was losing steam, and she didn't want to go home alone and sexually frustrated. "It's only you," she lied.

A slight cock of his head told her he wasn't sure he believed her. He wanted to. But . . .

"Right now, it's just you and me." She smiled enough to ease the apprehension coiling in his body. "I can get to where I want to go alone, but I'd rather do it with you." She arched toward him in a show of unity.

His eyes smoldered, and seemingly shoving aside his doubt, he quickened his pace. Sweat moistened the base of his spine, and she knew he had lost himself in the moment. She tightened her grip on her breast and moaned as the edge raced toward her faster than it ever had.

When she tumbled, she arched, allowing her body to give in completely to the sensations washing over her in rolling, hot waves.

Vaughan's body went rigid, and the muscles in his neck bunched as he bored deep into her. The tension in his back released, and his eyes glistened with the triumphant spark men had when they orgasmed.

He lowered down on his elbow and rolled on his back beside her. She closed her eyes again, nestled closer to his warmth, and drifted back to that fleeting place between the past and the present. She was not with her husband but with Vaughan; she could almost pretend she was happy like she used to be.

And these days, almost had to be good enough.

***

Nikki's heart beat in her chest as she shoved through the front door of her condo. In one hand, she clutched a grocery bag stuffed with the essentials: wine, aspirin, and coffee. In the other, she balanced a duffle, crammed with files she kept in her storage unit, and a pizza box.

She still couldn't believe that the skull belonged to Marsha Prince!

Nikki pushed her front door closed and crossed into the kitchen, dumping her purchases on the marble countertop.

After toeing off her shoes, she moved to her computer and pulled up her site. She had written and posted a quick recap of Marsha right after the detective and agent had left her. She checked the comment section and saw two dozen comments. Not stellar, but not terrible.

From the bag she removed the DVDs she had retrieved from storage. She arranged them in chronological order, starting with the first story she had filed on the Prince girl's disappearance. Today she would create a montage of videos for her site so that her audience could see what it had been like for her to cover it in real time.

She loaded a DVD in the disk drive, and as it queued, she poured herself a glass of wine and plopped three slices of pizza on a plate.

Six months ago, she would never have indulged in the carbs, but months of unemployment had translated into so many bad habits she now doubted she could fit into one of her trademark pencil skirts.

She sat at her small kitchen table and watched as the camera panned from the Princes' two-story home to her. For a moment, she hit pause, leaning in and staring at her face. Jesus, when had she ever been *that* young? She looked like Bambi caught in the headlights of a hunter. And the hair. Who had told her bangs looked good on her?

"Time marches on, McDonald."

She hit play and watched detectives cluster near the house as a grim-faced Hadley peeked out from the curtains of the large front bay window.

"I'm at the home of Larry and Edith Prince. Police are not saying much, but it appears that their nineteen-year-old daughter, Marsha, has vanished. My sources are telling me that the 911 call came in early morning, when Marsha's mother realized she'd not come home. I've spoken to several neighbors, who tell me that they saw Marsha Prince up to two days ago."

Over the course of the next several reports she had filed, neighbors and friends had had lots to say about the family. She'd learned of Mrs. Prince's multiple sclerosis and Larry's financial struggles, but most had conceded the Princes were a normal family. There had been potential sightings of Marsha and tips called into the hotline, but she had never been found.

Nikki drained her glass of wine and crossed back into the kitchen and brewed a pot of coffee. As much as she would like to finish the wine, she needed to start making a list of the people associated with this case.

Her attention shifted back and forth to the pictures she had of the girl and to the images she had taken of the blackened bones nestled in the chest filled with brittle tissue paper. She did not know the actual cause of death but wondered, given the state of the bones, if it even could be determined now.

But someone out there knew exactly how Marsha had died. And it was likely that someone had sent her to the remains because he or she wanted the girl's story known.

Her fear was that her friendly tipster would lose his nerve and remain as silent as he had been over the last eight weeks. Up until now, her contact had had all the power. Now she needed to get the upper hand. She quickly typed out a public plea on her website to her tipster, suggesting he was a coward if he did not contact her.

Her finger hovered over the "Post" button as she considered what kind of trouble she could be stirring up with an individual who could be unstable.

Seconds ticked, and her nerve actually wavered before she hit the button.

CHAPTER SEVEN

Tuesday, August 13, 2:30 a.m.
Alexandria, Virginia
The Day Of

Hadley had arrived home shortly after midnight, barely twenty minutes before Mark had pushed through the front door. She had lain in bed, listening to him move around downstairs, shower in the bath off the hallway, and change into jogger shorts and a T-shirt. The choice of clothing was for Skylar's benefit. If their daughter caught him on the sofa or downstairs, he could simply say he was out for an early run or had fallen asleep in front of the television. Mark did everything for that kid. He adored her, and Hadley knew if he had to choose between Skylar or her, their daughter would win hands down.

When their girl had had her troubles in Oregon, it had been Mark's idea to move back east. Hadley had not wanted to return to the East Coast but realized leaving Portland was better than facing the questions and stares. He had reached out to his company and requested a transfer.

Now as she rolled out of bed, minutes after three o'clock in the morning, she glanced briefly toward the spot where her husband had slept until last week. They had both agreed divorce was the only option available, and they were simply waiting for the best time to tell Skylar.

He had wanted to wait for a few more weeks to give Skylar a chance to settle into her school year. Hadley had insisted it be done by Friday.

Hadley knew her daughter well enough to know she was very smart and had to have sensed major problems in the marriage.

"Mom, why were the cops here?" Skylar asked. "I've been good. I've done everything you asked."

"They weren't here for you," Hadley said.

"Then why?"

A headache pulsed behind her eyes. "Don't worry about it."

Her daughter's temper snapped. "You only say that when there is a problem!"

Hadley now quickly made the bed, smoothing out all evidence of the separate sleeping arrangements. She dressed in jogging shorts, a bra, and a T-shirt, made a notation in a small notebook she used to track her workouts, and then tiptoed past Skylar's closed door and down the stairs. Mark lay on his side, his back pressed against the cushions and his arms crossed over his chest, as if trying to squeeze his large frame into the too-small space.

In three days, he would move out. All that was left to do was tell Skylar. Neither of them wanted to upend the girl's life. But Hadley needed a new challenge. A new *something* to consume her life and thoughts.

Poor Skylar. She had been born to a mother who was damaged. A mother who was OCD about so much irrational shit but who was powerless to ease her grip on control. She was a mother who kept secrets and lied because they made her feel safe and in control. A mother who recognized love but was so consumed by guilt she had forgotten what genuine emotion felt like. Maybe if Hadley had made different choices, Skylar would not have suffered.

Hadley slipped out the back door, closing it behind her but not bothering to lock the door. Even if someone broke into the house, Mark would hear it. And he would know what to do, because he always knew how to fix any problem.

He was Mark the Savior. The Fixer. The Jailer.

She stretched out her calves and Achilles tendons before easing out the back gate. She began with a slow and steady jog down the back street illuminated only by the light of a near full moon. Despite her warming up her muscles, the plantar fasciitis in her right heel sent pain bolting up her leg. Experience had taught her that the discomfort would continue for several miles, and when it vanished, she would miss it. She functioned best when she was hurting.

Her muscles groaned and pulled but finally relaxed, coaxed by the warm morning air. She drew in a deep breath. Normally, she ran five miles, but today she was tempted to go farther. Her body craved the activity that released the endorphins. She ran faster.

The image of Marsha's reconstructed face jostled into her thoughts. Though the sculpture was good, the face had an artificial look, much like a person prettied up for a coffin viewing. Real but not quite.

Each time she thought about Marsha's skull under the clay and paint, she imagined her sister watching her through the glassy brown eyes. Marsha's eyes had always been so trusting, because her sister had believed that no matter what, Hadley had her back.

Hadley stared up at the clear night sky and the full moon, remembering the moon had looked very much like this on the night Marsha had left. It had been clear, pure, and white. Almost perfect.

"Do you have to be such a bitch? You're never happy, are you?" Marsha asked. *"Hadley, it's not my fault."*

Hadley quickened her pace, trying to chase away memories of her sister. "Go away," she whispered.

Marsha's voice echoed again in her head. *I just wanted to go out and have fun. You should have warned me.*

"Shut up!" Hadley said.

Hadley pumped her arms harder. Ahead, a cat screeched, and another howled back. Sweat began to pool between her breasts.

The image of her sister's face flashed in her mind. The last time she had seen Marsha, her sister had been headed out the back door to meet a date at a club. Hadley could have said something. But she had not. She had remained silent as she'd watched Marsha drive off. It had never occurred to her that Marsha would not come home. She had thought maybe she would get knocked down a peg or two, but she would come home.

I trusted you! Marsha's voice echoed.

The memory of the bust's eyes stalked her. "You're dead. You're dead. And it's not my fault. Not my fault. Not my fault." She whispered the involuntary chant over and over as she pounded the pavement.

She tripped on a small pothole and had to take several quick steps to right herself. "Shit," she muttered as she refocused on the pavement.

One step. Two steps. Three steps.

The pain in her leg returned, and she let it lasso her thoughts. She ran for another hour, and when she entered her front door, her calf was on fire. The scent of coffee surprised her, and she wondered if her husband had set the timer on the coffee maker incorrectly again.

She limped up the stairs, not bothering a glance toward Mark. The upstairs was still dark, but she had walked this hallway so many times she knew every creak in the floor, the number of steps from the landing to her bedroom, and the location of all the light switches.

The digital display on her nightstand clock read 4:32 a.m. Good. She still had an hour before the house woke up.

She sat on the end of the bed and reached for her laces. As she ducked her head, she had the sense that someone was in the shadows, lurking, watching.

Hadley rose and walked toward her bedroom door. Her sister's name on her lips as she stared down the long quiet hallway. Her heart pounded in her chest. She listened but heard only the gurgle of the coffee maker downstairs. No one was there. And yet, something was definitely off.

She returned to her bedroom and readied to close and lock the door. But as she took hold of the knob and pushed it closed, the hair on the back of her neck rose. Her skin prickled. And then came the creak of floorboards only a few feet away.

The sound wasn't coming from the hallway but from behind her. Someone was in her room.

***

The phone woke Nikki McDonald, startling her from a hazy, restless sleep. Her body was still buzzing with too much caffeine, and her mind was crammed with ideas about the Marsha Prince story.

She reached automatically for the first of three cells on her nightstand. Blinking away the sleep, she focused on her phone.

What do you think of my tip?

She sat up so quickly the papers piled on her chest slid to the floor. She had received nothing from the tipster who had contacted her early in the summer through her website. And now, he was texting her.

Heart pounding, she drew in a breath. She gave out this cell number to anyone and everyone. It was the number she used when she worked a story, so no surprise that whoever her mystery person was, they had gotten ahold of it.

Nikki texted back: Who is this? How did you know Marsha Prince was in that storage room? She waited for the text bubbles. "Come on. Don't leave Mama hanging like that."

And then the trio of rolling bubbles appeared. I know a lot about Marsha Prince.

Who is this?

The bubbles vanished.

She typed, **Reward for more information.**

"Come on, come on." She gripped the phone for minutes, staring, waiting, before realizing whoever had contacted her might not be motivated by money. If coins were not going to do the trick, a few ego strokes might.

No one can tell your story like me.

Silence.

She fell back against the mattress, holding the phone to her chest. Whoever this was, this was contact number two. This mystery source was building up his nerve. He wanted something from her but was not ready to ask.

She swung her legs over the side of the bed. She dialed her contact in the police department.

"Manny Jackson."

"Manny, this is Nikki McDonald."

"Long time no talk." The rough edges softened as he was likely remembering the multiple rounds of bourbon she had bought him while working the Beltway Bomber story three years ago.

"Been on the move."

"So I hear."

She rose and paced, making herself smile. "Hey, Manny, got a favor to ask."

"You always have a favor to ask." He sounded more amused than put out.

"Hey, you scratch my back, and I'll scratch yours. Your department came off looking like heroes when I covered the bomber." The cops *had* been heroes. In cinematic fashion, they had found the bomb and disarmed it so quickly she had almost been disappointed. A little explosion or fire would have made for great footage, plus more airtime for her.

"You back on the job at the news station? For what it's worth, the gal who took your place looks like she's still in high school."

She pictured the brunette with the smooth olive skin. "Kelsey Jennings was in high school five years ago."

"Shit."

"I might have a shot at returning if you help me with this."

A sigh shuddered over the line. "What do you need?"

"Marsha Prince."

The beat of silence went from weary to charged, like she had struck a nerve, and it was sending shocks through his body. "What about her?"

This time her grin was real. "Vaughan came to see me today. He told me the skull I found shoved in the gray trunk was Marsha Prince. How did she die?"

He blew out a breath. "If the detectives know, they aren't telling."

"How long has she been dead?" When he hesitated, she added, "Do a down-and-out gal a solid, Manny."

He chuckled. "No one is sure. Now that they know who she is, they'll run more tests."

She paced the carpeted floor, glancing in the mirror as she passed. She sucked in her stomach. "What's the FBI's involvement?"

"Strictly support at this point. They did the bust and made the identification. Now, Ms. Prince is Alexandria PD Homicide's case."

"Thanks, Manny. I owe you a round."

"Make it two." In the background, a phone began to ring. "Got to go."

"Thanks, baby."

When the phone went dead, she pressed it to her chest and paced around the room. She owed Vaughan a phone call on this mysterious text, and she would tell him about it. Soon.

CHAPTER EIGHT

Tuesday, August 13, 5:30 a.m.
Northern Virginia
The Day Of

The instant Vaughan woke, he knew she was gone. He should not have been surprised. She never stayed long, but he'd thought last night would be different.

He swung his legs over the side of the bed and instantly spotted the note on the mirror. It was written on the back of the fast-food receipt in fluid and graceful handwriting.

Called a car. Didn't want to wake you.

Spencer. He knew how to make that woman's body tighten with desire and how to make her moan in a way that told him she was fully attuned to his body. But beyond that, she was still a complete stranger.

He flicked the edge of the note, surprised he had not awoken. Since he had become a cop and father, he had turned into a light sleeper. Both incarnations, like a doctor on call, were summoned at all times of the day and night. His ability to shake off sleep in seconds and then think clearly was well honed. But yesterday had been long, even for him.

He laid the note on his dresser as he glanced at the pillow that still held the impression of her head. It was not like him to be sentimental, but he was sorry he likely would not see her for a while.

He showered, and fifteen minutes later he was dressed, his badge and sidearm on his belt. As the coffee brewed, he scrambled five eggs before he realized Nate was gone. He toasted a bagel and ate alone at the kitchen table.

He filled a travel mug with more coffee and was on the road by six o'clock. Moonlight mingled with the lights looming over I-395 as he looped around the beltway and headed north toward his exit. The traffic was already building, and soon it would slow to a snail's pace.

With luck, the first wave of files from the Prince case would be in his office. He had been warned that there were a dozen file boxes, but he did not care. He also had the autopsy of the Jane Doe stabbed to death in the motel room to attend. It was going to be another long day.

Fifteen minutes later, he had parked and was in the break room, refilling his coffee. When he flipped on the lights of his office, there were six file boxes stacked in front of his desk. A green sticky note read *More to come*.

It was too early to call the medical examiner about his Jane Doe from the motel room, so he set his cup down and flipped through the first set of files.

He spent the next hour and a half reading through the detectives' notes. At the time of Marsha's disappearance, the detectives had exhausted every lead and tip that had come into the station, but in the end came up with nothing.

Vaughan juxtaposed the image of the blackened skull in the trunk and the smiling face of Marsha Prince. Only a monster would do this to a young, vibrant girl who had been Vaughan's son's age when she'd died.

When Nate had been a little boy, he had wanted assurance that monsters were not real. Before Vaughan could confirm they were, his ex-wife had been quick to tell the boy that they were only in storybooks.

But Nate had been savvy enough to know even then that she had lied. When Vaughan had been tucking Nate into bed that night, the boy had asked his father about the monsters.

Vaughan could not lie and had simply said, "I got your six, pal."

"I got yours, too, Dad."

A knock on Vaughan's door brought his attention to the present. Detective Cassidy Hughes stood in the doorway. He had worked with Hughes for a year now, and the two got on well. Short with a sinewy frame, Hughes had curly hair and always dressed in well-fitting clothes. Today it was snug jeans, a silk blouse, and heeled boots.

"Stop whatever you're doing," she said.

He cleared his throat and shut the dead girl's file. "What's up?"

"A real shit storm of biblical proportion."

***

Zoe stood in her kitchen, drinking coffee and staring at the still-packed boxes she had moved to her townhome six weeks ago.

Technically, she had the day off. Ramsey had told her to kick back for a few days after what had been an endless stream of weeks filled with different cities, police departments, and killers.

Try as she might, she had not been able to sleep more than a couple of hours, so she had risen and made coffee. As she sipped, she cared less about the flavor and more about the punch of caffeine to chase away the fatigue. She really did not want to unpack boxes today any more than she had during the other countless opportunities. Even an armchair psychologist would call this procrastination classic avoidance. She had legally claimed the property and sold a perfectly good condo, but for some reason she could not settle into living here.

She crossed the stone floor to the table nestled in the nook of a bay window and thumbed through the stack of mail. A glance out the wavy glass windowpanes, original to the 1801 house, showed a vivid blue sky.

Bright sunshine shone down on Prince Street's cobblestone road sloping toward the Potomac River less than a block away. She climbed the narrow staircase to her room, thinking she would slide back into bed and catch up on reading.

The stairs creaked and the banister wobbled a little as she climbed the stairs past the dozens of black-and-white photos featuring Uncle Jimmy in all the incarnations he had enjoyed during his eighty-two years.

Vaughan had hit the nail on the head when he had questioned why she was keeping this place. As tempting as it had been to sell, as it was worth millions even in its dilapidated state, giving it up felt disloyal to Uncle Jimmy and Jeff. Uncle Jimmy, who had raised Jeff, was her last tangible connection to him. However, the true cost of repairing and maintaining this home was beyond her means. So here she was, able neither to sell nor to keep. She was caught in no-man's-land.

The digital clock on the antique nightstand and her phone charger looked out of place next to the four-poster Queen Anne bed that dominated what had been a guest room.

The last time she had slept in this room had been the night Jeff had died. She had been unable to go home to the apartment they had shared, and Jimmy had been the only refuge that had felt remotely comforting. The old man had welcomed her in with open arms.

Before she had left for her last trip to Nashville, her single act of making this house her own had been to change the sheets on the guest bed, which, to her great relief, were seductively comfortable.

Hanging above the bed was one of the best forgeries she had ever seen of Monet's *Impression, Sunrise*. If Uncle Jimmy had known anything, it was how to paint the best fakes. Over the last few years, Zoe had often had dinner with Jimmy, and over a bottle of Chateaux Margaux, he had shared the tips of master forgers like himself. Jimmy had given her the skills to become the agent she was.

Her phone rang, and she fished it out of the back pocket of her jeans. Caller ID displayed *Jerrod Ramsey*. Her boss had a reputation for not sleeping, which she had been warned was a hazard of the job.

Zoe took another sip of coffee that had cooled. "Agent Ramsey, how did you know I was awake? It's my day off."

He chuckled as if she had made a joke. "You met with Vaughan yesterday?"

"I did." He never called for idle chatter. "Do I still have the next four days off?"

"Technically, you do. And technically, I've had five vacations in the last four years, but I've worked through every one of them."

She pressed the mug to her temple, grateful her plans to unpack today were officially shot. "What do you need?"

"Hadley Foster."

Her interest perked. "I met her yesterday. I went with Vaughan to make the death notice."

"She's missing, along with her daughter. The father is in surgery right now. He told the responding officer that he was stabbed by an unknown intruder."

There should have been a universal law forbidding evil on such beautiful days, she thought. "I can be at the residence in a half hour."

"Good. The media has already gotten wind of it, and I'm sure you realize there's a lot of pressure to find the mother and daughter as quickly as possible."

"Vaughan and I spoke to Nikki McDonald yesterday as well."

"She's no doubt leading the charge from the media."

"Understood. I'm on it."

He ended the call, and she quickly stripped and stepped into the shower. She toweled off, dressed in a dark pantsuit, and coiled her long auburn hair into a twist. She drained the last of her coffee and then, securing her badge and gun to her belt, grabbed her purse and headed down the stairs.

Out the back door, she cut across the long narrow backyard, past Jimmy's private garage, currently crammed full of God only knew what, and through the tall privacy gate to the street. Up a block, she found the spot where she had parked her Ford Explorer. She made a mental note to clean out the damn garage.

After tossing her bag in the car, she slid behind the wheel. She had thought after last night it would be a while before she would see Vaughan again, if ever. It had felt a little too personal, and a long break was in order. But here they were, working together again. At least this morning she had left him a note.

"No rest for the wicked," she muttered as she pulled out of the space.

***

AMBER ALERT

Seventeen-year-old female Skylar Foster and her mother, thirty-five-year-old Hadley Foster, are missing and considered in EXTREME DANGER. The family's 2017 black Lexus is missing and presumed stolen and was last seen in Alexandria, Virginia.

CHAPTER NINE

Tuesday, August 13, 8:00 a.m.
Alexandria, Virginia
One Hour after the 911 Call

The call played in Vaughan's mind as he scanned the Fosters' suburban street and the neatly maintained yards. Today, the safe, upscale neighborhood had been invaded by a collection of marked police cars parked on the street, the department's forensic van, and three news station vans. Channel 5 and their primary anchor, Rick McGuire, were on scene. No sign of Nikki McDonald yet.

He ducked under the tightly strung yellow crime scene tape and paused to speak to the uniformed officer. He extended his hand. "Oscar, what's going on?"

"It's a mess inside," he said.

Officer Aylor was young and had been in the department less than a year. The first homicide or truly gruesome death often shook up the rookies. He had wiped the blood from his hands, but his shirt and pants were stained.

Vaughan could still recall his first homicide. A woman had gutshot her husband. The smell of that scene had lingered with him for weeks. "I understand Mr. Foster called 911?"

"He did at 7:00 a.m. He was lying in the foyer when I arrived at 7:05 a.m. He was barely conscious, but he kept insisting that we find his wife and daughter."

"Did you ask for a description of the assailant?"

"Foster kept saying the guy wore a mask, and he didn't see his face."

"Did you search the premises?"

"The ambulance was seconds behind me, and when they took control of Mr. Foster, I searched the house. No sign of the wife, daughter, or perpetrator. But it's clear whatever went down happened in the master bedroom."

Vaughan would see for himself soon enough. "Thanks, Oscar. Good work."

"Thank you, sir."

Vaughan removed latex gloves from his pocket and slid them on his hands. As he climbed the front steps, he glanced left and right into the flower beds, thinking there might be footprints or a discarded item that would indicate what had happened here. It was the crime scene's job now to tell him the story.

When he saw nothing that caught his attention, he reached in another pocket and removed paper booties. When he reached the front door of the house, he slid the booties over his shoes.

"Detective Vaughan!" A woman called his name, and when he looked back, he saw Nikki McDonald. She was dressed in a lightweight red pantsuit that showed off her figure. Her hair hung loose around her face, and her makeup was flawless. "Do you have a comment or an update?"

"What time did you post your story?" It wasn't a matter of if but when with her.

"Five a.m. The story is up, as are the comments. Nothing unusual yet. Can I ask you a few questions?"

The release to the media had gone out minutes after he and Spencer had spoken to her, so she could not be blamed for revealing any secrets. "Not now."

"When can you talk to me?" Her high-heeled shoes clicked against the pavement as she walked up and down the yellow tape framing the sidewalk. Rick McGuire was crossing the street toward them.

Reminding himself he might need her, he kept his voice even and steady. "Soon. I don't know what I have yet."

Nikki glanced back at Rick, offered a small salute, and returned to her car as a Ford Explorer pulled up on the other side of the street, several houses down. Agent Spencer got out of the vehicle.

Her dark suit emphasized her long legs, which ate up the distance between them. Her gaze hitched on his briefly as she slid gloves on her hands. She climbed the stairs and slipped on the booties Vaughan handed her. "Thanks."

"Not how I expected to spend this morning," he said.

"You and me both."

"How did you hear about this?" he asked.

"Ramsey called a half hour ago. Can you give me a brief?"

"I just got here myself. All I know at this point is that the wife and daughter are missing, and the husband was transported to Alexandria Hospital a half hour ago. He was barely conscious but insisted a masked assailant took his wife and daughter."

"Did he recognize the intruder?" Spencer asked.

"No."

"And his injuries?"

"The uniformed officer stated he was semiconscious. The full extent of his injuries remains unknown."

"The press is going to eat this one up," Spencer said. "Young girl's remains found after eighteen years, and then her sister vanishes a day later. Christ, this is going to go nationwide."

"A little too coincidental."

"Yes, it is." Spencer stared up at the house, as if willing it to yield its secrets. Her gaze drifted to the edged grass along the sidewalk. "Did you notice yesterday how perfect Hadley kept her home? Not a speck of dust or misplaced item. And she didn't have a hair out of place or an extra ounce of fat on her body."

"She's a perfectionist."

"I think it's a coping mechanism," Spencer said. "She obsesses over the surface details because she doesn't want anyone to know how unkempt she is on the inside."

"My guess: she was wound pretty damn tight."

Spencer nodded. "And then we arrive with news that her sister is dead."

"Everyone has the potential to snap," he said.

"It's a matter of dialing up the right combination of events," she said.

"And I would say she was a prime candidate."

***

Inside the Foster residence, Zoe found herself face to face with a large bloodstain darkening the entrance floor. Several small splashes of blood dotted the pale-gray walls and family pictures encased in silver frames.

The floor was littered with bloody gauze pads, discarded bandage wrappers, and plastic syringe caps. Positioned by each were yellow evidence tags. The priority in any case involving a living victim was to treat the injured first. Invariably, EMTs, in their need to do their job, unintentionally destroyed a great deal of crime scene evidence.

Past the primary blood pool, her gaze followed the dotted trail that snaked its way through the living room, past the sofa, and to a door leading to what looked like a garage.

Vaughan shifted his attention back to the front door's lock. "The doorjamb and the lock have no marks indicating forced entry." He moved from window to window on the first floor, testing each to see if they were locked. They were. Next, he jostled the handle on a set of french doors. They weren't locked but had no signs of damage. "Whoever came into the house didn't force his way in."

She glanced toward the couch in the living room and noted the pillows that had been so neat yesterday were ruffled and appeared to have been hastily tossed back in place.

"We know very little about Hadley and Mark Foster after they left the area," she said. "That goes for the daughter, Skylar, too? Who knows what kind of trouble those three might have unwittingly brought to their home?"

"You really think this has something to do with Marsha Prince's identification?" he asked.

"I do. McDonald wasted no time posting the news."

"She scooped them all."

She looked out the front window, her gaze trailing toward Rick McGuire. "A bit of revenge against the station that canned her and the reporter who filed a complaint."

"Whoever messaged McDonald must have known the bones belonged to Marsha Prince."

"Our informant calls the media, waits for an identification, and then he swoops in and attacks the Fosters," she said.

"If he was looking for maximum attention, he's going to get it."

"We also have to consider that this had nothing to do with Prince's identification. Foster could have been stealing from his company, or he might have a drug problem for all we know at this time. A mistress. Who had a grudge against him? The three primary motivators for murder are money, sex, and revenge."

"Detective Hughes is already getting warrants for the Fosters' financials."

"Does the wife or daughter have a boyfriend?"

"Again, to be determined."

She peered out the front door for a security camera and pointed to a single-lens camera aimed at the front door. "That might tell us who paid them a call. It sends the recording to a computer or phone."

"Let's hope."

Zoe paused to study a painting of Hadley and Skylar when she was a toddler. She followed the blood trail up the carpeted stairs to the second floor landing. The blood led down the central hallway toward the end and what was presumably the master suite.

Lights from a camera flashed from the last room, and they moved down the hallway, pausing at the first door. The room appeared to be a man's study. The soft grays and whites gave way to browns, leathers, and heavy drapes. On the wall behind a heavy mahogany desk was a tall set of shelves that exhibited a series of professional awards as well as snapshots featuring Mark Foster displaying either a hunting or fishing conquest. There were papers assembled into piles around his desk.

"The man cave," Zoe said. "Lets the wife decorate the house, but this room is *his*. He knew those piles must drive her crazy."

"I grew up with three younger sisters," Vaughan said. "When you're the only guy in a house, it's nice to have your space."

"I don't see a computer." She crossed to the desk and discovered the computer cord still plugged in the wall. "I wonder if he backed it up somewhere?"

"I'll have Hughes look into it." He sent the detective a text.

She studied the pictures on Mark Foster's credenza more closely. "Judging by the scenery, Foster traveled out west to what looks like the Sierra Nevada Mountains, maybe Montana, or possibly Idaho. Just about froze my ass off the winter I was stationed in Butte."

"How long have you been with the bureau?"

"Six years in the bureau and two years on the criminal profiler squad." She shifted her gaze to another picture. "Mark Foster likes documenting his big game kills."

"That doesn't mean he's our guy."

"Didn't say he was. Just making an observation about the photos and the missing laptop, which might have footage of the intruder on it."

"Mark Foster knew Marsha Prince, and he was on my list of people to interview once I had my bearings on the case."

Zoe moved slowly and methodically when she collected homicide evidence. This was not a homicide yet, and she hoped it stayed that way. "Has an Amber Alert been issued for the girl?"

"Yes."

The first few hours a child or young adult went missing were golden. The circle of evidence was tight and the evidence fresh. The more time that elapsed, the larger that circle became and the more tainted the evidence.

An open datebook revealed several appointments with clients as well as a golf pro and a travel agent. Nothing out of the ordinary.

The two made their way to the next room. This room was decorated in soft purples and grays. The bed was covered in a paisley comforter and unmade. The large pillows were rumpled, and a nearly full cup of coffee sat on the nightstand. Jewelry was scattered over the dresser top, but the surface underneath was polished. In the bathroom, nail polishes were lined up in a neat row along the counter, and the rich supply of makeup was organized in clear containers. A hand towel was neatly folded on the rack.

"Skylar slept in her bed last night," Zoe said. "She was awake long enough to get a cup of coffee, bring it to her room, and take a couple of sips."

"And then all hell broke loose."

She walked around the room, searching for anything that was out of place. She had worked a missing persons case in Nevada, and the key to finding the fourteen-year-old girl had been a collection of coffee shop receipts that had led to the store clerk, who had become obsessed with her. The smallest detail could be the important piece.

"Do you see her cell phone?" Zoe asked.

"No."

"That's going to be critical."

"I hear ya. Kids all have social media pages, and most share far more than they should."

She fished out her phone and searched a couple of social media apps.

"How many apps do you have?" he asked.

"All of them. I routinely search people I'm investigating. I often learn more about a person from their online profiles than interviewing them or their associates." She paused and then nodded. "Here she is." Skylar's profile page on Instagram had been updated three days ago with a picture of the sun shining on an industrial building. The next update was several days before that, and it featured Skylar and a teenage boy. Their heads were tilted toward each other, and their outstretched hands each created the peace sign.

"Nate posts goofy pictures with his buddies. I worry about his posting enough," he said. "But if I had a girl to raise, I would likely have gone insane with worry."

"No pictures of her with her mother," Zoe said, scrolling through the collection. "There are pictures of Skylar with her dad in the spring, but nothing recently."

"Kids at that age are doing their best to distance themselves from their parents," he said.

"Maybe. Mother-and-daughter relationships can be strained even at the best of times."

As tempted as she was to ruffle the bedsheet and begin moving things around to look for the phone, she had to wait for the forensic team to process the room. "The phone was in her hand yesterday when she came into the house with her father. The case is pink and glittered."

As she walked around the girl's room, nothing caught her eye.

They left Skylar's room behind and continued along the blood trail, which grew heavier with each step closer to the master bedroom.

There were two forensic technicians in the room dressed in lightweight protective gear, gloves, and booties. One tech sketched the room layout while the other photographed.

What struck Zoe immediately was the explosion of red on the carpeting by the dresser. The blood not only pooled on the gray carpet, but it also arched in one defined, parabolic curve on the wall. The downward strike of a weapon created the wound, and drawing it back dispersed the blood. She pictured the knife blade going into the victim and tearing skin, and then, as the killer drew back the blade, the blood flinging onto the wall.

She doubted this blood belonged to the surviving husband, because whoever had been stabbed in this room had been struck in a major artery and immediately suffered massive blood loss. And judging by the profuse amount of blood staining the carpet, that injured party had fallen to their knees and then pitched forward onto the carpet face-first.

Just beyond the blood was a king-size bed that had been neatly made. The pillows were in place and the comforter smoothed.

One tech faced them. "Scene reminds me of the motel room. What are the chances of two similar stabbings in twenty-four hours?"

"Two stabbings in a densely populated area like this aren't out of the realm of possibilities," Zoe said.

"Bud, this is FBI special agent Zoe Spencer," Vaughan said. "Agent Spencer, this is Bud Clary, and his colleague is Mike Brown."

"Gentlemen," she said. "Feel free to kick us out if we get in the way."

Both men glanced at each other and then nodded to her. Having the FBI on scene always changed the dynamics of their interactions.

"What's your status of the motel scene?" Vaughan asked.

"We wrapped up late last night. But the room remains sealed should we need to double back."

Zoe suspected now that the Foster case was front and center, the faceless sex worker's death would sadly be shifted to a back burner. And judging by Vaughan's frown, this truth did not sit well with him.

"We've only started with the house," Bud said. "It'll take us a good twenty-four to forty-eight hours to process it. I've called Fiona so she can also join us. As you can see, there is blood through most of the house."

"Mind if we have a look?" Vaughan asked. "We won't touch."

"Much appreciated," Bud said. "Just follow the path I've marked."

"Will do," Vaughan said.

"Bud, let us know if you find cell phones or computers," Zoe said.

"Consider it done."

She looked past the techs, noting more studio-quality photos of the Foster family. In the early pictures, when Skylar had been about twelve, there was a black lab puppy in the picture; however, in later shots, the dog was gone. How old would the dog have been now? Five or six?

Zoe walked up to the entrance of the bathroom. The floor appeared wiped clean, and there was no visible blood. The towel rack was empty. "The towels are missing."

"Towels?" Bud asked.

"The bath towels. They were arranged neatly in Skylar's bathroom, but they aren't in here."

"Someone tried to stop the bleeding."

"Or clean up the floor," Zoe said.

"It was the same in Jane Doe's motel room," Bud offered. "The bathroom had been wiped clean, and towels were missing. He took the towels he used with him."

"Another similarity between the two crimes," Zoe said.

"They are hard to ignore," Vaughan said.

"A gut feeling?" she asked.

"Yeah."

"As long as you don't mix gut feelings with facts," she said.

The collection of perfume bottles was lined up perfectly on the marble countertop, and beside them was a small notebook that appeared to be a workout log. Today's date was written on the left side, but there were no miles logged. She looked back to the neatly made bed. "I would bet money, given Hadley's rigid schedule, she got up, dressed for her run, and then made the bed."

"If she was able to make the bed, where was Mark?" Vaughan asked.

"It's a three-bedroom house, and the extra room is Mark's office. The pillows on the couch looked creased. Maybe he'd been banished to the couch."

Vaughan tapped an index finger against his thigh, as if he was mentally cataloging and thumbing through the facts. "Bud, did the paramedics say what Mark Foster was wearing when they found him?"

"He was wearing his business suit pants, white shirt, and tie. His clothes are being tested for DNA as we speak," Bud said.

"Maybe he had been up early," Zoe said.

"Is there another shower in the house?" Vaughan asked.

"There's one off the upstairs hallway," Bud said. "It's dry, just like the one in the master bathroom. No one showered here this morning."

Zoe and Vaughan moved down the center staircase to the kitchen, where one coffee mug sat on the counter. It was an extra large cup and sported the Washington Redskins logo. It was half-full. She touched the cup and then the pot. "Both are ice cold."

"A man's mug, unless Hadley liked large cups of coffee."

"Fingerprints will tell us more."

Zoe shifted her attention to the wooden knife block on the counter. The set of knives was expensive, the type a chef would envy, and all the slots were filled except one. "This slot is for a boning knife."

"To cut meat?"

"Yes."

"Is there any sign of it in the dishwasher?"

She opened the stainless dishwasher door and peered inside to an empty interior. "No." She searched the drawers but didn't see it.

"It would have been handy enough for anyone to grab on their way upstairs."

"Agreed."

Vaughan peered out over the kitchen window, toward the backyard. "The privacy fence gate is ajar." He checked the door leading to the patio. It was unlocked.

But the blood trail led to a side door. Again, following what amounted to forensic bread crumbs, they opened the door and stepped into an empty garage big enough for one car.

"Yesterday when we were leaving, there was a black Lexus in the driveway that had not been there when we arrived."

"Mark's car," she said.

"Hadley and Skylar left via this exit," he said.

"The few cases I've worked like this one were always done by an acquaintance. It's time to talk to Mark Foster. He should be out of surgery soon."

Vaughan checked his watch. "Now you're talking. I've been ready to talk to Foster since the moment I stepped over the blood in the foyer."

CHAPTER TEN

Tuesday, August 13, 9:00 a.m.
Alexandria, Virginia
Two Hours after the 911 Call

Vaughan drove to the hospital with Spencer tailing behind. His phone rang. "Hughes, what do you have for me?"

"I've got the judge's signature. Now it's a matter of collecting the Fosters' financial data," she said.

With a missing child in the mix, everyone in the system was moving full steam ahead. "Great. The more we know about this family, the better. We need to trace the family's phones and find their Lexus. It's black, late model, and I'd bet money it has a GPS locator on it."

"I'll check it out." Someone in the background shouted Hughes's name, but she told him to wait. The homicide room was always busy, and there was never a recession in their business. Hughes, along with the rest, was juggling multiple cases. "I also heard from the medical examiner. Dr. Baldwin is going to do the autopsy on your Galina Grant."

"The Jane Doe stabbed in the motel room?"

"Yes. I ran her prints through AFIS, and no surprise, she'd been arrested for prostitution and drug charges multiple times." Pages flipped in the background, and he imagined her searching the battered red notebook she always carried. "She was nineteen and had been in the area for about six months. It wasn't her first time at this motel."

"When is her autopsy scheduled?" Vaughan asked.

"Three this afternoon."

"I want to be there." He took a sharp right, knowing Spencer kept pace. "But I've got to find Hadley and Skylar first."

"Understood. I can cover the autopsy, if it comes down to it," Hughes said.

"Thanks." Hughes was one of the best, but he already felt like he was shortchanging Galina Grant by handing this critical piece of the investigation off.

"Two stabbing cases in as many days. I hope this one doesn't come in threes."

No truer words were spoken. "Thanks, Hughes."

Spencer followed him down a side street and then to the hospital lot. He parked near the emergency entrance and waited for her. They entered through the automatic doors of the ER.

Inside the ER, the hum of conversations, patients, and staff in the half dozen registration bays mingled with the sound of monitors and a lobby television broadcasting a health-themed talk show. Vaughan made his way to an open registration desk.

The registrar, a woman in her early twenties, had ink-black hair and pale skin. "Can I help you?"

Vaughan removed his badge, holding it steady, and then introduced himself. "I need an update on Mark Foster."

She checked her computer, frowning as she juggled the restrictions of the HIPAA regulations and a cop's request. "Let me check with a nurse."

Vaughan tucked his badge back in his pocket. "Thanks."

He turned to find Spencer staring at the television with great interest. Curious, he walked toward her and realized she was watching a segment on brain aneurysms.

When she realized he had crossed the room to her, she shrugged and turned from the television. "My husband died from one."

"I'm sorry." She was still grieving for her dead husband. He shouldn't care that he was competing with a ghost, but he did.

She rolled her head from side to side, releasing the tension in her shoulders. "Thanks."

Double doors pushed open, and a young nurse wearing green scrubs appeared. After spotting Vaughan and Spencer, she strode toward them. "You're here for Mr. Foster?"

"That's right. Is he conscious yet?" Vaughan asked.

"We never had to put him under. We were able to stitch him up using only a local," the nurse said.

"I thought he was badly injured," Vaughan said.

"He was covered in a great deal of blood, but once we got him up to surgery, we discovered that the three wounds weren't life threatening."

"Where was he injured?" Vaughan asked.

"He was stabbed in the upper left arm and on the left side of his abdomen. They were nasty gashes. There was also a gash on his right arm."

"We'd like to see him now," Spencer said.

"Follow me." The nurse swiped her badge, and the three made their way down the wide hallway of the emergency room, past nurses and doctors who were darting in and out of curtained exam rooms. Beeping monitors blended with the sound of rattling wheels on a cart.

"How alert is he?" Spencer asked.

"Very," the nurse said. "He refused any kind of sedative other than the local. He's insisting on staying awake until he knows what happened to his wife and child."

"It's important that the media not talk to him right now," Vaughan said.

"This is a lockdown unit," the nurse said.

"Good," Vaughan said. "We want to control all the information disseminated to the public until Hadley and Skylar Foster are located."

"I understand. I will remind hospital security of the extra protocol."

The nurse walked to the end of the hallway, toward a uniformed police officer who stood outside a cubicle. The officer nodded to Vaughan and Spencer as the nurse pushed back the curtain.

Mark Foster lay in his bed, his eyes closed and his hands at his sides. He was hooked up to an IV and a monitor that beeped steadily. The shades over the window were drawn, and a nurse stood by his bed, checking his vitals.

"If you don't mind giving us the room," Vaughan said. "We'd like to talk to Mr. Foster."

Foster immediately opened his eyes, and he looked around, slightly wild eyed, first at his nurse and then at Vaughan and Spencer. "Have you found them? Please tell me you've found them?"

Vaughan approached him and waited for the nurse to leave the room before he sat by the bed. "We have not found your wife and daughter yet."

Foster closed his eyes, wiping away tears as he shook his head. "You've got to find them. They're my family. My life."

"I understand you're upset," Vaughan said. "And we are doing everything we can."

"How can you understand what I'm going through?" he said. "I've been gutted."

The man's furrowed brow, watery eyes, and trembling bottom lip told the story of a man who had suffered a crushing trauma. "Mr. Foster, can you tell me what happened?"

"I've told the uniformed officers my story at least twice." His jaw clenched and released. "We're wasting time. What are you doing to find my wife and child?"

"We have BOLOs out on both of them, we've issued an Amber Alert on your wife and daughter, and we've reached out to the surrounding

Mary Burton

jurisdictions. That means every cop in the DC metro area has Hadley's and Skylar's pictures, and they're looking for them."

Spencer shifted her body a little closer to Foster. "Sir, bear with me and tell me what you remember."

Foster pinched the bridge of his nose as he closed his eyes. "Jesus, how can a day that started off so good turn to shit so fast?"

"You said the day began well," Spencer prompted. "What time do you get up?"

Foster shoved out a breath. "I get up early every day. Today I slept in an extra hour because I worked late last night at the office. We have a big project due, and everyone is working overtime."

"What time did you get up?"

"Six. I normally run first, but not today. I got into the shower and stayed in longer than I normally do. Hadley finally hustled me out of the bathroom and told me she needed to get into the shower." He shook his head. "I invited her in and made a joke about saving water." He swallowed. "She got into the shower, which made us run even later."

Vaughan removed a small notebook from his pocket and flipped it to a clean page. Already the man's explanation didn't match the evidence, but it was still early, and there were no real red flags yet. "You both get dressed."

"Yeah. I finally stepped out of the shower and got dressed for work. Hadley lingered in the shower because she had to wash her hair. It's really thick, and she says it's always a production to wash and dry it."

"She keeps everything neat in the house," Spencer noted.

"She cleans up as she goes. She showers, she cleans the shower. Uses a towel, she washes it. Drives me crazy, but it keeps her calm."

"Was she going anywhere special today?" Spencer asked.

"To the gym. She's always at the gym. She teaches three or four classes a day."

"She washed her hair before her workout?" Spencer asked.

102

"Yeah. Like I said, she's a neat freak." Foster picked a loose thread in the sheet.

That might explain the pristine condition of the bathroom. She could have grabbed the towels and cleaned out the shower and the countertops. The towels could have been in the laundry room. He made a note to check.

"You got dressed." Spencer's voice was calm, unhurried. "Where was your daughter?"

"I heard Skylar moving around in her room as I went downstairs. She came and got a cup of coffee and then headed back upstairs. She was calling out to her mother for something. I was more interested in coffee and didn't stop to listen to my wife's response." He shook his head. "I should have listened."

"You did nothing wrong, Mr. Foster." She gave him a second to draw in a calming breath before saying, "Keep going."

"I was packing my briefcase when I remembered it's recycling day. I hustled out the back door and dragged the can around the side of the house to the curb. When I came back inside, I heard the screaming." He closed his eyes. "It was chilling. The sounds were god awful."

Spencer prodded him. "What happened?"

"I ran up the stairs two at a time." Foster's right foot moved back and forth, as if he was remembering the dash up the stairs. "That's when I saw them."

"What did you see?" Vaughan asked.

"There was a man. Dressed in black. He had a knife to my w-w-wife's throat." He stammered and closed his eyes. Tears ran down his cheeks.

"What did the man look like?" Vaughan asked.

"I'm not sure," Foster said.

Spencer jumped in, asking, "Was he taller or shorter than your wife?"

"Taller. At least six inches taller."

"Was the assailant fat or thin?" she asked.

"Medium build."

"Was he wearing a mask?"

"Yes."

"What color was the mask?"

"Black. It was a ski mask."

"Did you see the color of his skin around his eyes or on his neck?"

"It was tanned."

"African American? Hispanic?" she prompted.

"A white guy. His skin reminded me of someone who works in the sun a lot."

"Did he ever face you?" she asked. "Did you see his eyes?"

A sigh shuddered over Foster's lips, and he closed his eyes for a moment. "He glanced at me once very quickly before he used my wife's body like a shield."

"What did he want?" she asked.

"He wanted money and drugs."

"Do you keep either in the house?" she asked.

"Hadley keeps sedatives. She's always had trouble sleeping. And I don't keep cash in the house."

"What did the man's voice sound like?" Spencer asked. "Was his voice deep, high pitched?"

"Deep."

"Did he have an accent?"

"None that I heard."

"What about rings, scars, or tattoos?"

Foster opened his eyes. "I don't remember. I should, but I don't."

"You're doing better than you realize," she said.

"How did he get into the house, Mr. Foster?" Vaughan asked.

"It must have been the front door. I'd been on my way out to work, and I had unlocked it when I remembered the recycling. I left it open and didn't think twice about it. It was only open for a few minutes."

He pinched the bridge of his nose, shaking his head. "I should have locked it."

Vaughan didn't react with pity or condemnation as he gathered truths and potential lies. "Where was your daughter?"

"In her room. She must have been trying to get dressed."

"What happened next?" he asked.

"It all happened so fast. This animal dragged my wife forward. It was like in slow motion. I couldn't believe it. And then he slashed my arm."

"Did he speak at this time?" Spencer asked.

"He said he'd kill my wife if I moved. I wanted to tear his head off, but Hadley was crying and begging me to stand down."

"Your daughter should have been out of the shower and dressed by then," Vaughan said.

"She was."

"Why didn't Skylar call 911?" Vaughan asked.

"I don't know. I guess she didn't have her phone with her," he said.

"A teenager without a phone?" Spencer asked. "That's not very common these days."

"I guess it was in her room," Foster said.

Spencer said nothing, but the slow intake of breath told him she was not convinced. It was possible Skylar had not had her phone, but the phone records Hughes had already requested would give them a better idea of when and if she had been using the device that morning.

"What happened next?" Vaughan asked.

"He shoved my wife into the hallway, and she nearly stumbled onto my daughter as Skylar burst out of her room. He ordered them both to walk down the stairs and out the garage door."

The assailant had entered through the front door yet was leaving through a different exit. It would be risky to take two captives over new ground unless he'd been watching the house before the attack.

"Both my wife and daughter were screaming," Foster said. "I followed them down the stairs and, in a moment of desperation, lunged for the man. That's when he stabbed me."

"You were found collapsed at the front door," Vaughan said.

"I saw my car pull out of the driveway through the front window. My daughter was driving the car, and that monster was in the back seat with the knife to my wife's neck." Again, he closed his eyes. "The look on Skylar's face was pure terror."

"You were able to see all that?" Vaughan asked.

"Yes. Those moments will be burned in my brain forever." He shook his head. "I should have saved them. I shouldn't have let him order me around."

"You made a difficult split-second decision in a very stressful situation."

"I should have been stronger. But I got so dizzy and dropped to my knees."

"You called 911," Spencer said.

"I pressed the emergency button on my phone before I passed out," Foster said.

Vaughan scribbled key phrases on his notepad. "There was a huge bloodstain in your bedroom. Whose blood was that?"

Foster's gaze froze for a moment. "My wife's, I guess."

"You guess?" Vaughan asked. "It was a lot of blood."

"The man must have stabbed her right before I entered the room."

"And you didn't notice your wife bleeding out?" Spencer asked.

"Sure. I saw blood. But it all happened so damn fast," Foster insisted. "I'm having trouble remembering the details."

Vaughan was silent for a moment. "Has anyone made threats against you or your family before today?"

"No."

"Have you seen anyone hanging around the house?" he asked.

"No."

"Does your wife have any enemies?" Spencer asked.

"No! There were no red flags! I don't know who this guy was or why he came after us." Foster's face had paled, and the heart rate monitor spiked.

"How did your wife react to our visit yesterday?" Vaughan asked.

"She was a wreck," he said.

"Did she talk about her sister?" Spencer asked.

"No. She never talks about Marsha. I learned a long time ago not to bring up the subject of her sister."

"Why?"

He shook his head. "She and Marsha didn't always get along, and I think Hadley always felt guilty about that."

"Why did you move to Oregon after Marsha vanished?"

"I was accepted to Oregon State, and we needed to get out of this area. My parents offered to help us out, so we took it. Once Skylar was born out there, it started to feel like home."

"And then you came back here," Vaughan said.

Foster swallowed. "It was a chance for a better job. We thought enough time had passed, and the past had been forgotten."

"Was it?"

"I thought it was. But Hadley started having trouble sleeping again." He shook his head. "I don't see what this has to do with today."

The curtains slid back quickly, and a nurse appeared. Frowning, she crossed to Foster's bedside and checked his vitals and IV. "Officers, it's time to wrap this up."

"We have a few more questions," Vaughan said.

"They're going to have to wait," the nurse replied.

"I don't mind answering their questions," Foster said.

"This is not about what you want, sir. It's about what you need. This interview is ending for now. The detectives can come back in a few hours."

Hours. Not much time in the grand scheme, but for a kidnapping investigation, it often was the difference between a rescue and a recovery. "We'll be back soon."

Foster grabbed Vaughan's arm. "Find my family."

"Get some rest."

As Foster's arm dropped to the crisp white sheets, Spencer shot Vaughan a look but said nothing until the two were alone in the elevator. "We should have pressed harder."

He punched the lobby button. "He provided a generic description at best."

"High-adrenaline moments can blur details. Given a little more time, I can drill below the confusion. I can create a workable sketch."

"You can try. But I bet you end up with a sketch of an everyman."

"You don't believe him?" Spencer asked.

"It's the intangibles. The lame description. The minor injuries. The way he gripped my arm."

Her eyes lifted to his. "I've seen killers do that. They reach out to a detective either directly or through the media, because whatever they know is bubbling up inside of them, but they can't yet bring themselves to do it."

"Often our bodies react more truthfully than our words."

Spencer pursed her lips. "True."

"It sickens me, but I think he killed his family."

As much as Vaughan had disliked his crazy ex-wife, it had never occurred to him to kill her. And when she had been sick with cancer, he had taken vacation time and seen to it that Nate had visited her.

But motives for murder could be as complicated as they were very simple. He had seen people murdered for as little as fifteen dollars or a small traffic slight.

The elevator doors opened, silencing his response. They crossed the crowded lobby toward the exit and then to his car. "Let me check in with Hughes. The Fosters' financials and phone records are going to tell us more than Mark Foster."

"Okay." They both got into his vehicle.

He dialed the station, and Hughes picked up on the second ring. "You're on speakerphone," he said. "I'm here with Agent Spencer."

"Understood," Hughes said.

"Any word on the Fosters' 2017 Lexus and the phones?" Vaughan asked.

"You must be psychic. Just heard from the OnStar people. Hadley's car was located at a cemetery about five miles from the Foster house. No sign of either victim, but a uniform has secured the scene, and the forensic team is en route."

"What about the mother's and daughter's phones?" Spencer asked.

"The daughter's phone was found under her bed. It was on silent mode. The mother's device pinged to the exact location of the car," Hughes said.

"I want to see that car," Vaughan said. "We can be there in fifteen minutes."

"The forensic team should be there by then," Hughes said.

"Thanks, Hughes," he said. "You know the drill. Call me if you have anything."

"Will do," Hughes said.

Vaughan hung up. "Ride with me."

"Sure."

He started the car and maneuvered out of the parking lot. A red light caught them a block from the hospital.

"The assailant breaks into the Foster house, stabs Mr. and Mrs. Foster, and then escapes with both an injured woman and a hysterical teenager."

"And no one hears or sees anything?" she asked, incredulously. "Odds are Hadley and Skylar are already dead."

"I want to disagree, but I think you are right."

"The facts point that way the longer the search continues."

CHAPTER ELEVEN

Tuesday, August 13, 10:00 a.m.
Alexandria, Virginia
Three Hours after the 911 Call

The clock was ticking. And it was not lost on Zoe that the longer this search lasted, the less the chance that they would find either victim alive.

Vaughan maneuvered up King Street, a bustling central artery in Alexandria. Seconds later, they spotted the twin brick pillars of the cemetery entrance. He pulled through the gates, following the narrow road up a hill, past old tombstones, toward the flash of police lights.

Vaughan drove around the back side of a stone mausoleum, where two marked cars were nosed in toward the ring of yellow crime scene tape that established a generous perimeter around the late-model black Lexus.

The devil was in the details, as Uncle Jimmy used to say when he painted one of his masterpieces. Brush strokes, paint sources, even the type of canvas could betray his masterpieces as fakes.

The vehicle's glistening, polished exterior and the deep-black wheels suggested a recent cleaning. It was not surprising a man like Foster kept a clean car. He was an accountant in a prestigious firm, and he was paid to monitor the smallest details. He wanted his car to reflect that.

Zoe pulled on gloves as she approached the car's back passenger door, which was now open. The rusty scent of blood and leather heated in the morning sun drew her gaze toward the dark stains that puddled and ran over the back seat onto the custom floor mat. The buzz of a phone emanated from inside the car.

"Sounds like it's coming from the trunk," she said.

"It's rung several times in the last ten minutes," a uniformed officer said. "We're leaving it for forensic."

Vaughan tugged on his gloves, carefully opened the front door, and popped the trunk latch. Saving lives trumped preserving evidence, and he could not wait on the off chance Skylar or Hadley was alive and locked in the trunk.

A chill snaked down Zoe's spine as she braced for what they could find. Vaughan's grim expression mirrored her own sentiments. Silent, they walked to the back of the car, and he carefully opened the lid.

A ripple of tension passed over them both.

Both stood silent, staring in the trunk for a beat. No bodies—only an emergency roadside kit and an opened suitcase that was filled with Foster's clothes.

The one-two punch of relief and disappointment hit Zoe. "Why transfer them to another vehicle and risk discovery? If Foster's timeline is accurate, the assailant would have been transferring the women at the peak of the morning commute. A highly risky move, unless it wasn't originally part of the plan."

Vaughan looked back at the mausoleum, searching for security cameras. "There have to be cameras here. I'll have the uniforms check it out."

She angled around the trunk, back toward the rear seat. "Again, if Foster is telling the truth, and the blood in the room is his wife's, this must be hers as well. If Hadley Foster hasn't bled out, it won't be long," she said.

Vaughan turned to the officer. "Double-check with the area hospitals, and see if a woman matching Hadley Foster's description has been dropped off."

"Sure, Detective." The officer reached for his phone, dialing as he turned and stepped away.

The phone stopped ringing and started up again. Zoe searched the trunk, feeling along the interior until her fingers brushed the phone.

Gripping it by the edge, she faced Vaughan as he opened a plastic evidence bag. She studied the display and the name *Roger Dawson*. The call went to voicemail along with eight other missed calls.

Vaughan scribbled down the name and phone number. "Wonder what Roger Dawson wants?"

She hit callback and then speakerphone; then she said, "Let's find out."

On the second ring, a man said in a rush of exasperation, "Hadley, where have you been?"

"Mr. Dawson, this is FBI special agent Zoe Spencer, and I'm with Alexandria Police Department detective William Vaughan. Have you been trying to reach Hadley Foster?"

There was a pause on the other end before Dawson replied, "Yes. Is something wrong?"

"That's what we're trying to determine, Mr. Dawson," Zoe said. "Hadley appears to be missing."

"What do you mean, missing?" Dawson challenged.

"Exactly that, sir," she said. "There was a disturbance at the Foster home this morning, and Mrs. Foster and her daughter, Skylar, are missing."

"Where the hell is Mark?" Dawson demanded.

Zoe's gaze locked on Vaughan's raised brow. Like her, he heard concern usually reserved for loved ones.

Instead of answering the question, she asked, "Who are you to Hadley Foster?"

A hesitation crackled over the line. "We are good friends. Now please tell me what's going on. Where's Mark?"

Vaughan shook his head. "We'd rather talk to you in person. We'll come to you."

Another pause. Was Dawson in shock, or was he shifting to damage control?

"Yeah. Sure. I'm at my office on Duke Street." He recited the address of Weidner and Kyle, an accounting firm located on the building's first floor. The line went dead just as the forensic van rolled up on the scene.

"He's called her seven times in the last couple of hours," Zoe said.

"Did he leave messages?" Vaughan asked.

"Two. But her messages seem to be password protected."

Vaughan walked around the car and paused. "There's a hell of a scrape on this side."

She joined him and studied the long white graze. She touched her fingertip to the tail end of it and noticed traces of red paint. The right front tire was also noticeably low.

She looked back toward the corner of the mausoleum and spotted black scrape marks against an aluminum trash can. "The driver came flying around the corner and hit the post and then stopped here. Foster said his daughter was driving. A seventeen-year-old in a highly stressful hostage situation could easily have done this."

"All assumptions are based on the testimony of a man I don't trust."

"That's a given."

Her gaze roamed toward rolling green hills dotted with gray headstones. "Have an officer search the entire area. No telling what he'll find."

"Right."

She handed the phone to the forensic tech and then stripped off her bloodstained gloves and discarded them in a crime scene disposal bin by the van. "Let's see what Mr. Dawson can share with us."

***

Nikki drove to Fredericksburg in less than an hour. In the middle of the day, there was light traffic, and she pressed the speed limit, going well over eighty in some spots. It had not been too hard for her to find Becky Mahoney, Larry Prince's former secretary and lover. There were others who had known the Prince family back in the day, but there was nothing like an old flame to give the inside scoop. If Nikki was lucky, Becky would have some lingering animosity toward Prince and be very willing to talk.

The GPS took her to the south side of the city, down several winding roads undergoing construction, and then into a small neighborhood. She had not called ahead and was not surprised when no one answered the front door. She checked her watch, guessing that it might be hours before Becky Mahoney returned home. That gave her enough time to find a fast-food place. She pulled out of the neighborhood, and two miles down the main road, she spotted several drive-through restaurants. She picked the first and ordered a burger and a Diet Coke. She pulled into a parking space, and as she ate, she opened her file on the Prince case.

Back in the day, she had been sleeping with a cop who had helped her obtain copies of the detectives' case notes. What she had learned was that Larry Prince had been suspected of bribing state officials in exchange for the big contract he had won shortly before Marsha had vanished. However, there had not been enough evidence to bring charges. Some had whispered that Larry had broken a few key promises to local politicians. One detective had theorized that Marsha's disappearance was payback for Larry's disloyalty. It was all hearsay in the newsroom, but nothing could be proven, so no one had aired it. Today, she doubted her former colleagues would be so worried about lawsuits. Hell, at this stage, she was not really worried. As long as she attached *alleged* or *sources said*, she could wiggle out of just about anything.

Her stomach knotted, and her appetite vanished. She dropped the half-eaten burger in the bag and took a pull on the drinking straw. She leaned forward and opened the glove box, searching for the packet of cigarettes she always kept there. Technically, she had quit last year, but she had held on to this emergency stash as a kind of safety blanket. Her fingers skimmed over the crumpled packet. She'd thought she had one or two cigarettes left. It was empty.

"Shit."

She turned up the police scanner she had on the Alexandria Police Department and listened for chatter. Officers were being dispatched to a cemetery. She kept waiting to hear the name *Foster*. When the cops didn't say it, she knew something was up.

Glancing at the clock on the dash, she decided it was time to get back to Mahoney's house and have a chat with her. Afterward, she would haul ass back to the cemetery.

She pulled in front of the house just as a woman parked in the driveway. The woman was older and plumper than she remembered, but there was no missing Becky Mahoney's tall frame and bleached-blond hair.

Out of her car, she shouldered her backpack and hurried across the residential street. "Becky!"

The woman's head turned, and the automatic smile dimmed a fraction as Nikki got closer. Her eyes narrowed. "Do I know you?"

"We met years ago. I'm Nikki McDonald. I was a reporter for Channel Five in the DC market."

Becky's face flushed as she drew back, tightening her grip on her keys and purse strap. "I haven't been up there in years. And I don't talk about the time I lived up there."

"The news might not have reached you yet, but Marsha Prince's remains were found."

"I never had anything to do with Marsha's disappearance." Becky moved toward her front door, her hands trembling slightly as she tried to insert her house key.

Nikki noticed the bicycle in the front yard and the basketball hoop in the driveway. "I'm not trying to wreck what you have. It looks like you've moved on and left Larry in the dust."

Becky's shoulders hunched and her fingers stilled. "I have moved on. I choose not to think about Larry or his family."

"Please, talk to me," Nikki said. "I'm trying to figure out who killed that young girl."

"What difference does it make?" Becky said, whirling around. "She's dead, her parents are dead, and Hadley moved west years ago."

"Hadley moved back with her husband and daughter about a year ago. And now she and her kid are missing."

"What do you mean?"

"The cops are swarming all over her house as we speak. My sources tell me the interior is covered in blood."

Becky's face paled. "I don't know anything about that."

"We can't save Marsha, but maybe Hadley and her daughter can be helped."

Her annoyance seemed to slip away. "One doesn't have anything to do with the other."

"I'm not so sure about that. One sister is dead, and the other is in grave danger."

"I made a mistake with Larry," she said, stepping forward. "I thought I loved him and he me. But it was all a lie. I know what people thought about me, what you insinuated in some of your stories, but I never thought he had anything to do with his daughter's disappearance."

"You told the cops he was planning to leave the family for you." She had to strike a delicate balance. She wanted Becky to keep talking, but she also didn't want her sensitive questions to shut her down.

Her brows knotted. "I was wrong."

"I'm wondering if he figured the easiest thing to do was to get rid of his family. Maybe he started by killing Marsha, but for whatever reason, he lost his nerve."

Becky's mouth flattened into a frown as she shook her head. "That is the dumbest thing I've ever heard. Larry didn't like his wife, but he loved his girls."

"Someone messaged my website and told me exactly where to find Marsha Prince's remains."

Becky folded her arms over her chest. "That must have been a great scoop for you."

"I'm not going to lie. I could use a great story right now. But I keep thinking about Marsha. She had her whole life ahead of her. And now that Hadley and Skylar are missing, I wonder if the same person who killed Marsha is involved."

Becky shoved out a breath. She did not invite Nikki inside, but she also didn't disappear behind the now-opened door.

"Marsha worked in the office that last summer, right?" Nikki asked.

"Yeah. She took orders and even went out to price some of the jobs. Larry called her his smart daughter."

"How'd Hadley feel about her father not considering her as smart?"

"She never said anything, but I could see it bothered her. Marsha tried to downplay her father's compliments for Hadley's sake."

Nikki shifted tactics, knowing if she pressed on the crime, she would lose Becky altogether. "What was Hadley like in high school?"

"She seemed real sweet, but it all felt a little calculated to me. She worked in the front office in the afternoons when we needed the phones covered. I remember she could charm any customer."

"She was dating Mark then, right?"

"Yeah, Mark. They had been dating since junior year of high school, and we all thought they would get married. Larry wasn't crazy about the idea, but he liked Mark enough not to complain."

"Was she dating anyone else?"

"Well, no, not really. She loved Mark."

She could hear a small hesitation. "But?"

Becky was silent for a moment. "Hadley flirted with some of the guys. They were all fit, and some were cute. I think she went out with one guy."

"Do you remember his name?"

"No."

"What about Marsha? Was she dating anyone?" Nikki asked.

"Several of the guys had a thing for her. She was cute and nice."

"Any names come to mind?"

"No."

"Did the sisters go out with the same guy?"

"Yeah."

"And you don't remember his name?"

"No. I've done my best to forget about that entire time in my life."

"Did the two sisters get along?"

"No, not really, especially after their father told Hadley he wasn't sending her to college right away. She was furious with her father and Marsha."

"Would she have killed her sister?" Nikki asked.

The woman slowly shook her head. "I couldn't imagine Hadley getting her hands dirty like that."

"Would she have had someone else do it?"

"No. No. Hadley wasn't a killer."

"How do you know?"

"I just do." Becky opened the door wider. "Look, I'm married now to a good man, and I have a son. I don't want to get dragged back into all that mess. I don't want them to know about Larry."

"I won't pull you into this story. I'm just trying to figure out what happened to Marsha."

She shook her head. "You said something like that to me the first time, and then my name was all over the news."

"If I could just ask a few more questions—"

"No. I'm done. Don't ever come back." Becky slid behind the door and slammed it closed.

Nikki stared at the pineapple ornament attached to the door. It was not lost on her that the adornment symbolized hospitality. It certainly was not the first door slammed in her face, nor likely would it be the last.

CHAPTER TWELVE

Tuesday, August 13, 12:30 p.m.
Alexandria, Virginia
Just over Five Hours after the 911 Call

Vaughan parked in front of the ten-story office building where Roger Dawson worked. This strip of Duke Street straddled the new business district, filled with modern high-rise offices, and Old Town's historic section. The former was home to law firms, associations, and corporate headquarters; the latter was packed with brick and clapboard buildings originally built by tobacco traders generations ago.

Spencer matched his pace as they walked inside the sleek tiled lobby to the security desk. Each showed their credentials, and the guard on duty pointed them toward a bank of gold-plated elevators. The doors opened, and Vaughan pressed six.

"Is this the firm that Foster works for?" Spencer asked.

The elevator doors closed, and the car ascended. "No. I'm not sure how Mark figures into all this," Vaughan said, "but I can't wait to find out."

Each kept their theories to themselves as the elevator stopped and then opened to a large gilded sign that read **WEIDNER AND KYLE**. A receptionist verified their identification, escorted them toward the corner office, and knocked on the closed door before cracking it and saying, "Mr. Dawson. The police."

"Send them in."

Vaughan and Spencer entered and found themselves staring at a lean man wearing dark suit pants, a white shirt, and a blue tie. His dark hair was thinning, and thick round glasses magnified owlish dark-brown eyes.

A dozen diplomas hung on the wall, and a mahogany credenza featured Dawson in various scenarios, including a shot with Hadley and Mark Foster.

When the door closed, Dawson asked, "Tell me what is going on with Hadley. And where the hell is Mark? I called him after I got off the phone with you, and he's not picking up."

"Mr. Foster is in the hospital recovering from surgery," Vaughan said.

"Surgery? Has there been an accident?"

"Mr. Foster was attacked in his home at about seven o'clock this morning," Vaughan said.

"Jesus. Is he all right?"

"He appears to have suffered superficial wounds," Spencer said.

"Where are Hadley and Skylar?" Dawson asked.

"They're missing," Vaughan said. "We're hoping you might be able to tell us where they might be?"

"Missing." He shook his head. "How could they be missing? I just talked to Hadley last night."

"I noticed you called her several times this morning," Spencer said. "Are you two close?"

"She's a friend," he said quickly. "She's also my personal trainer. She was supposed to meet me at the gym this morning but missed our appointment. She never misses, and I became worried. If she's missing, how did you get her phone?"

Spencer ignored the question. "I've worked with a personal trainer for years," she said. "She missed one of our sessions last year, and I called her once. Not multiple times."

"I guess mine was better than yours. And I can be obsessive when I don't have an answer."

"Is she more than a personal trainer?" Vaughan asked.

"What do you mean? She and Mark are both my friends." Dawson reached for the cuff of his tailored shirt and tugged it.

"How did you two meet?" Vaughan asked.

"I met her through Mark. He and I have crossed paths professionally for years at various conferences. My ex-wife and Hadley are good friends."

"How long have you been divorced?" Spencer asked.

"Why are you asking me these questions?" Dawson challenged.

"Until we can locate Hadley and Skylar, I'm going to be asking a lot of nosy questions," Vaughan said. "You do want to help, don't you?"

"Of course, of course," he rushed to say. "I've been divorced a year. Have you asked Mark where his wife and daughter are?"

"He claims he doesn't know," Vaughan said.

Head shaking, Dawson dropped his gaze to the tips of his polished shoes. "Ask him again."

"What does that mean?" Vaughan asked.

"He and Hadley have not been getting on for at least a year," he said.

"She told you this?" Spencer asked.

"Sure. When you work out with someone three times a week for almost a year, you start to talk. I dished to her about my divorce, and in the last couple of months, she opened up about Mark."

"What specifically did she say?" Vaughan asked.

"She told me this in confidence," Dawson countered.

"You aren't doing her any favors by not talking to us," Vaughan said.

Dawson rubbed his thumb against a callus below his naked ring finger.

"The statistics for missing women are grim," Spencer said. "The longer it takes to find them, the worse their odds become."

"Mark was having an affair with a woman in his office. Her name is Veronica Manchester. She's a new accountant at his firm. Hadley found out about it, and she was angry. She was ready to take Skylar this past spring and leave him, but Mark swore he would break it off and turn it around."

"Did he?" Vaughan asked.

"That's what he told Hadley, and he did cut out the late-night work sessions," Dawson said. "But a month ago, he started working the long hours and stopped answering his phone when she called."

"Did she tell you this?" Spencer asked.

"She did."

"I'm not judging you, but I need to know if you two were having an affair," Vaughan said. "The faster I figure out who the players are, the faster I can find Hadley and Skylar."

Dawson pulled off his glasses, plucked a tissue from a box on his desk, and cleaned the lenses. Carefully, he settled his glasses back on his face. "I love Hadley. I wanted her to leave Mark. I wanted us to make a life together."

"How did she feel about you?" Spencer said.

"She felt the same way. She had been promising for weeks to tell him. But she was scared and having trouble working up the nerve. She was worried about breaking up Skylar's home life. Mark has been sleeping on the couch for the last few weeks."

"Do you know anyone who might have a grudge against Mark?" Spencer asked.

"No. He was very professional and well respected."

"Exactly what kind of accountant is he?" Vaughan asked.

"Forensic. He went into corporations and searched for missing money. He was quite good at it."

"Any clients who could have gotten angry with him?" Vaughan asked.

"How would I know?" Dawson asked.

"Hadley might have mentioned it during one of those personal training sessions," Spencer said.

Dawson's brow wrinkled, and he shifted his stance. "You're making what I have with Hadley sound cheap. We love each other. Rather than being here with me, you should be asking Mark what happened to his wife and daughter. He knows."

A fine line separated love and hate. He'd worked plenty of murders rooted in passion. "Did you and Mark ever have any arguments?"

"No. We actually get along well," he said.

"Did he know you were sleeping with his wife?"

Dawson straightened. "No. Hadley and I were discreet."

"Are you certain he didn't know?"

Dawson frowned. "I'm almost certain."

"Do the Fosters have a vacation home?" Vaughan asked.

"Hadley never wanted the responsibility of a second house."

"Is there some place she would go if she needed a place to hide or Mark needed a place to hide her?" Vaughan asked.

"Not that I know of."

"When is the last time you saw Hadley?" Spencer asked.

"That's none of your business," Dawson said.

"I'm trying to find this woman and her child," she clarified.

Dawson hesitated. "Last night. Mark works late on Monday nights."

Spencer showed no reaction. "Where were you two last night?"

He shoved out a breath. "There is a hotel in Crystal City where we stay. She left right before midnight, but I stayed the entire night."

Vaughan got the name and made a note to pull security footage. "Okay."

Spencer shifted directions, asking, "What do you know about Skylar Foster?"

"She's as smart as a whip. Hadley thinks she's going to get a full ride to a few top schools. When they first moved back, I used to see her quite a bit at the gym, but not too much in the last months."

"Did something change in the girl's life?" Vaughan asked.

"Hadley said Skylar has a boyfriend," Dawson said. "I don't know his name."

"Do you know where he lives or goes to school?" Spencer asked.

"Her high school, I think," Dawson said.

"Does Hadley have any close friends?" Spencer asked.

"I don't know. She likes to work out, and she looks after Skylar. She's always kept to herself."

"There was a news report about Marsha Prince," Spencer said. "Did you see it?"

"Yeah. I wasn't really paying attention. Girl died a long time ago, or something."

Vaughan shifted his stance. "Did Hadley ever talk about her family?"

"No. What does this girl have to do with Hadley and Skylar?" He looked genuinely frustrated.

"Marsha Prince was her sister. The girl was abducted and killed, and her remains were found back in June."

Dawson stilled, held up his hands, and took a step back. "What?"

"She never told you her sister was killed?" Spencer asked.

"Hell no! Jesus. She never told me she even had a sister. She said her parents died in a car accident."

"She wasn't truthful," Spencer said. "Her parents died of natural causes seventeen years ago. We met with her yesterday to inform her that her sister's remains had been identified."

Dawson shook his head. "She never said a word to me."

"Did Hadley make a habit of lying?" Spencer asked.

"Not to me."

"But to others?" Spencer asked.

"She worried too much about what people thought, so she tended to exaggerate."

Vaughan had crossed paths with many skilled liars, and if Dawson was one of them, he was in the top of his class. He handed Dawson a card. "Call me if you hear from Hadley or Skylar or if you think of anything."

Dawson glanced at the card, his face paling as he flicked the edge of the card. "Mark knows more than he's saying. Bet on it."

"Do you think Hadley summoned up the courage to talk to her husband about a divorce?" Spencer asked.

Tension rippled over Dawson's body as he pressed his fist to his lips. "I was pushing her to talk to him. She swore she'd ask Mark for a divorce this morning."

"Maybe she did just that," Vaughan said.

CHAPTER THIRTEEN

Tuesday, August 13, 2:00 p.m.
Alexandria, Virginia
Seven Hours after the 911 Call

Vaughan returned to the Foster house and discovered the news vans were still parked across the street, and the cop cars lining the curb had multiplied. As he parked, Spencer pulled in behind him.

Vaughan waited for Spencer to join him before they approached the house. Each donned latex gloves and entered the foyer. Bud Clary, still dressed in protective gear, was dusting for prints on the front window.

"Detective Vaughan," Bud said. "Agent Spencer."

"What have you found out so far?" Vaughan asked.

"The initial assault occurred in the bedroom, as I first thought. The victim was carried down the stairs and out the garage door to where the Lexus was parked. There's also a sizeable bloodstain by the entryway. Because Foster was found bleeding by the front entrance, we can assume that blood is his, but I can't confirm until I run DNA."

"You've sent off samples?" Vaughan asked.

"A couple of hours ago. We are collecting DNA from hair fibers in both the mother's and daughter's bathrooms as well as the blood drawn from Foster at the hospital. I'm also expediting the testing of the blood samples taken from the Lexus. It shouldn't be more than a few hours."

In the world of DNA matches, that was quick, but in the life of a missing kid, hours mattered.

"Bud, what about Skylar's phone?" Vaughan asked. "You said you found it?"

"That's correct," Bud said.

"Were you able to access it?" Spencer asked.

"No. But a Neil Bradford called shortly after we recovered it. I answered it. Bradford sounds like a young kid, and he says that he's her boyfriend."

Vaughan scribbled down the name and number for Bradford. "Where's the kid now?"

"He said he was calling from the local high school, and he was worried about Skylar because she was supposed to meet him."

"Thanks, Bud," Vaughan said.

Vaughan and Spencer walked into the house, and she moved directly toward the kitchen. She stood beside the Washington Redskins mug. "The cup's full, but he said he drank half the cup. It's a small detail, but they eventually add up."

Vaughan looked out the window toward the trash cans and the recycling bin. "Foster also said he put the recycling bin out."

Her gaze trailed past his toward the backyard and the blue-and-white plastic container filled with bottles. "There could have been another bin."

"There were no others on the street. Small detail number two."

"That blows his reasoning for leaving the front door unlocked."

"The sun's up at 6:19 a.m.," Vaughan said. "Folks in this neighborhood are getting up and going to work. It's busy around here, and someone should have seen a masked intruder. Foster called 911 at 7:00 a.m., which means the attack occurred at this peak time."

"Maybe Foster got the time wrong. Maybe he passed out after he was stabbed. Maybe whatever happened occurred much earlier," she said.

"Maybe. Fewer potential witnesses and less traffic between here and the cemetery. Want to start knocking on doors and talking to the neighbors?" he asked.

"I want to talk to Skylar's boyfriend first," she said. "If there's something wrong at home, a teenage girl is likely to confide in her boyfriend."

"He's in school now, but it won't be hard to pull him out of class to question him."

"Let's go."

***

Zoe relaxed back in her seat as Vaughan drove the fifteen minutes to the Alexandria public high school. Out of the car, Zoe and Vaughan crossed the lot to the main doors. Neither appeared to be interested in the small talk most cops attempted in a bid to get to know a new partner. And to be honest, it felt a little weird.

Better to keep their focus on finding Hadley and Skylar. Once they were found, she could chitchat all he wanted, or better, they simply could go their separate ways.

Through the front doors, they walked directly to the main office, where both showed their police credentials. The secretary ducked in the back and found the vice principal, who in turn consulted the principal.

Principal Fred Myers was in his midforties with a thick shock of gray hair. He wore a charcoal-gray suit and a red tie embossed with eagles, the school's mascot. Vaughan and Zoe both shook hands with him. "I understand you're looking for Neil Bradford?"

"Correct," Vaughan said.

"Can I ask what this is in reference to?" Myers asked.

"His girlfriend, Skylar Foster, and her mother are missing," Zoe said. "We're hoping he knows something."

He glanced in a folder. "Skylar's name is on the absent list this morning, and my attendance secretary has noted that no one at the house answered the phone."

"Is Skylar absent a lot?" Zoe asked.

"She has been tardy four times already, and we're only two weeks into the new school year."

"Was tardiness a problem last year?"

"No. She was the model student. But we see this kind of thing with seniors. They start to coast, though most have the sense to wait until they've made it to the winter holiday so their college applications don't suffer."

Vaughan offered a half smile. "What kind of student is Skylar Foster?"

"She's always been quiet. Last spring, she got into a fight with another girl at lunchtime. Both girls denied taking the first swing. Nothing was conclusive, so they both ended up with a three-day in-school suspension."

"Who was the girl?" Zoe asked.

"Jessica Harris. They used to be close friends but don't even acknowledge each other anymore."

"Is Jessica here today?" Zoe asked.

"She's home sick."

"Let's start with Neil Bradford. Can you get Neil for us?" Vaughan asked.

"Sure." He unclipped a small two-way radio from his hip and called to one of the classrooms, asking the boy to come to the office. "Neil is a really good kid. He's vice president of the student body and well on his way to being valedictorian."

Vaughan nodded but knew damn well from his cop experience that kids like these weren't always angels. "I have no doubt."

Principal Myers leaned in a fraction. "Detective Vaughan, have we met before? You look very familiar to me."

"We met at back-to-school night last fall. My son, Nate Vaughan, was a student here."

His eyes brightened with recognition. "Oh, yes, received a partial scholarship to James Madison University."

"That's right."

"Of course. I see the resemblance now. How's he doing?"

"I dropped him off at college yesterday. He looked ready to tackle the world."

"I heard his mother, your ex-wife, passed."

"Last year. She had cancer."

His words did not hitch or stutter, suggesting that their split had not been easy. It had been a year before Zoe could speak about Jeff's passing without tearing up or having to excuse herself. But Vaughan was cool, almost unmoved.

The door opened, and a tall, lanky boy stood at the threshold. He had dark hair, a smooth baby face, and a splash of freckles over the bridge of his nose.

When Zoe and Vaughan stood, the boy looked visibly nervous as he glanced toward his principal. "Did you call me, sir?"

"I did, Neil. Close the door," Principal Myers said in a soft tone.

The boy's shoulders hunched slightly, and his thick hair kept falling over his eyes, forcing him to shove it back with long fingers. "Is there a problem?"

"Neil, I'm Detective Vaughan, and this is Agent Spencer. There was a break-in at the Foster house."

"Is Skylar all right?" he asked quickly.

"She's missing." Zoe maintained a soft, even tone designed to calm. She needed the kid to remain focused.

The boy drew back, shaking his head. "I knew something was wrong. She always answers my texts and calls. *Always.*"

"We are doing our best to find her," Zoe said. "We're hoping you might know where she could be. Where does she go when she needs to get away from her home?"

Pale brows knotted. "She always came to my house when she wasn't here or at home. We hung out almost all the time."

"I know you must care about her very much," she said.

"I love her," he insisted.

"If she didn't go to your house, where would she go?" Zoe asked.

"Nowhere. She's always with me."

"What about Jessica Harris?" Zoe asked.

"Skylar and Jess don't speak anymore. They hate each other."

"Why?"

"I don't know. Skylar never would say. I think Jessica was jealous because Skylar was spending her time with me."

"How often did Skylar come by your house?" Zoe asked.

"A few nights a week."

"When was the last night she was there?" Zoe asked.

"Last night. Monday."

Hadley had been with Dawson. "Was everything all right at her house?"

Neil chewed the inside of his mouth. "I don't know."

Zoe deliberately softened her expression. "We aren't trying to get anyone in trouble, Neil. We're just trying to quickly find Skylar and her mother. We are very worried about them."

"Did you ask Mr. Foster?" the boy countered. "He should be able to help."

"Mr. Foster is in the hospital. He just came out of surgery," Vaughan asked.

The boy's worried expression took on a panicked edge. "Surgery? What happened?"

Zoe sidestepped the question. "Neil, were there problems in the Foster house?"

A ragged sigh shuddered through him. "Skylar said her parents fought a lot. That's why she came to my house. She wanted to get away from the yelling."

"What were they fighting about?" Vaughan asked.

"Mr. Foster wasn't doing so well at work, and Mrs. Foster is obsessed with being perfect. It drives her crazy when the house, Sky, or her husband aren't as meticulous as she is. The Fosters tried to hide their problems from Sky, but she knew them all."

"Was there anyone who might have been threatening the family?" Vaughan asked.

"I don't know about that." Neil hesitated and then added, "Skylar said her mother has been really weird for the last couple of months. She's been a nervous wreck and worried."

"Did Skylar say what upset her mother?" Vaughan asked.

"She didn't know. She said she asked her a bunch of times, but her mother said it was no big deal. Skylar said her mother always gets a little weird this time of year anyway."

"Why?" Zoe asked.

"Skylar says she always gets sad and quiet near the end of summer."

Marsha Prince had vanished in August. "You said she came to your house a few nights a week. What did Skylar do on the other nights?"

"She said homework and school functions."

"Do you know the passcode to her phone?" Zoe asked.

"Yeah, it's 1812. She's a history buff."

"Is there anyone who would want to hurt her?"

"I don't know who. Sky keeps to herself," Neil said. "We're pretty tight."

The kid saw the girl several nights a week but not all of them. "You have any trouble with her parents?" Zoe asked.

"No. I mean, I almost never talk to them. Mr. Foster is working, and Mrs. Foster is at the gym."

"When's the last time you saw them?" Vaughan asked.

"A few weeks ago. They seemed to be getting on fine. Mr. Foster gave me fifty bucks and asked me to take Skylar to a movie and dinner."

"Thank you, Neil." Vaughan wrote down his cell phone number on his business card and handed the boy his card. "If you hear of anything, call me. Doesn't matter when. If you have to get up and leave class, do it."

"Okay. What do I do now?" the boy asked. "Should I go and look for her?"

"No. You wait. And we're going to keep looking," Vaughan said.

"Do you think Sky is all right?" the boy asked. "She could be hurt or something."

"We don't know." Zoe thought about the blood in the Foster house. "That's why we're moving as fast as we can to find her."

"The more time that passes, the greater the chances that it won't end well," Vaughan said.

If his intent was to scare the boy, the kid's pale, drawn face said he had done just that. "Call us if you hear anything," Zoe said.

"Especially if she finds a way to reach you," Vaughan said. "You won't be protecting her by not telling us."

"I'll help. I promise."

Vaughan obtained Jessica Harris's address from the principal and instructed him to keep this conversation confidential and his eyes open.

Outside the school, the pair crossed to his vehicle and climbed inside.

"What did you think of Bradford?" Vaughan asked.

"He reads genuine," she said.

"Yeah."

As he backed out of the space, he called the forensic department and read off Skylar's passcode to her phone. "I need any texts or emails that might seem a bit off or troublesome."

Phone still pressed to his ear, Vaughan said to her, "He's pulling the phone right now."

"I'd bet money her life's secrets are on that phone," Zoe said.

They drove less than a block, and then Vaughan said, "Let me put you on speakerphone. I have Agent Spencer with me."

"Hello, Agent Spencer. This is Bud Clary."

"I'm surprised we found you in the lab," she said.

"Just barely," he said. "We just had the Fosters' Lexus towed to the forensic lab, and I was checking messages. That code you gave me for Skylar's phone worked."

"I'm interested in both text and email messages but also any apps that have encrypted messaging options." Several apps required an additional passcode to view communications. Keeping notes between friends seemed innocent enough until a predator twisted the app's intent and started a dialogue with an unsuspecting teen. There had been several instances of older men communicating with young teens and grooming them for sex or prostitution.

"The texts seem fairly ordinary," Bud said. "We have texts between Skylar and Neil Bradford. They tell each other how much they love the other or what they want to eat for dinner. Texts from Mom telling Skylar to be home for dinner."

"What about the apps?" Zoe asked.

He read them off. "I can open all of them but one. It has a messaging feature but requires a passcode."

"Try 1812."

"Nope. Doesn't work."

Frustration elbowed at Zoe. "She was born in 2002. Try that."

"No. Doesn't work."

"All right. We'll see if we can track down her passcode. Thanks," Zoe said.

He ended the call. "I have never been a fan of those apps."

"Me either."

He drove several more miles, turned on a couple of tree-lined side streets, and parked in front of Jessica Harris's house. Like the Foster house, it was older, made of brick, and in an affluent neighborhood.

They climbed the brick steps and rang the bell. Moments later, the door opened to a woman in her midfifties with dark hair streaked with gray at the temples. "May I help you?"

Vaughan and Zoe held up their badges and introduced themselves. "Yes. We are investigating the disappearance of Hadley and Skylar Foster. You are?"

The woman appeared taken aback by the news, and it took a moment before she cleared her throat and said, "Margaret Harris."

"We understand your daughter, Jessica, is a friend of Skylar's?" Zoe asked.

Mrs. Harris's hand tightened on the doorknob. "I saw it on the news. Jessica has not really seen Skylar since April."

"What about at school?" Zoe asked.

"I'm sure they pass each other in the hallways, but that's it. I don't see how she could help you."

"We are talking to everyone at this stage. Sometimes the smallest detail is important. Is Jessica home?" Vaughan asked.

"Yes. She had a fever this morning, so I kept her out."

"We'd like to talk to her," Zoe said.

"All right. Please come in." She escorted them to a neatly furnished living room bathed in several hues of white and beige. It was as perfect as it was cold.

"Can I get either of you a coffee?" Mrs. Harris asked.

"No, thank you," Vaughan said. "We just need to speak with Jessica."

"Of course." Mrs. Harris vanished into the house, her heeled shoes clicking on the tiled floor. Upstairs, a door opened and then closed.

"Let me interview Jessica," Zoe said. "I think she'll be more receptive to a female. And if not, you can give it a try."

"She's all yours."

The door upstairs opened and closed, and this time two sets of foot-steps sounded on the landing and down the stairs. Mrs. Harris appeared in the doorway along with her daughter, Jessica, a plump girl whose designer stressed jeans and loose-fitting burgundy top looked more uncomfortable than stylish. Long dark hair hung around her slumped shoulders. She pushed her glasses back up on her nose.

"Jessica," Zoe said. "I'm with the FBI, and Detective Vaughan is with the Alexandria Homicide team."

"I haven't really spoken to Skylar since last spring," she said.

"But you spent a lot of time with her, didn't you?" Zoe said.

The girl glanced to her mother, who nodded. "Yeah, we were pretty good friends."

"Why haven't you talked to her since last spring?" Zoe asked.

"Because she started dating Neil, and he just took over her life." Hints of bitterness sharpened the words.

Zoe glanced toward Vaughan, prompting him to say, "Mrs. Harris, would you join me in the kitchen? I have questions."

"I'm not leaving my daughter," she said.

"Agent Spencer is one of the best." A smile warmed his stark fea-tures. "She is simply on a fact-finding mission. Our goal is to find Skylar."

"People often remember different details if they aren't influenced by others," Zoe said. "It's not about deception or ill intent, but I interview witnesses alone."

"My daughter didn't see anything."

"Agreed," Zoe said. "But she's one of the very few people who knew Skylar well."

"If your daughter was missing, we'd be handling it exactly the same," Vaughan countered.

"It's okay, Mom," Jessica said. "I can answer a few questions."

"If you feel uncomfortable at any point, call out to me," Mrs. Harris said.

"I will."

When the two left the room, Zoe closed the door. "Mind if we have a seat?"

"Sure." Jessica sat in the middle of the sofa, and Zoe took the chair to her right.

"How long have you known Skylar?"

"We met last winter when she moved here. I'm new to the area, too. I think that's why we really hit it off."

"Why didn't she see you after she started dating Neil?" Zoe asked.

"I don't know. I called and called, but she always had an excuse. Finally, I gave up."

"When was that?"

"April fifth. It's her birthday. I got her a present and took it to her house. She accepted it but said she couldn't visit because she had to help her mom. I knew that was a lie. Mrs. Foster never asks for help."

"She's not the first girl to get swept up in her first relationship. But that doesn't mean it didn't hurt."

"Yeah, I guess."

"I found Skylar's social media accounts, and they look pretty normal. Were there others she didn't tell her parents about?"

"Yeah. She just didn't use her name."

"What name did she use?"

"Wild Blue. Like the sky." Saying the name out loud coaxed a quick, fleeting smile.

Zoe searched Wild Blue on a popular app designed for hiding communications and spotted the username. "Do you know her password?"

"I did, but I haven't looked at her profile for a while. I'm not sure if it still works. Do you want it?"

"Yes, I do."

Jessica rattled off the numbers and letters, which amounted to what appeared to be random numbers and initials.

Zoe texted the password to Bud Clary. He responded immediately, promising to get right back to her.

"Did Skylar ever talk about anyone other than Neil?"

"She used to talk to a guy on the phone."

"Who?"

The girl shook her head. "She never told me his name."

"Did you ever meet him?"

"No. She was kind of secretive about him. Do you think he is the one that took Skylar?"

"Maybe. I don't know," Zoe said.

"Is Skylar going to be okay?"

Even if they found her alive, her life would never be the same. "I hope so."

CHAPTER FOURTEEN

Tuesday, August 13, 3:00 p.m.
Alexandria, Virginia
Eight Hours after the 911 Call

When they stepped outside, Zoe slid on her sunglasses. The afternoon heat warmed her bones, and she was glad to be in the fresh air. Skylar and Hadley had been missing for about eight hours. In most cases like this, the perpetrator was not random but someone known to the family.

"Roger stated that Hadley is about to leave her husband. And Skylar liked to keep secrets, including a male friend no one had met," Zoe said.

"So much for the perfect family." As Vaughan unlocked the car and they both got inside, his phone rang. "It's Hughes." He answered and put her on speaker.

"We have Mrs. Foster's recent credit card. We've developed a list of stores she frequented, and uniforms are running down security footage," Hughes said.

"Key in on dates around the first week of July," Zoe said. "We have a report that Hadley Foster became more agitated about that time."

"Will do," Hughes said.

"What about arrests? Do any of the Fosters have arrest records?" Vaughan asked.

"Mark did missionary work in high school and then married Hadley. From then onward, they were the perfect couple. Skylar is their only child. The girl has no record here, but I'm reaching out to police in Portland, Oregon."

"Thanks. Keep us posted on the financials," Vaughan said to Hughes. "I know the uniforms have been knocking on doors all morning, but I still want to talk to some of the neighbors."

"Right," Hughes said. "Will keep you posted."

Twenty minutes later, Vaughan and Zoe were knocking on the door of the house that faced the Fosters' backyard. It belonged to Rodney and Sarah Pollard.

She glanced at Vaughan and noticed the frown lines around his eyes had deepened. Cases involving a missing child were stressful to everyone working the case, but for a guy like Vaughan, with a teenage son, it had to hit close to home.

Seconds later, footsteps sounded in the brick two-story house. Like the Fosters' house, the Pollards' home had been built about sixty or seventy years ago. The lawn was small but carefully manicured.

The door opened to a petite woman with salt-and-pepper hair draped over narrow shoulders. Worry darkened her eyes as she looked up at Vaughan and then Zoe.

"Are you police?" she asked.

"Yes, ma'am," Vaughan said. "This is FBI special agent Zoe Spencer, and I am Detective William Vaughan. We're working the case together."

"I've been worried sick since the officer knocked on my door this morning. Do you have any news about that poor family?"

"Mr. Foster is out of surgery and doing well. We're still looking for Mrs. Foster and her daughter. May we come in?"

"Of course you can," she said, stepping aside. "That poor family. My heart just breaks for them."

The house was decorated with traditional Queen Anne furniture, similar to Uncle Jimmy's tastes. The walls were painted a hunter green, more fitting with the colonial era of Alexandria, Virginia. There was a reproduction Matisse on the wall that she was tempted to look at more closely. Jimmy always said artists copying other painters signed their work in secret ways.

"How well do you know the Fosters?" Zoe asked.

"I see Hadley several times a week. We both are often coming and going at the same time, with just enough time to wave and smile. Last week, we were saying how nice it would be to go to the new wine bar on King Street. I don't know Mark that well. He, like my husband, works long hours."

"What does your husband do?" Vaughan asked.

"He's a lawyer."

"How long have you lived next to the Fosters?" Zoe asked.

"We moved here from Nevada about five years ago. And they moved here in January."

"Do you mind if I have a look out the back of your house?" Zoe asked.

"Go right ahead. As you can see, there's a very good view of the Fosters' house."

Zoe peered out the kitchen window, which overlooked the Foster house, and looked inside their family room. From this vantage point, it would have been impossible to see the front door, where Mark Foster had collapsed, or the interior entrance to the garage. And unless you were watching very closely, it would be easy to miss people passing in front of the narrow doorway visible from here.

"Did you notice a disturbance this morning?" Vaughan asked.

"I heard the family car pull out of their driveway very quickly. It was early. Maybe five or six."

"Which was it?" Zoe asked.

"I slept through my alarm, which is unusual. The sun hadn't risen."

"The sun rose at 6:13 a.m.," Zoe said.

"Then it must have been closer to five, because it was pretty dark." She shook her head, trailing Zoe's gaze with her own. "This is such a quiet neighborhood. We don't see trouble like this."

"Were you curious about what was happening at the Foster house?" Zoe asked. "Did the Fosters usually leave so early?"

"No, not that early," she said. "I wanted to call over and make sure everything was okay, but that felt too nosy. People are entitled to leave early if they want to. Now I wished I'd at least called."

"Did you see anyone looking at the house?" Vaughan asked. "Anyone in the neighborhood who didn't belong?"

"What kind of person are you talking about?" Mrs. Pollard asked.

"Anyone that didn't seem to fit," Zoe said.

"No one today," she said.

"What about yesterday or any day before?" Vaughan asked.

"Nothing. And I'm home all day and have a tendency to notice." She pressed a trembling fingertip to her mouth, shaking her head. "This is just so terrible. I've spoken to my husband, Rodney, on the phone, and he says you can call him anytime today. He is more than willing to talk to you. But if he'd seen anything out of the ordinary, he'd have said something to me. And he didn't."

Nothing out of the ordinary. A regular day, other than the car leaving the driveway quickly between five and six o'clock. Around five o'clock in the morning, the roads would have been easier to travel. Closer to six o'clock, and those times would have tripled.

Vaughan asked Mrs. Pollard a few more questions but got nowhere. The stress underscoring Vaughan's tone was growing more pronounced, and Zoe took the lead.

"Did Hadley ever talk about her family?"

"She mentioned that her sister died when she was a teenager. Said something about a car accident," Mrs. Pollard said. "It's odd that you should ask about her family. Normally, she had a bright smile on her face and a great disposition. But about a month ago, I saw her struggling with a garden hose, and she suddenly started to cry. I asked her if she was okay, and she said she'd run into someone who reminded her of her sister's death."

"Did she mention a name?" Zoe asked.

"No. In fact, it was like she caught herself and stopped talking. Next thing I knew, she was smiling like she didn't have a care in the world."

CHAPTER FIFTEEN

Tuesday, August 13, 3:30 p.m.
Alexandria, Virginia
Just over Eight Hours after the 911 Call

Vaughan and Spencer spent the next several hours knocking on doors and talking to the immediate neighbors. Another woman confirmed the Lexus had left well before dawn, closer to five than six. However, no one had seen anything unusual.

Their one and only witness to whatever had happened in the Foster home was Mark Foster. Now that he'd had a few hours to rest, it was time to talk with him again. They pushed through the hospital doors and made their way to the charge nurse on the floor. She told them Foster was conscious and threatening to check out if he couldn't talk to the cops again.

"Well, he's about to get his wish," Vaughan said. He thanked the nurse, and the two walked toward his room. Vaughan stopped to speak to the uniformed officer. "Has he said anything?"

The female cop rose from her chair and shook her head. "He yelled at the nurses about a half hour ago when they tried to give him a seda-tive. He refuses to turn off the television news."

"Any reactions to the news story?" Vaughan asked.

Mary Burton

She checked her phone. "We're starting to get calls. Some say they've seen the two, but the few we've followed up have been bogus. The networks have also posted Skylar's and Hadley's pictures on their websites and have listed both as missing and endangered. Nikki McDonald has updated her site four times today with video footage."

"Has he had any visitors?" Vaughan asked the nurse.

"A couple of reporters tried to get up to the floor, but hospital security stopped them. It is the beauty of a lockdown unit."

"Thanks," Vaughan said.

In the room, they found Foster sitting up in his bed, surfing the television channels. When Vaughan stepped inside the room, Foster shut off the television and faced them. His face was pale, and deep bags hung under bloodshot eyes. White bandages on his arm and chest stuck out from under his hospital gown.

"Have you found my wife and daughter?" he demanded.

"Not yet." Vaughan watched the man closely, knowing in his gut Foster was hiding something.

"What the hell have you been doing all morning? They've been gone for hours!" he shouted.

"We've been searching for your wife and daughter," Vaughan said calmly as he approached the bed.

"But you haven't found them!" Foster countered.

"We found your Lexus in a cemetery off of King Street. There was no sign of your family."

Foster closed his eyes and pressed his fingertips into his lids as he drew in a staggering breath. "This is a nightmare. We were all supposed to fly to the Caribbean over Thanksgiving. I had just bought the tickets."

Vaughan and Spencer exchanged glances. It was another small detail that he could easily verify. "I spoke to Roger Dawson. Did you know your wife was having an affair with him?"

146

Foster's brows drew together, and his jaw tightened. "I knew. Hadley and I have both made mistakes in our marriage, but we got past that."

"Dawson said your wife was planning to leave you." It was a pain Vaughan was familiar with, though by the time his ex-wife had decided to leave, he had been glad to see her go.

Foster swallowed and reached for a cup of water on the bedside table beside him. He slowly sipped through a straw. "He's lying. Hadley and I were solid."

"Skylar's boyfriend said you and your wife were fighting a great deal," Spencer said.

Foster folded his arms, wincing as he shifted. "That boy does not know what's going on in my house. What he's heard is from Skylar, who doesn't fully understand what she thinks she's heard. Aren't all teenage girls dramatic?"

"If she knew her parents' marriage was crumbling, she had a right to be upset," Spencer said.

"Sometimes Skylar overreacts," Foster explained.

Foster's repeated use of present tense could have been wishful thinking on his part, or it could have indicated he knew more than he was saying.

"From where I'm sitting," Vaughan said, "I'm looking at a guy with injuries that aren't that bad. His house and car are covered in blood, and his family is missing."

"What are you saying?" Foster demanded.

"Your neighbor said she spoke to your wife recently."

"Which neighbor?"

"Sarah Pollard. She said Hadley seemed upset about an encounter back in July. Hadley said the person she ran into reminded her of her sister's death."

"Sarah is the neighborhood gossip, and half her stories are wrong." He scraped his thumbnail against the side of the plastic water cup.

"Did Hadley ever talk about her sister?" Vaughan asked.

"Sometimes she has nightmares about Marsha, and they upset her."

"Did she talk about them?" Spencer asked.

"No. Every time I brought up her sister, Hadley would shut down. I wanted her to talk to a psychologist. She wouldn't but finally agreed to a prescription of sleeping pills."

"How well did you know Marsha?" Spencer asked.

"She was a nice gal. I didn't see her often because she was away at college."

"Did she date anyone that last summer?" Spencer asked.

"I'm sure she did. Guys liked Marsha, and Larry had a lot of men working for him who thought she was attractive," Foster said.

"Slater said you worked part time that last summer at the Prince paving company, correct? Do you remember any of the employees' names?"

"Larry used a lot of day laborers. How could I possibly remember them all?"

"Just thought your paths would have crossed," Vaughan said.

"I didn't socialize with them," Foster said.

"Did Hadley want to return to Alexandria?" Spencer asked.

"It took some convincing to get her to return to Alexandria last year. The area holds lots of bad memories. Why are you asking me about Marsha and my job transfer? Neither has anything to do with what happened to my family today."

Instead of answering, Spencer asked, "What might have triggered the recent dreams and her agitation?"

"I don't know." Foster dropped his head back against his pillow.

"Can you pinpoint the time?" Vaughan asked.

"It was around the Fourth of July weekend." He sounded weary, almost gutted.

"That's very specific."

"I remember because we were going to a party, and she said our cooler looked old, and we needed a new one. I told her it was fine, but she ran out to the hardware store to pick up a new one. After she got back, she didn't say much the entire weekend."

Vaughan noted the date. "Maybe she was sick."

"It's never good when Hadley is quiet. Something must have happened."

"Did you try to find out?" Spencer asked.

"I asked her a dozen times, but she kept saying she was fine."

"Could she have had a stalker?" Spencer asked.

His eyes brightened as he shook his head. "She could have. Do you think a stalker attacked us today?"

"I don't know," Vaughan said. "What do you think?"

"All I know is that I didn't hurt my wife and daughter, if that's what you are getting at. I love them both and would do anything to protect them. I would die for them."

"Even if your wife told you she was leaving?" Vaughan asked quietly. "You might not have meant to hurt her, but your temper flared. Maybe you walked out of the room to gather your temper, but as you stood in the kitchen and stared at the knives, your rage exploded. You lost it."

"That's not what happened," Foster said.

"You grabbed a knife and stabbed your wife," Vaughan pressed.

"No!"

"Your daughter must have gotten into the mix, and she had to be dealt with, too," Vaughan said. "Did she help you get her mother to the car? Maybe you told Skylar you needed to get Hadley to the hospital?"

"No!" Foster lurched forward and then immediately fell back against the sheets, his face contorted with pain, anger, and grief. "That is not true. I did not hurt my wife or daughter. I've always protected them."

Vaughan hadn't worked out all the details of what had happened this morning at the Foster home, but he was certain Foster was lying about all or part of it.

"Where are your wife and daughter now?" Spencer asked.

"I don't know!" Foster shouted. "I'm not saying another word until I have a lawyer."

Once a suspect invoked their right to legal counsel, it changed the dynamics of the conversation immediately. There were some in law enforcement who might have kept pushing at this point, but he would not. He did not want to risk a judge declaring his evidence inadmissible in court one day.

"Your wife and daughter need you to tell the truth," Spencer said.

"I'm not saying another word to either of you until I have a lawyer!" Foster shouted. "Get out of my room now, or I'm calling security and having you thrown out."

***

He sat back, watching the news anchor reading off a teleprompter as Marsha's picture appeared on the screen. Rubbing a callus on his palm, he fought back impatience as his heart beat faster. To calm himself, he closed his eyes and thought back to the girl's blood on his hands. He drew in several deep breaths until his pulse slowed.

The news anchor promised more details about Marsha in the coming days, but for now, she said police were focused on Hadley's and Skylar's disappearances. The news stations had moved on quickly to the next story.

He was frustrated that so little attention was being paid to Marsha. She had been his first. She had opened a new world to him when she had died. That made her special. And sharing her now with the world meant something.

Even now, Hadley had found a way to steal Marsha's thunder. She had always been jealous of her sister and hated it when Marsha was in the limelight.

This was all so typical of Hadley.

Still, he took comfort in knowing the discovery of Marsha's remains had to be eating Hadley alive. And he was glad.

***

There's a guy. Super cute. And when he flirts, he makes me forget about work, school, and everything. Not good, but what's a girl to do?

Marsha Prince, August 2001

CHAPTER SIXTEEN

Tuesday, August 13, 6:15 p.m.
Alexandria, Virginia
Eleven Hours after the 911 Call

When Zoe and Vaughan crossed the hospital lobby, a rush of frustration nudged her forward. "I want to see the Fosters' financials. I want to know where Hadley was on Fourth of July weekend. We might get lucky and find security footage from the hardware store. Maybe we'll get a look at who she ran into."

"I'll text Hughes and see what she's come up with so far," he said.

"Mark sounded a little indignant when you asked if he'd socialized with the day laborers. Easy to think he's just a snob, but I think it's more than that."

"Maybe he remembers more than he's saying." Vaughan's phone dinged with a text. "Hughes has footage from the July Fourth weekend and is now keying in on the hardware store." He typed several more lines. "She'll search all the private security cameras around that store."

As he walked around his car to unlock it, she leaned against the vehicle, absorbing the heat and chasing away the hospital's chill. "Did you see him perk up when you suggested that Hadley might have a stalker?"

"Reminded me of a drowning man who'd just spotted a life preserver."

"He was quite passionate about painting himself as his family's protector. And the pictures displayed in the Foster house suggest he did love his family very much."

"You chase forgers," Vaughan said. "You know better than anyone that pictures can lie. The more I'm around that guy, the less I believe him."

As he opened his door, a woman said, "Detective Vaughan!"

Vaughan slid on his sunglasses just as Zoe spotted Nikki McDonald heading toward them. "Ms. McDonald."

"What's going on with Mark Foster?" Nikki asked. "My sources tell me he's out of surgery and that he's talking."

"We have no comment at this time," Vaughan said.

"I also understand that you found the family vehicle," Nikki pressed.

Reporters had their sources within the police department, but unwanted leaks always frustrated law enforcement. "No comment."

"Come on, guys, I'm a part of this case. I found Marsha Prince's bones. You can't tell me that my discovery had nothing to do with what went on in the Foster house this morning."

Vaughan tightened his jaw and was silent for a moment before he shook his head. "Again, I can't comment. I have a missing woman and a teenage girl to find."

"I can help with that," Nikki said. "I still have a decent social media presence. I can put the word out. Ask for tips on the women. You know most people will talk to media before the cops."

"Speak to the department's public information officer, Britta Smith."

"Brit is great, but she's young," Nikki said. "She's never worked a case that's this high profile."

Zoe drew in a measured breath, knowing she would be willing to ask for help very soon if this case did not break. She sensed Vaughan, who was always pragmatic, would do the same. "I'll keep that in mind, Ms. McDonald. But right now, I have to find Hadley and Skylar Foster."

As he opened his car door, she rushed to say, "I was just down in Fredericksburg. I visited with Becky Mahoney. She was having an affair with Larry Prince just before his daughter went missing."

Annoyance surged through Zoe. The last thing she needed was a reporter interfering in one of her cases. "What did Mahoney say?" Zoe asked.

She locked eyes on Vaughan. "There were several guys in the shop who had a thing for Marsha."

"We've heard that," Vaughan said.

"Did you also hear that one of the guys went out with Hadley and Marsha?"

"Any idea what his name is or where he is?" Zoe asked.

"Not yet, but I'm looking for him. If I get a lead on the guy and he looks promising, I'll give it to you. But when these two women are found, I'm collecting on what you owe me."

"Why are you being so generous?" Vaughan asked.

"Getting kicked in the proverbial balls and tossed to the curb has a way of humbling your ass. Besides, whatever the hell is going on here is bigger than an evening newscast."

"It's a deal," Vaughan said.

Zoe and Vaughan slid into the car, and the heat coiled around her now like an unwelcome wool blanket. She glanced in the rearview mirror at the reporter and watched her walking into the hospital. "McDonald's greed and self-interest is oddly refreshing."

"We'll see if she sticks to her word." He started the engine and turned up the air-conditioning.

"A press conference would be a good move at this point," Zoe said.

"I know. I'm just not looking forward to the three-ring circus that will follow."

She understood his hesitation. Once they went public with the case's details and asked the public for tips and leads, they would be inundated with people with bad information or who wanted their fifteen minutes of fame.

***

Vaughan and Spencer crossed the marble entryway of Mark Foster's sleek office building, located on the edge of Old Town. He punched the elevator button, and they were soon riding the car to the sixth floor.

Vaughan had called ahead, and the receptionist quickly escorted them both back to a conference room that overlooked the historic section of the city.

They did not have long to wait before the door opened to an older man with a thick shock of gray hair and tanned skin. "I'm Simon Davenport. I own the company. We heard what happened at the Foster house today, and none of us can believe it."

Vaughan shook his hand. "We're hoping you can help us make sense of it."

"Sure. Anything."

"How long has Mark been with this company?"

"Fourteen years in the Portland office, and eight months here. We were lucky he wanted to move back east. He's one of the best forensic accountants in the business. If it's hidden, he'll find it."

"So the move was strictly job related?" Spencer asked.

"No, he said it was a family issue. I do know he took a substantial pay cut to move back to Virginia. He'll get a bonus at the end of the year if he performs, but in the interim, he took a financial hit."

"Did he complain about money issues?" Vaughan asked.

Davenport shook his head. "He didn't to me. But in the last few months, he's been working a lot of overtime to close a case. It has the potential for a tremendous payout."

"Did he talk about his family?" Spencer asked.

"Not so much about his wife, but he's crazy about his kid. I think the move back to the DC area was for the daughter."

"How so?"

"I learned from his Portland supervisor that the girl landed in some kind of legal trouble, and the family decided a fresh start was in order. From my perspective, it seemed to be working. The few times I met Skylar, she seemed like a delightful girl."

"Anything else you can tell us about Mark?" Spencer asked.

"He's worked closely with Veronica Manchester, and I would refer you to her, but she's on vacation now. I can try to track her down if you think that would help."

"I'm taking any lead I can get now."

"I'll have my secretary call."

"Is Mark the kind of guy who would stab his wife?" Spencer asked.

"Hell no. He's the last guy on the planet to hurt his family. He was very protective of them."

***

Zoe checked her messages while Vaughan maneuvered through the evening commuter traffic, which was in full form. Instead of the beltway, Vaughan opted for the web of side streets that he knew better than most. They were blocks from the police station when his phone rang.

Vaughan veered past a slow car in the left lane and answered the call. "Detective Vaughan."

His lips flattened into a grim line as he listened and continued to maneuver through traffic. He glanced toward the clock on the dash as he hung up. "They think they've found Hadley Foster in a motel dumpster."

"Are they certain it's Hadley?" Zoe asked.

"They aren't sure. The victim is a white female who is of similar height and build to Hadley. There are also lacerations on her chest and arms, suggesting she was stabbed to death."

"And Skylar?"

"No trace of her yet. The uniforms have started knocking on motel room doors all around the area."

Zoe dropped her head against the headrest and closed her eyes for a moment before she straightened. "What's the address of the motel?"

He rattled off the address while she plugged it into her phone. The motel was located on Bragg Street, near the Duke Street exit ramp.

They arrived fifteen minutes later and were greeted by six marked cars, including the captain's car. Vaughan parked, and the two got out, quickly tugging on gloves as they rounded the building.

The 1950s motel was one level and painted a light blue. The parking lot had several potholes, and there were weeds growing up through the sidewalk. It had seen better days.

The lot was filled with at least a dozen cars, which, considering the motel's sixty-seven-dollars-a-night price, was not surprising. In this area, there were few really cheap options for lodging.

"Galina Grant was found only a mile from here." Vaughan checked his watch and frowned. "I missed her autopsy today."

"You can't be everywhere, Vaughan."

"Tell that to Galina."

"If we're analyzing distance, this particular location is exactly 3.6 miles from the Foster residence and 1.2 miles from where we found the family's car," Zoe said.

"Foster could have stabbed his wife, dumped her, ditched the car, and run home by seven when he called 911, but it would have been tight."

"There are also serial killers who operate within a specific geographical area. They kill or dump bodies in places that are close to home and work."

"Maybe."

Yellow tape surrounded the dumpster, and as they approached, she could see that the responding officer had marked off what appeared to be a trail of dark dried blood that stopped a few feet short of the dumpster.

"Who called it in?" Zoe asked the uniformed officer.

"The motel manager," he said. "He was dumping trash and smelled the decomposition. He's had trouble with a local restaurant dumping bad meat here illegally, so he poked around, trying to find packaging so he could figure out who'd done it this time. That's when he saw the victim's hand. He backed right off after that."

The stench of death rose out of the dumpster. "In this heat and humidity, it's surprising she wasn't found earlier," she said.

"The body is badly bloated," the uniform said. "But hard to say how long she's been in there, given the heat and humidity." Nothing accelerated decomposition like August in Virginia.

Two forensic technicians set up a table as uniforms erected a tent to cover their work area. This scene would take a dozen or more hours to process, and if it was related to the Foster case, it meant a third crime scene was now in the lineup.

Zoe looked back at the motel, already wondering if there was security footage and how long the computer data would remain intact.

There was a growing collection of people across the street who had already gathered to watch, and she could not help but wonder if the killer stood among them. Some killers would return to their dump sites. In their minds, they shared an intimate bond with the victim because the killer was the victim's last contact with the living. No one could take that away.

Once the techs were set up, both Zoe and Vaughan were given booties and closer access to the dumpster to view the body.

As she approached the open side door, the air filled with death. Bracing herself, she looked inside the door. The bin was filled with white trash bags as well as a collection of beer bottles and a couple of broken chairs. When she scanned the space, she saw the collection of gold bracelets ringing a discolored slim wrist.

The forensic technician took pictures to document the surrounding area as well as the interior. Knowing this would go on for at least a half hour before anyone crawled into the dumpster, she shifted her attention to the crowd, which had grown to nearly a dozen.

She raised her phone and took video footage of everyone before she crossed the parking lot and held up her badge to the group of onlookers. There were two couples, a group of four women, and three single males.

"Why are you taking our pictures?" The question came from a midsize man wearing faded jeans, a plaid shirt, and work boots.

"I'm FBI special agent Spencer. I'm investigating a murder."

"But why do you care about us?" the man challenged.

"Perhaps you witnessed something. And your name, sir?"

"Rich Houston."

"And what are you doing here, Mr. Houston?" The man smelled of cigarette smoke, fast food, and beer.

"Enjoying the show like the rest of the crowd. Why do you care?"

"Do you live around here?" she asked.

"I'm staying at the motel. I'm a truck driver and had to pull in here when my rig broke down."

"How long have you been here?" Zoe asked.

"Three days. And before you ask, I didn't see nothing."

"Where are you based, Mr. Houston?" she asked.

"North Carolina. I make runs up and down the mid-Atlantic."

"I saw something," a woman to her left said.

Zoe kept her gaze on Houston a beat longer before turning. "And you are?"

"Theresa Kittredge. I work at the motel." Kittredge was in her early fifties and had a thin, wiry build with hunched shoulders.

"What did you see?" Zoe asked.

"A guy lingering by the dumpster."

She knew a dumpster in this area could easily see its share of illegal dumping. "What was he doing?"

"He opened the door and just stared inside."

"Did he put anything in the dumpster? Did he take anything out of it?"

"No. He just stood there." The afternoon sun caught the silver streaking her dark hair.

"When was this?"

"Yesterday."

"Any alarm bells go off for you?" Zoe asked.

"No. We get all kinds around here. I thought at first he was dumpster diving, because restaurants dump here sometimes. But like I said, he didn't take nothing."

"Did he see you?"

Kittredge rubbed her hands over her arms as if chilled. "No, I don't think so."

"What did he look like?"

She shrugged. "Average. Wore a ball cap and a full jacket, so it was hard to tell. I remember thinking in this heat that the jacket must have been miserable."

Eyewitnesses could be the most unreliable. Not only did people lie, but even the truth tellers did not always get it right. Human brains had a way of filling in details that fit their own personal worldviews.

Zoe scribbled down the woman's name and contact information. She spoke to the others standing around, but most were passersby and had nothing to add.

She approached the dumpster just as the first technician crawled through the door and stood over the body, which was covered in debris. He snapped more pictures before he handed out the broken chairs to another tech, who set them on an outstretched tarp.

It took another half hour before the trash and debris were cleared off the woman's body. The process was painstaking because the body lay under at least a dozen bags, which had to be carefully removed in case evidence was attached. Each sack was also opened on a nearby tarp and searched for any additional possible evidence.

The victim lay on its side, and sightless eyes stared from a discolored face that was drawn tight and also disfigured by what appeared to be animal activity. Her arms were crisscrossed, and her knees and ankles were drawn up toward her midsection. Her long blond hair was tucked neatly behind her ears.

She wore nice gold earrings, several rings on her exposed hand, and a bloodstained, gray, fitted athletic jacket that skimmed what appeared to be full breasts and a narrow, fit waist. Purple leggings covered athletic legs and matched the sneakers.

She looked very much like Hadley Foster.

But she was not Hadley.

And the odds of two random women who shared a similar look potentially dying within miles of each other were too slim to calculate.

"Galina Grant looks like this woman, and so does Hadley," Vaughan said.

The technician took dozens more pictures as well as sketches of the body and its position. Seemingly satisfied with his documentation, the tech carefully pulled the victim's hair away from her neck.

Zoe's gaze was drawn to the violent slash mark across the victim's long neck. The shriveled skin, though discolored by decomposition, was also eerily pale. It could be symptomatic of someone who had bled to death.

"Note the two-inch wound on her neck," the technician said. "Judging by the bloodstains soaking the front of her blouse, her attacker sliced an artery. The medical examiner will make the final call, but right now I'd say she bled to death."

Small yellow evidence tents marked the scattered blood spots in an unnatural trail that stopped ten feet from the dumpster. It stood in stark comparison to the massive stains in the house and Lexus.

"There's very little blood on the floor of the dumpster," Zoe said.

"I'd bet this woman was stabbed and bled out somewhere else before she was dumped here postmortem," Vaughan said.

"Why the dumpster? Was he making a statement or just being practical?" Zoe asked.

"He's done the deed, and now he has to get rid of her. He pulls up, likely late at night. When he's certain no one is watching, and any camera footage would be poor, he carries her from his car, dripping some blood as he goes, and lays her in the dumpster. Then he takes the time to tuck her hair behind her ears before he covers her in debris."

Absently, Zoe tucked her own hair behind her ear. "It's almost a loving kind of gesture."

Vaughan's scowl deepened. "Assuming it's the same guy, why dump this victim here, but leave Galina in the motel room?"

"He's evolving," she offered. "Different set of circumstances? Maybe he had more time with Galina. Maybe he was angry at this woman or another one who looked like her."

"And then he snatches Hadley and Skylar from their house?" Vaughan asked.

"Each kill is a little riskier than the last," Zoe suggested. "Because he's cocky? Reckless? Out of control? Or trying to cover up a motive."

"The first three are a given. This guy sat and ate a pizza on the end of the bed while Galina lay there, bleeding to death."

"If this murder and Galina's can be linked to Hadley and Skylar's abduction, it would help Mark Foster's case," Zoe said. "If I were his attorney, that's exactly how I'd present it to the jury."

"It's all a great theory, but we have no forensic proof," Vaughan said.

Zoe could feel the pieces of the real story swirling around but refusing to connect. "All the women look like Hadley."

"I'll have the forensic team see if anything from this dumpster transferred to any of Mark Foster's clothing or shoes. There's no way anyone could spend any time in there and not pick up something. I'll also put a call in to missing persons," Vaughan said. "For now, we have to stay focused on finding Hadley and Skylar."

Zoe nodded but continued to stare at the body, wondering who this woman was. Her clothes were intact, but that did not mean sexual assault had not been a motive. Some assailants redressed their victims after they were dead. But again, another question for the medical examiner.

Zoe watched as the technician covered the body's hands in paper evidence bags. Later, there would be finger scrapings, which hopefully would recover DNA for testing.

Finally, two technicians laid a fresh tarp over the exposed portion of the dumpster floor, lifted the body, and placed it on the plastic. If there was any DNA on the body, this would ensure it was not lost in transport.

Grabbing the ends, they lifted the tarp and body and handed it to the officers outside the dumpster, who then gently placed it on the asphalt of the parking lot.

Zoe knelt by the body and for the first time could see the truly deep gashes in her chest. To stab someone in the chest required close contact. This manner of death was as personal as it was violent.

"The reason behind a murder is generally simple," she said, thinking out loud. "Husband discovers affair. Wife confesses and demands a divorce. Husband hatches a plan for revenge that won't implicate him."

"You're saying this woman and Galina were decoys?" he wondered aloud.

"He knows he's going to kill his wife, so he sets it all up to look like a serial killer? Maybe he wanted the practice. One thing to plan murder but another to do it."

"That's one cold son of a bitch."

"Yes, it is," she said softly.

Zoe approached the forensic tech and gave him her card. "Have the medical examiner's office call me when they schedule this autopsy."

The guy tucked the card in his breast pocket. "Sure."

Zoe and Vaughan got into his car, and he started the engine. His phone rang. "It's Nikki McDonald."

"So soon? Should be interesting," Zoe said.

He accepted the call and put her on speakerphone. "Ms. McDonald. I don't have anything for you yet."

"I'm the gift that keeps on giving, Detective. Mr. Foster has a lawyer, a Rodney Pollard," Nikki said.

"Pollard is his neighbor," Vaughan replied.

"Well, Mr. Pollard showed up at the Alexandria Hospital a half hour ago and checked out Mr. Foster. They are planning a press conference at the Foster house in about thirty minutes. Seems they want to make a direct plea to the public for the safe return of Hadley and Skylar."

"How do you know this?" Zoe said.

"I have a few friends in the media who would love to have my footage of the Marsha Prince discovery. Which means they'll toss me the occasional bone. Regardless, I'm headed to the Foster house myself."

"Thanks for the heads-up," Vaughan said.

"Remember your friends." She hung up without waiting for a reply.

Vaughan muttered a curse as he dialed dispatch and requested a couple of marked cars be sent to the Foster house. "I need that crime scene preserved," he said to the dispatcher. "Spread the word that I don't want anyone in the home."

He pulled out onto Route One, into the sea of red taillights. Zoe drummed her fingers on the door handle as she reflected on the news.

"Interesting he's trying to circumvent the police," Zoe said.

"He's a desperate man."

"Desperate to find his family or shift blame?"

"Good question."

CHAPTER SEVENTEEN

Tuesday, August 13, 9:30 p.m.
Alexandria, Virginia
Just over Fourteen Hours after the 911 Call

Vaughan wove through various vehicles, tightening his hands on the steering wheel as he negotiated the snarled traffic. He dialed the police department's public information officer to get an update on the press situation.

"Britta Smith." The woman's voice was young but clear and direct.

"This is Detective Vaughan, and I have FBI special agent Zoe Spencer with me. You're on speakerphone."

"I know what you're going to ask," Britta said.

"I'm minutes from the Foster home." Vaughan flipped on his dashboard light and cut right, driving up the shoulder until he reached yet another shortcut.

"I'm in DC right now and have no chance of making it in time."

"What about Captain Preston?"

"He's on board with you taking the lead. He's spoken to Agent Ramsey, who wants Agent Spencer on site at the press conference as well."

"I can do that," Spencer said.

"Call me after it's finished," Britta said. "Nikki McDonald has already texted me and said she'll be livestreaming the event."

"Understood," Vaughan said before he hung up.

"Mr. Foster is putting his wife and daughter at risk by doing this. The abductor would have made contact by now if this attention is what he wanted. He could panic under the extra attention and kill one or both women," Spencer said.

"Do you think they're alive?" he asked.

She stared at the strip malls and cars racing past in a blur of whites, reds, and neon. "No."

They arrived at the Foster home, and Vaughan parked the car behind the forensic van that still had personnel working the interior of the home. He clenched his jaw as he calculated the next complication in this already convoluted case.

Out of the vehicle, the two crossed the street and approached the yellow crime scene tape, where Foster and Pollard faced off with a young uniformed officer. Foster was wearing a gray sweatshirt and pants, sneakers, and a Nationals ball cap. A sling was wrapped around his shoulder, holding up his injured arm, and he appeared to wince as he scooted to the door. Pollard, a portly man with thin graying hair, wore a charcoal-gray suit, a white shirt, a blue tie, and polished black shoes.

Nikki McDonald was on scene and ignoring another reporter who was trying to get her attention. Vaughan had to give her props for her dogged pursuit of this story.

Pollard glanced at Nikki and then Vaughan before he whispered a few words to Foster. Like a windup doll, Foster stumbled toward Vaughan.

"This is my house," Foster shouted. "I have a right to go inside. You can't keep me out!"

"Yes, we can, Mr. Foster," Vaughan said calmly. "This house is a crime scene, and we need to preserve as much evidence as we can."

A few of the neighbors appeared on their porches or in front windows. Two news vans rolled up at the end of the block with their reporters and camera crews spilling out of them.

"The house is covered in my wife's blood!" Foster shouted. "It's not right."

"No, sir, it's not right," Vaughan said. "But we have to tolerate it for now."

Rodney Pollard put his arm around Foster's shoulders. "Mark, you came here to make a statement. What do you want to say?"

The pain in Foster's eyes appeared genuine. Even if Foster had planned to murder his wife as Spencer had suggested, he certainly couldn't have been expecting this mess. "Yes, I have something to say."

The cameramen and reporters edged closer, but it was Nikki McDonald and her GoPro that made it to the prime spot first.

"I want my wife and daughter back," Foster said. "I will do whatever it takes to get her safely home. I love you both very much." Tears welled in his eyes and then spilled down his face. He wiped them away and clenched his fingers into fists. "Please don't hurt my girl."

Vaughan was struck immediately by his use of the singular. My *girl*, not my *girls*. *Her*. Not *them*. It could have been the meds and stress addling him.

Pollard looked at the cameras with the practiced confidence of a man who was comfortable with the spotlight. "Mr. Foster loves his family, and he's just as much a victim in this case as his wife and daughter. If anyone knows anything about Hadley or Skylar Foster, call the police or my office. We're prepared to pay a reward for any information leading to their safe return."

A reward would ensure twice the number of bogus calls.

"Detective Vaughan," Nikki said, "is there any link to this crime and the recent identification of Hadley Foster's sister?"

"No comment at this time."

All the reporters began to volley questions at Vaughan. The back-and-forth between media and law enforcement went on for another twenty minutes before Vaughan called a halt to the conference and ordered everyone to leave.

Foster's gaze held a mixture of sadness and anger. He appeared almost in a stupor. "Find my wife and daughter. There has to be someone out there who knows something."

Sarah Pollard stepped forward and laid her hand on Mark's. "Come to our house. You need to rest."

"I'm not leaving my own house." Foster snatched his arm from Mrs. Pollard's grip. "I have a right to be here."

Vaughan's frown deepened. "You're not helping your wife and daughter. Let us do our job."

"Come to our house," Pollard urged. "It's quiet, and you can sit down. You look like you can barely stand."

"I can't sleep or rest now," Foster said.

"No one is going to get any rest until Hadley and Skylar are found," Spencer said. "Let us escort you to the Pollard house."

Foster's shoulders slumped forward, as if whatever adrenaline had fueled him had run dry. They crossed the side alley between the two privacy fences and made their way up the Pollards' back steps into the sunroom that overlooked the Fosters' house. By the time Mark Foster sat, he was pale and drawn.

"I'll get us something to drink," Mrs. Pollard said.

"Thank you, dear," Pollard said.

Foster relaxed against large floral pillows that all but molded around his body. His face was pale, and his left hand trembled slightly. "Where are my wife and daughter?"

Vaughan asked Pollard, "Can you give us some privacy, please?"

"Pollard can stay," Foster said. "I need all the friends I can get now."

"I'm also his lawyer," Pollard said. "Mark is not talking to you without representation."

"Mr. Foster, do you feel like you need a lawyer?" Vaughan asked. "We are on the same side."

Foster looked toward his neighbor. "Rodney says the cops always assume the spouse did it. And I know that you see me as a suspect."

"We're here to find your family," Vaughan said.

"Your agenda is to close a case," Pollard said.

Spencer paid keen attention to Foster, as if she did not want to miss a second of his reactions. "Sir, we found a woman's body in a dumpster an hour ago."

Foster stared blankly at the ceiling for a moment, as if searching. Finally, he blinked and shook his head. "It can't be Hadley or Skylar."

Vaughan noted a sense of surety he had not expected. "Why do you say that?"

Foster leveled his gaze on Vaughan and, with a true sense of certainty, said, "Because Hadley cannot be dead. And Skylar has to be okay."

Vaughan had interviewed murderers who could look back on their own deeds in genuine disbelief. This was particularly true when the crime was intertwined with passion. The killer acted rashly and quickly and then, within minutes, could not believe what they had done.

But what struck him was a level of confidence that a man in his position just should not have.

"Were you able to make a solid visual identification of the body you found?" Pollard asked.

"Not yet," Spencer lied.

There was nothing in the rule book that said a cop could not lie to a suspect. "Animals got ahold of the body," Vaughan added.

The visual triggered more tears in Foster's eyes. They flowed down his flushed cheeks, and his hands trembled as if a chill coursed through his body. "My poor girls," he said. "They didn't deserve any of this. Our family was so close."

But it hadn't been. He'd been having an affair, and so had Hadley.

"Mr. Foster," Spencer said, "can you describe the man who broke into your house this morning?"

"I already have."

"Yes, sir, but can you do it again for me?"

A sigh shuddered through him. "I don't want to remember him."

Vaughan was certain if the shoe were on the other foot, he would be moving heaven and earth to remember key details.

"Mr. Foster," Spencer said, "let's start at the beginning. You were taking the recycling out."

"Yes."

"Your recycling bin was still in the backyard," she said.

"Then it was the trash," he said. "Tomorrow is trash day, and I knew I wouldn't have time."

She didn't argue but prompted him with, "You exited the house via the back door with the trash?"

"I started out the front door when I remembered the trash. I was in a rush and left it open as I hurried out the back."

"What happened next?" Spencer asked.

"I heard a scream."

"Your daughter's scream?" she asked.

"No. My wife. I raced upstairs, and there was a man in our room, holding a knife to her neck."

"What was your wife wearing?" she asked.

"Her purple workout tank and shorts."

Vaughan knew what Spencer was doing. She was peppering Foster with questions that he should remember easily if he was telling the truth.

"You said she'd already showered that morning," she said.

"She was going to the gym," Foster said.

"And your daughter?" she pressed. "Where was she again?"

"She was in another room."

"What room?" she asked.

"Her own. What does it matter where Skylar was?"

"It matters," Spencer said.

"You don't have to answer these questions, Mark," Pollard said. "The cops are fishing. And they're trying to trip you up on details. They are building a case against you."

More tears streamed down his face. "Skylar is such a good kid. She doesn't deserve any of this."

"No, sir, she doesn't," Vaughan said.

Pollard laid his hand on Foster's shoulder. "You need to take a break."

"Your wife and daughter don't have time," Vaughan said.

"Detective Vaughan, would you step outside with me?" Spencer said. Spencer's frustration bubbled under her blank expression.

"Sure."

He followed her out of the house, and when the two were outside, she crossed to the Fosters' fence and opened it. She walked directly to the trash can and raised the lid. It was half-full.

"Doesn't look like it was trash day either," she said.

"No, it does not."

"Foster is lying," she said.

"Divorces and children are expensive."

"With them both gone, it would clear the decks for a new life."

"Maybe," he said. "But we also have a potentially troubled kid who wasn't afraid to push the boundaries and could have brought all this upon her family."

CHAPTER EIGHTEEN

Tuesday, August 13, 10:00 p.m.
Alexandria, Virginia
Fifteen Hours after the 911 Call

It was as if Zoe had opened the puzzle box and dumped all the pieces onto a table. She had all she needed to create the picture featured on the box cover, but she had no idea how to connect them yet. "Have you tracked down any of her friends?"

Vaughan checked his notebook and nodded. "The place to go next is the gym. Apparently, Hadley spent most of her waking hours there."

"Agreed."

The trail of bread crumbs they were following was scattered at best. But it was all they had for now. "Right."

They drove to the gym located on King Street, parked in a lot behind the building, and pushed through the glass front doors and walked up to the front desk. A young woman wore a T-shirt that read KING STREET GYM. She had blond hair pulled into a perky ponytail and wore almost no makeup on flawless skin.

She looked up at both of them, smiling until she saw Vaughan's badge. "Is this about Hadley? We all just saw the news."

"Yes," Vaughan said. "She worked out here but was also an employee. I would assume she would have some acquaintances."

"She and Sharon hung out a lot. Sharon's the fitness director and has her office in the back. I'll show you."

"Did you know Hadley well?" Zoe glanced at her name tag. "Misty."

"I've only been here a few weeks. But she was always nice to me. I hope when I get to be her age, I'm in as good a shape."

When Zoe had been this kid's age, she'd still been dancing. In those days, she had felt invincible. Her body had responded when she had demanded it, and the aches and pains had been minor annoyances. She had been told she had tremendous potential, and she had begun to look at the more established dancers with a similar kind of awe. Never once had she pictured herself as anything other than a dancer.

They found Sharon sitting behind her desk when Misty knocked on the door. Sharon, like Misty and Hadley, was fit, her arms and legs finely toned. Zoe and Vaughan introduced themselves, and when Misty left, they sat in a pair of wire chairs next to a set of scales.

"I still can't believe Hadley is missing," Sharon said. "Who would do that to her?"

"That's what we're trying to figure out," Zoe said. "What can you tell us about Hadley?"

"She was a hard worker. If she wasn't training or teaching, she was working out. She never sat still. I asked her once if she ever relaxed, and she laughed and said she couldn't. I wonder if she knew something like this might happen."

"Did you know about her affair with Roger Dawson?" Zoe asked.

"Yes. It was hard to miss. Those two could barely keep their hands off of each other."

"Dawson said Hadley wanted to divorce her husband," Vaughan said.

Sharon shifted in her seat. "It sounds cheap when I hear you talk about it. But I think she loved Roger."

"She was going to leave Mark?" Zoe asked.

"Yes. She was only hesitating because of Skylar."

"Why?" Vaughan asked.

"Sky has been a handful the last ten or eleven months. Hadley caught her sneaking out, and she had grown very secretive. Hadley was getting frustrated with her. Last week, she said life would be easier if she'd never become a mom."

"Did she have a desk or a locker?" he asked.

"She did. I can show you." She rose, almost relieved to be getting out of the room. They walked past several doorways before Sharon pulled out a key and unlocked a door. She pushed it open and flipped on the lights.

The office was barely big enough to hold a small desk and two chairs. The desk was clean, except for a picture of Hadley and Skylar and an award. The picture had been taken at the beach and appeared to be as recent as this past summer. Both Hadley and Skylar had broad grins that lit up their faces.

"That was taken on the Eastern Shore," Sharon said. "She and Skylar went away for the weekend."

"Mark didn't go?" Zoe asked.

"She said he had to work." Sharon folded her arms. "Hadley wanted to be close to Skylar. That's why she entered them in the spring DC metro area fitness dance competition. They were both great and won first place. It was even in the papers."

"What was Hadley's relationship like with Mark?" Vaughan asked.

Sharon hesitated. "You know about his affair, right?"

"Yes," Zoe said.

"I can tell you that it really irked Hadley that Mark and Veronica still saw each other every day at work. I think that's what finally drove Hadley to Roger."

Zoe sat at the desk and opened the center drawer and found basic supplies: pens, pencils, paper clips, and rubber bands. She reached inside the drawer and patted her hand along the back edge but felt nothing. The next drawer contained Hadley's calendar with workout schedules. A pat down of this drawer also revealed nothing. The third and final drawer was deeper than the first two and contained fitness manuals.

She thumbed through each book and found only random notes that Hadley had made in neat handwriting along the edges that referenced questions about the book's content.

When she searched the back of the third drawer, her fingers skimmed over the edge of something. She removed a worn envelope and its contents.

The much-older picture featured a family of four, including Dad, Mom, and their two smiling blond daughters. There was no mistaking the girls. They were Hadley and Marsha.

All the Princes were smartly dressed and looked happy. This picture appeared to have been taken shortly before Marsha had vanished. She flipped it over, and written on the back were the words *I remember. Do you?*

"Remember what?" Vaughan asked.

"Good question. The photo is weathered and bears the photographer's embossed logo," Zoe said.

"Why would Hadley hide the picture in the back of an office desk drawer?" he asked. "If it upset her that much, why not just destroy it?"

"My guess is she wanted to, but something held her back," Zoe said. "Guilt. Remorse. Fear."

"Have you ever seen this picture?" Vaughan asked Sharon.

"About three weeks ago, I saw it on her desk, but as soon as I came in her office, she put it away."

"She would have been about seventeen when this was taken." Zoe showed the picture to Vaughan.

Interest flickered in his gaze, but he said nothing. He snapped a picture of the photo with his phone and removed a plastic evidence bag from his pocket. "Do you mind if I keep this?"

"No. No. If you think it will help find Hadley and Skylar," Sharon said.

"Thank you, Sharon," Zoe said. "Detective, are you ready?"

"Yes."

Neither spoke as the beat of music, the clink of weight machines, and the whoosh of elliptical trainers followed them out through the glass front doors. The parking lot was thinning as the ten o'clock closing time approached.

When they reached his car, she asked, "What did you make of the note?"

"Written by someone who knew Hadley before her sister vanished."

"What do you think the chances are that we'll pull a good print from the photo?"

"Slim. But it's worth a try."

CHAPTER NINETEEN

Tuesday, August 13, 10:30 p.m.
Alexandria, Virginia
Just over Fifteen Hours after the 911 Call

The police tip line lit up within minutes of the press conference, and as predicted, it was generating dozens of leads. Several callers said they had seen either one or both of the Foster women, but each time a uniformed officer followed up, the lead took them nowhere.

Vaughan was pulling into the police station when his phone rang. "It's the medical examiner."

Spencer checked her watch. "They've had the Jane Doe from the dumpster for two hours. And Galina Grant for almost two days."

"Detective Vaughan." It had been less than two days since he'd dropped Nate off at school, but it felt as if it had been a lifetime ago.

"This is Baldwin."

Phil Baldwin was the medical examiner, and the two had worked together on many cases. "Phil. Sorry I didn't get by today for the Grant autopsy."

"I watched the news and know you have your hands full. I wanted you to know the examination of Galina Grant is complete. As you suspected at the crime scene, it was the knife wound to her neck that killed her. Even if she'd been in an emergency room seconds after it happened, it would have been nearly impossible to save her."

That gave Vaughan little comfort. "I also sent a Jane Doe your way."

"After I conducted a preliminary external examination on this victim, I expedited her autopsy."

"Why?"

"Her wound patterns are almost identical to Galina Grant's."

Vaughan was silent for a moment as he weighed this new development. "Special Agent Zoe Spencer and I can be there in half an hour."

"I'll be waiting."

The drive west to the Commonwealth of Virginia Medical Examiner's Northern Virginia office took almost forty minutes. He looped around the I-495 beltway but was quickly brought to a standstill on I-66 thanks to a fender bender. It was past eleven o'clock before he pulled up in front of the modern building outfitted with large windows.

Both showed identification to the night guard, who called down to Baldwin. Minutes passed before the elevator doors opened and Baldwin stepped off. Dressed in scrubs, Baldwin was a tall man in his late thirties with wide-set shoulders and thick dark hair. A five-o'clock shadow blanketed his square jaw.

His athletic shoes squeaked slightly as he crossed the lobby. He extended his hand. "Vaughan. It's been a while since we've seen you in the cycling group."

"Launching Nate has been all-consuming for the last few weeks," Vaughan said.

"He has been delivered to college?" Baldwin asked.

"Thirty-six hours ago."

"I'd ask you if you missed him, but judging by the news, I'd say you've not had time."

Vaughan knew life would slow, and he would have real time to miss Nate. He dreaded it. "This is Special Agent Zoe Spencer."

"I believe we spoke on the phone over the summer," she said, extending her hand.

"The Jane Doe skull, a.k.a. Marsha Prince. I saw the pictures of your facial reconstruction work," he said. "Nice job."

"Thank you."

"As you know, I did examine the bones and found knife marks on one of the ribs."

"Can you inspect the bones again?" Spencer asked. "Look at the neck vertebrae especially."

"You think the same killer?" Baldwin asked.

"I don't want to rule it out," she said.

Baldwin nodded, letting out a sigh. "I can tell you how Jane Doe died. Come on down to the autopsy suite, and I'll brief you." They rode the elevators down a couple of floors. The doors opened to a long white hallway lit by high-wattage fixtures. Vents blasted cool air as they made their way to the storage room.

They each donned latex gloves as Baldwin crossed to a bank of drawers reserved for the dead. He opened number 202 and pulled out a slab that held a sheet-clad body.

Baldwin carefully drew back the sheet to expose a drawn face that was blackening due to decomposition. The chest was marked with a sutured Y incision.

"She's a Caucasian female in her mid- to late thirties," Baldwin said. "Judging by her teeth and bones, she enjoyed reasonably good health and nutrition. She was approximately five foot three inches tall, and she died as a result of multiple stab wounds. The lethal cut was across her neck, severing the carotid artery."

"Like Galina Grant?" Vaughan asked.

"Almost identical, and judging by the jagged marks on the wounds found on both women, I'd say a similar knife was used. The wounds were also deep. There were no minor stab wounds, which would have suggested hesitation."

"Which would suggest worry or inexperience," Spencer said. "This guy is comfortable with killing."

"I would agree," Baldwin said.

"Were you able to get fingerprints from Jane Doe?" Vaughan asked.

"Yes, we were able to get an impression of the right index finger and roll a print. It's with AFIS now, so we should know something within a few hours. And we also found a parking pass in the back pocket of her pants. Decomposition fluids made it tough to read, but one of my techs was able to confirm it was issued at the deck on the five hundred block of King Street."

"King Street?" Vaughan asked.

"Near Old Town," Baldwin said.

"And one block away from the gym where Hadley Foster worked."

Spencer's eyes darkened with interest. She dropped her gaze to her phone and pulled up the location on a map. "Was there a date on the pass?"

"We think the first week of August of this year, but the numbers are hard to read. Forensic is putting the paper under the microscope. Based on the insect activity found on the body and the body's state of decay, which would have been accelerated in this heat wave, I'd say she's been dead about seven to ten days."

"That matches with the parking pass," Spencer said.

"Yes," replied Baldwin.

"Anything else?" Vaughan asked.

"We found nothing else in her pockets or on her body. Hard to say at this point if she'd been sexually active or assaulted. We did pull some black hair fibers from her body, and they have been sent to the lab."

"Do you still have Galina Grant's body?" Vaughan asked.

"Yes." He carefully covered the body with a sheet and closed the drawer before moving to drawer 205. "We did locate Galina Grant's mother. She lives in Kansas but can't afford to travel here to claim the body, nor can she afford to bury her." He opened the drawer and peeled back the sheet to reveal Galina Grant.

Vaughan studied the young girl's still, drawn face, already blotchy with decomposition. Anger burned in him. No kid deserved to die like this.

"Jane Doe had good dental care, while Grant had a half dozen cavities," Baldwin said. "Radiology also revealed she'd suffered several broken bones, including her nose. That injury appeared to be within the last couple of months."

"There was a pizza box at the crime scene, and it contained only discarded onions and pepperoni."

"There was a partial slice of pizza in her stomach."

"Any pepperoni?" Vaughan asked.

"Yes, as a matter of fact."

So the killer hated the topping. "What else do you have, Doc?"

"Vaginal bruising confirms she had rough sexual intercourse before she died, but her partner wore a condom and didn't leave semen behind."

Spencer knitted her fingers together as she stared at Galina Grant. "She's so young."

"She was nineteen," Baldwin said.

"A little older than Skylar," Spencer said.

"Even like Marsha Prince when she died," Vaughan said. The evidence was creating a pattern that he feared painted the picture of a serial killer.

Vaughan's phone rang. It was Hughes. Turning and walking away, he pressed the phone to his ear. "Tell me you have something."

"I've matched Hadley Foster's credit card transactions with video footage from several stores. You might want to have a look."

"We're on our way."

They left the medical examiner's office, and as he drove east, back toward Alexandria, he glanced toward Spencer, who was sitting quietly, scrolling through her phone. "What do you think?"

Her naturally skeptical eyes swung around to meet his. "You have a killer who has a type. And he's been active for a long time."

"His capacity for violence is high. That's not easy to miss."

"He moves between jurisdictions and hunts prostitutes like Galina Grant. How many girls like Galina just vanish, and no one ever notices?"

"Too many." He tightened his grip on the wheel. "Marsha Prince, Hadley, and Skylar Foster aren't the kind of women whose disappearances go undetected."

"Marsha was murdered eighteen years ago. The world was not as connected, and forensic science was still developing. But I'd wager he learned from her that hunting in affluent neighborhoods would get him caught."

"So he shifted gears."

"For a time, yes."

"And then Hadley Foster returns to Alexandria," she said.

"She and Skylar were featured in the news in March when they won a fitness competition. Maybe seeing her stirred up memories."

"She starts him on a new killing spree."

"I would wager he has never stopped. In fact, I would wager seeing her agitated him and made him sloppy."

"It's all theories until we find Hadley and Skylar."

"Exactly." She slowly took in a breath, drawing his attention to the long lines of her neck. She had a grace and confidence that was hard to ignore. He liked the way she pinned her hair up.

"Are you hungry?"

"Starving. But I don't think we have time."

"I was thinking pizza."

She arched a brow. "Would this be a pizza place close to Galina Grant's crime scene?"

"Maybe. Pepperoni and onions work for you?"

"Sure."

"My kind of gal. Find the pizza place nearest the Bragg Street motel, and I'll buy."

She searched her phone. "There are three."

"We'll go with the closest."

She called in the order, and twenty minutes later, he walked through the front door of the pizza shop, his gaze traveling to the piles of delivery boxes piled behind the counter.

"Pizza for Vaughan," he said.

The slim Hispanic kid behind the counter rang up the order. Vaughan pulled up a picture of Galina. "Ever seen this girl?"

The kid frowned and looked from side to side, as if worried. "No."

"I'm not here to make trouble." He lifted the edge of his jacket, exposing his badge. "She was killed, and I'm trying to find her killer."

"I don't know her."

Vaughan scrolled to the picture of the pizza box. "You ever use boxes like this one?"

"No. We always got our name on our pizza boxes."

"Know anyone who uses this kind?" Vaughan asked.

"Maybe Gino's. It's three blocks from here."

"Thanks." He picked up the box, strode to his car, and set the pizza in the back seat.

The light from her phone sharpened the angles on her face as he slid behind the wheel. "Any luck?"

"Guy thinks maybe Gino's."

"Do you want me to call in an order?" she asked.

"Onions and pepperoni?"

"Done."

The drive to Gino's took less than five minutes, and when he pulled up, she reached for her purse. "I got it. Do me a favor and don't park in front of the store. This vehicle screams cop."

He chose a spot in the shadows that also gave him a clear view into the glass storefront of the pizza shop. "And if we aren't cops, what are we?"

"Not we. Me. I'll think of something. Stay in the car."

"You're the boss."

She rose out of the car, her long legs carrying her quickly across the lot. He watched Spencer inside the shop as she grinned and approached the cashier. Her expression brightened in a way that made it hard for the cashier or him not to notice.

The cashier, an older guy with white hair and a scruffy mustache, turned and selected her box from a tall stack.

When he handed her the ticket, she touched her hair and straightened her back a fraction, accentuating her breasts slightly. The man leaned in toward her, and the two spoke for several minutes before she smiled again and picked up the box and left. The cashier raised his phone, but his gaze lingered an extra beat on her ass.

She opened his back door and put her pizza box on top of his. "That your logo?"

He turned around. "Bingo."

"I thought so. Galina comes in several times a week. Loves her toppings. The last time he saw her was Monday."

"Was she with anyone?"

"She came in alone and paid cash. The shop has security cameras, so I suggest you get a warrant for the footage."

"Will do." Shaking his head, he put his car in drive. "He told you all this?"

"I said Galina was coming into real money, and there was a finder's fee for anyone that helped me."

Vaughan arrived at the police station minutes later, and with pizza boxes in hand, he followed her to his desk.

"Point the way to the ladies' room?"

"To your left, just past the break room."

"Perfect."

Like the cashier, he enjoyed watching her walk away.

When she vanished around the corner, he flipped his attention to his desk and the dozen pink slips. He sifted through the names and numbers, deciding they could all wait.

When Spencer returned, she held two sodas and several napkins. They opened the box from Gino's first, and each selected a slice. He sat behind his desk, and she, in front in a metal chair, scooted up close to the edge.

After they'd each sampled the second box of pizza, he asked, "What do you think?"

"If I were a hungry young girl, it would be amazing."

"Tell me you have not eaten all the pizza," Hughes said as she approached the desk with a computer tablet in hand.

"For you, we have plenty." Vaughan grinned.

"Bless you. I haven't eaten since breakfast." She pulled up a chair, grabbed a slice, and took a big bite before pressing several keys on her tablet. As Spencer reached for a second slice, Hughes asked, "How can you be so slim and eat so much? It's going to take me weeks to work off this meal."

"My dance instructors used to tell me I was fat," Spencer said.

Hughes snorted. "How much did you weigh when you danced?"

"One hundred fifteen pounds."

"I weighed that in the third grade," Hughes countered with a chuckle.

"They wanted me closer to one hundred."

"At your height?"

"The teachers liked thin and wispy," Spencer said.

Vaughan thought Spencer looked damn fantastic. "And how did you get to be a cop?"

"I broke my leg when I was eighteen and, while I was rehabbing, went to school to fill the extra time and fell in love with criminal science."

"Ballet's loss is the FBI's gain," Hughes said.

"So they tell me." Spencer took several bites of her food before asking, "What do you have for us, Detective Hughes?"

Hughes wiped her fingers off with a napkin and punched more buttons. "The first act of this story occurs on July first. Hadley and Skylar are shopping."

The image of the two in a dress shop appeared. They stood at the counter, and while Hadley paid the bill, the girl stared at her phone. The sales clerk seemed to speak to Skylar, but the girl didn't look up. Hadley nudged her, and the girl turned and walked out of the store.

Hughes pressed another button, changing the camera angle. "And then this happened."

Vaughan understood teenage hormones and moods, secretly glad he had a boy. As he watched the screen, he noticed a man who had been leaning against a store across the street began to follow them. The man wore a hat, a long-sleeve shirt, and dark pants.

"Did everybody see our man across the street?" Hughes asked.

Vaughan and Spencer nodded.

"On to act three. Hadley is at the hardware store. She bought a cooler that day. Her actual purchase was of no interest until I caught this." Hughes pressed a button. "Remember this is around the time her husband and neighbor said she started to act differently."

Hadley walked out of the store, and as she crossed the sidewalk, a man came up on her right. He was tall and lean like the man in the first video, and this time he walked directly toward her. When it became clear she had not noticed him, he called out to her. She lifted her gaze and at first appeared confused. Then she took a step back.

Grinning, the man moved closer, stopping less than three feet from her. Her confusion shifted to worry, and she gripped the handle of the cooler. She stumbled backward and then turned and ran toward her car. The stranger pulled a cigarette from his pocket and lit it up.

"Who is our mystery man?" Vaughan asked.

Hughes selected the man's face and enlarged it. "I don't know."

"Can you print that out for me?" Vaughan asked.

She dropped her gaze back to the list of phone numbers. "Sure."

When the printer across the room spat out the image, Hughes crossed to the machine, retrieved it, and handed it to Spencer.

"Judging by Hadley's expression, she knew this guy very well," Spencer said.

"We find this guy, we might find Skylar and Hadley?"

"Maybe," Spencer said.

This added a new dimension to their search. "I'll show the picture to the motel manager where Galina died. He said he didn't see who Galina showed up with, but he might still know this guy."

Hughes studied her computer notes. "FYI, Mark Foster called the same number sixteen times in the last two weeks. It's an unregistered phone, but I called it. The owner's voicemail was canned, and the inbox was full and didn't accept a message."

"Read it off to me?" Vaughan asked. As she did, he scribbled down the number.

"Mr. Foster's cell phone records indicated the last time he called this individual was seven days ago. They spoke for thirty-two minutes."

"What about Skylar's phone?" Vaughan asked.

"Most of her calls were to Neil Bradford," Hughes said. "And there is one more number that doesn't appear to be attached to a name. It has a North Carolina area code and, like the number Mark was calling, is a burner."

"One thing for Mark Foster to call a burner, but Skylar?" Spencer said.

"Not all kids can afford the better phones," Vaughan said.

He took several more bites of pizza and then dialed the number. "Let's see." It rang several times but never went to voicemail.

She nodded to the man's image on the screen.

"Kids from nice neighborhoods think they're invincible and trust too damn easily. They think that protective bubble will follow them everywhere."

CHAPTER TWENTY

Wednesday, August 14, 2:00 a.m.
Alexandria, Virginia
Nineteen Hours after the 911 Call

Zoe and Vaughan worked past three o'clock in the morning, reviewing the Fosters' financial and phone records. Fatigue was settling into her body, but she pushed through it, refusing to quit. A couple of times, he checked his watch and, when he caught her studying him, smiled sheepishly and admitted he had to remind himself that Nate wasn't home. She felt for the guy but knew there wasn't much she could say.

They had learned the Foster family enjoyed nice clothes, fancy restaurants, and expensive jewelry, but they were in deep debt. The house had two mortgages against it, and both Hadley's and Mark's credit cards were nearly maxed out.

Vaughan had also discovered that Mark had taken out a three-million-dollar life insurance policy on his wife a year ago. He was listed as the sole beneficiary.

By three in the morning, Zoe and Vaughan agreed to take a two-hour break so each could swing by their home to shower and change clothes.

He walked her to her car, and she drove back to her town house, cutting down the quiet streets of Old Town Alexandria. She parked and hurried down the brick sidewalk to her front door.

Zoe's ring of keys rattled in her hand as she twisted the old lock to the front door of her home. The hardware was brass and had stunning detail on both the handle and faceplate. However, it required finesse and jiggling to work, as if it really did not want her in the house.

She missed her modern condo with the doorman and the view of downtown Arlington and the Potomac. She also dreamed about the dual-head jet shower and the huge walk-in closet. Sure, it had had zero personality or history, but it had been convenient for work, which was what had kept her going after Jeff had died. And yet here she stood.

She closed the door behind her and hooked her purse strap on the end of the bullnose banister. Climbing the narrow staircase, she passed the wall cluttered with photo memories and paused to look at the picture of Jeff and his uncle. Both were still grinning.

It had been eight years since that picture had been taken, but it might as well have been a lifetime. She kissed her fingertips and pressed them to the picture.

As she climbed the last steps, she shrugged off her jacket and unbuttoned her blouse. She was anxious to peel off the smells of the day and wash away the lingering scents of the crime scene. She turned on the shower, knowing the old pipes needed time to coax out hot water. As the water ran, she stripped and unfastened her hair.

A glance to the right captured the large picture of her when she had been at her peak physical shape, leaning back against a tree. She would have tossed it, but it had been a favorite of Jeff's.

Zoe turned to the mirror and ran her hands over a belly no longer rock hard or perfectly flat. Her hips had also rounded since then, and the tone in her muscles had softened. She missed the ability to command her body to move in any direction and have it immediately obey.

She stepped under the hot spray, shifting her focus from the past to a very dark present that involved two missing women, a body in a motel room, and another stuffed in a dumpster.

She lathered her hair and washed. The warmth stoked the fatigue, and she was drawn to the unmade bed that waited for her. Instead, she turned the warm tap to cold, inhaling a breath as the chilled water smacked her skin and made her heart jump.

She switched off the water, quickly dried her hair, and dressed in a clean suit. The other would be dry-cleaned before she would consider wearing it again.

After heading downstairs, she made a cup of coffee and sipped it as she stared out her back window toward the long thin yard now overgrown with vines and weeds. She remembered visiting this house when she and her husband had first met a decade ago. It had been spring. The yard had been meticulously groomed, with its garden full of red and white tulips.

She popped a frozen bagel in the toaster, pleased with herself for stocking a few items in the freezer before she'd left for her last assignment. She set up her french press for another cup of coffee, knowing it would take at least two to shake off the dull headache.

As the bagel heated, she checked the fridge and pulled out a stick of butter. The toaster clicked off the seconds. Her phone rang; it was Vaughan.

She cleared her throat, doing her best to sound awake and alert. "Did you miss me?"

"Guess who our Jane Doe is."

Our. A dead body seemed such an odd thing to claim as a pair, but this was police work, and partners bonded over the strangest things. "Must be good—I can hear it in your voice."

"Veronica Manchester. Mr. Foster's office buddy."

A pulse of energy more powerful than any caffeine jolted her into high gear. "Do you have an address?"

"I do. I'm on my way there now. Care to join me?"

"You couldn't keep me away."

Fifteen minutes later, the black SUV pulled up in front of her townhome as she was wrestling with her backpack, freshly filled coffee mug, and the damn lock that required two hands. Coffee sloshed on her skin. She cursed, yanking on the door handle while turning the key. It was quite an art.

Shaking the coffee off her hands, she slid into the passenger seat.

"I can't get over the fact that you live on Captain's Row." He stared at her townhome with a tinge of disbelief. "What did Uncle Jimmy do?"

She set her mug in the coffee holder and clicked her seat belt in place. "James Malone was one of the best art forgers in the world. He made a fortune before he was arrested by the FBI. Law enforcement gave him a choice to either rot in a cell or help them. Jimmy didn't want his talent to go to waste nor his assets seized, so he put his heart and soul into finding forgeries while living quietly here, where no one was the wiser."

"He must have been talented."

"He was in his own right but was never a great commercial success. He decided to show the art world he was better than they were. And then taught me how to spot the fakes. His tutoring got me my job at the FBI."

"Why tell you his secrets?"

"He wanted the world to know. Didn't want his skills going to the grave."

"You going to sell the house? It's got to be worth a fortune."

"Maybe. Eventually. I have to clean it out, and that's going to take time."

"Looks pretty good to me."

"Don't be fooled by the outside."

"You could get two million right now even if it was crammed full of stuff."

"That stuff contains a lot of my history. And I want to figure that out before I make a decision." She shifted in her seat. "Now, if we are finished with the twenty questions about my strange inheritance, can we figure out who killed Veronica and abducted Hadley and Skylar Foster?"

He pulled onto the cobblestone street and drove toward the banks of the Potomac River. The moon was full and cast a bright light over the smooth waters that drifted past.

"What can you tell me about Veronica Manchester?" she asked.

"As you already know, she worked as a new accountant at Foster's firm. She was thirty-four and from the area. That's all I have so far."

He drove along Union Street and then worked his way back up toward King Street and I-395. Another ten minutes, and they were in Arlington, parking in front of a high-rise modern apartment building. In the lobby, they showed their badges to the guard at the desk.

"I'm Agent Vaughan. I called you about an hour ago. Agent Spencer and I are here to see Veronica Manchester's apartment."

"It's early," the guard said.

"I know it's early. I still need the apartment opened." He removed a piece of paper she knew was a search warrant from his breast pocket. She had to give Vaughan credit for finding a judge so quickly and getting a warrant executed.

"I'll take you up," the guard said. He spoke into a two-way radio and notified his partner to work the front desk. As soon as a second guard appeared from a side door, the trio took the center elevator up to the eighth floor.

"You know your residents pretty well?" Zoe asked.

"Yes. That's part of the job," the guard said.

"When is the last time you saw Veronica Manchester?" she pressed.

"At least a week ago."

"Did she travel a lot?" Vaughan asked.

"Not a lot. She works long hours and only recently started talking about a vacation to France, I think. She was real excited. I figured she was in France."

"Do residents notify you when they travel?"

"Most do, but not all."

The doors opened up to a simple carpeted hallway painted in light grays. At apartment number 806, the guard paused and typed a code into the keypad and pushed open the door.

The guard switched on the lights, and they found themselves staring at a modestly decorated one-thousand-square-foot apartment. She knew firsthand that rent in this area went for about three grand a month and was barely affordable on a cop's salary, including overtime.

"Do you mind leaving us?" Vaughan asked.

The guard glanced at the neatly folded search warrant and held it up. "Can I keep this?"

"It's your copy." Vaughan dug out his business card and handed it to the guard. "Any questions can be directed at me."

Zoe dug out her own card. "Or me."

The guard glanced at her card. "Does murder always get federal attention?"

"It does this time." She studied the guard a bit more.

The guard closed the apartment door behind him, leaving them alone. She walked into the galley-style kitchen and opened the refrigerator. The standard single-girl fare, including a box of old Chinese take-out, three bottles of white wine, and a container of expired strawberry yogurt, was staring back at her.

She checked cabinets and found a collection of plates, utensils, and pans that all looked fairly unused. The living room looked as if it had been furnished from a Pinterest page. A large piece hanging over the couch was made of rustic whitewashed wood and sported the word **Believe** in black scripted letters.

The single bedroom was off the living room and featured a queen-size bed covered in a rumpled coverlet. The pillow closest to the door still had the impression of a person's head, as did the pillow to its right. Two people had slept in this bed.

As Vaughan studied an open calendar on a small desk, she went into the bathroom and found a used towel hanging on the rack.

Draped on a shower door was a washcloth covered in old makeup. There was a collection of hair-care and makeup products on the counter. Off to the right of the feminine chaos was a man's razor and shaving cream. In the small trash can were two used condoms.

"Nice of her boyfriend to leave us a DNA sample," she said.

"I'll have forensic do a sweep," Vaughan said, texting.

As she searched the closet and bedroom, she found no connection to Mark Foster. And judging by Vaughan's silence, he had found nothing either.

"Most women have pictures of their boyfriends, right?" Vaughan asked.

"I'm sure some do, but many store photos on their phone," she said. "That's where we're likely to find her contacts as well. I suppose you've pinged her phone."

"I did. It's not putting off a signal."

"The guard said she has been gone at least a week, so if the phone is intact, the battery must be dead."

"There was no sign of her purse or keys in the dumpster," he said.

"It could have been stolen, or maybe the killer kept it as a memento."

"Saving mementos is the kind of behavior associated with serial killers."

"I know."

He shook his head. "A serial killer from Hadley Foster's past comes back, stabs Veronica, Galina, and then stabs her and takes her daughter."

She rubbed her hand over the back of her neck, massaging the tension from her muscles. "It's all just too coincidental."

He pulled the door closed, and it locked behind them. They made their way down the elevator, past the guard, and out the front door to the street. A coffee shop across the street had opened, and the glow of its warm light was too much for Zoe to resist.

"I'll treat you to a cup," she offered.

"I won't say no to that."

They crossed the street, which was only just filling with the morning rush hour, and walked through the front doors of the sleek shop. A young guy with dark hair swept back in a ponytail took their order and swiped her credit card. As they waited, she stared across the street at Veronica Manchester's apartment building and knew if she herself lived there, a place like this would be a daily stop.

She pulled up a picture of Veronica Manchester on her phone. "Don't suppose you ever saw this gal?"

"Sure, that's Veronica."

"She comes in here often?"

"It's her first stop every morning. I think she's on vacation."

"What makes you say that?" Vaughan asked.

"It's all she's talked about for the last few months. She just met a guy, and he was taking her to Spain or France."

"Her boyfriend ever come in here?" Zoe asked.

The guy shrugged. "No. But I saw him come out of her building with her pretty regularly."

"What's he look like?" she asked.

"Tall, fit. Maybe late thirties or early forties."

"They look serious?" she asked.

"She said he had just asked her to marry him."

"Nice," she said as she selected a picture on her phone. "They set a date?"

"I asked, but she was kind of vague. She said there was a lot of details to work out before they could settle on a date."

"He look like this?" She held up a picture of Mark Foster.

"Yeah. Maybe."

"Thanks."

As she and Vaughan walked across the street toward his car, Zoe said, "It's time we brought Mark Foster to the station for questioning. Dead girlfriend. Missing wife and daughter. It's not looking good."

"No, it certainly isn't."

***

Zoe checked her watch. "I want to go back to the Foster house and have another look. I want to revisit the Fosters' neighborhood. Someone there must know more about the family."

"Let's go."

They drove through the streets already heavy with traffic as the sun rose in the sky. She nestled in the seat, savoring the morning sky before dawn broke.

When Vaughan pulled up in front of the Foster house, there was a marked car outside, and the crime scene tape still maintained a tight perimeter around the yard. The news vans were gone for now, and the cluster of neighbors had cleared.

A woman walked her dog, a short mixed breed, on the other side of the street, while a man dressed in a charcoal-gray suit was opening his car door.

"Be right back." Zoe hurried across the street toward the man as he got behind the wheel. "I'm Agent Spencer, and I'm working the Foster case. Are you familiar with the family?"

The man was in his late fifties—handsome in a worn sort of way. "How could I not know? Cops and reporters have been swarming all over my lawn."

She let the comment go. "How well did you know the Fosters?"

"Casually. I work a lot of long hours. But I saw them at the neighbors' night out last week. They seemed normal enough."

"Can you clarify that?" she asked.

"Hadley was tense, but she's always been a little high strung, and Mark had had a few beers and was feeling no pain. Skylar looked bored like all the other teens did."

"Any idea why Hadley was always so uptight?"

"It's how some people just come wired," he said. "Knock on the front door and talk to my wife. She's up and knew Hadley better than me."

"Did you spend any time with Mark Foster?"

"No. Like I said, I work long hours." He checked his watch. "Speaking of which, I've got to get going. Go talk to Barb. She's pretty connected in the neighborhood."

"Thanks." Zoe walked to the front door, past a planter filled with yellow flowers and vines tumbling over the sides.

She knocked and heard the volume of a morning television newscast grow quieter as footsteps approached the door. The door opened to a heavyset blond woman in her forties.

"You're police," she said, somewhat startled. "I saw you yesterday at the Foster house."

"Agent Zoe Spencer. Your husband just told me you know Hadley Foster well."

"Sure, I'm Barb. Hadley and I didn't know each other that well, but Skylar and my daughter, Devon, used to hang out."

"But you spoke to Hadley from time to time?"

"Sure."

"Did Hadley ever sound like she was afraid for her life?"

"God, no."

"Did she ever mention that she wanted out of her marriage?"

"Who doesn't from time to time?" And then, as if she realized her quip had fallen flat, she added, "No."

"Can I speak with Devon?"

Barb shifted, twisted the ring on her finger, and then finally nodded. "Devon's in the kitchen, having breakfast. Please come in."

Zoe followed the woman through the house, past a collection of pictures and antique furniture. The place was clean and organized and stood in stark contrast to Uncle Jimmy's place on Prince Street. She wondered if she would ever have the time to give the house what it deserved.

"Devon, Agent Spencer would like to talk to you about Skylar."

Devon's long lean frame was hunched forward over a phone as she quickly typed a message. Her hair was jet black and fell over her face in a thick curtain. "What?"

"The police are here, Devon. Put the phone down, honey."

Zoe waited for the girl to type a few more words before she looked up, though she kept a firm grip on her phone. "You're friends with Skylar Foster?"

"Sure. I mean, we were super close for a little while, but she's all about her boyfriend now."

Zoe pulled out a chair and sat beside Devon. "Skylar is missing, Devon. And I'm doing everything I can to find her. What can you tell me about her?"

Devon looked up at her mother and then back at Zoe. "I don't know."

"Anything you can tell me about her. Habits, boyfriends, friends her parents might not have known about."

"She got along with everyone here okay. No big drama."

"What about back in Oregon?"

Devon was silent for a moment. "Well, she had a boyfriend out in Oregon, and he tried to break up with her. She said it really hurt her feelings, and she had a hard time letting go. Sky started following him around."

"She was stalking him?"

"When you say it that way, it sounds really creepy."

Was there a nice way to say it? "What did she do?"

"Sky got caught breaking into his house. I think she might have even trashed his room."

But was that the kind of offense that caused a family to uproot and move across the country? "Did she hurt anyone?"

"I don't think it was on purpose," Devon said.

"What happened?"

"She accidently hit him with her car. He's okay now, but I think it kind of scared everyone. She's on medicine now and doing better. She's going to be pissed when she finds out I told you this much."

"Do you remember the boyfriend's name?" Zoe asked.

"George Tate." Devon rushed to say, "She seems really happy with Neil."

"Has she made any threats against anyone you know in Alexandria?"

"No. She was always super sweet. And when she wanted, she could charm anyone."

"Thanks, Devon," Zoe said. "You've been a big help."

"It's weird what happened in the Foster house. Do you think Skylar is okay?"

"I hope so."

"She could be hiding out until the drama passes."

"Has Skylar run away before?"

"A couple of times, but only for a few hours, and it was always to Jessica's or my house. We'd eat ice cream and talk about how her parents sucked. She didn't like to be around them when they fought."

"I never saw them fight," Barb said.

"They were super careful that no one heard them," Devon said. "They wanted everyone to think they were perfect."

"Is that what Skylar said?" Zoe asked.

"Yeah. She hated that they were always getting into it."

"What did they fight about?"

"Money, mostly. Mrs. Foster liked to buy things. And I think Mr. Foster wasn't making the money he used to," Devon said.

"I never knew any of this," Barb said.

"Did Mr. Foster ever threaten his wife?" Zoe asked.

"No. At least not that she told me."

Kids absorbed more than most parents realized. Zoe fished two cards from her pocket and handed one to Barb and one to Devon. "If you think of anything else, call me."

"Of course."

"She's going to turn up," Devon said. "She always does."

"I hope so," Zoe said.

Outside, Zoe called Bud Clary. When he answered, she asked, "What's the status of the messages on Skylar's phone?"

"She'd been in contact with a guy by the name of Mr. Fix It," Bud said.

"Really?"

"He's told her multiple times how special she is and how much he loves her. Let me read an exchange."

"Fire away."

Wild Blue: My mother is leaving my father.

Mr. Fix It: I told you she would.

Wild Blue: How am I going to survive without my family.

Mr. Fix It: I'll be your family now.

"Damn it," she said. "Thanks, Bud."

She returned to the house and rang the bell. Barb answered it. "I have one more quick question for Devon."

"Sure." Barb called to her daughter, who came down the stairs.

"Sorry to bother you again. Have you heard of a guy named Mr. Fix It? Skylar was messaging him through an app."

"No, she never mentioned him to me."

"Are you sure?"

"Yeah."

"Okay, thanks again." When Zoe found Vaughan, his phone was to his ear and he was frowning, deepening the lines around his mouth and eyes. She imagined in a few years those lines would be permanently etched into his face, and the flecks of gray in his hair would be thickened. At least on him, the extra wear looked good. He was a hard man to ignore.

When she reached Vaughan, he said in a weary tone, "Agent Spencer and I will be right there."

"What is it?" she asked.

He tucked the phone in his breast pocket. "A couple of morning joggers on the W&OD Trail found a body in Waterfront Park. It matches the description of Hadley Foster."

The fifty-mile trail, which followed an old railroad bed, started thirty miles to the west in Loudon County and meandered along the Potomac River to Mount Vernon. "Any sign of Skylar?"

"No."

CHAPTER
TWENTY-ONE

Wednesday, August 14, 9:00 a.m.
Alexandria, Virginia
Twenty-Six Hours after the 911 Call

By the time Zoe and Vaughan arrived at the thirty-acre park ten minutes later, she had briefed him on Skylar's conversation with Mr. Fix It. His grim expression mirrored her own worries for the girl and her mother.

Flashing lights and a dozen cop cars greeted them. They parked and moved toward the yellow tape, ducking under it, and headed for the grassy shoreline along a wide creek. The sun was already high in the sky, and the air was heating up. Another hot, humid day.

Zoe tugged on latex gloves and moved directly to the shore. She spotted the white athletic shoe and then the jogging shorts. Slowly, her gaze trailed up the trim body to the face of Hadley Foster, which stared, sightless, up to the clear blue sky.

A deep sense of sadness and disappointment washed over her as she studied the knife wounds slashing the woman's neck and arms. Cops tried to be cynical and hardened about how these cases played out, but that did not stop them from hoping they could beat the odds. For just a moment, she allowed outrage and disgust to roil inside her before she carefully shoved both inside an already brimming box deep within her. Hadley Foster's body had to now be considered strictly as evidence.

Her gaze lowered to the woman's hands. One lay in the water and was already discolored and bloated. Water did terrible things to the dead. The other hand was on shore and still in fairly good shape. The nails, though dirty now, were not broken or chipped. Her hands weren't scraped or cut.

As the water gently lapped against the side of the body, she inventoried the knife wounds and counted three in the chest and neck region. The direct frontal attack, combined with the absence of defensive wounds, suggested to Zoe that Hadley had either recognized her attacker or been caught completely by surprise. And considering that the initial attack had occurred in her bedroom, perhaps it was a combination of both.

Her thoughts pivoted back to Mark Foster. The man had been having an affair. His ex-girlfriend was now on ice at the medical examiner's office. His own wounds had been superficial. He was in debt. His kid had exhibited unstable behavior. There was already enough probable cause to hold him for questioning.

But until she knew where Skylar Foster was, she would tread carefully. Foster already had a lawyer and, at this point, was a desperate man with little to lose.

Vaughan approached the body and crouched like a lion stalking prey. He removed a pen from his breast pocket and pushed back the collar of Hadley's workout jacket so that they both had a clear view of the knife wound that sliced directly across the jugular vein.

"Foster said the assailant had a knife to Hadley's throat," she said.

Thick, dried brown blood caked her throat, making it impossible to see if there were any small nicks on Hadley's neck. All that was visible now was a large gaping wound that appeared to have been slashed in an upward motion.

"Any word on the Quick-DNA testing on the blood in the Foster house?" Zoe asked.

Vaughan rose and called the forensic department, nodding, listening, and thanking the person on the other end. "The blood in the master bathroom and in the Lexus is Hadley Foster's."

"Any sign of Mark's blood in either location?" she asked.

"So far, his was only found by the front door," he said. "But that could change. It's going to take weeks to test it all."

"What about in the trail leading to the garage?" Zoe asked.

"All Hadley."

The end corner of a terry cloth bath towel caught her attention. It matched the hand towels in the Fosters' master bathroom. "The towel looks as if it were used to stop the bleeding. Why would the assailant try to stop the bleeding?"

"Maybe Skylar tried to save her mother. Perhaps the assailant wanted to contain the blood until he disposed of her."

"Mark Foster never said their attacker or Skylar ran into the bathroom for a towel."

Vaughan's eyes glinted with skepticism. "He could have forgotten the detail in all the confusion."

"Do you really believe that?" she asked.

"My job is to play devil's advocate."

"If this was done by a stranger like this Mr. Fix It, and Hadley knew her daughter was in the house, why didn't she fight her attacker?" Zoe countered.

"Maybe she was scared. Maybe she froze. Maybe it all happened so fast she never saw it coming."

"It's all possible."

"And then her killer laid her down on the back seat of the Lexus and, if we can believe Mark Foster, had Skylar drive them here."

"We need to find Mr. Fix It." Zoe noticed the marbling on Hadley's chest. When the heart stopped pumping, the blood pooled at the lowest point in the body. If Hadley had been faceup—as she might have been if she had still been alive—her back would have been black and blue.

In this case, it was her chest. "He tossed her in the back seat facedown because he knew she was dead by the time they got her to the car."

Zoe lifted her gaze to the creek that wound through the park. On the other side was a thick stand of trees and a couple of picnic tables. "How long do you think she's been near the water?"

"Twenty-four hours plus," Vaughan replied.

"You need to have some of your officers search the waters close to the shore. The placement of Hadley's body looks rushed. And if I were a killer and needed to get rid of a knife, I might be tempted to throw it in the creek in the hopes it would get carried away."

"I'll have them on it right now."

She opened her social media apps on her phone and checked Skylar Foster's accounts. There had still been no activity since late Monday night, eight hours before the reported stabbing.

"Is there any sign of the girl in the park?" Zoe asked.

"Not yet, but they're bringing in a cadaver dog to search the entire area."

"How did he get away from the park with Skylar?" Zoe asked. "He could have dragged her, but she doesn't strike me as the kind of kid that wouldn't fight back."

"Maybe it was Mr. Fix It," he said. "We know they were in communication. Maybe she got in his car willingly."

There were many fragments that simply did not fit. "Maybe."

The two watched as the forensic team took pictures, made sketches, and then lifted the body and placed it on a tarp. Rigor mortis had stiffened the limbs, and the belly was beginning to bloat.

The technician searched Hadley's pockets, finding loose change in the right pocket and a single house key in the left.

"She had just gotten back from her run, but she didn't shower," Zoe said. "The bathroom was so clean because she'd not used it yet, and neither had Foster."

The autopsy technicians laid a body bag beside the remains and unzipped it. Working in tandem, the two men lifted the body into the plastic bag as a forensic tech took pictures.

"Before this leaks to the press, we need to inform Mark Foster we've found his wife," Zoe said. "I want to see his reaction when he receives the news."

"We better go now, because this isn't going to stay a secret long," Vaughan said.

The two drove to the Pollard house, parked, and approached the front door. Vaughan rang the bell, and almost immediately, footsteps sounded in the hallway. They both stood back from the door, eyeing the peephole and ensuring whoever was looking out from the other side could plainly see them. The door latch slid back, and a dead bolt turned before the door swung open.

A faintly welcoming smile on Mrs. Pollard's face did little to soften the dark undereye smudges left behind after a sleepless last night. "Officers, how can I help you?"

"Is Mark Foster still here?" Vaughan asked.

"Yes. He's in the sunroom, resting."

"We'd like to see Foster," he said.

Any hint of hospitality slipped away, and Zoe was not sure Mrs. Pollard would let them inside. "My husband isn't here now. He had to go into the office and won't be back for a few hours."

"We have news for Mr. Foster," Vaughan said. "He doesn't have to speak, only listen."

Her brow wrinkled, and then she stepped aside before leading the two down the center hallway to a room filled with plants, floral prints, and sunshine streaming in through the glass.

Foster was sitting in a rocker, facing the back side of his house. He was dressed in a pair of ill-fitting dark sweats, an oversize T-shirt, and a pair of house slippers.

"Mr. Foster?" Vaughan asked.

Foster winced as he rose to his feet and cradled his arm as he shuf-
fled toward them. Beard stubble covered his chin. His hair, which had
been flawless when they had first met, looked as if he had spent the
night pulling his fingers through it. "Has there been any word on my
wife and daughter?"

"Yes, sir," Vaughan said. "We've found your wife."

Zoe studied Foster's blank expression as Vaughan approached the man.

"We found her body an hour ago," Vaughan said.

Mrs. Pollard drew in a sharp breath and pressed trembling fingers
to her lips. "Oh my God. That poor woman."

Foster lowered into the chair and dropped his face into his hands,
hiding his expression. "This is a nightmare. My wife has to be all right."

"I'm afraid not," he said.

"Jesus." Foster threaded trembling fingers through his hair and then
looked up, tears streaming. "What about Skylar? Have you found her?"

Zoe noted a keen desperation in the words.

"No, sir, we have not found Skylar. So far there are no leads. Has
your daughter made any attempt to contact you?"

"No," Foster said. "If she had, I would have said something to you."

"Would you?" Vaughan asked.

"Of course I would!" Foster shouted. "I want my daughter found.
I love her more than anything. I'm not sure what you're insinuating,
but I don't like it."

"I'm trying to solve this case and bring your daughter home alive,"
Vaughan said. "You've had the night to think about all this. Have you
thought of anything that might be of help to us?"

"No. And I haven't slept at all." Foster leaned back and let his head
drop against the chair.

"That's true," Mrs. Pollard said. "He paced all night. Rodney was
up with him until almost 2:00 a.m. The man is devastated."

"Can you go over again for me what happened yesterday?" Vaughan
asked.

"I told you. Twice," Foster said.

"Do it again." Vaughan's polite tone had sharpened.

"I was on my way to work when I remembered the trash. I took out the trash, and when I came in the back door, I heard my wife scream. I ran upstairs and found her standing in our bedroom. There was a man standing behind her, holding a knife to her throat."

"Had he stabbed her at that point?" Vaughan asked.

"Stabbed her?" Foster asked.

"Your bedroom is covered in blood." It was common to ask the same question several times. People who told the truth didn't have trouble with details. Liars sometimes did.

Foster closed his eyes and didn't answer.

"Mr. Foster, where was your wife stabbed?" she pressed.

"It must have been in the bedroom!" Foster almost shouted.

"Where were her wounds?" Zoe asked.

"I don't know." He pressed his fingers to his temples. "There was blood on her shirt and around her neck."

"Was she fighting to get free?" Zoe asked.

"Her eyes were wide with shock and fear. She was terrified."

"Was she reaching for the knife?" Zoe asked.

"I don't know. I suppose."

"Did she speak to you?" Zoe asked.

"Why do you keep asking me about my wife? Shouldn't you be out there finding her killer and my daughter?"

"We need all the facts from you," she said.

"I've given them to you. But clearly, it's not what you want to hear, so you keep asking me over and over again."

"Sometimes people remember more in the hours and days after an event," Zoe said. That was true, but she was more interested to see if Foster's story changed.

Vaughan drew in a breath. "Who is Mr. Fix It?"

"I have no idea," Foster said.

"Your daughter has been in communication with him."

"Where? How?"

"An app on her phone," he said. "We were lucky enough to get the password from her friend Jessica; otherwise, we never would have read their messages."

"Who the hell is he?"

"We have no idea." Vaughan shifted his stance. "Mr. Foster, I'd like you to come down to the station."

"Why? Am I under arrest?" he demanded.

"No." Not yet. "We have more questions for you," Vaughan said.

Mark Foster shook his head, his wild eyes darting around as if he were a caged animal. "I'm not going anywhere. Not until I talk to Rodney. Not until I find my daughter."

Mrs. Pollard's head bobbled in agreement. "Rodney always knows what to do."

"He's my lawyer now," Foster added.

"Your daughter is still missing," Vaughan said. "There's still hope to find her."

Foster closed his eyes. "Her mother is dead. Murdered. That poor girl is never going to be the same."

Zoe was struck by the comment. "You need to tell us everything you know so we can find Skylar."

Foster stared at the gauze wrapped around his arm. "None of this is her fault. That kid didn't deserve this disaster."

Zoe sensed a small crack in whatever armor Foster had fashioned around himself. She needed to drive a wedge into that microscopic crevice and work it back and forth until it widened. She could sense the truth lurking under the surface. "Of course she doesn't deserve this. No kid deserves to see her mother stabbed and likely die in front of her. She must be in a state of shock."

"I love that little girl," he said. "I would do anything for her."

She heard the genuine affection in his voice. "We know you do. That's why we have to find her. We have to help her."

"Let us help Skylar," Vaughan said.

Foster was silent for a long moment, and then finally he shook his head, as if shoring up that tiny breach in his defenses. "Skylar is tough. She's going to be fine. She'll get through this."

"You say that as if it's a certainty," Zoe said.

"It is." He swallowed hard. "It has to be."

"Come to the station with us." Vaughan made the order sound like a request. Technically, Foster was lawyered up, and they would have to tread carefully. This case was already a tangled mess, and the knots were more likely to tighten than loosen.

Foster shook his head. "No. I'm not going anywhere with you. I need to speak to Rodney."

Mrs. Pollard stood a little taller. "I'm calling Rodney. And in the meantime, I need you both to leave my house."

Zoe and Vaughan made no move to leave. This was not the first time either had been thrown out of a suspect's house or had pushed the boundaries to get a witness to talk.

"Teenage girls like to talk," Zoe said. "Not necessarily to their parents but to their friends and boyfriends. They unburden even the deepest, darkest family secrets."

Foster leaned back in his chair, puffing his chest as if to make himself look stronger. "There are no secrets to share," he said.

"There are always secrets," she continued. "How long had you been having an affair with Veronica?"

His lips flattened into a grim line. "Six months. I'm not proud of it at all, and for the record, I broke up with her a few days ago."

That would have been a neat trick, considering she was dead. "You spoke to her?"

"I sent a text. What does this have to do with my daughter?"

"When is the last time you spoke directly to Veronica?" Zoe asked.

"It's been weeks." Foster shoved out a breath. "Why are we talking about Veronica?"

Either he didn't know about Veronica, or he was a very good actor; regardless, she wouldn't press the point until she found Skylar. "When girls feel ignored or unimportant, they can reach out to other people."

"Hadley and I had our problems, but we loved our daughter."

"Did she know you two had decided to separate?" Zoe asked.

"No. We were always careful to keep our adult conversations private."

"Have you heard the saying 'Little pitchers have big ears'?"

"What the hell does that mean?"

"It means she heard a lot more than you realized," Zoe said.

"I don't believe you. Hadley and I made mistakes in our marriage, but we always kept Skylar out of it."

"You didn't keep anything from her," Zoe pressed as Mrs. Pollard rose and grabbed her cell phone from the kitchen. "I'm guessing she heard a real whopper of a secret recently. Maybe it's why she tried to kill her boyfriend back in Oregon."

Foster's face paled. "That was an accident."

"And the stalking?" Zoe asked. "Was she stalking her ex-boyfriend?"

"No. The boy was making up lies to hurt her." His jaw tightened and his fists clenched. "You're trying to provoke me."

Zoe pushed back. "Something bubbled over in your home yesterday. What was it?"

"I'm calling Rodney," Mrs. Pollard said. "This is harassment." She began dialing and then raised the phone to her ear.

Zoe leaned closer, knowing she now had seconds before she and Vaughan would have no legal reason to remain. "What happened yesterday? What cracked in that house? There was a lot of pain and secrets. Something blew the lid off this pressure cooker."

Foster's eyes darkened as invisible weights seemed to grow on his shoulders. Tears streamed down his cheeks. His lips twitched, as if the words clamored at the tip of his tongue and begged to be spoken.

"Mark," Mrs. Pollard said. "Rodney is on the phone. He wants to talk to you."

And just like that, Foster seemed to catch himself and draw back. He looked shaken, as if he realized he had nearly stepped over the edge of the cliff. Mrs. Pollard pressed her cell into his hand, and he raised it to his ear.

She could not hear Pollard, but it was enough to buttress the man's failing reserves.

"Okay. I won't say a word," he said. "I understand. Not a word." He ended the call and handed the phone back to Mrs. Pollard. "I'm going upstairs now. I'm tired."

He rose on trembling legs, turned, and vanished around the corner in the kitchen.

Time was up.

For now.

Mrs. Pollard escorted them to the front door, and as they stepped over the threshold, she said, "Don't come back to my house unless my husband is here."

The door slammed, and they walked slowly toward Vaughan's car.

***

Nikki lowered down in the seat of her car and stayed out of sight as Detective Vaughan and Agent Spencer exited the Pollard house. She had been reviewing her questions for Foster when the two had arrived, and judging by their grim faces going into and leaving the Pollard house, she suspected something had broken in the case.

She reached for her cell and dialed Manny's number. He answered on the fourth ring. "I know you're busy," she rushed to say.

"Up to my ass in alligators."

She crossed her fingers. "I heard about the break in the Foster case."

"How the hell did you hear?" he said, dropping his voice.

A chorus of ringing phones and fast-paced conversations buzzed in the background. It sounded like all hell was breaking loose on his end. She could only assume that Hadley, Skylar, or both had been found dead.

"I'm good at what I do." And then, taking a risk, she asked, "Did they transport the body yet?"

He sighed into the phone. "Yes."

"Was it the mother or daughter?"

He cursed and lowered his voice. "You've got to stop calling me. I can't keep feeding you information."

She drew in a slow breath. "Manny, how long have we known each other? Almost twenty years. You know I don't burn my sources." She could hear him on the other end and knew he couldn't fault her statement. "This will never come back on you."

"It was Hadley."

"Thanks."

"Yeah, sure." He hung up, cutting her off from the chaos on his end and leaving her to sit in the silence of the car.

She texted the number of her tipster. Did you kill Hadley?

She sat for several minutes, hoping for a response. The air conditioner hummed as she lifted her gaze toward the Pollard house for a sign of Foster.

"What the hell were you expecting, McDonald?" she muttered.

She slid the phone in her purse and shut off the engine. Grabbing her notebook, she hurried across the street and up the front steps of the house and rang the bell.

Footsteps sounded; curtains fluttered and then dropped. Whoever was on the other side of the door did not open it.

"I'm Nikki McDonald, a reporter, not a cop," she said. "I'm Mr. Foster's chance to talk directly to the world. I can help him."

Floorboards shifted, and then the footsteps moved away from the door.

"Don't go. Let me help."

The footsteps grew faint and then silent. She dug one of her cards out of her purse and shoved it in the doorjamb.

As she turned from the doorway and descended the stairs, her phone chimed with a text. She fished out the phone and read it. Hadley deserved it.

Did Marsha deserve it?

Seconds passed, and then, No. But it was still fun killing her.

Let me interview you.

You don't want to get too close to me.

I'm not afraid. That wasn't true, but this story was getting too big to let fear get in the way.

You should be.

***

He calls himself Mr. Fix It. And that's true. He's a marvel in an odd sort of way. Daddy would flip if he knew he'd asked me out. And that I said yes.

Marsha, August 2001

CHAPTER
TWENTY-TWO

Wednesday, August 14, 11:00 a.m.
Alexandria, Virginia
Twenty-Eight Hours after the 911 Call

"What else do we know about Hadley's past?" Zoe asked. She and Vaughan had returned to the police station and were huddled by Hughes's desk. "In the surveillance tape taken outside the hardware store, Hadley had the look of a woman who had seen a ghost."

Hughes reached for a folder in one of the stacks and opened it on a pile of other folders. She rummaged through a few pages. "She and her parents moved to Alexandria when she was five. She and her sister grew up in this area and attended the local public school. She was a solid A/B student and was squeaky clean until she got a speeding ticket when she was seventeen. It should have been a straightforward ticket, but her boyfriend, who was with her at the time, got an attitude with the cop. The officer ended up arresting them both. Her father got her off, but he left the boyfriend in jail."

"Are we talking about Mark?" Vaughan asked.

"No. According to police records, the boyfriend's name was Jason Dalton."

"Jason Dalton?" Zoe asked. "A Jason Dalton worked for Prince Paving. He knew Marsha and Hadley."

Vaughan rubbed the back of his neck. "He's the one who vanished before Marsha did."

"Yes. Do you have a better picture of Jason Dalton?" Zoe asked.

Hughes pulled up his mug shot on her computer. Jason Dalton stared at the camera. Thick blond hair brushed his collar and fell over the tops of blue eyes that lit up with a grin that looked more mischievous than daunting. He had the look of a young Matthew McConaughey or Bradley Cooper. He was also the man who had confronted Hadley at the hardware store.

Zoe studied the contours of the man's face and the tilt of his head. His look would have been very charming to a girl or woman. Hadn't there also been a guy in the shop who'd dated both sisters? "Hadley and Mark married a month after Marsha Prince went missing. When was Skylar born?"

Hughes sifted through her papers. "Seven months after her parents married."

"Skylar would have been conceived about the time of the arrest?" Zoe said.

Hughes nodded. "That's correct."

"Jason figures out he and Hadley had a daughter and reaches out to Skylar," Vaughan suggested.

"That's assuming the two had a romantic relationship," Hughes said.

Zoe pulled up a picture of Skylar on her phone and held it up next to Jason's. There were striking similarities in the eyes and around the mouth. "The messages to Skylar that Bud read off to us were from a Mr. Fix It. Could Jason be our Mr. Fix It?" Zoe asked.

"Hughes, tell me you know where Jason Dalton is living now," Vaughan said.

Hughes grinned. "You're going to owe me dinner."

"I'll even toss in drinks," Vaughan said.

"Jason Dalton was brought up on assault charges down in Florida in 2007 and ended up doing ten years in prison. He moved back to the area last year and currently lives in Arlington and works at Danville Auto Repair."

"So he would have been in the area when Hadley and Skylar won the fitness competition in the spring. He could easily have seen the mention in the local paper," Vaughan said. "And Jason Dalton sees her."

Hughes scribbled down the address on a sticky note and handed it to Vaughan. "Home and work addresses. Be careful. The guy had a reputation in prison for being tied to several killings, but nothing stuck."

"Maybe he got tired of just texting with Skylar," Vaughan said. "Maybe he got tired of watching another man raise his kid."

"Now you need to ask me about Skylar's credit card receipts," Hughes said.

"Fire away," Vaughan said.

"Around April of this year, she started taking Uber over to Arlington and buying a late dinner in a little Italian place one block from where Jason Dalton works."

"Skylar has been having a late dinner with him?" Zoe asked.

"Two entrées were on the receipts," Hughes said.

"Jason snaps, puts on a mask, and enters the Foster house. Knifes Mark and takes mother and daughter," Vaughan said.

"If he stabbed Hadley, why take her with him?" Hughes asked.

"Maybe Skylar was upset, and he took Hadley along to keep her calm," Zoe said.

"Hadley dies, he dumps the body, and he vanishes with his kid." Vaughan flicked his finger over the edge of the Post-it Note. "We need to get over to that mechanic's shop and see if Mr. Dalton is there."

Zoe stepped out of the cubicle. "Let's go."

***

Twenty-five minutes later, Vaughan parked across the street from Danville Auto Repair, where Jason Dalton worked. The double-bay mechanic's shop looked like it dated back to the sixties. There were at least a dozen cars parked in the lot, and both lifts in the bays sported late-model luxury cars.

The whir of a pneumatic drill buzzed as they pushed through the glass front door and approached the counter with several work orders and keys set on it. Behind it hung a collection of papers and receipts, all overlapping what looked like a swimsuit calendar from 1990.

Vaughan knocked on the counter and, when no one appeared, moved around the counter toward a door. He knocked again and was rewarded with a gruff, "Be right out!"

Vaughan stepped back, his hands at his sides, but his fingers tensed as if he was mentally assessing the potential dangers. She was doing the same. Every cop who came into a new environment needed to be on their game and aware that just their presence alone could trigger serious trouble. And given Jason Dalton's prison record and his confrontation with Hadley in July, there was no telling what could happen.

Vaughan always scored well on his department's firearm qualifications. He had heard Spencer could hold her own with the best of them. But today, he did not want to find out who could put the bad guy down first. Skylar had to be found, and dead suspects did not talk.

The door opened, and a tall birdlike man in his midfifties with muscled arms built by a life of turning a wrench came around the corner. His slicked-back hair was unusually dark, almost gun-barrel blue. His name tag read *Bob*.

The man's eyes narrowed the instant he looked them both over. He knew they were cops right away. The pair reached for their badges and held them up, showing no expressions but watching his every move.

"What can I do for you?" he asked.

"I'm Detective Vaughan, and this is Agent Spencer. You are?"

"Steve Jenkins." When the mechanic noticed their puzzlement, he added, "Bob used to work for me. This was the only clean shirt I had."

"Steve," Vaughan said. "Jason Dalton's parole officer said he works for you."

"That's right. For about a year. Is he in some kind of trouble?"

"No," Vaughan replied. "We're searching for a missing girl and believe he might be able to help us."

"Is that the kid they been plastering on the news for the last twenty-four hours?"

"Yes," he said.

"What does Dalton have to do with a girl like that?" Steve asked.

"That's what we're trying to determine," Vaughan said.

Nodding, Steve ducked his head in the bay and called out Jason's name before facing them again. "He'll be right here. I can tell you he's been working long hours at the garage. If you're looking for someone to vouch for him, I'm your guy."

"We appreciate that," Vaughan said.

Jason Dalton stepped through the garage bay door, wiping his greasy hands on a clean towel. He was a tall man with large biceps that strained the edges of his short-sleeve blue shirt. The full-sleeve tattoos running down each arm were likely prison ink. His hair was as long as it had been when he had been arrested for speeding with Hadley, and the lines at the creases of his eyes were a little deeper, but he was still a good-looking guy.

Wariness sharpened the blue eyes for an instant. Vaughan could almost hear the man's defenses slamming into place before Jason's mouth curled into a grin. "What can I do for you?"

Vaughan introduced himself and Spencer. "We'd like to talk to you about Skylar Foster."

His smile faded. "We've had the news playing in the garage. Have you found her?"

"Not yet. That's why we're here," he said.

Jason shoved the rag in his back pocket. "Boss, you mind if I step outside for a moment with these good folks?"

Steve glanced at the clock. "Don't take too long."

Jason grinned and winked. "No, sir."

The trio stepped outside and around the side of the building. Jason removed a pack of cigarettes and lit one. Smoke curled around his face as he exhaled slowly.

"You dated Hadley Foster in high school?" Vaughan asked.

"No. I knew her, and I worked for her father, but we didn't date," he said.

"How long did you work for Prince Paving?" Vaughan asked.

Jason scratched the back of his neck. "About a year. It was a good job, and Larry was a decent boss."

"You quit a couple of weeks before Marsha Prince vanished," Vaughan said.

"My leaving had nothing to do with Marsha. I simply got a better job offer in Florida. I liked Larry, but he didn't pay top dollar."

"Hadley was with you when you were arrested for speeding," Spencer challenged.

"We had dinner once," Jason said. "That night, as a matter of fact. We didn't see each other again."

"If I ran a DNA test, would yours match as Skylar's biological father?" Spencer's gaze was as blunt and direct as her question.

Jason's intake of breath was slow as he stared at the glowing tip of his cigarette. "If I had a one-night stand with Hadley, so what? That was eighteen years ago. It has nothing to do with now."

"It might have something to do with Skylar and Hadley's disappearance," Vaughan said.

"I don't see how it could," Jason said.

"Have you been communicating with Skylar through a secured phone app?" Spencer asked.

"That's not against the law," Jason said.

"No, it's not," she said. "Did you?"

Jason inhaled deeply. "Yeah, Skylar and I started texting in the spring."

"Do you have any idea where she might be?" Vaughan asked.

"No." He exhaled. "Have you asked her dad where the hell she is?"

"Where would Skylar go if she were in trouble and wanted to hide?" Vaughan asked.

"She's got that boyfriend, Neil, wrapped around her little finger. You should ask him."

"We did," Spencer said.

"Ask again. If Sky was going to reach out to anyone, it would be that pencil neck."

"When did Skylar find out you were her biological father?" Spencer asked.

"The kid is very smart. She always knew she wasn't like Mark."

"How so?" Spencer asked.

"Temperament. Interests. Apparently, kids like Sky sense when they don't exactly fit into a family." Another inhale and exhale of smoke. "Anyway, she tested her DNA against Mark's, and it proved her instincts were right."

"Did she ask her mother?" Spencer inquired.

"No. Like I said, Sky's no fool. She knows Hadley would never come clean with her. Sky dug around in Hadley's old papers in the attic and found a picture of Hadley and me. The kid looks like me. There's no getting around that. I came out of work one day, and the kid was standing there. She asked me to dinner. We hit it off."

"Why did you come back to Virginia after your release from prison?"

"It's where I grew up. It's home, for what it's worth."

"Can you account for your whereabouts over the last forty-eight hours?" Vaughan asked.

"Working mostly. You met the boss. Steve doesn't like giving much time off. And he'll tell you I arrived at work yesterday about 5:00 a.m. and worked straight through until 6:00 p.m. The security cameras picked up me arriving, working, and leaving. Steve will give you a copy."

"Why did you approach Hadley back in July at the hardware store?" Spencer asked.

"I recognized her. Is there something wrong with talking to an old friend?"

"She looked a little spooked in the video footage."

"I'm sure I startled her. It's been eighteen years." He checked his watch. "If you don't wrap up this interview soon, my pay is going to be docked."

"If my kid were missing, I'd be pretty upset," Vaughan said.

"I'm worried. But I learned in prison not to wear my heart on my sleeve." He flicked the growing ash off the tip of his cigarette and inhaled again. "Sky is a tough kid. And I'll say it again. She's smart. She'll turn up."

"Speaking of tough, we found Hadley Foster's body this morning," Vaughan said with no emotion. "She was stabbed to death."

Jason dropped his cigarette butt to the asphalt and ground it with the tip of his worn boot. "I'm sorry to hear that. I didn't wish her any harm. Did you find Skylar?"

"Not yet," Vaughan said.

Relief softened his features.

Spencer's expression was unreadable. "Hadley moves back to Virginia in January. You find out you had a daughter with her. Marsha's body is discovered. You confront Hadley, and a month later she's murdered."

Jason flashed a grin and wagged his finger at her. "None of that has anything to do with me, Agent Spencer."

"I'm bothered by your proximity to the sisters who are both now dead," Spencer said.

"Mark also knew both the Prince sisters. Mark might appear to be a saint, but he's not. Five will get you ten; he finally had it up to his ears with Hadley's spending, whining, and whoring. He just shut her up for good."

"What was Marsha Prince like?" Spencer asked.

"Pretty. Smart." A smile flickered on his lips. "She was the sweeter of the two Prince girls."

"Did Marsha get along with Hadley?" Spencer asked.

"Hadley was not fond of her sister."

"How do you know that?" Vaughan asked.

"She made it pretty clear when the two were in the office at the same time."

"Any idea who would have killed Marsha?" Vaughan asked.

Jason sniffed. "None."

Steve appeared at the side door and tapped his index finger on his watch.

Jason raised a hand. "On the way, boss."

Vaughan handed him his card. "If you do hear from Skylar, call me."

"Yeah, sure." He turned. "I can't lose this job, or my probation officer will send me right back inside."

"Do you care about Skylar?" Spencer asked.

He blew out a breath. "Yeah, I do. She's my flesh and blood, and I'm proud of her."

"How did you feel when you realized Hadley and Mark had kept your daughter from you for all these years?" Vaughan asked.

"I wasn't thrilled. If I'd known about her, maybe things would have been different for me."

"I'd have been pissed," Vaughan said.

Jason shrugged. "Not much I could do about it."

"But it still bothered you, didn't it?" Vaughan pressed.

"I got better things to worry about than Hadley's lies."

Vaughan studied him a moment, seeing the subtle tension in his jaw, before he shrugged and broke eye contact. "If she contacts you, let us know," Vaughan said.

Jason nodded. "Same. Tell me when she's found."

Vaughan watched as Jason returned to the garage and turned his attention back to a car on the lift. He and Spencer found Steve and obtained the security footage before heading back to his car.

Vaughan fired up the air-conditioning as she hooked her seat belt. "If Nate were missing, I'd be tearing this town apart."

The cool air felt good against her hot skin. "I sensed pride when he said she shared his blood. She carries his DNA, and that matters to him. And I would bet money he was furious when he found out about Skylar."

"He has a solid alibi for yesterday morning."

"Yes, he does. How does Veronica figure into this?" she asked.

"Veronica looked like Hadley. So did Galina. Maybe whoever took Hadley and Skylar was just practicing on Veronica and Galina."

***

Nikki McDonald had left her apartment early this morning, knowing the drive north to Baltimore could take extralong in the morning commute. As much as she had dreaded the predawn drive up I-95, she had set up an interview in a coffee shop with Rose Howard, Hadley Foster's first cousin. Rose and Hadley had gone to high school together, and Rose's mother, Julie, had been Larry's older sister. The family had left the Alexandria area six months before Marsha's murder.

She ordered a large coffee and found a seat in the back corner so she had a good view of the front door. When the front doorbells jingled, she noticed a woman who shared many of Hadley Foster's features. She was shorter and not as lean as her cousin, but the blue eyes and full lips were almost identical.

Nikki stood and crossed the room. "Rose?"

The woman was dressed in a dark suit and carried a leather briefcase. "Ms. McDonald."

"Yes."

"I don't have a lot of time."

"Understood. What kind of coffee do you like?"

Minutes later, they were sitting at a corner table, each stirring sweetener into their coffees.

"It was weird seeing Hadley's face on the television," Rose said.

"You weren't any more shocked than I." She sipped, knowing this fourth cup would send her heart rate into overdrive. "I was trying to find Marsha's killer, but it blew up in this awful mess with her sister and her family."

Rose tapped her manicured finger on the side of the cup. "I'm ashamed to say I'd almost forgotten about my cousin. It's been so long. Why do you care?"

"It's an unsolved mystery," Nikki said. "It's bad enough being murdered, but to be forgotten and have the guilty walk free is unforgivable."

"I don't see how I can help you," Rose said. "I was Hadley's cousin but had next to no contact with my uncle Larry, his wife, or the other kids."

"The families didn't get together at the holidays or birthdays?"

"No. Larry and Mom had a falling-out long before I came along. I never told Mom I hung out with Hadley, because I sensed she'd have been pissed."

"What was Hadley like?"

"Like any other teenager. Selfish. Funny. Full of life."

"What was she like with Mark?"

"I think she liked him well enough, but at the time, he served a purpose."

"And what was that?"

"A ticket out of her house. Her father approved of him, and Larry didn't like many of the guys she brought around. And his family had money. Hadley liked money."

"Was there anyone who threatened Marsha? Was she afraid of anyone?"

"I think there were several guys who worked for Larry who weren't the best. The asphalt business was damn hard work and attracted a bunch of roughnecks. Men who could work long hours in horrible heat. They weren't choirboys."

"Marsha and Hadley both worked in his office."

"They did. Their father paid them less and worked them harder, seeing how they were the owner's family. Marsha accepted it because she was getting a good education. Hadley really started to resent her father after he told her she wouldn't be able to go off to college."

"Was Hadley angry enough to kill her sister?"

Rose sat back, shaking her head. "I want to be fair to Hadley. My goal is not to trash her now that she can't defend herself. I know how the media can be. But she could be really selfish and petty at times."

"What about Mark? The cops think he might have stabbed Hadley. Could he have also killed Marsha?"

"Mark was always the nice guy. He wanted to protect Hadley. Besides, he was away at some kind of football camp when Marsha vanished."

"I know Hadley was dating another guy the summer her daughter was conceived," Nikki said.

"Yeah, Jason." Rose sat back, eyeing Nikki. "You're good at doing your homework." She sipped her coffee, as if trying to figure out how much to tell, and then, with a small shrug, said, "Hadley was stepping out on Mark with Jason. It wasn't a lot, just once or twice. I think she liked the idea he was edgy and dangerous. For a while, she had a tiger by the tail, and she liked it."

"Can you spell Jason's last name for me?" Nikki asked.

"Dalton: D-a-l-t-o-n."

"Right, that's what I thought," she lied. "When Marsha went missing, Hadley said nothing to the police about Jason," Nikki said.

"If she had, then Mark would have found out about Jason, and she didn't want that to happen." Rose tapped the side of her cup, hesitating about what she was going to say next. "Once, Marsha told me she kept a diary. She kept it hidden under the floorboard of her bedroom closet. Maybe you should go look? It might still be there."

CHAPTER
TWENTY-THREE

Wednesday, August 14, Noon
Alexandria, Virginia
Twenty-Nine Hours after the 911 Call

Zoe and Vaughan arrived at the medical examiner's office, and within fifteen minutes, they were gowned up and standing in front of a stainless steel gurney with the draped remains of Hadley Prince Foster.

The room was thick with the scent of death and decay. Some cops liked to put Vicks on their upper lips to mask the smell, but Zoe had learned over the years that there was no escaping death. Keep breathing it for a few minutes, and the body's olfactory system would adjust and block out the smell. The trick was not to get a big lungful up front and then fight it.

Baldwin adjusted his eye protection and mask as he moved to the head of the first table, where a sheet-clad body lay. He pulled back the sheet to reveal the pale, slim body of Hadley Foster. Ravaged by the August heat, rodents, and insects, her skin barely looked human. The eyes, hooded by drooping lids, were milky white. The jaw gaped open in an odd deathly expression of surprise.

"I'm going to autopsy this afternoon and do a complete workup. I also can tell you with almost certainty that the knife wound to her neck severed an artery and caused her to bleed out in minutes."

Like Galina, she'd suffered an irrevocable injury that a doctor could not have fixed in time. "Any signs of drugs? Sexual assault?" Zoe asked.

"No. She did have intercourse shortly before her death, and we were able to collect DNA. It's been sent off for processing. We'll let you know if there's a match."

"Do you have an estimate for her time of death?" Vaughan asked.

"Based on her liver temperature, I'd say between 4:00 and 9:00 a.m. yesterday," Baldwin replied.

"Mark Foster placed the 911 call at 7:00 a.m.," Vaughan said.

Zoe felt a sense of relief when the doctor pulled the sheet back over the victim. She could handle death but was never truly comfortable with it.

"As you have likely noticed, Hadley Foster's knife wounds are not similar to Veronica Manchester's and Galina Grant's. In the first two cases, the knife wounds were deeper, as if they were more aggressive, and in each case, there is a distinct neck wound. Hadley's wounds, though deadly, weren't as deep, and the cut to her neck appeared to be a glancing and not a direct blow. All her significant wounds center around her heart."

"Different people?" Zoe asked.

"Maybe," Baldwin said.

"Or different circumstances," Vaughan said. "The killer was alone with the first two, but he had Mark and Skylar to contend with in Hadley's case."

"Why open himself up for a challenge?" the doctor asked.

"Assuming it's the same perpetrator, I would say he's raising the stakes to keep his adrenaline rush," Zoe said.

"What about the type of knife?" Vaughan asked.

"Similar knives were used in the first two killings. They were serrated, wide, like a hunting knife. But the knife used on Hadley Foster was smooth, long, and narrow."

"Similar to the boning knife missing from the block in the Fosters' kitchen." Zoe pulled up the pictures taken of Mark Foster's injuries at the hospital yesterday. "These are the wounds the husband sustained."

Baldwin examined them. "His wounds are even narrower, suggesting a smaller knife than the one used on his wife."

"You're saying the knife that killed Hadley is not the same one used against Mark Foster?" Vaughan asked.

"I can't say with one hundred percent certainty, but the wounds vary enough to make me suspicious," the doctor said.

"Anything you can tell us about Hadley Foster we don't already know?" Zoe asked.

"Not really. She was healthy and in peak shape, just like the other women."

"What about a toxicology screen?" Zoe asked.

"Blood's been drawn and sent off, but that'll take a couple of weeks," Baldwin replied.

"We don't have weeks," Vaughan said. "Skylar has been missing almost thirty hours, and the golden hours have long passed."

"I wish I could tell you more," Baldwin said.

"Thanks, Doc," Zoe said.

Vaughan's phone rang, and Captain Preston's name appeared on the display. "Captain." He listened, his frown deepening. He ended the call.

"Mark Foster just showed up in Captain Preston's office."

"What does he want?"

"He wants to tell us what really happened yesterday."

***

Nikki pulled into a parking lot and around the side of the building across from Jason's garage. After removing an ice pick from her purse, she drove it into a tire and, when the air hissed out, smiled. Back in the car, Nikki circled the block a couple of times, and when the tire light lit up her dashboard, she drove toward the auto shop.

She parked in front and walked into the main office. A man behind the counter looked up, and she explained, "I have a flat. I don't know if I picked up a nail or what, but it's going flat fast, and I have a meeting out in Fairfax in an hour. Can you help me?"

"Sure, pull around back to the last bay on the right. I'll get Jason to change it for you."

"Perfect."

She maneuvered the car around to the back and edged toward the empty bay; she shut off the engine but left the keys in the ignition as she waited. She had done some reading on Jason Dalton. He was on probation and had done time in Florida for assault charges after a bar fight. He had put a guy in a coma. He had been sentenced to twenty years, but thanks to budget cuts and his demonstrated remorse to the parole board, he had been released early.

When he came around, his head was ducked, and he was wiping grease from his hands, but the instant she saw him, she had to admit he was a fine-looking man. He was long, lean, and muscled, and the tattoos on his arms and the thick shock of hair gave him a bad-boy look few women could ignore.

The instant their gazes locked, she knew he recognized her. Though she had been off the air four months now, most who lived here had probably spent more time with her each day than they had with many of their friends and, sometimes, family.

He acknowledged her with a nod and a grin she found utterly charming. He moved to the left rear tire, which was now completely deflated. He knelt and ran his finger over the tire and whistled. "Looks like someone is out to get you."

"Why do you say that?" she asked, moving closer.

"Sidewall has a puncture that's not from a nail."

"Are you kidding me?"

"I would not kid you, ma'am."

She didn't want to overplay. The less said, the better. "If I had the time, I'd be pissed or worried, but I don't. How soon can you fix it?"

He rose up, threading long calloused fingers through his hair. "I'll get it up on the lift right now and pop the tire. Give me fifteen minutes."

"You're an angel."

He shook his head as he slid behind the wheel of her car. "Not even close. But thank you for saying so."

Jason held out his open palm, and she dropped her keys in his hand. He drove her car onto the lift and then got out to operate the controls.

He moved with an ease that telegraphed confidence that she bet had made Marsha and Hadley melt. Far from the metrosexual males she had worked with at the station, he was rugged. No buffed nails or facials for this guy. Given a different set of circumstances, she might have taken him for a whirl.

With a pneumatic drill, he removed the lug bolts and pulled the tire off as if it weighed nothing. On the workbench, he inspected it. "Whoever did this destroyed the tire. There's no patching it."

"Seriously?" Had she really destroyed her tire? And how much was that going to cost her?

"Yep." He grinned, regarding her with eyes that danced with humor. "You know, if you wanted to ask me questions, you could have just asked. You didn't need to ruin a good tire."

Nikki could have tried to bolster up her pretense, but she knew the time had come to cut her losses. "Do you have a new tire?"

He moved a few inches closer. "A hundred and fifty bucks will cover the tire and the labor."

"Fine." She was fairly sure her credit card had not fully maxed out.

"Be right back."

He returned minutes later with a new tire. "Shouldn't take long now."

"You know why I'm here. Mind if I ask you a few questions while I wait?"

"Fire away, sugar."

"How long did you work with Larry Prince?"

"About nine months, give or take." He hefted the new tire onto the car and hand tightened the lug nuts.

"Why did you quit a couple of weeks before Marsha Prince vanished?"

"I quit because he was cutting back my hours. I couldn't make my rent, so I headed to Florida to work for a friend."

"And ended up doing time in prison."

He looked over his shoulder at her and grinned. "Shit happens."

"Did you kill Marsha Prince?"

"Cops were here earlier asking me the same question. The answer is the same. No, I did not."

"Were you sleeping with her?"

He reached for the drill, and its whir-whir silenced her questions for a moment. "She was of age, and the sex was consensual. I've always liked the ladies, and the good Lord has seen to it that they like me back."

"Who do you think killed her?"

"I always thought Hadley did. She was always jealous of her sister, and they fought a lot that last summer." He set the drill down and turned the tire. Satisfied, he lowered the lift.

"What did they fight about?"

"Anything that was bugging Hadley at the time. She was a manipulator. Face of an angel. Heart of the devil. Someone you wanted to tread softly around."

"Could Mark have killed Marsha?"

"I don't think he had the stones."

"Could Mark have killed Hadley?"

Jason paused, staring at the tire. "Like I said, I don't think he had the stones, but if there was a woman who could tune a man up and piss him off to the point of murder, it was Hadley."

"What about Skylar?"

The humor in his eyes dimmed. "That kid is a survivor. She's alive and well."

"That sounds like wishful thinking."

"It's not. It's fact."

"I did a little research on the woman who owned the storage unit. She has no idea how the trunk got there."

"That so?"

"It really was a perfect hiding place. She's eighty-eight, and it's not likely she keeps up with her unit or visits very often."

He stared at her with an intensity that made her feel as if they were the only two people in the world. "That's fascinating."

"Someone wanted me to find Marsha. But what keeps chewing on me is why now? Why after all this time?"

"I'm not the kind of guy to ask a complicated question like that. I'm a simple man at heart." He rested his hands on his hips. "How about you and I get a drink tonight after I get off work? I might have all kinds of good things to tell you."

She smiled. "How about I take a rain check on the invitation?"

"I'm always here, sugar."

CHAPTER
TWENTY-FOUR

Wednesday, August 14, 4:30 p.m.
Alexandria, Virginia
Thirty-Three Hours after the 911 Call

When Vaughan and Spencer arrived at the police station, they went directly to Captain Preston's office. The captain, in his midforties, was tall, with a naturally dark complexion, and wore a perpetually skeptical glare. Vaughan knocked, and the captain waved them in as he rose and said, "That's right. Do what you can. Now I got to call you back."

Preston's phone's receiver landed in the cradle with a firm click as he rubbed the back of his neck. "Foster showed up thirty minutes ago. He said he wants to confess to his wife's and daughter's murders. But I'll warn you, he seems like he's high on pain medications."

"So we can't use anything he says in court," Vaughan said.

Spencer shook her head. "Has he said where he stashed Skylar's body?" she pressed.

Preston pursed his lips, as if pausing to control anger. "He said it doesn't matter where his daughter's body is now. She's with the angels."

"The hell it doesn't," Vaughan growled. "I want to know what happened to that kid."

"That's what I thought." Preston nodded in the direction of the interview rooms. "He's all yours."

"I'm on it." Vaughan stopped in the doorway, his mind already turning with questions. "Does Foster drink coffee or soda?"

"Coffee," Preston said. "One sugar."

"Thanks."

Vaughan paused at the break room and made a fresh pot of coffee. He offered a cup to Spencer, but she declined, and he then poured one for Foster and the other one for himself. A packet of sugar and a stir stick, and he was ready to go. He had learned a long time ago that if you wanted a man to talk about his crimes, he had to believe you were his friend.

"This doesn't make sense," Spencer said. "It's too easy. All of a sudden, he wants to talk? What about his lawyer? He can't be happy about this."

His eyebrows knitted. "Sometimes it simply is. Let me talk to him alone. I don't want this to seem like an interrogation."

"I'll be across the hall, watching on closed-circuit television."

"Perfect."

Legal pad tucked under his arm, he entered the small interview room, where Mark Foster sat at the table. Foster cradled an empty foam cup marred by small divots dug out by his thumbnail.

Vaughan set the fresh cup of coffee, sugar, and stir stick in front of him and then sat kitty-corner to him. "Thought you could use this," he said.

Foster blinked slowly and nodded. "Thanks."

Vaughan sat back in his seat and casually sipped coffee he really did not want. There was an art to looking calm and friendly when all he wanted to do was reach across the table and grab him by the collar.

"Can I get you anything else?" Vaughan asked. "Are you hungry? I could get us a pizza or burgers."

Foster let a breath trickle out over clenched teeth. He swayed slightly. "No. I don't need anything else."

Vaughan carefully sipped the coffee, categorizing the dozens of questions that demanded to be asked. Instead of firing the first, he paused, knowing if he built a rapport, Foster might believe they were on the same side. The goal now was not to get a pound of flesh but to find the girl.

"I know you've been under a tremendous amount of stress," he said. "I can't imagine how difficult the last few days have been."

"It's been the worst time in my life," Foster said, dropping his gaze to his cup. "Never did I think I'd be here."

"I believe you." Vaughan set his cup down and reached for a pen in his breast pocket. He clicked the end of it and let the silence settle between them, knowing it could coax some kind of conversation.

Foster reached for the sugar packet and carefully tore off the top, poured it into the cup, and stirred. "Hadley hated it when I used sugar. She said it was poison for the body."

"You've got to live a little," he said, forcing a smile.

Images of Hadley Foster's mutilated body, as well as the dead bodies of Galina Grant and Veronica Manchester, crowded around him. He took a mental step back from the memories as he added sugar to his coffee.

"That's exactly what I used to tell her." Foster took a sip and set the cup down carefully.

"Was she always so set in her ways? Disciplined, I guess?"

"Not when we first met." His mind seemed to drift. "She was carefree and so much fun. In those days, I woke up and fell asleep thinking about her."

"When a woman gets in your blood, it's hard to shake," Vaughan said truthfully.

Foster looked up. "A teenage boy never had a chance against Hadley Prince. She blew into my life like a hurricane, and I was never the same."

He leaned back, shifting tactics again. "How did you meet Hadley?"

"She was running a register at her father's shop. Once I saw her, I applied for a job."

"You worked there for a summer, right?"

"Yeah."

"Marsha also worked there."

"Yes."

"Before we talk about Hadley, I'd like to talk about Marsha Prince." Vaughan would work the conversation around to Hadley in a minute. "Were she and Hadley close?"

"On the surface, but Hadley resented Marsha because their dad's business had been profitable enough to send her to Georgetown. The tables turned when it was Hadley's time to go. Marsha was still going back to Georgetown, and Hadley was headed to community college, if she was lucky."

"Did they fight?"

"Sure. Sisters fight. But Marsha didn't instigate the trouble. Hadley did."

"I have three sisters. My sister Kendra was always the one stirring the pot." He sipped his coffee. "But Kendra would never kill any of our other sisters."

Foster's brow tightened with a frown as he stared into his cup. "And Hadley wouldn't have killed Marsha. I always believed that deep down she loved Marsha. Hadley was never the same after Marsha vanished. She carried tremendous guilt over all the fights she picked with her sister."

"It must have thrown her off after our visit," Vaughan said.

"She was a mess. I couldn't get her to calm down. I was supposed to go back to the office and offered to stay home, but she insisted I go. She wanted to be alone."

"But she wasn't alone that night, was she?"

He frowned and blinked, as if trying to remember. "No, I guess not."

"When you got home that night, did you realize she'd been with Roger Dawson?"

He shook his head. "No. She was home when I got home. We didn't speak until the morning."

Vaughan reached for a memory, hoping it would appeal to Foster. "When my marriage went south, it didn't happen right away." The sincerity of his own words surprised him, and it wasn't lost on him that he was having this conversation with a suspect in front of Spencer. "It was a slow and steady downhill slide."

Foster's hand trembled a little when he took a sip of coffee. "It sneaks up so slowly you don't see it coming."

Again he let the silence simmer. "Is that when you reached out to Veronica Manchester?"

He looked up, his gaze earnest. "Yes, but I broke it off."

"Did you? Your phone records recorded multiple conversations recently, and we found no text that suggested a breakup."

"Maybe it wasn't a text. Maybe I called her from the office phone. I just don't remember."

"Where is she now?" he asked casually.

"Vacation. In France."

"She kept in touch with her friends while she was traveling?"

"Not that I heard of."

Vaughan tapped a finger on the table, trying to figure out if this guy was telling the truth or playing him for a fool. DNA, surveillance tapes, and possible new eyewitness testimonies would eventually tell the story, but what he needed now was to find Skylar.

"Tell us about yesterday. How did it start?" Vaughan asked.

"Like it always does." Foster sipped his coffee. "It was very ordinary. I got up, and Hadley wasn't in bed but out for a run. She likes to get up early and get a workout in before she sees her clients."

"She's dedicated."

"More likely, obsessed."

"Did that bother you?" Vaughan asked.

"Not when we first married. I knew she was carrying the guilt over Marsha. I thought it would get better, but it only got worse, and after a while, it bugged the hell out of me." The frown lines on Foster's face deepened, and he looked as if he was ready to slip back into his brooding silence.

Vaughan scratched his chin. "You wake up. She's out running."

He dropped his gaze to the coffee. "I went downstairs to make coffee. I checked email on my phone, and when the pot was brewed, I took a cup up to Skylar. She's always slow to wake up."

"You were downstairs having your coffee?"

"Yes, and then I went upstairs for a shower and to get dressed for work. I had an early morning. While I was putting on my tie, I heard Hadley come upstairs."

Vaughan sensed the truth was thinning and the lies growing. "What happened next?"

Foster swallowed more coffee and, for a long moment, stared at a deep scratch in the wooden table. "After I gave Sky her coffee, Hadley called out to me. She was pissed about something, and I chose not to answer. It only fueled her anger, and she blurted out that she loved Roger and was leaving. I don't remember much after that. I was angry because we were supposed to be trying to fix our marriage for Skylar's sake. I saw white and barely remember going to the kitchen and getting the boning knife. I came back, and I stabbed that bitch in our bedroom."

"Where was Skylar?" Vaughan asked.

Mention of his daughter's name made him stiffen. He closed his eyes, as if trying to block out the image of her.

The pain crimping the man's face felt genuine. His pain was real. But murder and regret often went hand in hand. Lashing out in the heat of the moment often led to a lifetime of regret. Murderers were people. They did suffer guilt. But that sense of remorse did not exonerate them from punishment.

"Skylar screamed. She was standing behind me and saw what I'd done to her mother." Foster pressed his fingers to his temples and rubbed slowly in clockwise circles. "Hadley was making the worst gurgling sound. She was struggling so hard to breathe. The look in her eyes." He swallowed. "She was shocked."

"What did Skylar do next?"

"Nothing. She kept screaming. I had to stop the sounds. I didn't think, but I reacted. I told her to help me get her mother in the car. I told her we had to get to the hospital."

None of the neighbors he'd spoken to had reported screaming. "Did you intend to go to the hospital?"

"At first, yes. Sky got in the back seat with Hadley. She was cradling her mother's head as I drove. Skylar kept saying, 'Daddy, help me. Mommy's not breathing.'"

It was another lie. He knew from the examination of Hadley's body that she had been facedown in the back seat. Once he had Foster's version of events, he would compare every word of it to the evidence. "But you didn't make it to the hospital."

"Skylar said Hadley stopped breathing. She said there was no pulse. I pulled into the entrance of the park and checked Hadley. She was dead. The hospital was pointless. I panicked because I didn't want to go to jail. I picked her up in my arms, carried her to the creek bank, and laid her down. I threw the knife into the creek."

"Where was Skylar?"

"She was in the car. At first she was quiet, but then she started screaming. She was making so much noise. I just wanted her to be quiet. I put my hand over her mouth. She struggled. I kept pressing harder and harder, and then finally she crumpled in my arms. It was too late when I realized she had suffocated."

"Where did you take her body?"

"I don't remember. I was in shock and just started driving. I remember leaving her somewhere safe. And then I went home. I stabbed myself and made up the story about the attacker."

Vaughan studied the man for a few moments. "Mr. Foster, we need to find Skylar."

"I don't know where she is," he stammered. "I don't remember."

"How many pain meds have you taken, Mr. Foster?" Vaughan asked.

"I don't know. I got a little confused and took an extra, but I am clearheaded."

"You told me yesterday a masked intruder broke into your house."

"I panicked. I didn't know what to say. Now I do."

"You're inebriated. You need to go home and sober up, and then we can talk again."

"Why? I'm telling you the truth," he said. "I just confessed to two murders! Case is closed. You win. Isn't that what you want from me?"

"It's not a win until I have the truth," Vaughan said.

Foster slumped back in his chair. "It is the truth. It's all my fault."

"If you killed your daughter, where is Skylar's body?" Vaughan pressed.

"I don't remember!" Foster shouted.

Foster was not in his right mind. Vaughan was sure of it. And he was not convinced that Foster had killed his child. So why was he putting them through this dog and pony show? Was he trying to protect Skylar in some way?

Vaughan shifted in his seat, slowly tapping his index finger on the table. "Veronica Manchester is not on vacation, Mr. Foster. She's dead."

Foster stared at him with a blank expression. "What?"

"She was stabbed to death roughly ten days ago, and her body was dropped in a dumpster. Did you kill her as well?"

Foster's face turned ashen, like a guy who had just taken a right cross. "No. I didn't kill her."

"Who would?" he asked.

Foster's gaze took on a wild expression, as if he was witnessing a litany of dark scenarios. "I have no idea."

"When did you find out that Skylar was not your biological child?" Vaughan asked, matter of fact.

"What the hell?" Foster whispered. "Skylar is *my* daughter."

"I have no doubt you love her. You raised her. But you're not her biological father."

Foster folded his arms. "She's dead, so it doesn't matter."

"We know Skylar was in communication with a man through a password-encoded app on her phone. We also know she was having weekly meals near a garage where Jason Dalton now works."

"I love Skylar. That will never change."

Several times, he had used a present tense verb when referring to his daughter. "Was Hadley sleeping with Jason Dalton back in high school?"

Foster dug his thumbnail into a scratch on the table. "When she told me she was pregnant, I saw it as a sign of hope. I thought the baby would help her get over her sister's death." He swallowed. "I guess that's been bubbling under the surface all these years, and that's why I killed them both."

"Did you tell your attorney you were coming here today?" Vaughan asked.

"No."

"Why not?"

"He'd have tried to stop me." Foster chewed on the end of his thumbnail.

"You aren't in your right mind, and your story is not matching up with what I've seen at your house. As time goes on, I will get more forensic data, and I'll get a clearer picture of what really happened in that house."

As Foster studied him closely, the color drained from his face. "I should call Pollard."

"That would be a good idea. I'll arrange it."

"Shouldn't you read me my rights?" Foster asked.

"You're not under arrest." He leaned forward. "When my son was born, I felt on top of the world. I wasn't more than a kid myself, but I loved that boy from the start. Was it that way with Skylar?"

Tears rolled down his cheeks. "I was a goner the first time she smiled at me."

"I'd do anything to protect my boy."

"What are you getting at?" Foster asked.

"Where is Skylar?"

Foster was silent for a moment, and then he sat back and drank more coffee. "I don't remember."

Vaughan rose and closed the interview room door behind him. Spencer came out of the room across the hallway. They walked down the hall and away from the door.

Before she could speak, he said, "He's lying."

She shook her head. "He spoke about his wife's death with vivid detail. But when he spoke about his daughter's death, the tone and description deviated significantly. I think Skylar is still alive."

"But where?"

"He's stashed her somewhere. I don't know if she's locked up or just in hiding. But he doesn't want us to talk to her."

"Because she knows exactly what happened?"

"You know as well as I do that something more happened in that house yesterday."

He rubbed the tension from the back of his neck. "Absolutely."

"We'll talk to him again in a few hours. I want him to sober up here and think about what he's told us. His first set of lies didn't work, and I want him to realize this set won't either. Right now, we need to talk to forensics and see what they have."

"All right."

Twenty minutes later, they stepped through the doors of the forensic department. Bud Clary was leaning over a microscope when Vaughan knocked on the door.

"Bud," he said. "What do you have for me?"

"Detective." Bud leaned back and slid his glasses to the top of his head. "We've just finished collecting evidence at the Foster house. It's going to take time to process all of it."

"That's the problem," Vaughan said. "I don't have time. Mr. Foster just confessed to killing his wife and daughter."

Bud's mouth bunched in a frown. "Where's the girl?"

"That's the thing. He doesn't remember. He claims he suffocated her and dumped the body. I was hoping there might be some forensic insight you could offer."

"Right now, all my evidence could be used to support his story."

Spencer's phone dinged, and seconds after she glanced at it, she held up her hand. "Hold on, folks. I think I might have found Skylar."

"How?"

"Jessica Harris just texted me. Neil came by to see her. He wanted to borrow some of her clothes. She thinks he's taking the clothes to Skylar."

"Quite the detective," Vaughan said.

"Give me Neil's cell number," Bud said. "And I'll ping his location."

CHAPTER
TWENTY-FIVE

Wednesday, August 14, 5:00 p.m.
Alexandria, Virginia
Thirty-Four Hours after the 911 Call

When Vaughan and Spencer pulled up in front of the motel, two marked police cars were positioned across the street, per Vaughan's instructions. He had not wanted to arrive at the location hot, because given the amount of blood found at the Foster home, he was assuming that Skylar was being held hostage, and her abductor might kill her. Four marked cars and as many uniformed officers were primed and ready as soon as he gave the signal.

Spencer got out of the vehicle and walked carefully into the manager's office. Her body language appeared relaxed to anyone glancing into the room, and when she leaned forward, blocking the view of her hands, he knew she was showing him her badge. The manager's stiff nod came seconds before he placed a key card on the counter.

Spencer came out, nodding to Vaughan as he got out of his car. He approached room number 210 from the west side, and Spencer moved in from the east. They each stood by the door. A television blared inside, and the faint scent of pizza drifted out.

Each removed their weapons from their side holsters, and Spencer carefully slid the key card into the lock. She removed the card with a small click as he slowly pressed down on the handle. They exchanged glances and then slammed open the door, guns drawn.

They found Neil Bradford on the bed with a piece of pizza in his mouth. He was sitting cross-legged, watching an old episode of *The Walking Dead*. The shower was running in the bathroom.

"What the hell," the kid said as he moved to scramble off the bed.

"Don't move," Vaughan warned. "Tell whomever is in the bathroom to come out."

At this point, who the second person was did not matter as much as controlling the scene and figuring out who he was dealing with.

The zombies on the screen screeched and howled as the human defenders fought them with spears and axes. Neil blinked and dropped his slice of pizza to the box in the center of the bed.

Vaughan moved closer to the bed with his weapon pointed. "Do it!"

"Hey, come out here." Neil's voice broke, and he had to clear it before he could speak again. "Come out here, now!"

The shower shut off, and seconds later, the door opened to a cloud of steam and the scent of herbal shampoo. Both Vaughan and Spencer tensed and waited.

Skylar Foster had wrapped her body in a big white towel and had another around her hair. She stared at them both with a mixture of shock and even a little annoyance.

"What's going on?" she asked.

Lights flashing from the marked cars now bounced off the motel room walls. "You remember me, Skylar? I'm Detective Vaughan. Alexandria Homicide."

Whatever annoyance he thought he saw vanished, and she said quickly, "I remember you. How's my mom?"

Spencer stepped forward and moved past the girl to check the bathroom. When she indicated it was clear, he said, "Do you have clothes you can put on, Skylar?"

"Yeah, Neil brought me some from Jessica."

Spencer holstered her weapon and then picked up the small red duffel, opened it, and then handed it to the girl. "Go change."

Skylar's gaze shifted to Neil, who scrambled toward the end of the bed. "Neil?"

"Go on, Sky," the boy said. "We knew we'd have to talk to the police sooner or later."

The girl clutched the bag close to her chest and vanished into the bathroom.

Vaughan holstered his weapon. "Neil, you were supposed to call me if you had any leads."

"We planned to call you, but she was so upset. I just wanted to give her a little time."

"We've had all the surrounding police forces looking for her," Spencer said. "Withholding information is a crime."

"She only called me about two hours ago," he said quickly. "We were going to call any minute. I swear."

"After the pizza? After her shower? When exactly?" Vaughan asked.

"Soon." The boy's voice raised an octave as his fear took root.

"How long have you been here?" Vaughan asked.

"I just arrived twenty minutes ago."

"And she's only just getting in the shower?" Spencer asked.

"She said she's been sleeping since she checked in."

"When was that?"

"I don't know."

"How did she get here?" Vaughan asked.

"I don't know."

"You weren't curious?" he pressed.

"Well, yeah, but I thought she would want to shower and eat first before we talked."

"What did she look like when you arrived?" Vaughan asked.

"Exhausted. I had to pound on the door to wake her up. She could barely keep her eyes open."

"Where are the clothes she was wearing?" Spencer asked.

"In the dumpster behind the motel. She wanted me to get rid of them right away," Neil said.

Vaughan radioed to a uniform and asked him to check the dumpster. "Did they have blood on them?"

"Yes. But it's not like I was hiding anything. I put them in a plastic bag, so they'll be easy to find. She just wanted them out of the room."

He picked up a cell phone from the nightstand. It was password protected. "Did you bring her this phone?"

"No. She had it already."

"Where did she get it?" Vaughan asked.

"I don't know."

Of course he didn't. "Open it."

"No." Neil puffed out his chest in a show of defiance, and Vaughan could not decide if the kid was a patsy or a master manipulator. So far, none of this case made sense.

An old air-conditioning unit hummed as Vaughan let his size crowd the boy. "I don't want to toss you in a jail cell, but I will."

The boy blinked and shifted his stance. "You can't just arrest me."

Vaughan reached for his cuffs. "You are a material witness, and I can hold you in the city jail for up to twenty-four hours." He leaned forward. "Do you have any idea of what kind of guys comes through that jail on any given night?" He grinned as the boy's eyes widened with worry. His comment had intended to summon frightening images, and it had.

"I'm coming right out!" Sky shouted. "Just wait!"

That last comment told him she did not want the boyfriend alone with the cops too long.

"Agent Spencer, why don't you talk to Sky when she gets out of the room? Neil and I are going to the dumpster to catch up and get that bag of clothes." He clamped his hand on the boy's shoulder, feeling the kid's muscles flinch.

"I want to stay with Sky," Neil said in a show of fresh bravado.

"How old are you, son?" Vaughan asked.

"Eighteen."

"And Sky is seventeen." Vaughan shook his head.

"She's only six months younger than me," the boy protested.

"But in the eyes of the law, you're an adult and she's a minor. Right now, those six months mean you would be tried as an adult in court."

"For what?"

"Hiding a material witness, for starters. Aiding and abetting. Perhaps statutory rape. Give me a little time, and I'll come up with other charges."

"I want to call my mom," Neil said.

"Once we find that bag, I'll let you call your mother. For now, it's just you and me, chatting as we walk to the dumpster."

The bathroom door opened, and Sky appeared. She'd dressed in faded jeans and a high school sweatshirt, and she'd attempted to run a comb through her hair but appeared too rushed to have finished the job.

As Sky moved toward Neil, Agent Spencer blocked her path. "I need a word with you."

"I want to go home," Skylar said. "I want to see my parents."

Spencer exchanged a glance with Vaughan and then said simply, "First, we talk."

The girl folded her arms and managed a pout likely perfected when she was a toddler. "Why do I have to stay here? Why can't I leave? I've done nothing wrong," she insisted.

"A lot of people have been looking for you," Spencer said.

"Why?"

"You and I are going to talk about that."

Vaughan pushed the boy outside a little more forcefully than he intended. He turned back to the motel door in time to see Spencer close it.

***

Zoe again blocked the girl's exit as she tried to follow Vaughan and Neil outside. "We need to talk."

"You can't hold me here," Skylar said. "I want to see my mom and dad, too."

"I've called an ambulance for you. And now we're going to wait."

"I don't need an ambulance," Skylar said. "I want to see my mom and dad."

Zoe took the girl's hand, noting the shallow slice across her palm. It wasn't a bad cut. The edges of the skin were already knitting together, and she doubted it would leave a scar. "How did you get that?"

The girl snatched her hand back. "I don't know."

"How could you not know?"

The girl pressed her fingertips to her temple and closed her eyes. "I've been asleep for so long. I just woke up, and I'm really confused."

"Have you been here since yesterday morning?"

"Yeah, I guess."

"How did you get here?"

"I'm not sure. It's all really confusing. I've barely been able to keep my eyes open. Where are my mom and dad?"

Hadley's stabbing would have been horrific to witness and certainly could have affected the girl's ability to recall. The likelihood that this state of confusion would last was slim. There was also the possibility that the girl knew exactly what had happened and was lying. At this stage, she couldn't determine which scenario was more likely.

"I know you're rattled, Skylar, but I need you to tell me about yesterday."

She closed her eyes, her brow scrunching, like a little girl playing hide-and-seek. "Dad brought me coffee."

"Did he always bring you coffee?"

"Yes."

"Where was your mother?" Zoe asked.

"Out for a run. She runs a lot."

"And then what happened?"

She closed her eyes. "I had a bad dream."

"About?"

"My mother was screaming." She opened her eyes, studying her palm, and traced the red line that slashed across her pink skin still wrinkled from the shower. After a pause, she looked up at Zoe. "Was it a dream?"

"No." Her tone was soft, but she was keenly aware of the girl's reaction.

An anguished cry escaped her lips as she sat down on the edge of the unmade bed. She ran a trembling finger through her damp hair. "Where is she?"

The air stilled. "Do you remember yesterday morning? Do you know how you got the blood on your clothes?"

She traced the red line slashing across her palm. "I thought the blood was mine. It's from the cut on my hand."

"Why was your mother screaming?"

"She was in pain." Skylar pressed her fingers to her temples and shook her head. "I remember hearing Dad shouting. He told me to run. To save myself."

"From what?"

"There was a man." She drew in a stuttering breath. "The man attacked Mom."

"Who was the man?"

"I don't know. I'd never seen him before."

Zoe shifted to more detail-specific questions. "How tall was he?"

"Taller than Mom."

"What was he wearing?"

"Black, I think. He was a white guy."

"What color was his hair?"

"Like sandy. And he had a weird tattoo on his hand. But I never got a look at his face." She closed her eyes, her head jerking slightly as if a vivid memory had assailed her. "He kept asking for money. Dad said he could have whatever he wanted as long as he left us alone."

"How did you cut your hand?"

Again, she studied the gash. "I couldn't just leave Mom. I ran past Dad toward the man and Mom. I guess that's when I got cut."

"You were close enough for him to slash your palm. Do you remember what he smelled like?"

Her nose wrinkled. "He didn't smell good."

"What did the knife look like?" Zoe asked.

"It was from our kitchen. Mom uses it to cut meat all the time."

"Are you sure?"

"Yes." The girl looked up at Zoe, her eyes clearing and getting sharper. "Where is my mom? Is she in the hospital?"

There was no more avoiding the answer. "Skylar, your mother is dead. I'm sorry, but she didn't survive her injuries."

Tears spilled down her cheeks. "Mom cannot be dead. She can't."

"I'm sorry." The girl leaned toward Zoe, needing a hug. Zoe wrapped her arms around her. Sobs racked the girl's body.

When Skylar finally drew back, her eyes were puffy and red.

"I want to see my dad," Skylar said.

"Do you have any other friends and family you can stay with?" Zoe asked.

"No. Why can't I stay with my dad?"

"Because your father confessed to killing your mother."

The girl shook her head with a force that rang true. "My father didn't kill my mother. He loved her. There was another man in the room who killed Mom."

"Why would he confess?"

"I don't know."

The complicated relationship of the Fosters was not a subject she wanted to press with this young girl, but now was the optimal time, when defenses were not erected and the truth had a way of slipping out. "When is the last time you saw Roger Dawson?"

Skylar blinked. "I don't know. Mom trains with him at the gym. Why would he be at our house?"

"What about Jason Dalton?"

The girl's eyes widened for an instant and then narrowed. She was calculating, measuring her words now. "Jason."

"Jason. You have dinner with him at least once a week. He works at a garage in Arlington."

"How do you know that?"

"I've seen your messages you sent through an app on your phone."

"It's password protected."

"Jessica remembered your old password."

Her brows wrinkled. "I forgot I told her."

"Why were you meeting with Jason?" she asked.

"My dad is Mark Foster, and he loves me and would do anything for me. Jason is my biological father," she said.

"How did you find out about Jason?"

"I found a picture of him and Mom."

"What picture?"

"I'd never seen it before. Someone mailed it to Mom, I think." The girl's eyes sharpened. "Jason didn't kill Mom, if that's what you're getting at."

"How can you be sure? You said you didn't see the attacker's face."

"I *know* Jason wouldn't do that." The girl stepped toward Zoe, her fists clenched. "I want out of here now. I want to see my dad." The last words shrieked across the room, and seconds later, the door snapped open.

Zoe had pressed this interview as far as she could. "Okay."

Vaughan stood at the threshold. "The ambulance is here."

"I want to see my dad," Skylar said. "I don't need to see a doctor. Dad didn't kill Mom. I need to see him."

"First, the paramedics have to check you out," Zoe said. "Then we'll arrange for you to see your father."

"Where is Neil?" the girl demanded. "I want to see Neil."

Vaughan jerked his thumb over his shoulder, toward the marked cars and the flashing lights. "Sitting in the back of one of the squad cars, waiting for his mother."

"Why? He didn't do anything," Skylar protested. "None of this is his fault. Why are you punishing him?"

Zoe didn't let the girl maneuver past her. "He should have told us you were here."

Skylar pushed around Zoe but halted when she came face to face with Vaughan standing in the doorway. "He wanted to call you right away, but I begged him to come to me first! I was scared and hungry and just needed a little time."

"Neil is going to be fine. For now, let the paramedics check your hand," he said, undaunted.

She curled the fingers of her right hand into a fist. "And then can I see my dad?"

"We'll see," Vaughan said.

CHAPTER
TWENTY-SIX

Wednesday, August 14, 7:00 p.m.
Alexandria, Virginia
Thirty-Six Hours after the 911 Call

The ambulance carrying Skylar Foster whisked away, leaving Vaughan and Spencer standing on the sidewalk outside the motel room. Vaughan had given the forensic team the bag containing Skylar's clothes and shoes he had retrieved from the dumpster. The forensic team was now also in possession of the burner phone Skylar had used to text Neil. She had not said how she'd obtained it, but the expectation was that once they had analyzed it, they would know more.

Vaughan had spoken to the motel office clerk and had learned a man had appeared yesterday in his office with a ball cap on his head, wearing a thick overcoat. When asked if he had been suspicious about the man, the clerk had shrugged. He got all types of nutcases here.

Neil's mother had arrived on the scene. She had been upset and had had no idea why her son would keep such secrets from her. Vaughan had advised her that the boy was not facing charges yet. That could all change in the next few minutes.

"Neil doesn't strike me as the aggressive kind," Spencer said as she watched Mrs. Bradford's Volvo drive off. "If anything, he takes his marching orders from Skylar. Did you notice how he kept looking to her, as if for guidance?"

"I did. He just about lost it when I opened the back of the squad car. He kept asking about Skylar, as if he couldn't function without her."

"What about Mark Foster?" Spencer asked. "Why would he lie about killing his wife and daughter if he knew the girl was alive? It was a matter of time before we realized he was lying."

"Maybe that's all he wanted—time."

"For what?" Spencer asked.

"I'm not sure yet. First, I want to know if his prints are in that motel room."

"You think he stashed his daughter there?"

"I do," Vaughan said.

"Neil said she was groggy. Do you think Foster drugged her?"

"Blood test will tell us that," he said. "But it would make sense. It would have kept her quiet. Again, he was buying time. We need to get to the hospital. I know the press will be there in force soon, if they aren't already there."

"They can't get to the kid while she's being looked at, correct?" Spencer asked.

"I've posted two uniforms outside her room. That should hold off even Nikki McDonald. We've got about twenty minutes. Let's grab a bite to eat. We're going to need it." His phone rang. He didn't recognize the number, but he had handed his card out so much during his investigations he knew he should answer. "Detective Vaughan."

Silence crackled over the line, but he could hear breathing.

"This is Detective Vaughan. Who is this?"

Spencer shifted her attention to him, her head cocked as she waited.

"This is Jewel."

259

The voice was soft and sounded as if it belonged to a young woman. "What can I do for you, Jewel?"

"I was a friend of Galina's."

"Galina." He watched Spencer's gaze soften. "I'm sorry for your loss."

"We tried to have each other's backs. I let her down."

"How did you get my card, Jewel?"

"One of the girls you talked to knows Galina. We're friends."

"What can I do for you, Jewel?" he asked.

"I saw her on Sunday. I saw the car she got into before she vanished."

Tension rippled through him. "Did you get a good look at the driver?"

"I did."

He beckoned Spencer forward. "Would you sit down and talk to someone who might draw a picture of him?"

More silence.

"Galina seemed like a sweet kid," he said. "And she was too damn young to die."

"I'm working in a motel off of Telegraph Road. There's a diner across the street."

"We'll meet you there right now."

Another sigh and a sob. "Okay. Fifteen minutes, but I can't stay more than a half hour, or I'll get in trouble."

"We'll make it work." As he and Spencer hurried to his car, he explained.

"I have a pad and pencil in my bag. I'll be able to get some kind of sketch."

He started the engine and pulled onto the busy side street. The lights of the city passed, and headlights up ahead blurred into a long red line.

Spencer rubbed her eyes. She shifted in her seat. She looked tired, but like him, she would keep going until they had cracked this case.

He found the diner Jewel had described. The lot was crowded, and when they entered, most of the booths were filled.

Spencer nodded toward a lone girl in the far-right corner. "I bet that's her."

"She looks like she's a kid."

"Most of these girls are in their teens." She moved down the row of booths to the back of the diner. "Jewel?"

The girl shifted and looked at Spencer and then him. "Detective Vaughan?"

"That's me. Can we sit?"

"Yeah."

Spencer flagged a waitress and ordered three burgers and sodas before she slid into the booth next to Vaughan. "I know I could eat, and I bet you could, too, Jewel."

The girl clasped her hands together and leaned forward a fraction, as if she could bolt out of the booth at any second. "I'm hungry."

The waitress appeared with the three sodas and set them on the table. "Burgers will be right up."

Jewel took a long pull of her drink and seemed to relax a fraction. "Thanks."

"We appreciate you talking to us," Vaughan said. "We're going to need help if we're going to figure out who killed Galina."

Jewel dropped her gaze to her soda and took another long pull on the straw. "No one is going to remember she was a nice person. They won't think past what she had to do to live."

"I want people to know she mattered," Vaughan said.

Spencer set her untouched glass of soda in front of the girl and then removed a small sketch pad and pencil from her bag. "Maybe if you can talk to me a little about her last customer, I can draw a picture of his face."

Jewel studied the blank paper. "You can do that?"

"I'm pretty good at it."

"I don't remember that many details," Jewel said. "I only saw him once for just a few seconds."

"Don't worry about that. Why don't I just ask you a few questions. We might be able to figure out what he looked like together. You want to give it a try?"

"Sure. Why not?"

Before Spencer could ask the first question, the burgers arrived, and for several minutes, the three sat at the table, eating. He and Spencer were hungry, and he suspected the girl was starving, as she quickly crammed a handful of french fries in her mouth. He watched as she squirted extra ketchup on her burger and then took a big bite.

Jewel's plate was empty when she said, "What's your first question?"

"Tell me about your last moments with Galina," Spencer said.

Jewel's brow knotted. "How is that going to help?"

"Trust me," Spencer said.

"We had been up all night working a party. Not a fancy one, but it was at a hotel that had a conference of insurance men. Galina and I were in a great mood because we'd made good money."

"Where was the hotel?" Spencer asked.

She rattled off the name and address. "Nothing real fancy."

"What was it like when you two stepped outside?"

"Hot. But the heat felt good. We'd been inside for over twenty-four hours, and the air-conditioning was on full blast. The bright sun and fresh air was nice."

"What time of day was this?" Spencer asked.

"About noon on Sunday."

"What did you two do next?" she asked.

"She wanted to order a pizza. I wanted to go to bed, but we shared a ride to Gino's. We hugged, and she said she would come back to our room soon."

"And when did the man approach?" she asked.

"He stopped as she was walking up to the front door of Gino's. I saw him show her a roll of cash. I heard her tell him she wanted pizza, and he gave her money to buy it. When he turned to get in his car to wait for her, I saw his face for a second."

"Was he tall, thin, fat?"

"Lean. He wore jeans, a long-sleeve shirt, and a hat."

"Did the hat cover his hair?"

"No, I saw some of it around his ears. It was dark."

"Was his face round or slim?"

"Slim." Absently, she brushed her fingers over her chin, as if remembering. "He wore a ball cap and dark sunglasses. Like the ones pilots wear."

"Aviator sunglasses?"

"Yes."

Spencer drew the narrow face of a man with a hat. "What about his mouth?"

Jewel's phone dinged with a text, and she looked down, her brow knotting. "I can't stay much longer."

Spencer asked as her pencil hovered over the paper, "Were his lips full or thin?"

"Thin." Jewel typed a text.

"Was his nose wide or narrow?"

"Kind of in between." She slid across the booth. "I can't stay. I got to go."

"Can I have your phone number?" Vaughan said as Spencer continued to draw. "I want to keep in touch."

Jewel glanced at the picture. "His nose was wider at the base. And his lips were twisted up in a kind of smile."

"Excellent," Spencer said as she modified what she had drawn.

Jewel rose. "I have your number. I'll call when I can. We can keep trying."

"When?" Vaughan asked.

"Soon. I promise." The girl hoisted her purse on her shoulder and darted out of the restaurant.

He sat back, frustrated, wondering if they had just been played for a meal or if Jewel had really seen Galina's attacker. "What do you think?"

Spencer laid the sketch on the table. "Have a look for yourself."

He looked at the angled jaw of a man wearing sunglasses and a hat. "Nondescript and unusable."

"I usually spend hours, not minutes, with a witness. Give me some time later tonight, and maybe I can refine this a little."

"I can leak it to the media that we have a sketch," he said.

"It was a hot day," she said. "Someone might have noticed him, and if you can find any surveillance footage, I can use elements of the images to create a full picture if none capture his entire face."

"Lots of limited options." Vaughan received a text from Hughes. Pollard arrived at the station. Foster has recanted. Claims medications confused him. He showed it to Spencer. And then read Hughes's next text. "Pollard heard from Neil's mother about Skylar. He's now arguing that we coerced Foster's confession."

"He came to us," Spencer said.

"Pollard claims we lured him to the station on the pretense we had information about his daughter. Pain and stress, coupled with those medications, jumbled his client's thoughts, and nothing he says is admissible."

"I've seen some clever legal maneuvering over the years, but that is one of the best."

"He'll be out in less than an hour."

"That'll give us a chance to speak to Skylar before he can catch up with her and they can get their stories straight."

***

Zoe and Vaughan arrived at the emergency room and made their way through the maze of curtained-off exam rooms, toward the uniformed officer who stood outside of Skylar's room.

"Let me talk to her alone," Zoe said. "I want to ask her about the man who attacked her mother. I'm curious how much detail she can provide."

"Sure."

Zoe pushed back the curtains and found the young girl lying in bed. She was hooked up to an IV, and her hand had been bandaged. She had the channel selector in her other hand and was flipping through channels every other second.

"Skylar," Zoe said. "How are you doing?"

The girl did not take her gaze off the screen. "I want to get out of here and go home."

"You can't go home," she said. "They'll be releasing you in the morning. When you do leave, would you be willing to stay at the Bradford house?"

She drew in a breath. "Yes. I like the Bradfords. They're normal."

"And your family was not," Zoe countered.

"Yeah, you could say that," the girl said.

"Why's that?"

Blue eyes glinted. "My mother was stabbed to death. *Duh.*"

"*Before* the stabbing," Zoe said. "What wasn't right about your family?"

"Both my parents were cheating on each other. That's kind of sick. They said they loved each other, but they couldn't have. I love Neil and would never cheat on him."

"He seems devoted to you."

She clicked the channel selector through several more stations. "He *is* devoted to me. We love each other. We would die for each other."

"Tell me about your boyfriend back in Oregon," Zoe said.

Skylar glared at her for a split second. "George was a nice guy."

"Then why did you try to hurt him?"

"No," she said. "It was an accident. I was confused."

It was the argument that Mark Foster was now using. "Is that why your family moved to Alexandria?"

"My dad got a job transfer."

Zoe reached for the channel selector and took it from the girl's hand. She turned off the television. "What do you remember about yesterday?"

"I heard my mother screaming, and I came out of my bedroom. I saw him stab my mother."

"I want to see my daughter!" Mark Foster's voice boomed from the hallway. "You cannot keep me from my child!"

Skylar sat up straight and tried to get out of her bed, but her IV stopped her. "Daddy! I'm in here!"

The door slammed open, and Mark Foster rushed into the room. Out in the hallway, Pollard and Vaughan were arguing.

"Skylar!" Foster shouted. He hurried across the room, cupping his injured arm. "My God, honey, are you all right?"

Skylar's eyes welled with tears as she wrapped her arms around her father's neck. "Daddy, I was so frightened. Where is Mommy?"

He tightened his hold. "She's gone, honey. She's gone."

Skylar began to weep. "I want my mom," she said.

Zoe watched the two carefully. She sensed there was tremendous relief, which should have felt normal. They had both been through a terrible ordeal. Before she could put her finger on what troubled her about the two, Vaughan pressed into the room with Pollard on his heels.

"I'm so sorry, honey," Foster said. "I'm so sorry she's gone."

"What are we going to do, Daddy?" she sobbed.

"I'll fix this," Foster said. "I will absolutely fix this."

Pollard cleared his throat. "Mark, I don't want you to say anything else."

"Mr. Foster," Vaughan said. "You wanted to see your daughter, and now you have. Now I need for you to say goodbye."

Foster kissed his daughter on the cheek in a tender, loving way. "I'll take care of everything."

"Daddy, don't go," she said.

He smoothed back her blond hair, as if she were just a small child. "I love you more than anything. I want you to always remember that."

Pollard took Foster by the arm, as if he sensed his client might once again incriminate himself. "We'll be back soon. But we have to go now."

Foster kissed Skylar one more time. He was weeping when he let go of her hand and followed Pollard out into the hallway.

"Daddy," Skylar cried as she reached to pull her IV out. "I want my daddy and mommy."

"You can't leave right now," Zoe said.

"I don't want to be here."

"You have to stay until we can work out who can take you."

"Mrs. Bradford will take me. She's nice."

A knock on the door had her turning to see the officer standing next to Neil. The boy's gaze went to Skylar, and the worry in her gaze melted. She cried harder, and he rushed across the small space to her.

"Can we be alone?" Neil asked.

"Please," Skylar said. "I'll tell you all you want to know, but I can't right now."

"I'll be outside." Zoe stepped into the hallway and spotted a woman in her fifties who shared Neil's eyes and lean frame. "Mrs. Bradford," she said.

"This is such a mess. Poor Skylar," she offered. "And Mark looks destroyed."

She had no doubt that even if he had killed his wife in the heat of the moment, the man was now suffering terrible grief.

Zoe handed the woman her notebook. "I'll likely be paying you a visit tomorrow. Can I have your address?"

"Yes." Mrs. Bradford scribbled down her address and handed the notebook back to Zoe.

Vaughan gave Mrs. Bradford his card. "I'm advising you not to talk to the media until we have all the details of this case closed."

She tucked the card in her wallet. "I have no plans to speak to anyone."

"We also don't want Mark spending time alone with his daughter," Vaughan said. "They are the only two witnesses to Hadley's death, and I don't want one story influencing the other."

"Okay."

Neil stepped out of Skylar's room. His lips were drawn into a grim line, and his skin looked ashen. "She wants to leave with us tonight."

"She can't," Zoe said. "But you and your mom can pick her up in the morning if she's ready."

"Neil, get some sleep tonight," Vaughan said. "The next few days are going to be hectic, and you're going to need your rest." He turned to the boy's mother. "You may want to keep both the kids out of school tomorrow."

"Yes. That's a wise idea." She wrapped her arm around her son's shoulder and drew him close to her. "Thank you both."

Vaughan watched mother and son leave, and when they rounded the corner, he said, "The forensic department won't have anything to report until morning. For now, there's not much we can do. I'll drop you at your place."

"That would be great," she said, smiling. "Thank you."

Finding Skylar alive and uninjured would go down in the books as a win. And it was. But Zoe knew happy endings were rare. The girl's ordeal was far from over. She had lost her mother and had been deeply traumatized. She had a long road ahead of her. And there were too many questions that remained unanswered, and until she could answer those, she wouldn't mark this case a true win.

CHAPTER
TWENTY-SEVEN

Wednesday, August 14, 10:00 p.m.
Alexandria, Virginia
Thirty-Nine Hours after the 911 Call

Zoe sat silent as Vaughan pulled up in front of Zoe's townhome, sliding into a parking spot. The moonlight shone in through the window, illuminating the side of his face, accentuating the angles. She had never thought it was a handsome face, but it was the flaws that made it so attractive to her.

"We don't have to be at the lab until nine, so get some sleep," Vaughan said.

"Sleep. It's all I've dreamed about for days, and now I'm so wired I can barely sit still. Want to come in and see the place?"

He studied her a beat and then, "Sure. I'd like that."

"I'll warn you—it's a relic."

He shut off the engine and followed her up the small set of brick steps and watched as she wrestled the old key in the lock and was forced to pull on the handle before the bolt would wriggle free.

Zoe clicked on the entry light switch, which spit out enough light to make the space maneuverable but not enough to really bring it to life.

He looked around the space, jingling his keys in his hands as he walked around the small front room. The ceiling looked lower at night. He walked to the bookshelf and ran his finger along the spines of several books, including titles from Mark Twain, Ernest Hemingway, and F. Scott Fitzgerald. "This is an impressive collection."

"Feel free to take any that catch your eye," she said. "There are hundreds of books in this house. Jimmy was an avid reader."

He removed a book, gently opened the red leather cover, and thumbed through yellow pages. "This is a first edition."

"Like I said. He liked his books." She dropped her purse and keys on a beautiful mahogany table and kicked off her shoes. "Can I get you something to drink? Coffee? Whiskey?"

He ran his fingertip over the book's cover, wondering how many generations had read it before him. "A small whiskey would be good."

She flipped on more lights in the kitchen and opened the cabinet, removing two crystal glass tumblers and a bottle of Glenfiddich single malt Scotch whiskey, aged twenty-one years. She poured a couple of fingers in each, crossed, and handed him a glass.

He sipped, enjoying the smoothness. "This your stock or Uncle Jimmy's?"

"Mine. I like a good drink."

"Puts my stock to shame." He took another sip and swirled the amber contents around. "Damn, that's good."

She sipped from her glass, savoring its warmth and flavors. "What book did you pick?"

He held it up so she could see the gold embossed letters on the spine. "*Silas Marner*."

"Can't say I've read it."

"It's been a while for me," he said. "Never had a first edition."

"If Jimmy owned it, there's a good chance it's a fake."

Chuckling, he set it down on the small Queen Anne round table. "I'll borrow it. It'll give me an excuse to come back here."

She stared at him over the rim, feeling a surge of desire, just like she did each time they were alone like this.

He downed the last of his glass and set it down next to the book. He ran his hand over her arm and watched as she sipped the remains of her drink. Slowly, he took her glass and set it beside his before cupping her face in his hands and kissing her on the lips.

It was a tender kiss. Not hurried or rushed but almost exploratory. He was never one to be rushed, and the idea of him taking his time with her tonight sent a shiver down her spine. She wrapped her arms around his neck and leaned into the kiss.

He wrapped his arms around her waist and drew her closer to him. She could feel his erection hard against her. It had been too long since she had enjoyed a man and allowed herself to feel.

Vaughan ran his calloused fingers over her long slim neck and up to the clip holding up her hair. He tugged at the band holding the braid and unraveled her hair, which tumbled around her shoulders in a wave of curls. He ran his fingers through her hair, spreading it over her shoulders.

She reached for his tie and gently tugged and loosened it as he unbuttoned the top button of his shirt. She pressed her fingertips against his chest and kissed his lips.

"Where's your bedroom?" he asked.

She could hear the urgency in his voice. "Top of the stairs."

His eyes glinted like glass. "Tell me it's not Uncle Jimmy's room."

She chuckled. "No, it's not. I took the front bedroom. It's a little noisy, but it's all mine."

"Good."

He took her by the hand and led her up the stairs, glancing only briefly at the pictures on the walls and noting the empty spots. He did not ask her why she had removed the pictures from the wall, but she knew he had noticed. Later, he might ask, but for now, he did not appear interested in talking.

She turned on the bedside light, which cast a soft glow over the room and the rumpled sheets she had not bothered to make this morning. As he removed his badge and gun from his belt, she did the same. Each set a weapon on a nightstand, his on the left, closest to the door, and hers on the right.

As he unbuttoned his shirt, he walked to the picture leaning against the wall. In the photo, Zoe was dressed in a black tutu and stood on tiptoe in silver satin toe shoes. Her long arms were outstretched, and her head was angled toward the sky. He stared with clear interest. "This is you?"

"In my glory." She did not want to talk about the past. She wanted to focus on now. "When I dreamed of being a prima ballerina."

His gaze lingered on the image. "How old were you?"

"Seventeen. It was shortly before my accident."

"I'm sorry."

"Don't be. I found a way to reinvent myself." She unfastened the buttons on her blouse, not the least bit interested in rehashing her dancing years. "It led me to law enforcement. To here."

He raised his gaze to hers and very slowly lowered it over her body, resting finally on the pale crests of her breasts peeking out over a lace bra. "Your body is perfect."

"Maybe not perfect, but not as lumbering as my instructors suggested."

He crossed the room and smoothed his hands over her shoulders. "They were morons."

A chuckle rumbled in her throat. "Perhaps that was one of the words I used as I left for the last time."

He hooked his thumb into the strap of her bra and tugged it off her shoulder. The lace cup gapped, revealing more of her breast. He traced the top of the soft flesh, sending a ripple of desire shooting through her.

"I bet you were one of the best." His voice had grown husky.

"Not one of the best. But really damn good." She dropped her gaze to the tip of his finger and watched as it skimmed over her skin. Longing warmed her body. She hungered for what came next.

Vaughan stepped back and carefully removed his shirt, his stare never wavering from her face. She unhooked the back of her bra and let the lace fall to the ground. She stepped forward and skimmed her hands over his shoulders, relishing the strength in them.

He kissed her lips again. Like the last kiss, this was gentle, testing. She leaned into him and pressed her naked breasts against his chest. Immediately he deepened the kiss.

She reached for the buckle on his belt and deftly unfastened it. She slid her hand under the waistband, but she did not reach for him. She let her fingers linger in promise of what would soon happen. For the first time in a long time, she wanted to savor the desire and delay her release.

The next minutes passed in a blur of sensations as their clothes slid from their bodies and piled on the floor. When she stepped out of her panties, he rested his hands on her bare hips, and then began to slowly caress the curves of her body.

He tugged her toward the bed and pulled back the covers, watching as she climbed into the center. He moved on top of her and, pulling up the covers, nestled with her under the coverlet. His erection pressed against her as she cupped her breasts and then opened her legs. He kissed her on the lips and then on the top of her breasts, as she again skimmed her fingers toward his erection. His groan was a mixture of pain and pure pleasure.

This time, she wrapped her long fingers around his shaft and moved her hand up and down in a slow and steady pace. He drew in a breath and grabbed her hand, pinning it and the other above her head as he leaned forward and suckled her right nipple.

She hissed in a breath and arched as a soft curse escaped her lips. "You are too deliberate."

"I thought you liked deliberate?" he asked.

She felt his grin against her breast as he looked up at her. "I do, but it's more difficult than I imagined."

The spark in his gaze told her he delighted in her frustration. "I have a reputation for examining all the details. I don't rush."

"Time to shift to the bigger picture now, Detective." Her voice had a breathless edge.

He pulled his hand between her breasts and down her flat belly to the small nest of curls. "But details matter. I've heard you say it several times."

"So do results." She cupped her breasts and knew he liked watching, that this deliberately slow attack on her senses was getting harder for him to maintain.

She opened her legs and pressed her mound against his erection, and when she saw the slight glimmer in his gaze darkening, she knew the time for teasing had ended. He reached for his erection and pressed it to her moist center.

He pushed into her body with a hard thrust. The invasion sent a wave of sensations rushing up through her like a crashing wave.

He paused. "You like that?"

"Yes." A blush warmed her cheeks. She felt so alive. "I like it very much."

He covered her body with his, moving in and out with hard, deep thrusts as he kissed her fully on the lips. Her body would take all of him. Her breathing quickened, and she could feel herself rushing to the edge. She was within seconds of release when he slowed his pace and suckled her nipple. She grew wetter.

His fingers moved in slow, steady circles. Reading the nuances of her tense muscles, he seemed to sense what brought her closer to orgasm and what delayed it. And every time she thought she would tumble, he stopped, kissed her, and stole her breath. Anticipation swirled around her as she anxiously waited for him to begin again.

He ran moist fingertips over her thigh. "Such beautiful legs. I've admired those legs since the first day I saw you."

"Did you?"

"You were wearing black heels during that first class you taught at the bureau."

Were they really talking about her shoes right now? "I always wear black heels."

"I know. By my guess, you have at least three different pairs."

Zoe lost count of how long he teased her, but he knew intimately her rhythms. When she really thought she would go mad with wanting, he hastened his tempo. This time when the edge came, they both plummeted over it. Delightful spasms rippled over her. He drove into her, moaning with desire. She gripped his arms and pressed her pelvis upward.

Zoe opened her eyes and locked on Vaughan's gaze. For the first time, she saw him and not Jeff. In her mind, a distant door closed, and she did not race to reopen it. But this time, the sweetness outpaced the bitterness.

***

When Zoe awoke, the night sky was blanketed with stars. Moonlight bathed the row of houses across the street. She turned to her right.

She reached for her cell and saw that it was 4:26 a.m. Too early to get up, and yet her mind was fully awake and her body growing more restless by the second.

The sound of footsteps downstairs had her reaching for her robe and her gun. As she slid on the terry cloth and cinched the waist tight, she tiptoed across the room, taking inventory as she moved. All of Vaughan's clothes were gone.

At the top of the stairs, she saw the soft glow of a light that appeared to be coming from the kitchen. Barefoot, she tightened her grip on her weapon. She stepped over the third step from the bottom to avoid its creak.

As she crossed through the living room, she spotted Vaughan's jacket and caught the first whiff of coffee in the kitchen.

She lowered her weapon and stepped into the kitchen to find Vaughan sitting at her small kitchen table. He was reading *Silas Marner*.

"I just made a pot," he said.

She set her weapon on the counter, removed a bone china cup from the cabinet, and filled it with coffee. "You will never get back to sleep if you drink coffee this early."

"I never would have gotten back to sleep either way." He closed his book. "I don't sleep much. Haven't since Nate was born."

She wrapped her fingers around the cup, savoring the warmth. "I love to sleep. But I can't remember the last time I slept late."

Zoe sat across from him, sipped her coffee, and crossed her legs, knowing the folds of the robe would slip away.

He dropped his gaze to her leg and smoothed his hand over her thigh and then over the knee that still bore the scar of her surgery. He traced his finger over the light-pink semicircle. "Does it ever bother you?" he asked.

"Not really. Distance running is a thing of the past, and I can predict rainy days before they happen. I've gotten used to the minor aches and pains."

He nodded toward the stack of photos she had pulled off the walls barely two days ago. "I'm assuming he was your husband."

"Jeff. He was one hell of a cop. And an all-around good guy. He was healthy as a horse and had finished a marathon three days before he died. They tell me he was at the courthouse to get a search warrant when the first headache brought him to his knees. We'd just spoken, and he had said he was on the way to our favorite restaurant." She set her cup down with deliberate care. "I'd been waiting at the restaurant for thirty minutes when his captain called me."

"I'm sorry." He kept his hand on her knee.

She pushed away the images of that restaurant and the days and years that followed. "Life isn't always a party. I'm guessing you're not a single parent by choice."

"Divorce. It was better for everyone, but I know it hurt Nate."

"How old was he when you and your wife divorced?"

"Five. Motherhood and being a cop's wife were too much for her."

"The principal at the school mentioned that she died."

"Long after the divorce. I was sorry for Nate," he said. "Despite it all, she was his mother."

Zoe laid her hand over his. "I'm sorry for him and you. She was the mother of your child."

"Yeah."

They sat together for several seconds. "We still have a couple of hours to kill before we have to be at the lab. We could catch a few hours of sleep."

He held up his empty cup. "I'll never get back to sleep."

"Neither will I."

He slid his hand up under the robe and ran his fingers over her soft curls. She reached for the belt on her robe and undid it. It slid from her shoulders and settled on her chair.

She rose and stood between his legs. He cupped her buttocks and again suckled that nipple. The last time he had tortured her with wanting. Now it was her turn.

She lowered to her knees, and as she ran her tongue over her lips, she unfastened his belt. She cupped his erection and teased it with the underside of her thumb.

"I won't last long if you keep that up." His tone was seasoned with a dark humor.

She smiled. "Two can play this game."

CHAPTER
TWENTY-EIGHT

Wednesday, August 14, 11:00 p.m.
Arlington, Virginia
Forty Hours after the 911 Call

He should be satisfied. Hadley Foster was lying in cold storage in the medical examiner's office, covered in knife wounds. That beautiful body she had worked so hard to maintain, the Botox injections, and the acrylic nails had been reduced to a lump of decaying skin and bones. Eventually, she would be dust.

He had dreamed about and planned for this moment for weeks, months, hell, even years. He should feel like he was on top of the world. He had won, and the cops would never nail him for the crime. It did not get any better than that.

But instead of elation, he felt let down, like a kid seconds after the Christmas Day presents were opened. That's it? No more goodies? Now what dark fantasies would he dream about to get him off each morning?

He sat in his car, staring blindly at the strip of bars in Arlington. They weren't the fancy clubs of the young, upwardly mobile hotshots

I See You

hoping to make it big in the nation's capital or strike it rich with one of the consulting firms. No, these bars served the working man. The guys and gals who built the upscale, modern buildings, cleaned the toilets, or cut the lawns. They were the invisible people. The ones their betters did not want to acknowledge.

He liked moving and hunting among the unseen because they were the easiest to murder. And right now, he needed a kill more than anything.

His phone dinged with a text saying that his "date" for the evening was waiting for him on the corner. He had agreed to pay extra if she came to the motel room of his choosing and not the one she normally worked out of. He wanted home-field advantage. Besides, there was something about fucking on sheets after another guy that disgusted him.

A rap on the window, and he looked to see the woman. He'd ordered a blonde, preferably with blue eyes and a small frame. Big tits were good, but it was hard to get the entire package each time. As long as this one looked a little like Hadley, that would be enough.

The woman waiting for him now was a little too tall for his tastes, and her tits were not spectacular, but she was blond. A good fuck would take the edge off the raw anger clawing at his insides.

He clicked the lock button open, and she slid into the car, tossing him a practiced smile seen by more men than even she could count. As he nodded, he locked the car doors. The click made her flinch, but she kept smiling. A pro.

"Where're we going?" A heavy dose of cheap perfume filled the car as she snapped on her seat belt.

He was amused she was concerned about highway safety, considering she had gotten into a stranger's car. "I have a room. It's a few blocks from here."

"You've paid for three hours. That includes travel time."

279

"I get that." He put the car in drive and slowly pulled away from the curb. He wove through the traffic, careful not to look rushed. He wanted his driving to be as nondescript as his vehicle.

She fussed with the hem of her short skirt, running her hand over the fishnet covering her exposed thigh in a practiced way. With her hand on the door, she relaxed back into her seat. "Feels good to sit down."

"I thought you girls didn't walk the streets anymore. I thought it was all phone calls and shit."

"It is. But it's been a long night." She coiled a blond curl around her finger.

The stoplight turned yellow, so he slowed. It turned red, and he reached for the radio and switched on a rock station. Sometimes when he played the older stuff, it reminded him of when he was younger. In those days, he had still been angry, but he'd also had hope he would get his shit together and live the dream. Now he knew the dream was nothing but smoke and mirrors.

He adjusted his tight grip on the steering wheel several times before the light turned green. He pressed the accelerator and drove two more blocks to his motel. It was an older place, but what he liked about it was the front desk took cash. It also did not have cameras.

He shut off the car engine and unhooked his seat belt. "I'm on the first floor."

That automatic smile returned, and when he unlocked the car doors, she reached to open hers. As she rose, he glanced at her ass. He would bet she was already thinking about what moves she would run through with him so she could get him off fast so she could catch a little sleep.

He moved around the car and met up with her, and the two walked toward the room. Her heels clicked on the sidewalk, and a side-eye glance caught the swell of those tits in the V of her low-cut top. She already was working him, and they had not even gotten inside the room.

He opened the door, clicked on the light, and waited for her to enter. He closed the door behind him and watched as she set her purse by the edge of the bed closest to the door. She walked to the bathroom, looked inside, and then faced him. "What's your pleasure?"

"Take your clothes off," he said.

She sat on the edge of the bed, unzipped her boots, and set them by her purse. She must have learned the hard way to lay out her clothes and plan for a quick exit.

His dick grew hard as she reached for the edge of her top and pulled it over her head, exposing big floppy tits with big pink areolae that conjured images of a milk cow. Not Hadley.

She wiggled her hips and pushed off her short skirt, leaving her only in a black thong, which she also removed. Again, the clothes were piled neatly with her other belongings.

She rose, reached for the comb in her hair. "How do you want it?"

"Leave your hair up. Lie on the bed," he said.

"On my back?"

"Yes. I want to see your face."

She hesitated a moment, as if something in his tone bothered her. A girl like her would have to be smart if she wanted to survive on the street. "And then what?"

"Stretch your arms out," he said.

As she got on the bed and lay down, slowly extending her arms to either edge of the headboard, he straddled her. His dick was hard, but it was not throbbing, and he feared if he kept looking at that damn face of hers, he would lose it altogether.

He closed his eyes, pictured Hadley, and ran his fingers over her belly and up to the breasts. When his fingers skimmed the pink, large tits, he squeezed hard. She whimpered and squirmed under him.

He pinched again, this time taking a big handful of each breast in his hands and clamping down hard.

"Fuck me," she whispered.

Her words were not an invitation but an acceptance that this job was not going to be as easy as she had first thought. He was hurting her. And his dick got a little harder.

His hands moved up her chest to her neck, and he wrapped his fingers around it. He tightened his hold, remembering the times when he'd had Hadley under him. This woman felt different. Tauter. Sinewy. Pissed that this woman was not Hadley, he tightened his hold.

"Not so rough, baby," she whispered. "We have over two hours to go."

The sound of her voice broke the moment, and something inside of him clicked. No matter how much he pretended, there was no bringing back Hadley. She was gone forever.

But that did not mean the night was going to be a complete loss.

He released her neck, now marred by the red impression of his fingers. "Sorry."

Worry skimmed her gaze. "It's okay, baby. Why don't you lay down and let Kiki do her magic on you?"

"I bet you've got some moves," he said.

"I do, baby. Kiki is one of the best. I have a five-star rating." She rubbed her fingers over his thighs. "Take these pants off, and let me show you how I got those five stars."

He rose up off the bed, but instead of reaching for his belt buckle, he opened the nightstand. Beside the Bible was a gag, a set of handcuffs, and a knife.

Kiki glanced toward the drawer, and when she saw the toys, she started rolling toward her clothes and the door, gripping the hair comb in her hand. In seconds, she was on her feet and running toward the door, snatching her clothes from the chair as she passed.

He raced after her and grabbed her by the wrist. He tightened his grip and yanked her back. She stumbled, righted herself, and, in a swift move, brought the hair comb around and jabbed the sharp edges into the front of his chest. The pain stunned him, and he released her hand.

She twisted the door handle and opened it a fraction before he lunged again. But she was ready for him, and this time, she drove the sharp comb up under his arm. She twisted, forcing him to stumble back.

Before he could right himself, she opened the door and dashed into the night, naked and with her clothes bundled in her arms.

He took a step outside, ready to chase her, when he saw a cop car drive by the motel. There were several hookers standing outside who ran toward the naked girl and surrounded her.

With no choice but to retreat, he slammed the door. Blood streamed down the front and sides of his chest. It stained his pants and the tops of his feet. He dashed to the bathroom, grabbing a small towel and pressing it into his wounds.

Heart hammering in his chest, he shifted into damage control as he slid on his shoes and grabbed the handcuffs and gag. He opened the door, saw that the lot was clear for the moment, and started running.

"Fuck you, Hadley."

CHAPTER
TWENTY-NINE

Thursday, August 15, 8:00 a.m.
Alexandria, Virginia
Forty-Nine Hours after the 911 Call

As soon as Vaughan and Spencer left her townhome, he was on the phone with the hospital to check on Skylar's physical state. He wanted to interview her again about what had happened at her home two days ago.

The hospital's receptionist put him in touch with the nurse on Skylar's floor, who informed him that Mrs. Bradford had picked up Skylar and taken her to her home. He unlocked the car, and the two slid in as he dialed Mrs. Bradford's number.

The call went to voicemail. "Mrs. Bradford, this is Detective Vaughan. I'll be by later today. Remember, no media. And the girl does not see her father without a social worker or me present."

He hung up and pulled into traffic. "I want to talk to the forensic department first. At this point, I need to have as many facts in hand as possible before I talk to Skylar or her father again."

"Neither one of them has given us the full story. If he truly killed her mother, why is she protecting him?"

"He's the only parent she has left."

The two had time for a quick breakfast in a King Street bakery, and then they drove to the lab just as Bud was laying out two jackets on the light table. He recognized the clothes as belonging to the Foster family. Bud stood over the light table and clipped off a small piece of fabric from a blood-soaked exercise top.

The first set of clothes belonged to Hadley. They included jogging shorts, an exercise top, socks, and shoes. The second set were Skylar's, and to his surprise, they were jeans, a black shirt, a dark hoodie, and running shoes. And then at the end were Mark Foster's dress shirt, slacks, tie, socks, and shoes. Paramedic and emergency room personnel had cut Foster's clothes off him.

All the clothes were doused in blood. Hadley's were the worst by far, followed by Skylar's and finally Foster's. It would take weeks of testing to determine whose blood was on whom.

"All my testing is preliminary at this point," Bud said. "We're talking Quick-DNA, and I still have a mountain of evidence that'll require more testing before I can finalize my reports."

"The quick-and-dirty version will work for now," Vaughan countered.

Bud adjusted the glasses perched on his nose. "The blood on Hadley Foster's body so far belongs predominantly to Hadley Foster," Bud said. "Considering the medical examiner estimated Hadley lost over fifty percent of her blood volume, this makes sense. Hadley's injury was such that she would have drenched anyone or anything that came in close contact with her as she was dying."

"Skylar had a cut on her hand," Vaughan said.

"Like I said, it will take time to sort the blood on Hadley's clothes. For now, I can't differentiate between the two."

"That conclusion also includes the back seat of the Lexus?" Spencer asked.

"It does. There is some blood that belongs to Skylar, but most of it was Hadley Foster's."

"Where did you find Skylar's blood?" Vaughan asked.

"In the front seat, on the steering wheel," Bud said.

"Fitting Foster's first narrative that the girl drove her mother and the assailant away from the house," Vaughan said.

"It could be interpreted that way," Bud said.

"Did you get a chance to pull Jason's DNA from his prison records and compare it to Skylar's?" Spencer asked.

"It's a match," Bud said. "He's her biological father."

"The blue eyes and high cheekbones they share are not a fluke," Spencer said.

"Appears so," Bud said.

"Is there any of Mark Foster's blood on Skylar's or Hadley's clothes?" Vaughan asked.

"No," Bud said. "So far, his blood seems to be contained to his clothes, by the garage, and on the floor by the front entryway."

"What about Skylar's clothes?" Vaughan asked.

"She's soaked in her mother's blood," Bud said. "And there are also traces of her own blood on her clothes."

"All could fit the narrative of a masked intruder who forced the girl to leave with her mother," Spencer said.

"Which leads me back to Mark Foster's story," Bud said, pointing to stains on Hadley's outfit. "Hadley's clothes were doused in her own sweat. These were the clothes she wore while she was running. She did not shower and change as her husband said."

"She was killed shortly after her run," Spencer said, more to herself.

"Why doesn't it surprise me that Foster lied?" Vaughan asked.

"Foster's clothes were also stained with sweat," Bud said.

"That could have been the result of chasing after his family's attacker or the trauma of a stabbing," Vaughan said.

"Very true," Bud said. "But there was a significant amount of perspiration, which is what caught my attention. Makes me think he did a good bit of running himself. Also, his shoes are badly scuffed on the bottoms."

"They could be an old pair," Vaughan challenged. Smoking guns rarely arrived fully formed but slowly in a collection of small facts that paired together to create a mosaic that told a narrative.

"The scuffs are well defined," Bud said.

"There's no record of him getting a ride from the car's location to his home," Vaughan said. "It's a solid four miles between the car's location and their house. He'd have to be one hell of a runner to get back home, especially in the summer heat and humidity."

"He's fit," Spencer countered. "Plus, his body would have been surging with adrenaline. Maybe he could have covered that ground in a little over a half hour. It would explain the sweat and the scuffs."

"He panics, puts both in the car," Vaughan said. "Maybe he did want to save Hadley, but she bleeds out. Now he has to protect his daughter and save himself. Stashes the kid, dumps the body, and runs home."

"But there are no traces of his wife's blood on his suit clothes," Bud said.

"He was sleeping on the couch," Spencer said. "Guessing he was wearing a T-shirt and shorts in case his daughter happened in on him in the middle of the night. He was dressed in those clothes when Hadley was stabbed."

"Where are the clothes soaked in his wife's blood?" Vaughan asked. "And where did he clean up?"

Bud grinned. "I might be able to help with that one. We found traces of Hadley's blood in Skylar's motel room shower. We attributed that to Skylar's shower, but her father could have cleaned up there as well."

"Foster had a suitcase full of clothes in the trunk of the Lexus," Spencer said.

"He dumps Hadley's body and then takes Skylar to a motel. He dopes her up, showers, changes, ditches the bloody clothes, and runs home. He has time to stab himself and call 911 by 7:00 a.m."

"Where's the knife he stabbed himself with?" Spencer asked.

"It has to be in the house close to where he was found," Vaughan said.

"Are Veronica Manchester's or Galina Grant's knife wounds similar to Foster's?" Vaughan asked.

"I can't rule that out definitely," Bud said. "I studied pictures of the wound patterns on both women. The knife used to kill them had a shorter and wider blade."

"Any DNA pulled from Veronica Manchester's or Galina Grant's bodies?" Vaughan asked.

"Hair fibers. Semen samples. All of it's been sent off for testing, but that could take weeks. Do you still think the two cases are linked to Hadley Foster's murder?"

"All the women had a very similar look, lived within twenty miles of each other, and two of the three knew Mark Foster," Vaughan said.

"It could be a coincidence," Bud offered.

Vaughan raised a brow. "How often do those really happen?"

"Almost never."

***

Nikki parked in front of the nondescript trilevel home on the tree-lined Alexandria street. A **FOR RENT** sign was in the front yard, left worn and brittle by the August heat. As the AC blew against her skin, she felt oddly flushed as she stared at the house where the Princes had lived seventeen years ago.

She grabbed her bag and got out of the car, wondering where the years had gone. She simply had not noticed the time zooming past until she had seen herself on tape and now. Shit. She felt old.

Within seconds, the day's heat made her perspire as she walked past the sign and up the brick sidewalk covered with weeds growing up through the cracks in the mortar. Her hand slid along the wrought iron railing as she climbed the stairs. Memories flashed as the day's heat seemed to close in on her. There had been a tremendous amount of chaos and confusion when Marsha Prince had first gone missing. The area had been swarming with cops, and many of the neighbors had been terrified that their own children might be at risk. Many had not wanted to talk to her for fear their children would be targeted by the unseen assailant.

A car door closed behind her, bringing her back to the present. She turned to see a trim young woman dressed in a bright-red dress and sensible heels with a flash of gold at her wrists and ears. The woman's hair was swept into a practical ponytail.

Nikki found a smile as she pulled back her shoulders. "Ms. Westwood?"

Sure, quick heeled steps clicked over the cracked sidewalk. "Yes. Romi Westwood. I'm with the property-management company, and this house is one of my listings." Green eyes narrowed. "You're the reporter."

"I am."

"Weren't you put on leave or something?"

"I was." She sidestepped any explanations or apologies. "I would like to see the house. Is that possible?"

A frustrated sigh shuddered over her lips. "You aren't interested in renting it, are you?"

"I should have been more forthcoming on the phone, but no, I'm not interested in renting. I'm working a story about the Prince sisters."

Romi shook her head, her expression a mixture of annoyance and curiosity. "I knew it was too good to be true. This house has always been difficult to rent."

"With so many people coming and going from the Northern Virginia market, I'm surprised it's an issue."

"You would think the house was cursed." The young woman dropped her gaze to her phone.

As Romi seemed to tune her out, Nikki said, "You heard I was the one who found Marsha Prince's body, right?"

Romi looked up. "I don't watch the news. Bums me out too much."

"Yeah, well, I'm the one who got the tip and discovered the skeletal remains in a trunk." She added the last bit as a teaser, hoping to appeal to the darkness that lingered in everyone. "I'm trying to figure out who killed Marsha Prince."

"Does it really matter?" Romi asked. "I mean, it's been years."

"I think it does matter," Nikki said with an edge to her tone. "Especially now that her sister, Hadley Foster, was found murdered."

"So, like, you think the murders are connected?"

"Seems a little odd, don't you think? Two sisters murdered?"

"Yeah, I guess." Her phone dinged with another text, and she dropped her gaze again to the screen.

"If you show me the house, think of the stories you can share with your colleagues and on social media."

Romi looked up and then shrugged. "I'm here, so I might as well show you around."

"That would be great."

"So, what are you looking for?" Romi knelt by a locked box by the door, punched in a key code, and then removed a key.

"I'll know it when I see it," Nikki said.

Romi unlocked the front door and pushed it open. The air in the house was thick, stale, and hot. "We turned the AC off to save money."

Nikki's shoes clicked on the clean, polished floors as she moved to the middle of the empty living room. She glanced down the hallway toward several doors, remembering what Rose had told her. "Do you have any idea which room belonged to Marsha?"

"You'd know better than me."

"I never was allowed in the house. Her parents weren't fond of the media."

"It's a three-bedroom house," Romi said. "Can't be too hard to figure out."

"True." Nikki moved down the center hallway and stopped in the first bedroom. Opening the closet, she checked the floor and the baseboards, but all were affixed firmly in place. She repeated the process in the next room and found nothing. When she entered the third, she was again reminded of empty vaults and fools' errands. Still, her body hummed with excitement.

In the final bedroom closet, Nikki knelt and ran her hands over the floor and the baseboards. The wood was smooth, but as she came around the last side, she noticed a small ridge. Looking closer, she saw the tiny seam. She removed a small multitool from her purse and worked it behind a baseboard that had likely been painted over several times since the Prince family lived here.

"What are you doing?" Romi asked, her patience with this adventure thinning.

"I'm not sure." Nikki could sympathize. This entire adventure felt bogus. But still, she kept pulling on the section of wood.

"This is getting a little weird," Romi said.

And then the wood gave way, and she saw the opening beneath it. After grabbing a small flashlight from her purse, she shined it inside the small dark hole.

The shifting of feet told her Romi had leaned forward, intrigued.

When Nikki initially did not see anything, she pushed her hand into the darkness.

"You're going to put your hand in there?" Romi asked.

"Nothing ventured, nothing gained."

"Nasty."

Nikki opened the video app on her phone. "Can you do me a favor and tape this?"

"Sure, why not?"

For the camera shot, Nikki started the process over. She first tugged on latex gloves and inserted her hand through the opening. Her fingertips slid against the subfloor coated with grease and dirt from five decades. She'd been at the top of her game five months ago, and here she was, rooting on her hands and knees with a hand shoved in a black hole up to her forearm. Oh, how the mighty did fall.

At the very back, she felt a plastic bag filled with what appeared to be paper.

Removing the packet, she felt a sense of triumph. She had just taken another big step toward reclaiming the life she had. She looked up into the camera to make sure Romi was getting this.

"Shouldn't we wait for the cops? This could be some kind of evidence."

"I'm calling them as soon as I open it." She pulled out the pile of banded papers and looked at the first page. Blood rushed to her head, and she absorbed what she was reading. "Holy shit."

***

Vaughan and Spencer met Hughes in her office, and she had already prepared several surveillance clips for them to see. She downed the last of her coffee and looked up at them, her green eyes bloodshot.

"Don't you two look chipper," Hughes said. "Must be nice getting some sleep."

"Don't be hatin', Hughes," Vaughan said with a grin.

Her chair squeaked as she leaned back. "Yours truly has been up all night long reviewing video footage from multiple surveillance cameras. I'm amazed at all the cameras out there that are always watching."

"What about Jason Dalton and the garage surveillance footage?" Spencer asked. "Do the recordings back up his story?"

"I did have a look at them all, and he was exactly where he said he was, working at the garage," Hughes said.

"Meaning he could not have been the one who killed Hadley Foster," Spencer said.

"Not unless he can teleport," Hughes said. "I thought Foster said he killed his wife?"

"He's sobered up now and not talking to us," Vaughan said.

Hughes leaned back and grinned. "Then ask me what else I saw in the tapes."

"I can tell by your expression, Hughes, that you found something," Vaughan said.

"Let's start with Veronica Manchester." Hughes leaned forward, pushing aside several empty snack-size potato chip bags, and opened a file on her desktop. "This video surveillance follows the trail of Veronica Manchester's last few days."

She clicked on a file, and an image of Veronica frozen in midstep at the Pentagon City Mall appeared. In the clip, Veronica was walking out of the Jazz dress shop, a large shopping bag resting on her arm. She reached into her purse and removed her cell and held it up to her ear. She stopped, frowned, and looked around and then started moving at a fast pace toward the mall exit. She vanished out of sight.

Hughes clicked on another screen. "This was taken outside the north mall exit, which was the direction she appeared to be moving in when she left the dress shop."

In this clip, Veronica exited the mall and crossed the lot toward a dark SUV. As she approached the car, the window came down. She paused to talk to the driver, who, at first glance, was not visible to the viewer.

"Wait for it," Hughes said.

The door opened, and Mark Foster got out. He glanced from side to side, and then he kissed Veronica on the lips.

"What date was that?"

"Two days before she 'went on vacation.'"

Hughes zeroed in on the car near the SUV. "Does this car look familiar?"

Spencer nodded. "It's Hadley Foster's."

"And the driver is Skylar. She was following her father. She must have seen him kiss Veronica," Vaughan said.

"Might be coincidental for the girl to just show up at the mall. But I wouldn't bet the farm on it," Hughes said.

"Good work," Vaughan said.

"Oh, I'm not finished yet. Let me replay Foster's 911 call."

7:00 a.m.

911: 911, what's your emergency?

Caller: My wife has been stabbed. Kidnapped, along with our daughter.

911: Sir, what is your name and location?

Caller: I'm Mark Foster, and I'm at my home. Hurry.

911: Mr. Foster, are you injured?

Caller: I've been stabbed. My wife and daughter have been kidnapped.

"Now that we are reminded of the timeline, you're going to find this interesting," Hughes said as she clicked on another clip. "We were also able to pull the security footage from the neighbor's home located on a diagonal to the back of the Fosters' house." She pulled up the image.

The black-and-white footage featured the Fosters' backyard. It was dark, but there was a full moon.

The back door to the Foster home opened, and Hadley Foster appeared. She stretched, rolled her head from side to side, and jogged toward the back gate.

"What time was this?" Spencer asked.

"It was at 3:15 a.m.," Hughes said.

"That's almost four hours before the 911 call," Vaughan said.

"A lot earlier than we first thought," Spencer said.

"Hadley reappeared in her backyard at 4:20 a.m. through the same entrance," Hughes continued. As Hadley walked up the back sidewalk, she pressed a hand to her side, as if she had a stitch. She vanished into the house. "Now watch the shadows by the toolshed."

Both Vaughan and Spencer observed the inky darkness shrouding the back corners of the yard. It was totally still, and then seconds after Hadley went into the house, something moved. It was impossible to make out who was there, but it was clear there was something.

"An animal?" Vaughan asked.

"That's what I thought at first. Keep watching." Seconds later, a figure appeared wearing jeans and a hoodie. They both waited and watched, willing the figure to step into the light.

And then a security light tripped, and the face of Skylar Foster came into view.

"Skylar was up," Spencer said.

"What the hell was Skylar doing outside?" Vaughan asked.

"Teenagers aren't always asleep in their own beds," Spencer said. "She could have been sneaking home."

"From where?" Vaughan asked.

"Neil Bradford is the logical choice," Spencer said. "But who knows."

"Mark said she was in her room when the attack happened," Vaughan said.

"We know she was following her father to the mall. Stands to reason she could be following her mother when she went out early," Hughes said.

The timeline of events came more into focus for Vaughan. "Hadley arrives home. Skylar is on her heels. Mark is sleeping on the couch and wakes up. He sees them both. Maybe he thought the daughter had gone to sleep. He and the wife get into it. It goes sideways, and he stabs her?"

Hughes leaned back in her chair. "Still doesn't rule out that masked intruder. If I were Mark, I'd claim their attacker held them hostage for a couple of hours."

"I don't think whatever happened in Hadley and Mark's bedroom was planned," Spencer said.

"Why do you say that?" Vaughan asked.

"Foster's fabricating his story as he goes along. He wasn't expecting the stabbing, the tossing of the body and knife, nor stashing his kid in the motel room. Foster was in a full-blown panic that morning. He comes by the station to confess until you impress upon him that you're still going to follow the forensic evidence. Then he seems to shift gears."

"What the hell is he hiding?" Vaughan asked.

CHAPTER THIRTY

Thursday, August 15, 9:00 a.m.
Fifty Hours after the 911 Call
Alexandria, Virginia

Zoe and Vaughan rang the bell of the Bradford house. She listened as determined footsteps echoed inside, seconds before curtains covering the windows to their right fluttered. Mrs. Bradford opened the door.

Mrs. Bradford's face was as pale as it was grim, and Zoe guessed she had not slept much last night. "Come in. I've been expecting you since I received your voicemail. Sorry I didn't call back. It's been a mess here today."

"What's happening?" Zoe asked.

"My phone is ringing off the hook. The reporters are calling non-stop. I finally had to turn my phone off. Neil had to do the same. Nikki McDonald is the most persistent."

"I hope you've not spoken to any of them," Vaughan said.

"No. I have no desire to be the center of a media circus," Mrs. Bradford said. "I just want all this to die down."

"How's Skylar?" Zoe asked.

"She's doing pretty well, I think. She was up during the night, pacing. I asked if I could get her anything, but she said no. She's trying to appear brave."

"Where is she?" Zoe asked.

"In the basement den with Neil. They've been hunkered down in there because there are no windows, and they're watching a movie. Can I get either of you coffee or water?"

"No, thank you, ma'am," Vaughan said.

They made their way through a modest home filled with pictures of Neil that documented most of the major moments in his life.

"Is Neil your only child?" Zoe asked.

"Yes. I wanted more, but my husband liked the idea of focusing on the one."

"Where is your husband now?" Zoe asked.

"He's traveling for work. He's in sales."

"I don't see any pictures of him," Zoe said.

"Andy hates having his picture taken. Says he has a mug that will break any good camera. I don't agree. Neil is the spitting image of him."

She descended the stairs, past wood-paneled walls, toward a low ceiling. "Make sure you duck. The ceiling is lower than we'd like, but digging down six more inches was too expensive, so we duck."

"How long have you lived in the area?" Vaughan asked.

"We've been here about a year. We were in Kansas, but my husband's company transferred him. The high school is new for both Neil and Skylar. I think that's what drew each to the other."

"Did you spend any time with the Fosters?" Zoe asked.

"No. We didn't know her parents very well, but Hadley was always nice to me."

"When was the last time you saw Hadley alive?" he asked.

"Alive." She pressed her fingertips to her temple. "God, I can't believe I'm talking about her in those terms."

"I know it can be difficult."

She straightened her shoulders. "It was about three weeks ago. I ran into her while I was getting coffee. We had a lovely time and chatted about family."

"And it was a pleasant meeting?"

"I suppose it was. I had to go to the restroom, and when I came back, she was gone. I thought it odd, but when I called her, she apologized and said it was an emergency."

"You said a few weeks ago?"

"That's right."

"And where were you?"

"The coffee shop in Arlington."

Vaughan jotted a note, and she suspected he would be checking the date against Hadley's credit card receipts as well as any area security cameras. All that they had learned about Hadley so far was that she had kept a tight rein on her life until about three weeks ago, when her life had gone off the rails.

Mrs. Bradford led them into the basement room, where they found the young couple curled up on the plaid sofa in the den, watching a horror movie dating back to the eighties. The movie was a cheesy horror film, and it struck her as odd that a girl who had seen her mother knifed to death forty-eight hours ago was now watching a slasher movie.

Skylar absently ate popcorn from a bowl as she snuggled close to Neil, who had wrapped a protective arm around the girl. If this had been any other teenage couple, she would have thought the scene normal. This scenario troubled her.

"Skylar," Vaughan said.

The girl's gaze lingered on the wide-screen television a quick beat, and she muted it before she pulled away from Neil. "Detective Vaughan."

"Skylar, we need to talk."

A frown furrowed her brow. "We did talk. Did something change?"

"Nothing has changed," he said. "But when we talked, we only skimmed the surface. I need to talk to you face to face now. And Neil and Mrs. Bradford, I would like you to excuse us."

"I think we should stay," Neil said, straightening his scrawny frame like he was a puffer fish intimidating its challenger.

"It's okay, Neil," Skylar said. "I can handle this. After the last couple of days, a few questions won't be a big deal."

In the background, the killer slashed at the girls, and they ran for their lives. Vaughan turned off the television. He said nothing and waited for Neil and his mother to leave.

Neil rose up off the couch, kissed Skylar on her lips, and nodded for his mother to follow. "We'll be right upstairs if you need us."

The door upstairs squeaked closed but did not quite click into place. Vaughan and Zoe sat across from Skylar, who remained curled on the couch and reached for a soft blue blanket to pull it over her legs.

"Skylar. Tell me what happened two days ago," Vaughan said.

She pulled the blanket up closer to her chin. "My father told you what happened. A masked man broke into our house."

"Walk us through the morning," Zoe said.

The girl closed her eyes, a small sigh slipping over her lips. "I was in my room, getting ready for school. Dad brought me coffee."

"How was he dressed?" Vaughan asked.

"He was wearing his suit. He gave me my coffee, and then he remembered the recycling. He left. I took a couple of sips, and then I heard the screaming. I ran out of my room, and Mom was on the floor. A man was standing over her."

Zoe knew Vaughan wanted the girl to repeat the story. She had been given enough time to settle in a little; now was the time to amend it. She had not.

"Skylar, that version of events doesn't fit with what we've found," Vaughan said.

"What do you mean, it doesn't fit?" she asked.

The girl had the face of an angel, and when she looked up at them, it was with pure innocence mingled with pain and confusion.

"We pulled surveillance footage from your neighbor's house. We saw you follow your mother into the house. Why didn't you tell us that you'd been outside?"

Skylar closed her eyes for a moment, and when she opened them, she was nodding. "I forgot about that. I'm in shock, I guess. And I'm still scared. I didn't want anyone to know where I'd been."

"Where had you been?" Zoe asked.

"With Neil." She dropped her voice a fraction. "We were in his family van. I know Monday nights are the easiest to get away without being noticed."

"Why Mondays?" Vaughan asked.

"Mom was seeing a guy. Dad works late. He always has a big report to turn in on Tuesdays."

"Where were you and Neil parked?" Vaughan asked.

"There's a park close by. We didn't want our parents to know." She rubbed her fingertips against her temples. "I should have told you, but I didn't think that it mattered. I went right upstairs and went to sleep. That's why I was slow getting out of bed when Dad woke me up at 6:00 a.m."

"How did you end up at the motel room?" Vaughan asked.

"I'm not really sure. I think I was drugged."

"Who gave you the drugs?"

"I guess Dad did," she said softly. "Next thing I know, it was twenty-four hours later."

"Who is Mr. Fix It?" Zoe asked.

Skylar was silent as she seemed to gauge her words. "Jason."

"Jason Dalton," Vaughan clarified.

"Yes."

"Did he contact your mother ever?" Vaughan asked.

"I don't know."

"Would seeing him upset your mother?" Zoe knew the answer to the question but wanted to hear it from her.

"I don't know," Skylar said. "It didn't take much to upset my mom."

"Maybe seeing a former boyfriend would do it?" he said.

The girl's gaze sharpened for just an instant, and if Zoe had not been watching, she would have missed it, because on its heels came a flood of tears. Sobs now racked the girl's body.

"Did you share details of your parents' marriage with him?" Vaughan asked.

"I don't know," Skylar said. "Where's my dad? I want to see my dad again."

"Did you tell Jason about your mother and father?" he asked again.

"I want my dad!" More tears rushed down her face. "I want my dad. I want to see him."

"You can't. Not right now. You both are witnesses in the case. You two are the only ones who know what happened to your mother."

"We've both told you what happened!" She sounded more agitated.

"Yes, you both did. And the stories conflict."

"I just said I was confused."

"About?"

"Everything."

But father and daughter were both spinning stories that did not match all the facts. Each got portions right. Now he had to figure out why they had left pieces out.

"I'm very tired," Skylar said. "I don't want to talk anymore. When are they going to bury my mom?" she asked.

"I don't know yet," Vaughan said.

"I miss Mom. I miss her so much." She continued to weep.

The girl's words were perfectly reasonable given what she had been through, but the moment felt almost identical to the one that had played out in the hospital. As if it had been rehearsed.

Mrs. Bradford, who had clearly been listening, came into the room, scowling. For a mild-mannered woman, she looked particularly fierce, as if she were a mama bear ready to defend her cub. "It's time you both go. I know you have a job to do, but right now, this girl needs rest. She's had a terrible shock and needs time to heal."

"We'll be back tomorrow," Zoe said. "There is so much more we need to discuss."

"Call me in the morning, and we'll see. Now leave, or I'm calling social services and my friend the judge."

Zoe and Vaughan exchanged glances and, with little choice, knew they had to go.

"We'll see you tomorrow," Zoe said to Skylar.

The girl was already reaching for the channel selector and aiming it at the television. A click, and the slasher movie reappeared.

Zoe and Vaughan left the house, and once they were sitting in his car, both found themselves staring back at the house.

"She's totally distanced herself emotionally from what has happened," Zoe said.

"That girl is smarter than she lets on. She also remembers more than she's saying."

"Agreed. I want to talk to Jason Dalton again. He's had quite a bit of contact with Skylar this year."

"He acted like he didn't care about her."

"I don't believe him." Her phone rang. "Nikki McDonald is calling."

CHAPTER THIRTY-ONE

Thursday, August 15, 11:00 a.m.
Fifty-Two Hours after the 911 Call
Alexandria, Virginia

Zoe and Vaughan walked through the front door of the police station to find Nikki McDonald pacing. The reporter appeared impatient to the point of agitation, but Zoe found she had very little patience of her own.

"Ms. McDonald," Vaughan said.

"Finally," she said.

"I didn't realize it was an emergency," he said.

"Is there somewhere we can talk?" she asked. "I have news about Marsha Prince."

Vaughan's jaw tightened as he nodded. "Come upstairs."

"Agent Spencer," Nikki said. "I know you'll want to hear this."

The trio made their way up the elevator to a second-story conference room. As they sat at a small conference table, Vaughan closed the door and asked as they sat, "What do you have?"

"I've been chasing old leads on the Marsha Prince case since Agent Spencer identified her," she said. "I spoke to Larry Prince's former secretary, Hadley, and Marsha's cousin. I even visited their old house."

"Why?" Vaughan asked.

"The cousin remembered that Marsha used to keep a diary. She also remembered she kept it hidden in the closet in her room. Long story short, I found the diary." She reached in her bag and pulled out a plastic bag containing a stack of banded papers.

Zoe and Vaughan both pulled latex gloves from their pockets and tugged them on. "Did you wear gloves when you handled this?"

"I sure did. And in full disclosure, I've photographed the contents."

"I assume you've read it?" Vaughan asked.

"That's exactly why I'm here." She sat back, folding her arms over her chest and looking very pleased. "Basically, Hadley wasn't just mildly resentful of Marsha, as several have suggested. Hadley hated her sister."

"Says who?"

"Marsha, in her diary."

"And you're sure Marsha wrote it?" Zoe asked.

"I am, but I'm sure you'll need a handwriting expert to confirm it."

"Continue," Vaughan said.

"Marsha details several occasions when Hadley either followed her around, spread lies, or out-and-out punched her. Even their cousin mentioned that no one wanted to get on Hadley's bad side. I'm not sure she'd have told me about the diary if Hadley were still alive."

"Did Hadley hate her sister enough to kill her?" Zoe asked.

"I don't know if she had the nerve to pull it off herself," Nikki said. "Marsha's entries suggest Hadley wasn't the type to do her own dirty work."

"Like Mark?" Zoe asked.

"I don't think Mark was her boy. He truly respected Marsha. Plus, he was a bit of a Boy Scout. He was always calming Hadley down and keeping her from doing something stupid." Nikki drew in a breath. "I have no proof," Nikki said. "But if I were you, I'd take a hard look or two at Jason Dalton."

"Dalton." Like Nikki said, there was no solid proof yet of his involvement, but more and more indicators were pointing toward him.

Nikki raised a brow as she dropped her gaze to her phone. "Marsha's last entry was dated August second, 2001. It read: *I'm a little nervous. He asked me out. Not my kind of guy at all. But that smile makes it so tempting. Hadley heard me talking to him and was actually nice to me. She said he's cool and that I should go.*" She looked up. "Who do we know with the killer smile?"

"Jason," Zoe said.

"He strikes me as the bad boy who acts before he thinks. Aggressive, and not just with men," Nikki said.

"But we know from the garage video footage that he couldn't have attacked Hadley in her home," Vaughan said.

Nikki shook her head. "The only murder I'm chasing is Marsha Prince's. And I think Jason is your boy for that one."

***

When Zoe and Vaughan pulled up to the garage, Jason was parking a late-model sports car on the side lot. He got out, walked to the front desk, and left the key with his boss.

As Zoe and Vaughan approached, he reached for a rag in his back pocket and wiped his hands. "I heard Mark confessed."

"Did you hear that he also recanted and is out?" Vaughan replied. "He's still maintaining there was a masked intruder."

"I hope you don't believe his bullshit," Jason said.

"I don't believe anyone at this point unless it's substantiated," Vaughan countered.

Jason eyed them warily. "How's Skylar?"

"She's staying with friends," Zoe said. "She's holding up as well as can be expected."

"Probably at her boyfriend's house. She's got a lot of her mother in her. She likes having a man in tow."

"Tell me more about Hadley and her sister, Marsha," Vaughan said.

"What does Marsha have to do with any of this?"

"You knew her pretty well, didn't you?" Zoe asked.

Jason walked over to the soda machine, fed in four quarters, and made a selection. The can rattled through its insides and dropped down the chute with a clunk. He grabbed the can, popped the top, and took a long drink. "Sure, I knew her. She wasn't around as much as Hadley."

"But you were sleeping with her." Zoe couldn't confirm this yet, but she let the statement sit.

"Who says?" Jason demanded.

"Marsha. It turns out she kept a journal about you."

"I hope she said nice things." Jason shrugged and then grinned. "Sure, we slept together once. We had fun, but I was smart enough to know that we were going in separate directions."

"You were sleeping with both sisters," Zoe said.

"Why not?" Jason said. "We were young and having fun. I gave as good as I got."

"Which sister did you sleep with first?" Zoe asked.

"Does it matter?" Jason asked.

"I think it does," Zoe said. "I think you slept with Hadley, and she saw something in you that spooked her. She keeps it secret because she didn't want to lose Mark. She gets wind that Marsha is falling for your charms, and Hadley, knowing what's in store for Marsha, puts in a good word for you. Maybe she just wanted to rattle her sister. I don't think she planned on her sister dying."

"You keep forgetting that I was gone by the time Marsha went missing," Jason said.

"You had quit your job at Prince Paving," she said. "But there's no proof you weren't in Northern Virginia."

"I was in Florida," he said, his grin widening.

"Did you know Hadley was pregnant with your child when she married Mark?" she asked.

His grin faltered. "Look, young love ain't the kind of love that really stands the test of time," Jason said. "I moved on. And she sure did."

"With your kid," Zoe pressed. "That must have really stung when you realized she'd taken your kid. I bet when you realized you'd been cheated out of your kid's life, you were pissed."

He dropped his gaze to his calloused palm. "Sure, I was mad. But remember, I was here at the shop under a 2000 Ford pickup truck when she was murdered. You must have looked at the footage; otherwise, I'd be wearing cuffs by now." His eyes narrowed as he regarded them. "I see what's going on now. You can't pin Hadley's murder on me, so you're going to blame me for Marsha's death."

"Did you kill her?"

His gaze locked on hers, and his body stilled as if he was struggling for control. "Doesn't matter what I say. You're going to manufacture evidence and pin it on me."

Sometimes people communicated more without even realizing it. And Jason had done just that.

***

Nikki was sitting on the floor of her living room, staring at the images she had made of Marsha Prince's diary. It had been one thing to see images of the girl and another to hear what others said. But to read her own words brought the girl to life. It stirred a sadness in Nikki she had not expected.

Her phone dinged with a text. She glanced toward it, and when she saw Mark Foster's name, she sat taller, imagining herself at her desk.

If you want the real story, meet me at my house.

As her mind spun with possible scenarios, she typed quickly. The real story?

About Marsha. Hadley. All of it.

She unfolded her legs, her knees groaning slightly as she straightened. When?

Now. I won't be here much longer.

Give me fifteen minutes.

She dashed toward her front door, sliding her feet into sandals and shoving her cameras and keys into her purse. Her apartment front door slammed behind her, and she rushed to the elevator, hitting the down button a half dozen times. The elevator car creaked up the shaft and finally arrived. With the door open, she dashed inside and pounded the first floor button while the doors slowly closed.

The next few minutes were a race to her car and out of the lot. When she pulled up in front of the Fosters' house, her heart was pounding. It had taken her twenty minutes to get there.

"Shit." She hurried up the front walk and stopped at the yellow tape blocking the entrance. She knocked several times and rang the bell. When she heard no sounds of life inside, she had the vague notion that she had been played.

She then moved around the side of the house, through the privacy fence gate, and up the back stairs to the door. She twisted the handle, and it turned.

Getting caught at an active murder scene would not get her any favors, but given that she had very little to lose right now, she stepped into the kitchen. The large room had been designed to be airy and bright, but the air-conditioning had been turned off, creating a stuffy heat that made the large room feel oppressive. Anything that could have fingerprints was covered with the graphite dust used by the crime scene technicians. The coffeepot was still half-full. Yellow tents marked the trail of blood through the kitchen and toward the garage.

"Mr. Foster. Mr. Foster? It's Nikki McDonald."

Somewhere in the house, a clock ticked. Careful to step over the trail of blood, she moved through the downstairs, looking in each room. Outside, she heard a dog bark and a car door slam.

"Mr. Foster?"

She climbed the stairs and stopped at the first door, which was slightly ajar. She pressed her knuckles gently to the door, not wanting to leave her fingerprints. The hinges squeaked open. The skin on the back of her neck tingled. Six months ago, she would not have taken this kind of risk. She would have been behind her anchor desk, reading the news. But six months ago, she'd been collecting a fat paycheck and was not desperate to get back in the game. Instinct shouted at her to run. Desperation told it to shut the hell up.

She moved down the hallway to the bedroom and paused as she stared at the large stain of darkened, dried blood. "Mr. Foster."

No one responded, but she noticed the light in the bathroom was on. She edged toward the door. And then she smelled it. It was blood. Fresh blood. She pressed open the door with her knuckle, and her gaze went immediately to the bathroom. Mark Foster lay in the dry tub. His wrists had been cut, and he appeared dead.

Her nerves crumbling and her stomach tumbling, she backed out of the room, ran down the stairs, and called the cops.

***

As Vaughan was driving back to the station, his phone display lit up with Nikki McDonald's number. Vaughan was tempted to ignore it. The woman had inserted herself into the Marsha Prince investigation, and though the diary appeared genuine, he knew if the case went to court, there could be claims that the reporter had manufactured or tampered with the entries. He did not believe she had, but by her not calling him first, she'd opened them both up to scrutiny.

"Ms. McDonald?" he said.

Spencer lifted her gaze from her phone and looked at him, her head tilted slightly.

"Detective Vaughan, I'm at the Foster home." She sounded breathless, agitated.

"What are you doing there?" he demanded. "It's an active crime scene."

"Foster contacted me. I came here to see him."

"He shouldn't be there either." As he reached the next red light, he did a U-turn and headed back in the direction of the Fosters' home.

"Look, I'm not calling to debate the finer points of crime scene protection," she said. "You need to get here quickly. Mark Foster is dead."

"Dead?"

"I called 911, and the uniforms are here," she said. "I'm on the front porch."

"We're on our way."

"Foster is dead," Spencer said, more to herself. "How?"

"We'll find out soon enough."

Vaughan pressed the accelerator, flipped on his grille lights, and covered the six miles in minutes. He pulled up in front of the house behind three marked cars, lights flashing. He and Spencer got out and quickly approached a uniformed officer.

"How long have you been here?" Vaughan asked the young officer.

"Five minutes. Paramedics have been called, but there's no way Foster is alive."

"How did he die?" Vaughan asked.

"He cut his wrists."

Vaughan looked past the officer toward Nikki, who was standing next to one of the police vehicles. Her arms were folded over her chest. Her expression was a mixture of interest and worry.

"Ms. McDonald," Vaughan said.

"Detective. Agent."

"What are you doing here?" he asked. "Why did you enter the residence?"

"Foster said he'd give me an exclusive interview. He said he had a lot to tell me, but not a lot of time."

"Tell you what?"

"I wish I knew." She pulled in a breath, as if inhaling a cigarette. "He was dead when I found him."

"Did you disturb anything while you were in the room?" Vaughan asked.

"You'll find my fingerprints on the back door, but I didn't touch anything else. When I found Foster, I called the cops right away and got the hell out."

"Why didn't you call when he first contacted you?" he asked.

She leveled her gaze on him. "Because I'm chasing a story, Detective. Like you, I want to do my job the best I can."

"When you say he contacted you, how did he do it?" Spencer asked.

"He texted."

"Could he have sent you the text at the beginning of the summer regarding Marsha Prince's remains?"

"It's not the same number. I double-checked."

"What else have you found out during your investigation?" he asked.

"I've given it all to you."

"Were you wearing your camera when you entered the house?"

"No. I didn't want to spook him."

"How did you know the text really was from Foster?" Vaughan asked.

"I wasn't sure." A grin tugged at the edges of her lips. "But you know how it is: you got to play to win."

"Can I see your phone?" Vaughan asked.

She dug it out of her purse and handed it to him. The screen saver image featured a PR shot of Nikki at the station.

"Password?" he asked.

"Search warrant?" she countered.

"I'm not in the mood for games," he said.

"Neither am I," she said. "What little I have of a life, I have on that phone, and I'd rather not give it over to the cops."

"I can get a warrant."

She grabbed her phone back. "And that will take time."

"I want the number of the person who texted you."

Nikki typed quickly, and seconds later, his phone dinged with several texts. "Why would he kill himself if he didn't murder Hadley and Marsha Prince?"

Vaughan turned away from the reporter. "No comment."

Vaughan and Spencer pulled on latex gloves.

"Why come here?" Spencer asked. "Why not make a run for it?"

"If the guy had any good memories, they'd have been wrapped up in this house," Vaughan said.

They each had their hands on their weapons as they approached the back door. Vaughan took point while Spencer covered him as they went through the house toward the study.

A clock ticked in the hallway. The two exchanged glances and moved forward; he checked the living and dining rooms while Spencer stood watch. They continued this methodical search through the downstairs and garage before they climbed the stairs to the second floor.

Skylar's room was untouched. Like the other parts of the house, there was no sign that Foster had been here.

They entered the master bedroom. Vaughan stepped around the earlier bloodstain and glanced toward the red arch of spray on the wall before he checked the last space in the house.

He pushed open the bathroom door and instantly smelled the copper scent of blood in the room. This was not stale but fresh.

He rounded the corner and found Mark Foster lying in the tub. He had slashed both wrists.

Holstering his weapon, he reached for a pulse. Foster's skin was pale, cold to the touch. There was no heartbeat. Foster's wounds were from his wrists up his forearms. They were deep and deliberate with no hesitation.

"The paramedics are two minutes away," she said.

"He's gone."

"Why did he summon her here?" she asked.

"I don't know."

"Do you see any kind of note?"

He stepped back from the body and scanned the room. That's when he spotted the mirror over the double vanity. The words were written in Hadley's red lipstick. They read *I did it. I'm sorry.*

CHAPTER
THIRTY-TWO

Thursday, August 15, 6:00 p.m.
Fifty-Nine Hours after the 911 Call
Alexandria, Virginia

Within hours, the brass was considering the Hadley Foster case on the way to being closed. Captain Preston was calling it open and shut. Wife had been having an affair, told the husband she was leaving, and he lost it and stabbed her to death. Only after had he realized what a shit storm he had created. He had tried to cover it up by stashing his kid, ditching his wife's body, and creating a narrative that involved a masked stranger. The nonthreatening cuts to his arms were self-inflicted.

Zoe crossed the parking lot of the police station to her car. She did not trust the open-and-shut verdict in this case. There was likely enough evidence to have convicted Mark Foster, but the pieces felt forced.

Her phone rang, and an unknown number popped up. "Agent Spencer."

"This is Jewel," she said softly.

"Jewel, how are you?"

"Okay." In the background, another girl was speaking, and Jewel's reply to her was too muffled for Zoe to make it out.

"What's going on?"

"There's another girl like Galina."

Zoe closed her eyes. "Was she killed?"

"No. She got away."

Adrenaline rushed through Zoe. "Did she see his face?"

"Yes. She got a good look at him. Can we try the sketch again? I can bring her to you."

"Where do you want to meet?"

"There's a motel down on Route One."

"I'll come right now."

"Just you," Jewel said. "My friend is spooked by men right now."

"Okay."

Twenty minutes later, Zoe swung through a drive-through to pick up burgers and sodas and then parked in front of the room Jewel had indicated. She grabbed her bag, which held her sketch pad and pencils, and knocked on a door with chipped blue paint and tarnished brass numbers. She moved her jacket away from the grip of her holstered gun and stepped back to the side. A chain rattled on the other side.

Jewel peered at her through the cracked door with wide dark eyes that telegraphed a mixture of fear and relief. "I wasn't sure you'd come."

"I said I would." She held up the burgers. "Can I come in?"

Jewel glanced back in the room, as if to get approval, and then nodded. "Yes."

As she stepped into the dimly lit room, her gaze skipped from Jewel to the young girl standing by the bathroom. Not more than sixteen, the girl was thin, and her long hair was dyed a brassy blond. Mascara was smudged under her eyes, as if she had been crying.

"I'm Agent Zoe Spencer," she said.

The girl sniffed. "I'm Kiki."

"Are you all right? Are you hurt?" Zoe asked.

"I'm not hurt," Kiki said.

Zoe's attention shifted to the bathroom, and instinct had her crossing to it and checking to make sure it was empty.

"We're alone," Jewel said.

"Kiki, did you tell Jewel what happened to you?" Zoe asked.

"I told a few of the girls, to warn them. When word got to Jewel, she told me about you."

Zoe motioned toward a round table and the two chairs by the front window. She set the bag of food down along with the drinks and took a seat. "Girls, sit and eat now. It's still hot."

The girls hurried forward, and both sat in their chairs and reached for a bag.

"I'm always so hungry," Kiki said.

"I had the clerk supersize the orders," Zoe said. "Eat as much as you want."

She did not offer advice about nutrition or taking the time to eat. She knew the girls were not going hungry by choice.

Zoe removed her sketch pad and flipped to a clean page as the girls bit into the burgers. She sat on the edge of the bed.

"The picture you did for me wasn't good," Jewel said. "But Kiki saw him better. He got right in her face."

"Was he a customer?" Zoe asked.

"Yeah," Kiki said. "I've seen him around in the last few months but never got picked. Last night, when he picked me, I almost didn't go. I was so nervous and afraid."

"We get this kind of extra sense on the street," Jewel said. "But sometimes we have to ignore it for the money."

"I understand. It's a hard choice."

Kiki grabbed a cluster of french fries. "I'm not going to do this forever. I'm saving my money."

Zoe wanted to believe that was true, but the statistics were against both girls. "Mind if I start asking you a couple of questions about this guy?"

Kiki gripped her burger with both hands, pausing with it inches from her mouth. "Can I keep eating?"

"Of course. I want you to be relaxed. Jewel, do me a favor and let her give her entire description before you speak, okay?" She would have sent Jewel away but feared Kiki would not stay without her.

"Sure. I won't say a word," Jewel said.

As the girls ate, Zoe began with questions about where Kiki had met this john. She asked questions about what the girl was wearing, the weather, the other girls working on the street near her, and details about the motel room.

Zoe slowly shifted her questions to the assailant's description. She began with the shape of his face. They talked about round and ovals, and when they decided on a round face, she began to ask questions about his eyes. The color was important, but also the shape. Did his eyes turn down? Were the eyes set wide or narrow? Were the lids hooded? When Kiki was not sure, Zoe drew examples until they settled on a shape.

Next, it was the nose and then the mouth. She spent time shaping and reshaping the lips and then angling and straightening the nose. This back-and-forth went on for almost two hours. Zoe was so focused on the details she did not take the time to look at the complete image.

Finally, when she completed the sketch and studied it closely, her own reaction to the drawing surprised her. Carefully, she turned it around to show the girls.

"Is this the man?" Zoe asked.

Jewel chewed her nail as she leaned forward and studied the picture. She did not answer but looked toward Kiki, whose complexion had grown ashen.

"Kiki, is this him?" Zoe asked.

Kiki nodded slowly, studying the image closely. "Yeah, that's him. That's him."

Zoe drew in a breath as she reached for her phone and called Vaughan. Her call went to voicemail. Frustrated, she texted him the picture along with the question, Jewel's friend Kiki and I just created this image. I know who it is. Do you?

***

Fifteen minutes later, Zoe parked on the Arlington side street. She sat in her car, watching the business, noting the lights were on in the bays and that loud music played inside. As she checked her phone again, a text from Vaughan appeared.

He wrote, En route.

She replied, Positioned outside.

Wait for me.

Understood.

Seconds after she hit send, a male figure passed in front of the garage bay window, and she heard the clang of tools and several curses. The music went silent, the lights began to click off, and she realized he was leaving.

Instead of watching him drive away, she got out of her vehicle. Placing her hand on her weapon, she blocked the path between the front door and the single car in the lot.

The door opened to Jason Dalton. He looked startled to see her but recovered quickly and grinned. "Agent Spencer."

"It's late to be working, isn't it?" she asked.

"I work late all the time." He scratched his chin as he looked around. "The overtime comes in handy. What are you doing here alone?"

"I have just a few questions. It shouldn't take long." Vaughan was minutes out, and if she could stall Jason, then she would have her backup.

"What kind of questions?" he asked. "Fun ones, I hope."

"Questions about the Foster case."

He held up his hands. "I heard Mark killed himself. That must mean the case is closed, right?"

"Not quite," she said.

"What else is there to talk about?" he asked.

"Kiki. Do you remember her?" She studied his gaze closely and raised her hand to the grip of her weapon.

He shrugged, his head tilting as he regarded her. "No. Should I?"

"She's a prostitute. One of her johns attacked her, but she got away."

Blue eyes narrowed. "What does that have to do with me?"

"Kiki remembered the face of the john very clearly. I was able to make a sketch based on her descriptions."

"I don't believe you," he said. "Half those hookers are on drugs and don't know up from down."

She reached in her pocket and pulled out her phone, which now displayed the image of him. "Have a look for yourself."

He studied the picture and smiled. "Is that supposed to be me?"

"Yes."

"It looks like me, but I'm better looking than that." He flexed his fingers. "You just drew a picture to screw with me, right?"

"No. It's based on witness testimony."

"A whore from the street." He shook his head. "You can pay them to describe anything you want."

"The cops won't rely totally on the sketch," she said. "What they will do is cross-check your DNA with any that was found on Galina or Veronica."

"That sounds a little like a witch hunt. Sounds like you're looking for an excuse to come after me. I'm an ex-con and an easy target, right? You also going to try to nail me for Marsha's murder?"

"When the DNA comes back, then we'll know for sure. But for now, the sketch is enough to detain you."

"Is this supposed to rattle me and make me confess?" He looked amused.

She drew her weapon, knowing he could close the distance between them in seconds. "You kill girls like Galina because they're easy and no one misses them. Veronica would have been a challenge, because sooner or later someone would have missed her."

He glanced at the gun and then back at her. "I don't know a Veronica."

"All the victims look like Hadley and Marsha."

"We keep coming back to Marsha. You have a one-track mind, Agent Spencer. Is the gun really necessary?"

She ignored the question and held the gun steady. "Marsha was young and pretty and trusting. Was she your first kill? Did you save her bones out of sentiment, or maybe it was proof you were the one behind all the media headlines?"

He reached for his car keys. "You're good at spinning stories, Agent. I haven't done any of the stuff you're talking about. The press would call this harassment."

She tensed and took a step back but kept pressing with her statements. "I think Veronica was a two for one. She just happened to be your type, and you knew she was Mark's girlfriend. Maybe Skylar was upset that her daddy was messing around. Maybe you just wanted to hurt Mark."

"I don't like Mark. That's no secret. But I don't care who he sleeps with. That was between Hadley and him."

"Galina was convenient and easy. But after her, I'm surprised you went after Kiki. Were you stressed out? Does killing help you feel in control?"

The frown lines around his mouth deepened. "This has been fun, but it's now boring me. It's been a long day, and I want to go home."

She prayed Vaughan was close. "You're under arrest."

He laughed. "You're full of shit. Now, unless you have a warrant, I'm leaving. I been working for ten hours, and I'm beat. And I don't have time to play cops and robbers with you."

"Stay right where you are, Mr. Dalton. Detective Vaughan is minutes away, and he wants to talk to you."

"Minutes away? Shit, that's a lifetime." He took a step toward his car, but in the next instant, he stopped and pivoted toward her.

The next few seconds slowed to a crawling pace. She caught the glint of a blade. As she locked him in her sights, he lunged. The blade slashed through the air, slicing through the tendons and muscles on her forearm. Pain cut through her body, and blood soaked the sleeve of her blouse. The fingers in her right hand went numb and were unresponsive.

Adrenaline pumped and dulled the pain in her arm. But she knew that wouldn't last. Soon, her arm would burn, and what little advantage she still had would vanish.

She had practiced scenarios like this thousands of times, and muscle memory kicked in. She angled her body back a couple of steps, giving herself the space to shift the gun to her left hand and regain her footing. The grip felt slightly awkward in her left hand, but again, countless practice sessions with her nondominant hand kicked in. She tightened her hold and leveled the gun, refusing to allow any thoughts or emotions to dull her focus.

He raised the knife and lunged forward, ready to plunge the blade into her. She tweaked the angle of her sights, caught him in her crosshairs, and fired.

CHAPTER
THIRTY-THREE

Thursday, August 15, 11:00 p.m.
Sixty-Four Hours after the 911 Call

Zoe stood on the sidewalk, her heart pounding as blood soaked her blouse, pants, and arm. Her breathing was rapid and shallow as she tried to settle herself. Agents went their entire careers without firing their weapons, and she had just fired hers point-blank into a man's chest.

She heard police sirens in the distance, shoved aside the emotions that were sure to come later, and hurried toward her attacker. He lay on his back, staring up at her, his eyes focused sharply on her. She quickly kicked the knife out of his reach and pointed her weapon at his blood-stained chest should he make any move toward her. She did not have the strength or dexterity now in her right hand to cuff him. "Jason, can you hear me?"

He blinked, but it was a slow, lumbering move that suggested he was slipping.

"Did you kill Marsha?"

He closed his eyes as a slight smile tugged the edge of his lips. The color in his face drained.

"Jason, did you kill Marsha? Don't come clean for me, but do it for Skylar."

His eyes opened at the sound of his daughter's name. He looked at her and then slowly nodded and smiled before he closed his eyes. His breathing quickly grew shallow and faded.

The lights of a cop car flashed around her, and she heard her name. She did not move or look back as she kept her gaze locked on Jason.

"Zoe!" It was Vaughan. "Zoe, are you all right?"

She did not dare look toward him. "I'm fine. You need to check for a pulse. He took a round to the chest."

He reached for his cuffs, moving past her as he grabbed Jason's hands and secured them before he pressed his fingertips to the man's throat. "He's dead."

She slowly lowered her weapon and took a step back. "He came at me with that knife."

Vaughan took Zoe's weapon from her and then called in the shooting. "You're bleeding. Did he stab you?"

"He tried. I'm fine." She dared a glance down at her arm and tried to wiggle her fingers. They did not move.

Flashing blue-and-white lights mingled with the now-screaming police sirens. Two police cruisers barreled toward the garage, one from the south and the other from the north. They came to a stop, nose to nose, in front of the building.

"This is FBI special agent Zoe Spencer," Vaughan said to the uniformed officer. "She and I have been working a case."

Her mouth was dry, and the trembling in her hands was seeping through her body. Intellectually, she understood this was the adrenaline dump, her body's reaction to the attack.

Blowing a breath between her lips, she reached for her badge and held it up. Her right arm burned, and she realized just how badly she was injured.

The paramedics arrived and unloaded a stretcher and supplies. One raced toward Jason as Vaughan led Zoe back toward the ambulance.

The paramedic pulled on fresh gloves and had her sit on the edge of the truck. "You're going to need stitches, likely surgery," the paramedic said. "It's a nasty gash."

"How deep is it?" She watched as a uniformed cop secured the scene with yellow tape.

"Deep enough," the paramedic replied.

"Is there tendon damage?"

"Too soon to tell."

As Vaughan stood beside her, she tried to move the fingers on her right hand again. They remained unresponsive.

"You'll be fine," Vaughan said. "They'll get you patched up."

"I've been down this road before. It doesn't end well."

"Don't borrow trouble," he said.

She looked up at him, searching for something that would assure her she had come through this, but the look of concern darkening his gaze told her just how much she stood to lose.

The paramedic applied a bandage to her cut, and as he pressed, pain burned through her, and she hissed in a breath. "Easy now."

Vaughan laid a hand on her knee. It was steady and sure and brought her gaze into focus on the worry etched deep in his face. "Let's get you to the hospital, and then we'll figure this out."

She closed her eyes, knowing this was the kind of injury that could end a career. God, but she had worked so hard to rebuild her life after her leg injury. If she could not be an agent, where would she go? *Not again,* she prayed.

***

Vaughan's temper was stretched thin. Seeing Spencer covered in blood was something he never wanted to repeat. He followed the ambulance to the hospital, and he stayed with her. Both of them were silent as the doctor examined her wound and then made quick arrangements for a surgeon. He knew she was worried about future use of her hand and her career. The quieter and more reserved she became, the angrier he grew. Finally, when the doctors told him he had to leave, he was ready to argue, but Hughes appeared on scene, and she reminded him he had a job to do. He kissed Spencer and left, determined to dig up whatever he could find on Jason Dalton.

That vow rested heavily on his shoulders now as he handed the search warrant to the rotund building manager, who appeared half-asleep. Searching the apartment was the first step to figuring out what had driven Jason to attack Spencer with a knife and likely Veronica and Galina.

The manager handed Vaughan back his warrant and unlocked the front door of the apartment.

Vaughan reached in and turned on the light. "Thanks. I'll take it from here."

"Sure."

Vaughan and Hughes stepped into the small studio apartment. It was simply furnished with a couch, a television, and a coffee table covered with a couple of old pizza boxes. Clothes were scattered on the floor, and the trash can beside the couch was filled with beer cans.

"For once, I'd like to deal with a criminal who keeps his place clean," Hughes said. "It smells like a pigsty in here."

The walls were bare, and the curtains that covered the windows were a bland beige that looked like they came with the unit. He walked to the window and pushed back the curtain. The view featured two dumpsters and several parking spaces filled with boats and campers.

He moved to the kitchen and found more pizza boxes and empty Chinese takeout. More beer cans in the overflowing trash can, and dirty dishes were piled in the sink.

"Let's look at the bedroom," he said.

It took less than ten steps to cross from the kitchen to the closed door. He turned the knob and discovered the door was locked. The lock was a standard issue with a small opening in its center.

Vaughan ran his gloved fingers over the top of the door until they skimmed over a small metal skewer. He pressed the end of it in the hole, and the lock on the other side popped open.

"Not exactly state-of-the-art security," Hughes quipped.

"Just enough to keep any visitors from wandering into his room."

He flipped on the light. There was a double bed with no sheets and a rumpled comforter. The nightstand was an old crate box with a small lamp that looked like it had been a find at Goodwill. He crossed the carpeted floor, stepping around more clothes and shoes to open the closet door. It was a walk-in closet with a pull-down entry into the attic.

He switched on the light, and the bulb flickered. Instantly, he was taken aback. The side walls of the large closet were filled with pictures of women. The pictures were divided into two categories. The first set appeared to have been taken before his incarceration. The second set after, and most likely in the past year. In the older set of photos, there were pictures of Marsha and Hadley Prince. Both were young, vibrant, smiling teenagers, and they looked remarkably alike.

Hadley was also featured in the newer images. He had taken pictures of her coming out of the gym, at the grocery store, and jogging along the river. He'd been watching her for months.

It struck Vaughan how much Hadley had changed from the first set of images to the second. She was still fit and still stunning, but the former spark in her gaze had dulled. Most would say that was due to age and time. It happened to everyone. But he had to think the rigid control she'd maintained over her life was a reflection of something deeper and darker.

"There are driver's licenses of Galina Grant, Veronica Manchester, and Marsha Prince," Hughes said. "It's his trophy room."

He leaned forward and studied the DMV photo of Marsha Prince. She had rich, glowing skin, bright brown eyes, and a broad smile. It had been taken back in the day when the pictures were in color and one could smile. "I keep thinking about that blackened skull found in the storage unit trunk."

"I contacted Helen Saunders's apartment manager, and he found her original application. Apparently, he's been looking for it. Nikki McDonald offered a bounty on it."

"I give the woman points for her investigative skills. What did you find?"

"Ms. Saunders listed a Marjorie Dalton as her emergency contact. She was Jason's grandaunt."

"That explains why he chose her unit to store the bones."

"But why did he torch them and save them in the first place?"

Vaughan shook his head. "Maybe she was his first. Maybe he thought if he kept her, he'd have some kind of hold on Hadley." He searched the piles. "Is there anything for Hadley Foster?" he asked.

"I haven't seen anything yet, beyond the creepy stalker pictures," she said. "But it could be here."

"Dalton was recorded on video surveillance at the garage when Hadley Foster was murdered, so he couldn't have killed her."

"Do you really think Mark killed his wife?"

"I don't know." Vaughan reached for a bag and discovered several burner phones inside. It would take time, but he would bet money they would find links to Nikki's phone and Skylar's. "Time to find out what really happened in the Foster house."

***

Zoe was not at the hospital long before a surgeon was called into her room. She was asked to wiggle her fingers, something she could not do. And it seemed the harder she tried, the less they responded. She went into surgery that evening to have the muscle, tendons, and, most importantly, the nerves repaired.

The surgery was finished by midnight, and back in her room, she was left with the entire night to think about how she would be able to do her job without a fully functioning right hand. The new world she had created for herself would go the way of the old, wiped away by a violent moment that would echo through her life forever.

Vaughan knocked on her hospital room door at four o'clock in the morning.

"Enter," she said.

"The nurses told me you weren't sleeping."

Cupping her arm, she shifted her position and sat up. "Tell me you've talked to the doctor and that there's no nerve damage. He wasn't saying much to me earlier."

He came to her bedside and pulled up a chair. "The tendon and muscle were repaired. We won't know about permanent nerve damage for a while. Until then, you'll be in a cast. I'm sorry."

Sorry never did her any good. "Water under the bridge. When can I get out of here?"

"You've only been out of surgery for a few hours."

"Like I said, when can I get out of here?"

"Tomorrow, if all goes well."

"I'd rather leave now." She pushed herself into a sitting position, pausing as her head spun. "Where are my clothes?"

Vaughan arched a brow. "You'll stay put if you want that wound to heal properly."

"Can you at least raise my head?" Zoe asked. "I'd like to sit up a little more."

Vaughan pressed a button on the side of the bed, and her head slowly rose as Vaughan approached. At least sitting up, she didn't feel so helpless. "Tell me about the case."

As the nurse closed the door behind her, he opened with an update of what he and Hughes had found at Jason's apartment. She listened, locking on his words as if she needed an anchor. Finally, he shifted to the shooting. "Your left-handed shot was textbook center mass."

"I'm lucky."

"You're good." He leaned forward. "The knife was found. We've already found his fingerprints on it and your blood. What happened?"

"I saw him preparing to leave, and I approached. He attacked. The entire exchange lasted only minutes."

"Did he say anything?" Vaughan asked.

"Not much. When I showed Dalton the sketch, he was calm and challenged me to prove it. His demeanor was nonchalant. I think he planned to kill me the instant he saw me standing outside the garage."

Vaughan frowned, his fingers drawing into a fist before he relaxed them. "The forensic team is searching for signs that he'd been in the Foster home but so far have found nothing. Mark Foster's toxicological screen came back. He had high levels of sleeping pills in his system."

"So did he kill himself?"

"Good question."

CHAPTER
THIRTY-FOUR

Sunday, August 18, 4:00 p.m.

Two days postsurgery, Zoe probably should have been inside with her feet up. But inactivity would have given her time to worry about the hand that still felt numb as well as the inquiry into the Dalton shooting. It was a recipe for insanity.

She sat in a wooden card chair by her garage, her arm in a sling, watching the two men she had found on Craigslist willing to haul away her junk. She had been holding on to all of Jimmy's things as if she were protecting a piece of the past. But she knew it was time to let some of the memories go.

She'd also never thought she would be giddy at the thought of parking her car, but knowing she would not have to circle the block or hoof it through the rain was just this side of nirvana.

The crewman carried out a large cardboard box, set it at her feet, and opened it. This had been their process. They hauled and opened, and she then inspected. So far, what she had found had ended up on the donation pile.

As she opened the latest box, she almost did not bother to glance inside until her gaze landed on a neatly folded shirt that had belonged to Jeff.

She gently ran her fingers over the worn flannel. The softness triggered memories of Jeff laughing and teasing her out of a mood she had slipped into after she had received a B instead of an A in one of her classes. He had coaxed that smile, and they had ended up in bed. When he had first died, that memory had not only taunted her but reminded her of everything they would never share again. Uncle Jimmy had told her to put Jeff's things away and come back to them later, but she had tossed his clothes into a box and dumped them on the curb.

"Jimmy. You're a sneaky one," she whispered.

She raised the shirt to her nose, unmindful of the heat as she inhaled deeply. For just a moment, she caught a faint whiff of Jeff's spicy aftershave.

How could you love someone so much and forget so much about them? Tears welled in her eyes. One escaped down her cheek before she caught herself. Carefully, she placed the shirt back into the box and closed the lid. She would always love Jeff and wonder what it would have been like to grow old with him. But he was gone. And for the first time in a long time, she was grateful to be alive.

"Is that for the junk truck, ma'am?" the man asked.

Zoe cleared her throat. "These are good clothes. I want these donated."

"Will do." He reached for the box and lifted it.

As he turned, she stood quickly. "Wait."

"Ma'am?"

She opened the top and removed the flannel shirt. "The rest can go."

"You sure?"

"Yes."

She sat back in her chair, holding the shirt close, and watched as the men cleared out the last of the items and closed up the truck. She walked into the now-empty garage. Her phone rang. It was Vaughan.

"Ready?" he asked.

"I am."

"I've arranged with social services and Mrs. Bradford to be present when we talk to her. I don't want to take any shortcuts with this one."

"Me neither."

"See you in fifteen."

When he pulled down her street right on time, she was ready, having changed into a loose pair of black pants and a simple button-up blouse. It was not fashionable, but it was all she could manage with the cast now.

When she climbed into his car, he kissed her. "You look better every day. How's the hand?"

"Stubbornly silent. But I'm on a quarter of the pain meds now. So, progress. Have you spoken to Bud?"

He reached for a manila folder and handed it to her. "You should enjoy reading this."

She had enough time to read through the file before Mrs. Bradford arrived with Skylar at the police station. She had retained the services of a court-appointed attorney, Tara Ellison, a tall slim woman in her early thirties.

Skylar was wearing a peach-colored top, white capris, and sandals, and she had swept her blond hair into a ponytail so like the one Hadley had worn.

"Thank you for coming, Skylar," Zoe said.

"What is this about?" Ms. Ellison said. "Her parents' cases are nearly closed."

"Not quite." Zoe opened the file Vaughan had given her.

"This entire case started with a text. Someone sent Nikki McDonald a message telling her where Marsha Prince's remains could be found. I was able to re-create her face before she could be identified." She flipped through pages and then pointed to a row of numbers. "I've spent the last couple of days trying to figure out who sent her that text. Who knew Marsha was dead?"

"I don't know what else my client can tell you. The woman died before Skylar Foster was born," Ms. Ellison said.

"Jason Dalton admitted that he was angry when he learned Hadley had kept his daughter from him. He strikes up a relationship with Skylar, and they texted on a secured app. Over the course of the last six months, he did a good job of stoking her frustrations. Skylar, you weren't happy with your parents, and Jason made it worse."

"He listened," she said. "He was a friend."

"I've had a chance to read all your exchanges with Jason. He didn't sound like he had your best interests at heart. *Your mother can be a bitch. Even her own sister hated her.* Those don't sound like supportive texts," Zoe said.

Skylar brushed back a lock of blond hair. "It was the truth. She wasn't the nicest person sometimes."

"I believe that," Zoe said. "You made a comment once that she got drunk sometimes and she talked. Did she let it slip that she felt guilty about her sister?"

"Don't answer that, Skylar," Ms. Ellison said.

"Did you tell Jason? We now know from the burner phones we found in his apartment that he texted Nikki McDonald the tip."

"The text Mr. Dalton sent has nothing to do with my client," Ms. Ellison said.

"Jason might have been trying to turn you against your parents, but you were also working him. You confided details about your mother to Jason because you were mad at her. What you didn't realize was that you opened a bigger can of worms than you had imagined. The more you told Jason about your mother, the madder he got. You woke a sleeping monster. Did you also tell him about Veronica and your father? Is that why he killed her?"

"You can never prove this," Ms. Ellison said.

"No, I might not," Zoe said. "But I can prove who killed Hadley Foster."

"Mark Foster confessed," Mrs. Bradford said.

"He did," Zoe said. "We found the knife he used to stab himself shoved in a planter."

"See, that proves my point," Ms. Ellison said.

"It wasn't the knife that killed Hadley. But we found that knife. It was in the creek near where her body was found. We've been in a drought, so the waters weren't deep. We think Mark did throw the murder weapon into the creek, thinking it would get swept away, but it didn't. Some of the blood on the knife was washed away, but as I've said many times before, blood travels into all kinds of cracks and crevices."

Skylar folded her arms over her chest.

"For whatever reason, I think your mother announced she was moving out of the house," Zoe said. "When you reached out to Jason and brought him into your mother's life, I think it set off a chain reaction in her mind. She needed to escape her life, and maybe she talked to Mark Foster about leaving, but he knew after the family's move from Oregon, he couldn't afford to leave. We know Mark was sleeping on the couch. Maybe she decided Roger Dawson was the guy to take her away."

"I don't know what you're talking about," Skylar said.

"Whatever the reason, Hadley said she told Mark she was leaving. Did they have a fight after we told her Marsha's body had been found?"

Skylar didn't speak but simply stared at Zoe.

"You lost your temper. You were waiting for her when she came back from her morning run. And I think you two fought. Maybe you tried to reason with her. Maybe you tried to convince her that Jason wasn't a bad guy. Whatever the reason, I bet you didn't want your life upended again."

"I liked living here," Skylar said.

Zoe nodded. "But you didn't convince her, and she left you in the kitchen. That's when you grabbed the knife from the butcher block and followed her upstairs and stabbed her. Your father realized what had happened, but he was too late to save Hadley, so he tried to fix it. He put you and your mother in the car and dropped you at the motel. He gave you sleeping pills to keep you quiet while he dumped your mother's body and then parked near your motel. He showered in your room and ran home. He stabbed himself and at 7:00 a.m. called 911 and reported the attack from the intruder."

"That's a nice story," Skylar said. "But I loved my mom. I never would have hurt her."

"I don't think you planned it. But I think you snapped when she said she was leaving, and your temper got the better of you."

"No," Skylar said.

"When you stab someone, your hand gets slick with blood." Zoe held up her left hand and slowly flexed the fingers. "And if you aren't careful, the blade can slip. It's not uncommon for the attacker to cut themselves and leave their own blood on the knife or, in this case, in the handle's crevices."

"I use that knife at home all the time," Skylar said. "I've cut my hand on it before. And my dad confessed. He left a note and everything."

"Mark did it to protect you. Jason might have tried to convince you otherwise, but in Mark Foster's mind, you were his little girl. I wonder if he knew all along that the baby Hadley was carrying wasn't his. I think that's why they moved out west. He would have kept you both in Oregon if not for the trouble you got into. The only reason he came back here was because of the job. Maybe he thought the past was over and done, and you three could live a happy life here now."

Tears welled in the young girl's eyes. "No."

"And then you test your DNA and show up at Jason's garage. He knew from the moment he met you he would use you to get back at Hadley. Maybe he didn't know how, but he figured sooner or later, he could turn you against your mother."

Her shoulders drew back as she inhaled. "No. Jason wouldn't do that. And I did love my mom."

"We now have DNA evidence that proves Jason stabbed to death Veronica Manchester and Galina Grant. Both the women look very much like your mother, and we think he was using them as surrogates."

For the first time, the defiance burning in the girl's gaze cooled. "Jason wouldn't do that."

"He did do that. I can't prove it, but I also think he killed your mother's sister, Marsha. Cops didn't take a hard look at him because he'd quit his job at Prince Paving and moved away."

"You are lying," Skylar whispered.

"Jason knew Mark was having an affair with Veronica. I'm not sure why he killed her. Maybe because he knew her death would eventually cast suspicion on Mark, or maybe she just looked so much like Hadley he couldn't resist. And Galina Grant was just an easy target who had the misfortune to be Jason's type."

"Jason isn't a monster. I'm not a monster. I loved my mother."

"I have no doubt you loved your mother," Zoe said. "And I bet if you could take back those few moments when you stabbed her, you would."

Skylar looked as if she would say something, but then her face hardened in a way that reminded Zoe of Jason. "No, you're wrong. I wouldn't take it back."

The girl was still very young and had suffered multiple traumas. She could live to regret those words. And then Zoe reminded herself that Jason hadn't been much older than Skylar when he'd killed Marsha.

Vaughan rose. "Skylar Foster, you have the right to remain silent."

EPILOGUE

The house had a lighter feel, as if for the first time in a decade, it had taken a deep breath. Zoe stood in the living room, arranging the furniture she had had reupholstered while a crew had stripped the old wallpaper, painted the walls a soft gray, and buffed the wood floors. Remodeling the living room and her bedroom certainly was not a complete renovation, but she could tackle the rooms bit by bit.

Her front doorbell rang, and she glanced out the window to see Vaughan. She smiled. It had been a week since they had seen each other, and she realized how much she had missed him.

She opened the door, and he leaned in and gave her a kiss with the kind of familiarity shared by close couples. "This is a nice surprise," she said.

"I had DNA results I wanted to share with you."

"How romantic." She laughed.

"I thought you'd be impressed." He stepped into the room and kissed her again.

Smiling, she stepped back. "What do you think of the room?"

He nodded with approval. "This looks great."

"Crews just left yesterday, and the furniture was returned this morning. Now I just have to figure out what to do with it all."

"I can help."

"I could use the extra muscle."

"How's the arm?"

"Still sore. But better." She flexed her fingers. "It's getting better each day. How was parents' weekend?"

"Nate is doing really well. I also think he has a girlfriend."

She removed two cold sodas and handed one to him. "Good for him."

"As long as his grades don't suffer." He popped the top of the soda.

"Spoken like a dad." Vaughan's dedication to his son was one of his qualities she admired most.

"I'd like you to meet him."

"That would be nice."

"He'll be home the week of Thanksgiving."

She crossed her fingers. "Barring a case, so will I."

"Nate's used to holiday dinners being delayed for a case. If you can be flexible that week, we'll make it work."

She wanted to make it work. "Then we will."

He kissed her lips softly. "Can I tempt you with those DNA results now?"

"You know how to charm a girl."

He took another pull on the soda can. "I reached out to Andrea Jamison in the FBI's ViCAP division. I kept going back to a point you and Dr. Baldwin made about Veronica and Galina's killer."

"We thought he was comfortable with killing."

"Exactly."

"What did you discover?"

"I provided Andrea—Andy, as she likes to be called—with Dalton's approximate locations over the last couple of years and asked if there were blond women who had been stabbed in or near those areas. I asked her to key in on sex workers. Turns out Andy is good at tracking patterns."

"And?"

"She found ten cases that fit the criteria."

"Ten murders." In all honesty, she was surprised the number was not higher, given the rate of this summer's killing spree. "Was DNA collected on any of the cases?"

"Most of the bodies were too degraded, but there was DNA collected on two. They had been submitted for testing, but with the backlog in the local lab, they hadn't been analyzed yet."

"And now?"

"One was a match to Jason Dalton."

"Really?" She felt no satisfaction knowing her theory had been proven.

"I suspect some of the other victims were his as well, but we may never know," he said. "The consolation is that he won't be killing any more women."

"What about Skylar? Is she going to be charged with Hadley Foster's murder?" Zoe asked.

"There is talk of filing manslaughter charges, but there's little political will to prosecute Skylar."

"The girl is a natural manipulator like Jason." Zoe was not happy, but she also saw the logic. "The cops have a confession from Mark, which, true or not, carries a great deal of weight with the courts. Do you think he killed himself?"

"He might have. Mark loved Skylar, and he wanted to protect her. He knew she'd killed Hadley, and he figured the only way to help her was to take the blame himself."

Foster had simply been trying to do right by his wife and daughter, as he always had. "That doesn't explain how Hadley's blood got on Skylar."

"Skylar's attorney said she had been trying to save her mother after the father's attack."

"Did you see the interview the girl gave with Nikki McDonald?" she asked.

"I did. Skylar has the face of an angel." He flicked his finger against the can's tab.

Zoe shook her head. "Do you think she'll do it again?"

"It wouldn't surprise me," he said. "The girl is missing an emotional chip."

The apple did not fall far from her biological father's tree. "Mrs. Bradford and her son, Neil, are standing behind her."

"Sleep with an open eye," Vaughan cautioned.

"I feel like we lost this one."

He took her soda can from her, set it beside his on the kitchen counter, and then pulled her into his arms. "Jason is dead. He's not going to kill any more women. We take the victories where we can." He kissed her on the mouth.

She leaned into the kiss, savoring the touch of his lips.

"And we can enjoy what we have together," he said.

Her life as a dancer and then as a wife to Jeff had ended forever. There was no going back. But she was still an FBI agent, and not only was she good at what she did, but she liked it.

And there was Vaughan. With him, a new door had opened to new possibilities. For the first time in a long time, she wasn't desperate to recapture what she'd had. She was ready to step through this new door and see what waited for her.

"I like that idea very much," she said.

ABOUT THE AUTHOR

Photo © 2015 Studio FBJ

New York Times and *USA Today* bestselling novelist Mary Burton is the popular author of thirty-five romance and suspense novels as well as five novellas. She currently lives in Virginia with her husband and three miniature dachshunds. Visit her at www.maryburton.com.